MARK GREANEY

AGENT IN PLACE

sphere

SPHERE

First published in the United States in 2018 by Berkley,
an imprint of Penguin Random House LLC
First published in Great Britain in 2018 by Sphere
This paperback edition published in 2018 by Sphere

1 3 5 7 9 10 8 6 4 2

A CIP catalogue record for this book
is available from the British Library.

ISBN 978-0-7515-7001-4

Printed and bound in Great Britain
by Clays Ltd, Elcograf S.p.A

Papers used by Sphere are from well-managed forests
and other responsible sources.

Sphere
An imprint of
Little, Brown Book Group
Carmelite House
50 Victoria Embankment
London EC4Y 0DZ

An Hachette UK Company
www.hachette.co.uk

www.littlebrown.co.uk

To you, the reader

ACKNOWLEDGEMENTS

I would like to thank Lt. Col Rip Rawlings (USMC); Amanda Schulter; Scott Swanson; Mike Cowan; Mystery Mike Bursaw; Jon Harvey; Jon Griffin; Joshua Hood; John Busby; Nick Ciubotariu; Dan Newberry and the staff at Bangsteel in Wytheville, VA; James Yeager; Jay Gibson and everyone at Tactical Response in Camden, TN; Chris Clarke; Devon Greaney; Devin Greaney; the Tulsa Greaneys; and Dorothy Greaney.

Thanks to my agent, Scott Miller, and the team at Trident Media; my editor, Tom Colgan; Loren Jaggers; Jin Yu; Grace House; and the rest of the team at Penguin Random House. Also thanks to Jon Cassir and the team at CAA.

Experience, that most brutal of teachers. But you learn, my God, do you learn.

C. S. LEWIS

You may not be interested in war, but war is interested in you.

LEON TROTSKY

CHARACTERS

AHMED AL-AZZAM: President of Syria

JAMAL AL-AZZAM: Late father of Ahmed al-Azzam, former president of Syria

SHAKIRA AL-AZZAM: First lady of Syria

BIANCA MEDINA: Spanish fashion model, mistress of Ahmed al-Azzam

DR. TAREK HALABY: Cardiac surgeon, co-director of the Free Syria Exile Union, husband of Rima Halaby

DR. RIMA HALABY: Cardiac surgeon, co-director of the Free Syria Exile Union, wife of Tarek Halaby

VINCENT VOLAND: Former intelligence officer, DGSE, Directorate-General for External Security (French Foreign Intelligence Service), and DGSI, Directorate-General for Internal Security (French Domestic Intelligence Service)

SEBASTIAN DREXLER: (Code name: Eric) Swiss intelligence officer, employee of Meier Privatbank

HENRI SAUVAGE: Captain, Police Judiciaire, French National Police

FOSS: Lieutenant Intern, Police Judiciaire, French National Police

ALLARD: Lieutenant, Police Judiciaire, French National Police

CLEMENT: Lieutenant, Police Judiciaire, French National Police

MALIK: Foreign intelligence operative of GIS, General Intelligence Service, Syrian External Security Division

LARS KLOSSNER: Owner of Klossner Welt Ausbildungs GMBH, security and private military contractor

VAN WYK: KWA, private military contractor/team leader

SAUNDERS: KWA, private military contractor

BROZ: KWA, private military contractor

WALID: Major in Desert Hawks Brigade (pro-regime Syrian militia)

PAUL BOYER: Former French Foreign Legionnaire, private security officer

ROBERT "ROBBY" ANDERSON: Captain, U.S. Army 10th Special Forces Group

STEFAN MEIER: Vice president, Meier Privatbank

JAMAL MEDINA: Infant son of Bianca Medina

YASMIN SAMARA: Nanny to Jamal Medina

DR. SHAWKAT SADDIQI: Trauma surgeon, Syrian resistance sympathizer

ABDUL BASSET RAHAL: Syrian resistance fighter with the Free Syrian Army

MATTHEW HANLEY: Director, National Clandestine Service, Central Intelligence Agency

AGENT IN PLACE

PROLOGUE

The prisoners were slaughtered one by one, with efficiency as true as a ticking clock. Two dozen dead now, and the executioner was just hitting his stride.

The scene of the massacre was one of abject horror: the stench of fresh blood, the cloying smell of bodies floating in the brown lake, the viscous brain matter splattered and thickening on the sun-blanched pier.

Above the slaughter the rocky hillside sparkled in the midday heat, the reflection of broken glass and twisted metal jutting out of the wreckage of a battle fought months ago. Many had died, and the few vanquished who survived had run for their lives and left the ruined land to the victors.

The black flags of ISIS hung in the town square now, and they waved from the rooftops of the wrecked buildings and whipped in the back of most every pickup truck that rolled through the broken streets: certainly every vehicle that was filled to capacity with young bearded men wearing cheap tactical gear and brandishing weapons, eyes wild with the fervency of their sickening death cult.

Here by the lake, between the broken hillside and the water, ran a narrow shoreline of salt flat and brown brush. Forty-three condemned men in orange jumpsuits knelt, the remainder of the sixty-seven who had been trucked here just twenty minutes earlier.

The captives were surrounded by masked fighters holding rifles at the

3

ready; the prisoners' wrists were tied with rough cord in front of their bodies, and they were all lashed together by a long rope. This removed the chance that any one of them would get up and leg it, though it hardly mattered. Nobody was going to run. It was nearly a hundred kilometers across the dead ground of war-torn Syria to the Turkish border, so what chance would they have if they ran?

No one entwined and kneeling here would resist the fate that awaited him. There was no use to it, and virtually all these men understood that their last few moments left on this foul Earth would be better spent praying.

The executioner wore a pair of daggers in his belt, but these were just for show. The real tool of choice for the slaughter wasn't the blades; it was the Avtomat Kalashnikova, model 74U, held in the arms of the hooded executioner standing at the end of the pier.

As had been the routine for the past twenty minutes, two guards shoved a prisoner to his knees next to the executioner, the masked man pointed the muzzle of his weapon behind the condemned man's right ear, and then, without a pause or a comment or a moment's hesitation, he pulled the trigger.

Sanguine spray erupted from the captive's head, and the body snapped forward, the mangled face leading the way down to the water. It crashed into the surface of the lake, just like so many before it, and just like so many more, waiting on the shore for their turn to die.

And a videographer on the shoreline recorded it all for posterity.

The shrinking row of prisoners remained passive, kneeling on the lakeside, over a dozen armed men at the ready standing on all sides of them. Some flinched with the rifle's report; others flinched with the sound of the splash, knowing their ruined dead bodies would follow suit in moments; and soon two armed ISIS fighters walked down the fifteen-meter-long wooden pier, stepped onto the rocky shoreline, and took the closest man in orange by his shoulders. Two more captors had just cut him from the rope tied around his waist, so the walking crew hefted the condemned from his knees to his feet and guided him back down the pier, shoving him onward if he slowed for an instant. The doomed man prayed softly in Arabic as he walked with his hands secured in front of him, his eyes on the wooden planks at his feet, not on the water, not on the dozens of bodies floating just off the end of the pier . . . not on his dead friends and comrades.

The walk was thirty seconds in duration, and then the prisoner's sandaled feet stopped in the pool of blood at the end of the wooden planks. Here the lead executioner waited, his Kalashnikov hanging low from the sling around his neck.

The executioner said nothing. The prisoner in orange knelt; he showed no emotion but only continued to pray, his eyes closed now.

The two men who had delivered him here took a step back; their own boots and pants and even the ammunition racks on their chests were covered in blood splatter, and they kept their weapons raised, barrels just behind their prisoner's ears, but they did not fire. They looked on while the executioner raised his Kalashnikov, glanced towards the cameraman back at the edge of the pier to make certain he was getting all this, and then shot the young man in his right temple.

Half of the man's head exploded, spewing outwards three meters above the water; the body spun and tipped forward and dropped into the bloodred lake face-first with a splash that was identical to the twenty-five other splashes that preceded it.

The escort team had already turned away to take the next man in the rapidly shrinking row of prisoners.

Forty-two now.

There were Iraqis and Syrians and Turks in the row left to be killed this morning on the banks of al-Azzam Lake, and soon the escorts had their hands on the shoulders of a twenty-eight-year-old with matted hair curled in an afro, blood smeared on his face, and a black eye, and they pulled him up and along, beginning his short stroll to his death.

That left forty-one in the row of tied and kneeling men in orange jumpsuits, and the next man to wait his turn looked much the same as the others. Filthy tangled dark hair in his eyes, flecked with bits of rubble and glass. His head down in supplication, his gaze averted from the impossibly horrific scene going on before him. Blood was caked on his bearded face from the beating he had taken in the makeshift prison the night before, and his nose was swollen; a punch to his jaw had left it scraped and bruised, and he was unable to open it fully. He also had a savage cut above his right ear and a bloody gash over his left eye.

Still, he was not much worse off from the rest of the prisoners still alive.

5

The main difference between him and the others was a small distinction and would serve as no comfort to them. He'd die first, and they'd die after.

. . .

The prisoner to the left of the man with the beaten face raised his head now, defying the orders of the captors, and he looked at the horror around him. His name was Abdul Basset Rahal, and he was Syrian, a rebel soldier in the Free Syrian Army; he had been captured late the afternoon before along with the prisoner with the beaten face who was next in line to die. Rahal was a brave twenty-four-year-old, but he was scared now; he was human, after all. Still, he took solace in the fact that he would be martyred by his death, like all of the others save for the man on his right. Rahal felt sadness for the beaten man at his shoulder, because he had done so much to help; he had been a lion in battle, a true hero in their righteous cause, and now he would die without achieving martyrdom.

Because he was no Muslim.

Abdul Basset Rahal had only met the man the day before yesterday, but already the Syrian thought of the American as a fellow warrior, a kindred spirit, and yes . . . even as a friend.

The Syrian found some peace in the fact that he would share his last few breaths with this great soldier, and peace in the fact that the ISIS captors had not learned that this man was a Westerner, because they certainly would have made a bigger show of his death for the camera, and whatever manner they would have chosen, it would have been so much more horrible than a simple rifle shot to the temple.

The American was lucky; he'd get a bullet to the brain and then it would be over.

Rahal looked back down at the salty shore between his knees as the two escorts returned.

The American was cut away from the others; there was a scuffle of boots on the rocks, and then the American was grabbed by both shoulders, yanked to a standing position, and pushed away, hauled off along the waterline and towards the pier.

Rahal called out to him, careful to speak in Arabic, because although he spoke English fluently, doing so would tip off the ISIS monsters of the American's true origins.

"Habibi!" Friend! "I swear it has been my great honor to fight and die alongside you."

For his words Rahal received a rifle butt to the back of his head, knocking him onto his face and pulling other prisoners down with him by the rope tied around their waists.

But the American either had not heard him or did not understand, or perhaps his jaw was just swollen shut, because he made no reply.

. . .

Courtland Gentry's bare feet slapped along the wooden pier; the coarse twine wrapped around his wrists in front of him bit into his skin. The AK barrels held by the men at his sides jabbed against his low back, and he felt the eyes of the other fourteen ISIS gunmen behind him. He'd counted them when they got out of the trucks, and he counted them again as he was brought to the water's edge with the others.

He passed the unarmed cameraman and kept going, glanced up now, and focused his eyes on the blood-drenched far edge of the pier. The masked man with the wired-stock AK and the daggers in his belt beckoned him with a bored wave of his rifle; he was a thick man, but even so, Gentry could see that the executioner had his chest puffed out, no doubt for the video and the attention paid to him by all on the hillside, confederate and enemy alike.

The American prisoner continued forward; his fate lay at the end of this pier.

The walk was short . . . as if fate were anxious to get on with its day.

One step past the executioner Gentry was forced to his knees; he slipped in the gore coating the wooden planks but recovered. He knelt with his head bowed and gazed down three feet to the surface of the lake, the water swirling bloodred in the brown. The body of the most recent victim had drifted a few yards away, and this meant the American wouldn't crash into him as he himself went into the lake, not that this gave him any great consolation at all.

The escorts behind him took a half step back, their gun barrels close to

7

his head, and then Court heard the sling swivels of the executioner's rifle as the man lifted the weapon and trained it behind his right ear.

This was it.

Courtland Gentry lifted his head, squared his chin, and fixed his eyes in resolution.

"Here we go," he whispered.

. . .

Abdul Basset Rahal, the young Syrian who would be the next to die, did not watch the execution of the American warrior. He just closed his eyes and listened for the boom of the rifle. When it came, it seemed louder than all the others now that he was focused fully on the sound, and the report had only just trailed away when the splash came.

Al-Azzam Lake had accepted its newest victim, and the Syrian knew it was now his time to walk to the edge of the bloody pier.

CHAPTER 1

ONE WEEK EARLIER

Cimetière du Père-Lachaise is the most visited cemetery in the world, but the Paris landmark was all but deserted on this rainy, gray, and cool weekday morning. An elderly couple fed squirrels on the cobblestones; a dozen young people stood solemnly in front of Jim Morrison's fenced-off but simple plot. A group of German hipsters lounged among the graves surrounding Oscar Wilde's tomb, and a lone man took photos of the statue of Euterpe, the muse of music, as she wept above composer Frédéric Chopin's mausoleum.

There might have been seventy-five visitors in all on the property, but the cemetery spread over one hundred hilly and wooded acres, so anyone who wanted privacy could find it easily here in the warren of tombs, crypts, cobblestoned lanes, and old oak.

And one man had done just that. A dark-complected fifty-five-year-old with thinning gray hair sat alone a few rows up the hill from Molière's tomb, on a small bench that one had to either know about or stumble upon to locate. His name was Dr. Tarek Halaby, and there wasn't much about the man to make him stand out from the average Parisian of Middle Eastern descent, although someone with knowledge of fashion might pick up on the fact that his raincoat was a Kiton that ran north of two thousand euros, and

9

they might therefore come to the quite reasonable assumption that this was a man of significant means.

As he sat there in the stillness of the cemetery, Halaby pulled out his wallet and looked at a small photo he kept there. A young man and a young woman standing together, smiling into the lens, with hope and intelligence in their eyes that said the future was theirs to command.

For twenty seconds Halaby stared at the photo, till drops of rain began to fall, splashing on the image and blurring the smiling faces.

He dried the photo off with this thumb, put his wallet back in his coat, and looked up to the sky. He lifted his umbrella and got ready to pop it open, but then the phone he'd placed on the bench next to him buzzed and lit up.

He forgot about the impending shower, put down the umbrella, and read the text.

Crematorium. Alone. Lose the goons.

The man in the raincoat sat up straighter and looked around nervously. He saw no one: only tombs and gravestones and trees and birds.

Cold sweat formed on the back of his collar.

He stood, but before he began walking he sent a reply.

I am alone.

A new text appeared, and the man in the raincoat felt his heart pummel the inside of his chest.

Two men with guns in their coats at the entrance. Two more fifty meters east of you. They go . . . or I go.

Dr. Halaby stared at the phone a moment before typing out his reply with fingers that trembled.

Of course.

He placed a call, held the phone to his ear, and spoke in French. "He sees you, and he won't do this with you here. Take the others, go get a coffee, and wait for my call." A pause. "It's fine."

The man ended the call, slipped the phone into his raincoat, and began walking up the hill towards the crematorium.

. . .

Five minutes later Dr. Halaby held his umbrella over his head while he walked through the steady rain. The huge crematorium of Père-Lachaise was higher on the hill, another sixty meters on, but Halaby was still making his way through the narrow passages between the tall mausoleums all around. As he advanced, his eyes fixed on another man, himself holding an umbrella. He appeared around the side of the huge crematorium, then stepped into a parking lot between Halaby and the building. Halaby expected the man to continue in his direction, so he was surprised when he instead climbed into a small work truck and drove off to the west.

Halaby was doubly surprised to hear a voice behind him now, not three meters away, coming from a recess between a pair of crypts.

"Stop there. Don't turn around." The man spoke English, softly, his voice barely louder than the sound of rain hitting Halaby's umbrella.

"As you say," the doctor replied, standing still now, doing his best to keep his hands from shaking. He was partially shielded on three sides by the marble walls of crypts, and in front of him row after row of waist-high tombstones jutted from the wet grass.

The voice behind him said, "You brought it?"

Halaby was Syrian, he lived in France, but his English was good. "As instructed. It is in my front pants pocket. Shall I reach for it?"

"Well . . . *I'm* not putting my hand down your pants."

"Yes." Tarek Halaby reached into his pocket slowly and retrieved a blue badge in a plastic case hanging from a lanyard. There was also a folded sheet of paper with an address on it. He held both items back over his shoulder. "The badge will get you into the event. VIP access. As you know, there is no photo. You will have to provide that yourself."

The man behind him took the badge and the paper. "Anything new to report?"

Halaby detected the American accent now, and he knew this was, for certain, the man who had come so highly recommended. He didn't know much about the American other than his reputation. He had been told that this asset was a legend in the world of espionage and covert ops, so *of course* he would be thorough in his preparations, exacting in his demands.

Halaby replied, "All is the same as in the information you were given yesterday."

"Security around the target?"

"As you were told. Five men."

"And the threat?"

"Also the same as before. No more than four hostiles. Five, at most."

"Five is more than four."

Now Halaby swallowed. "Yes . . . well . . . I was told *probably* just four hostiles, so the intelligence is not certain. But it is no worry, because the hostiles will not act until tomorrow, and you will proceed tonight. *Won't* you?"

The asset did not answer the question. "And the target? Still departing France tomorrow?"

"This is unchanged. The flight leaves at one p.m. Again, tonight is the last night where we can—"

"The address written on this paper. Is this the RP?"

"The . . . the *what*?"

"The rally point."

"I'm sorry. I do not know what this means."

Halaby thought he heard a soft sigh of frustration from the other man. Then, "Is this where I go when it's done?"

"Oh . . . Yes. It is the address of our safe house here in Paris."

There was a longer pause now. A grackle landed on a tombstone just a few meters in front of the man with the umbrella, and the rain picked up even more.

Finally the American asset spoke again, but his voice sounded less sure than before. "The man I talked to on the phone. He was French. You are not French."

"The one who you spoke with, the one who hired you through the service in Monte Carlo . . . he works for me."

Halaby heard soft wet footsteps and then the American came into view around the umbrella. He was in his thirties, a touch shorter than Halaby's six feet, with a dark beard and a simple black raincoat. The hood hung low over his eyes; rainwater dripped off it in front of his face.

The American said, "You are Dr. Tarek Halaby, aren't you?"

Halaby's heart began pumping wildly upon hearing this dangerous man uttering his name. "*Oui*, that is correct." He switched his umbrella to his left hand and extended his right.

The asset did not move to accept the handshake. "You are the director of the Free Syria Exile Union."

"Co-director, actually. My wife shares the title."

"You supply medical equipment, medicine, food, water, and blankets to civilians and resistance fighters in Syria."

"Well . . . originally, yes. Relief used to be our only mandate. But we are now involved with more direct opposition of the regime of Ahmed al-Azzam." Halaby spoke through a nervous smile now. "As you know, we haven't hired you to deliver blankets."

The American continued eyeing him, adding to Halaby's disquiet. "One more question."

"Yes, of course."

"How the *hell* are you still alive?"

The rain beat down ceaselessly on the umbrella and the marble structures around the two men. Halaby said, "I . . . I don't understand."

"A hell of a lot of people would love to see you dead. The Syrian government, the Islamic State, the Russians, Hezbollah, the Iranians. And yet you came this morning in person to meet with a man you did not know. And you are here alone."

Halaby answered defensively. "You asked me to send my people away."

"If I asked you to shoot yourself in the face, would you do it?"

Halaby tried to control his breathing. With all the conviction he could muster, he said, "I am not afraid." The truth was he was stone-cold terrified, but he did his best to hide it. "I was told you are the best there is. Why on earth should I be afraid?"

"Because I bet you were told I am the best there is at killing."

Halaby blanched but recovered quickly. "Well . . . we are on the same side, are we not?"

"I am taking money to do a job. That's not exactly a side, is it?"

The older man forced a smile. "Then I guess I should hope the *other* side didn't offer you more to eliminate me." When the American did not return the smile, he added, "It was important I met you. I wanted you to know how crucial tonight is for our movement."

The American seemed to be thinking things over, as if he might just drop the badge in the mud, turn away, and forget this entire affair. Instead he just said, "Trust will get you killed."

Even though he was scared, Halaby realized he was under scrutiny now, and he knew he had to assert himself to earn the respect of this man. He brought his shoulders back and his chin up. "Well, monsieur, if you are here to kill me, get on with it, and if not, let's end this meeting, because you and I both have a lot to do today."

The man in the hooded raincoat sniffed. He was not to be rushed. His eyes shifted around the cemetery for a moment, and then they locked back on the doctor. "I support what you are doing. I took this job because I wanted to help."

Halaby let out a soft breath of relief.

"And that's why it pisses me off to learn that you're an amateur. You're going to get your ass killed long before you or the Free Syria Exile Union actually accomplishes anything. Dudes like you don't last long as revolutionaries unless you take extreme measures to protect yourself and your operation."

Halaby had never been referred to as "dude" in his life, but he did not interact often with Americans outside the occasional surgical symposium. He said, "I am quite aware of the danger. Hiring you, I was told, was the right decision. I hope you will prove me right. By our actions we can, perhaps, deal a serious blow to the Syrian regime and hasten the end of this cruel war. Nothing you could do for our cause could be more important than tonight here in Paris." Halaby raised an eyebrow. "Unless I could persuade you to go to Syria yourself to eliminate President Azzam."

The remark was clearly a joke, but the asset did not laugh. "I said I support what you're doing. I didn't say I was suicidal. Trust me, you'll never get my ass into *that* hellhole."

"That hellhole . . . is my home."

"Well . . . it's not mine."

Both men listened to the rain for a moment, and then Halaby said, "*Please*, monsieur, help us succeed tonight. *Here*."

After another bout of silence, the American in the hooded coat said, "Pull all surveillance on the target. I'll take over. And watch your back. If no one is actively targeting you yet, that will probably change after tonight." He turned away and began moving off around the tombstones to the west.

Halaby called after him, causing him to stop after only a few steps. "You asked me how it is I am still alive."

The American did not turn back. He just stood there, facing away.

"My wife has a philosophy about this. She thinks all the best and bravest of my people died in the first years of the conflict. An entire generation of heroes. Now . . . those of us who are left after seven years of fighting . . . we are the ones who were too afraid to get involved in the beginning.

"My wife says the resistance leaders of today aren't in power now because we are the strongest. The boldest. The most capable. We are in power now, *alive* now, simply because we are all that remain."

The asset began walking again, drifting off through the tombstones, but he spoke over the sound of the rain. "No offense, doc, but I think your wife might be on to something."

Tarek Halaby realized he'd never really studied the man's face, and now, thirty seconds after looking right at him, he doubted he'd recognize him if they met again.

Soon the American disappeared from view through the rain and the dead.

CHAPTER 2

The small and spartan 15th Arrondissement apartment saw no natural light when the sun was out, but on a rainy afternoon like this, the third-floor walk-up appeared positively subterranean inside except for a single lamp on a desk in the corner.

A man sat alone under the lamplight, hunched over the desk, listening to the rain on the nearby shuttered window while he worked. He looked up from his project when he heard a noise over the water dripping off the roof. It was the sound of footsteps in the private courtyard outside, and then the echo of a door slamming shut.

The man rose silently and moved to the window, opened the shutters a few inches, and looked down, his right hand hovering over the grip of the Glock pistol in his waistband.

He saw the origin of the noise instantly. The old woman from apartment 2C stood in the rain, lifted the lid to a garbage can, and poured a full pan of used cat litter into the can. She closed the lid again and returned to the door to the stairwell, and it slammed behind her several seconds after she headed back inside.

Courtland Gentry scanned the entire scene below him now, slowly and carefully, then took a calming breath. He closed the shutters, returned to his chair, then leaned back over his project.

There were a few items lying on the table next to his backpack. Coiled climbing ropes, a gun-cleaning kit. The blue badge given to him by the man in the cemetery lay on the desk before him, under the bright light. Next to it was a passport-quality photo of himself: a two-inch-square shot of him wearing the same clothes he wore now. A charcoal suit coat, a white shirt with a spread collar, and a black tie. Taking his time to check the image carefully, he determined it wasn't perfect, but it was good enough to pass normal scrutiny.

The apartment was all but bare; no personal items lay about, only items needed for today's operation. On his left, just five feet from where he sat, a blue tablecloth was attached low on the wall with pushpins, and a few feet in front of it a camera sat on the seat of a wooden chair. A fluorescent desk lamp stood on the wooden floor pointed towards the tablecloth. Five minutes earlier Court had turned on the light, pressed the ten-second delay on the camera, sat on the floor in front of the blue background, and stared into the lens until the camera clicked. After that he flipped the light back off and printed the image out on the color printer in the corner that he'd purchased for this single two-inch-square image.

Now he took a pair of tweezers and used a craft store glue stick to affix his picture in place on the ID, then pressed down on it with the bottom of a plastic cup from the kitchen, taking his time to make sure it was secure so the corners would not peel.

While he waited he did a few neck rolls to relax. He wasn't a fan of the arts and crafts work that came with his job; he was slow and meticulous with it, and this sort of thing stressed him out. Only by necessity, and only over a long period of time, had he gotten good at it.

Court had served for over a decade in the Central Intelligence Agency, then five more years in the private sector as an assassin for hire. When CIA was running him, he could order up docs, credos, credit cards, and fully backstopped legends with little trouble. But working as a solo act, he'd had to either find private "paper hangers" or create what he needed himself.

Sometimes he was forced to rely solely on his clients to provide the documents for his needs, but today was something of a hybrid situation. His client had been able to procure an authentic badge that would get him into the event he needed to infiltrate, but Court didn't trust his client enough to pass over a photo of himself for them to complete the project.

He'd do the work himself to maintain his personal security.

17

Court had become something of a hybrid himself. He was back with the CIA in an ad hoc contract role, but he retained the autonomy to accept freelance work when he so desired. And today was one hundred percent freelance. Langley had no idea where Court was, or what he was doing, and that was by design. Court didn't know if they'd approve of today's mission, and he didn't give a damn.

For a long time he'd wanted to do something to support the fight against the Syrian regime, and this was his way of doing it without going into Syria. A mission *into* Syria, Court had determined via study of the situation and his many years of personal experience as an intelligence and operational asset . . . would be a fool's errand.

He'd taken this job from a handler based in Monte Carlo who, for a twenty percent finder's fee, served as a cutout in the initial negotiations between the contractor and the client. Court decided the work asked of him looked like it would be difficult but doable. As an additional bonus, the job was in Paris, and Paris was probably Court's favorite city in the world.

But now he couldn't help but worry about the amateurish behavior of his clients. Yes, they seemed to have some top-flight intelligence about his target tonight, but their operational tradecraft was all wrong.

Still . . . the job itself felt right, and that was why Court was here. He'd recently completed a mission in Southeast Asia with flying colors, but the operation had left him angry, empty. The United States had come out the ultimate victors, thanks to Court's actions, and that was the plan, but it was an ugly op, and Court's own actions on the mission left him feeling angry and conflicted. Now he wanted to feel positive about what he was doing, like back in the days before his reconciliation with the Agency.

Court believed in this Paris job, so despite his misgivings about the danger, he would continue on.

He'd earned the moniker Gray Man for his ability to remain low profile, in the shadows, while still completing his arduous assignments. He had the skill to succeed. He believed in his plan, and he believed in his skill to make it through tonight to see the sunrise tomorrow; he told himself all he had to do was keep his eyes open to avoid getting burned by his employer's bad practices.

This was his first work in two months; he'd been lying low, first in Slovenia, then in Austria. He'd spent his time training and hiding, reading and thinking. He was in as good physical shape as he'd been in years, and he'd focused intensely on the physical side of his development recently, because he had concerns he had lost a step mentally. No, it wasn't PTSD or concussions or early-onset dementia that threatened to slow him . . . it was something *much* more debilitating.

It was a woman.

He'd met her on his last operation, spent just a few days with her, but still he could *not* get her out of his mind. She was a Russian intelligence officer, now in the hands of the CIA and buttoned up in some safe house back in the States, and this meant there might be even less chance of him seeing her again than if she'd been working at the Lubyanka in Moscow.

If ever a relationship was doomed to failure, Court acknowledged, it was this one. But he had feelings for her, to the extent he wondered if he was the same person he was before he met her. Had he lost that step? Would he hesitate in danger? Was he open to compromise now that there was someone out there who actually meant something to him?

As he worked on his forged ID badge, Court considered all this for the thousandth time in the past two months. And for the thousand and first time, he admonished himself.

Jesus, Gentry. Turn that shit off. Thoughts like these will get you killed.

This was no life for a man in love. Court saw himself as an instrument, a tool, mission-focused in the extreme. The woman on his mind was on the other side of the globe, embroiled in her own issues, no doubt, and he knew he'd do well to forget about her so he could operate at one hundred percent.

He knew he needed to remain mentally sharp. Especially today, because shit was going to get crazy before the night was through.

The man in the darkened apartment shook off concerns of his diminished mental alertness and climbed into a black two-piece motorcycle rain suit, pulling the rubbery material over the Armani. Then he hefted a pair of black backpacks, locked the door to his apartment on the way out, and made his way down the dark and narrow staircase towards the street.

Paris shone in the afternoon sun, the buildings and streets still glistening from the rain shower that blew out of the area a half hour earlier. Cars rolled by the majestic seventeenth- and eighteenth-century architecture of the 8th Arrondissement, just north of the Seine and within a few blocks east of the imposing Arc de Triomphe.

The Hôtel Potocki on Avenue de Friedland was a structure that would have stood out as a magnificent showpiece in most any other city on Earth, but here in Paris, the Potocki was just another beautiful building on just another beautiful block full of beautiful buildings. It had been built as a palace two hundred years earlier for a family of Polish nobility who made it their life's work to erect ornate residences all over Europe, and they'd spared no expense to illustrate their wealth and power to the Parisians. Even today it remained one of the most elegant mansions in the city, rented out as a high-dollar venue for parties, events, and private get-togethers of the elite.

This afternoon the entrances to the building were surrounded by crowds, all holding their camera phones high in hopes of catching images of the attendees of the exclusive function inside. In addition to the hundreds of onlookers, photographers and reporters milled about, limo drivers stood by their freshly polished vehicles in nearby lots, and private security manned the streets and sidewalks.

But the real action was inside. Through the monumental bronze doors cast by Christofle, up the grand marble staircase, and in the opulent Salle des Lustre, some three hundred well-dressed men and women sat around a long glowing runway that ran below and between rows of crystal chandeliers. The room was packed shoulder-to-shoulder, and thumping music and flashing lights gave an energetic, almost manic feel to the scene.

The announcer proclaimed the arrival of the winter collection, the crowd leaned in, and, one at a time, lithe models began marching authoritatively out onto the catwalk wearing dramatic velvet capes, thigh-high boots, and embroidered chiffon dresses.

The hum of the crowd was unmistakably approving.

In the ninth row, to the right of the runway, sitting at the southern end of the room and holding a camera and an iPad, a man in a charcoal

Armani suit sat next to an elderly woman with a small poodle nestled in her arms. The man's eyeglasses were as refined as his silk tie and handkerchief, and he looked on at the procession traversing the catwalk just like everyone else, craning his head, nodding along with each new look, and tapping notes into his tablet.

The man had avoided the majority of the cameras, and even the lights from the runway did not reach to him in his seat. He was just a face in the crowd. No one in the room was focusing on him, and other than the guard who scanned his pass and the roving waitress with the silver tray of champagne flutes, he'd had no interaction with anyone in the building, though he'd entered a full ninety minutes earlier.

As a new model stepped out from the wings and proceeded down the catwalk, the man in the Armani suit focused intently for a moment, then looked away.

Not her, he told himself.

He took a moment to look around the room again, and not for the first time in the last hour and a half, Court Gentry told himself that this was probably pretty much what his version of hell would look like. Through the too-bright lights he saw the vapid eyes, and through the too-loud music he heard the insipid discussions on inane topics all around him in multiple languages, conversations that he felt made him dumber by the minute for having been forced to listen to them.

The focus on the clothes and the colors and the style and "the scene" was nearly a foreign tongue to him, but he understood enough to know he didn't give a damn about anything being discussed, anywhere in the building. He couldn't imagine anything more annoying than the crowd he sat in, the words from their mouths, the oohs and ahhs about a bunch of clothes no one off a runway would ever wear, *anywhere*, and no one who'd ever eaten a sandwich in their life could fit into in the first place.

Everyone else here insisted on referring to this as Paris Fashion Week, but still, Court was pretty sure he was in hell.

This was the Zuhair Murad show of the Haute Couture Collection, and Court had done just enough study on the designer and his work to pass relaxed scrutiny as a member of the alternative fashion press. His cover was as a freelancer, sent to get impressions and images of the periphery of

Fashion Week for an online style magazine, to chronicle the guests and the clothes and the "scene," whatever the hell that was.

Court looked around. A coked-up sixty-year-old man with a horror-show facelift and eyeliner danced in his chair on the other side of the runway, sloshing half his champagne on the leg of the nineteen-year-old boy seated next to him.

To the extent Court had a scene at all, this sure as shit wasn't it.

But it was Court's job to fit in, no matter what the surroundings, and he did his job well. He was invisible here, because it was his job to be so, just as it had been his job to remain invisible while riding the Metro in D.C., roaming the streets of Hong Kong, or piloting a yacht off Minorca.

His eyes flicked back to the runway, and as the beautiful women came out one by one, he continued scanning them.

Not her. Not her. Not her, either.

His attention moved from the slow procession of models and off the runway entirely. Two athletic men with dark suits and dark hair entered the hall on his right from an access door near the entrance to the stage. They stood back against the wall, scanning the crowd. Court pinged on them instantly, and his eyes casually followed them as they moved closer to the curtain where the models emerged.

Across the lights of the runway he saw another pair of goons, similarly attired, both dark and swarthy. They stood close to the action, and directly behind them a few seated men and women called out to them to try to get them to move.

A security man attached to the venue stepped over to the pair on the far side and ushered them a few feet closer to the wall. They complied, more or less, but they remained within reach of the models on the stage and runway.

And then a tall female model with coal-black hair marched out from behind the wings in a black chiffon dress with silver piping. She was as beautiful as all the others, perhaps even more intense and serious about her work than the rest as she moved up the runway. Through the flashing of dozens of cameras, she marched her stilettos to the beat of an old David Bowie song souped up with industrial techno. Court noticed all four of the big men looking up at her, and then he noticed all four men turning and scanning the crowd. They didn't follow her walk down the length of the raised platform, but their eyes stayed on the three hundred or so in the audience.

Court turned his attention away from the bodyguards, and he focused again on the model.

She was utterly stunning. And she was his target.

CHAPTER 3

Court had her bio down cold. Her name was Bianca Medina; she was twenty-six, positively ancient for a model, although she was one of the most gorgeous women Court had ever laid eyes on, striking even on a runway full of stunning women.

There was a confidence in her moves that he, a complete layman in the world of fashion modeling, recognized instantly.

He raised his camera, pointed it at her, and took a few shots like the rest of the crowd holding cameras, but quickly he turned the lens to the first duo of security men at the back wall. He took several pictures, then shifted in his seat a little and got a few shots of the pair on his right, on his side of the runway.

Private security protection was not the norm for the models here at the Zuhair Murad show, but Court knew things about Bianca Medina no one else in the room did, and for that reason he knew she didn't have much in common with the other women walking the runway today.

She showcased her dress and left through the sequined curtain at the rear of the stage. The security men disappeared through the stage doors at the same moment she did, no doubt forming around her backstage to escort her to her dressing area. Court assumed she'd be hustled into another outfit and sent back out onto the runway in minutes, but he'd seen all he needed to see, so he stood and left the Salle des Lustre.

As he headed down the grand staircase on his way to a side entrance of the Hôtel Potocki, he thought about what he'd just learned. He'd been told Medina would have her own security team of five men, but he'd needed to test the accuracy of this information he'd been given on this assignment. With his own eyes he'd seen four bodyguards, and he assumed another man would be waiting outside in a vehicle, so his intel appeared to be accurate.

Good, he thought. His client's tradecraft might have been amateurish, but it seemed, so far, at least, that his intelligence product was solid.

Court exited the building, passed by dozens of mostly young men and women clambering to get a look at a famous guest or a beautiful model at the side exit, then he walked two blocks to his black 2010 Yamaha XJ6 motorcycle, left in a lot on the Rue Chateaubriand. Here he unlocked the top case on the back of his bike and then took off his Armani jacket. After kicking out of his leather wingtips, he pulled the two-piece motorcycle rain suit from the case and put it on in seconds, then slipped into a pair of black tennis shoes. He crammed his coat and shoes in the case and relocked it, donned his black helmet, lowered the smoked visor, and climbed aboard the bike.

He drove around to the back of the venue, having already scoped out the exit the models were using for the fashion show. Here he parked fifty yards from the door but remained on his motorcycle, and he steeled himself for a long wait.

• • •

Court sat on his bike, his attention shifting from the Hôtel Potocki to the passing vehicles on the roads to the windows and roofs of buildings in the neighborhood. Every now and then a car would roll up to the rear door and someone would either climb out of the vehicle and step into the building or step out of the building and climb into the vehicle; the three dozen or so onlookers on the sidewalk crowded behind the rope and kept back by a security man took pictures of the action. But despite the movement, Court saw no hint of his target.

An hour and forty minutes after Court took up his watch, a silver Cadillac Escalade pulled up by the rear door of the Potocki, and the employee access door opened in symmetry with the big vehicle's arrival. Court locked his eyes to the scene now, thinking this looked like it could be a trained security movement in action. Just as he suspected, a pair of Bianca Medina's bodyguards stepped out of the building and looked around at the small crowd and the street, and then the model herself appeared. Her hands held her camel raincoat tight against her neck, her massive bag swung from her shoulder, and she walked with a determined gait. She kept her head down; many in the crowd took pictures of her because she *looked* famous, even if they didn't know who, in fact, she was.

In five seconds she was ensconced in the SUV, and it was moving as soon as the last door closed.

Court fired up his bike and followed the Escalade to the east.

. . .

The Yamaha wound through the thick early-evening traffic on the Avenue de Friedland following 150 yards back from the Escalade. He found himself too far behind at one point, so he ignored the lane markers and darted through the gridlock at an intersection, swaying left and right as needed to keep his momentum while the cars and trucks around the motorcycle moved at a snail's pace.

Court kept his head on a swivel, his eyes firing down to his mirrors, making sure there wasn't a chase car working with Medina's protection element, or even another group targeting and following the model and her entourage. He'd satisfied himself he hadn't been compromised, but his tradecraft skills caused him to resatisfy himself of his own personal security every few seconds.

They were heading east, and this indicated to Court that they weren't going to one of three hotels with rooms reserved for models in the Zuhair Murad show. He'd doubted from the beginning his target would have much contact with the other women and girls, and this just confirmed his suspicion.

He wasn't surprised she was steering clear of the more public places; he just leaned lower on his bike and told himself he couldn't lose her now, because he probably wouldn't be able to reacquire the woman if the Escalade disappeared in the traffic.

Fortunately for the man on the motorcycle, the drive to his target's next destination was only ten minutes. The Cadillac pulled up in front of an open set of red arched doors at 7 Rue Tronchet. Court had just made the turn in front of L'eglise de la Madeleine, a massive Roman Catholic church here in the 8th Arrondissement, when he saw Bianca's long black hair emerge from the silver SUV. She marched through the open doorway surrounded by four of her five bodyguards.

He continued heading north, past the scene, and only looked into the arch to see a darkened forecourt and confirm that there was no signage or other indicators of what sort of building Medina was entering.

Court rolled his bike up onto the curb a block to the north and parked it next to a public toilet. From here he could still see the front of the building at 7 Rue Tronchet across the street, but he was out of range of any possible cameras around the building.

He pulled out his phone without removing his helmet. He pushed some buttons and waited for the call to be answered. Soon a male voice with a French accent spoke into Court's Bluetooth earpiece.

"Oui?"

"Sept Rue Tronchet."

"Est vous sûr?" Are you sure?

"Bien sûr." Of course.

There was a slight delay as his contact did some research on his end about the location, so Court took the time to check his own security here. It seemed to be a typical cloudy spring afternoon on a typical central Paris intersection, which meant a lot of traffic, both pedestrian and automobile, and quite a few people just standing around. There were window shoppers, smokers standing in front of shops and office buildings, men and women selling out of food kiosks and newsstands.

But within ten seconds of the beginning of his scan, a pair of men on the opposite sidewalk set off Court's internal alarm. They were on motorcycles next to each other, one man on a black Honda and the other on a red Suzuki, and they scanned the area, much like Court himself was now doing.

Court looked around at the buildings behind the pair, tried to come up with a legitimate reason they would pick that part of the sidewalk to park, and came up with nothing. A women's clothing store. A perfumery. A shop that made and sold high-end confectionery.

Sure . . . these guys could be out picking up gifts for wives or girl-friends. But they had no bags with them, only backpacks with webbing on the outside used to strap more gear on, a feature common with military and police personnel.

He put them in their late thirties or early forties; they were relatively fit men, one bearded with wavy brown hair and the other completely bald and clean-shaven. There was a hard edge to both that was easily apparent to Court, even from this distance. They weren't military—not active duty, anyway—and they certainly weren't beat cops, but Court wondered if they might be attached to the police or government in some capacity.

Their backpacks and helmets looked well used, but both their motorcycles appeared to be almost new. He had the impression that these guys could handle more powerful bikes than the ones they were sitting on, so he pegged the motorcycles as rentals.

As Court concentrated on remaining subtle—performing the balancing act of surveilling two people while at the same time remaining sensitive to any possible countersurveillance—his earpiece came alive again with a response from the Frenchman.

"*Sept* Rue Tronchet is a *hôtel particulier*. A private guesthouse for wealthy travelers visiting Paris. Four suites. Five floors. Minimal security . . . but cameras in the lobby, stairs, and lift. Good locks, no easy roof access."

"My problem. Not yours."

"*D'accord.*" *Agreed.* "What do you need?"

"A car. Somewhere within three blocks of the target location."

"It will be delivered. You will be texted with the drop-off location."

"Okay." And then: "Question . . . Do you have any eyes trailing the target?"

"*Non.* You demanded we discontinue surveillance."

"You're certain your guys are clear of this scene?"

"Absolutely so. We did not have any idea she would be going to Rue Tronchet. All our assets are accounted for. Why . . . ? Is there a problem?"

Court looked up to the two bikers again. The brown-haired man on the Honda was gone; he must have headed off to the south, otherwise Court would have seen him race past. And the bald man on the Suzuki was just now putting his helmet on. In seconds he fired up his bike and rolled off to the north.

"'Allo?"

Court asked, "Who else might be interested in the target? Caucasians. Europeans."

After a pause the Frenchman said, "No one. Certainly no Caucasians that I can think of. None."

But Court was less sure now than he had been about the pair. Court was certain they hadn't ID'd him, so he couldn't imagine why they would leave like this if, indeed, they had been following Medina or holding surveillance on her building. And, try as he might, Court couldn't find anyone else in the crowd who looked like they might have replaced these two in coverage.

"'Allo?" the man said again.

"It's nothing," Court replied, though he wasn't at all sure. "Just deliver the car and text me the location."

Court made to hang up when he heard the man speak.

"When do you think you will be able to—"

Court ended the call.

He started the Yamaha again, brushing off lingering thoughts of the two men. He drove off to circle the block and try to find a better place for surveillance, because he was certain this was his target's residence for the evening, and *this* would be the evening he'd come for her.

CHAPTER 4

At ten p.m. Bianca Medina left her private apartment on the Rue Tronchet, climbed into her silver Escalade with her full security detail, and rode in silence for the ten-minute journey to a two-Michelin-star restaurant on the Rue Lord Byron.

Here she was escorted into an ornate private room by the maître d', the door was closed, and she dined alone.

Well, not really alone.

Three of her five minders sat at the two other tables in the room, with a fourth man just beyond the door to the main dining room, and the fifth with the Escalade outside.

The men around her did not make eye contact with Bianca, nor she with them. There was little talking between the protectee and any of her protectors and no real conversation whatsoever. The detail and the principal had a prickly relationship that no one in the mix seemed anxious to rectify.

Bianca sat at her candlelit table, nursed a flute of champagne, and picked at a salad with no dressing. She alternatively nibbled on her food and thumbed a copy of French *Vogue* she'd pulled out of her handbag. Bianca was from Spain, but she spoke French and English fluently, having lived in Paris and New York working as a model, dividing her time between the two fashion meccas for nearly a decade before all but retiring three years earlier.

Her waiter was a handsome man in his midtwenties, a few years younger than her and a thousand times more upbeat and talkative, and he was clearly fascinated by the sullen-looking beauty with the expensive jewelry and the big security entourage. He attempted to flirt with her at every opportunity, showing himself not to be intimidated by either her magnificence or the gruff men surrounding her.

Bianca had ignored his early attempts at small talk, but this Casanova wasn't one to take no for an answer, so the more curt she became, the more he wanted to break through her tough exterior.

As he removed her salad plate and replaced her silverware, he asked, "Are you in town on vacation?"

"Work," she said, not even looking up from *Vogue*.

"Of course. You must be here for Fashion Week."

She did not reply.

"A supermodel. I would surely recognize you if I spent more time following celebrity magazines."

Nothing.

After a pause, the waiter leaned a little closer. "Madame . . . I just have to say it—"

She flipped a page in her magazine. "No, monsieur . . . whatever it is, you do not."

The handsome waiter hesitated again, surprised at the remark, but he recovered. He somehow didn't get the hint that Bianca was not a woman to be toyed with. "Forgive me, but while I understand why a true beauty like you must be well protected, I don't understand why you can't give just a little smile. It is always sad to dine alone, *c'est vrai*, but a perfect woman in a perfect restaurant in a perfect city should, at least, try to find a way to be happy."

Bianca lifted her eyes from the magazine only now, but not to look at the Frenchman. Instead she just glanced towards Shalish, the leader of her security detail, sitting alone at a candlelit table by the door to the dining room. He had certainly heard the exchange, she knew, because Shalish missed nothing.

Shalish, in turn, looked to his two men, and Bianca turned her attention to the waiter now. In French she said, "Go away. Come back with food, or don't come back at all."

31

The waiter was used to women playing hard to get, but he clearly was *not* used to such cruel rejection. After a moment's pause, he bowed curtly and turned on his heels, heading towards the door.

Shalish glared at the waiter as the young man passed by. As Bianca began to look back down to her magazine, she saw two of her bodyguards standing—off the look from their boss, no doubt—and following the young man out the door.

Ten seconds later she heard an exclamation in the kitchen, then a clanking of plates and glasses.

She could picture the scene. The waiter was either up against the wall or down on the floor, and he was in pain. She imagined the good-looking man would be sent home for the evening, perhaps to tend to a black eye or a sore shoulder joint.

To the guards around her, to the restaurant staff, and most certainly to the waiter with the wounded body and pride, Bianca Medina appeared to be a cold and cruel bitch, but as far as she was concerned, she'd done the would-be Lothario a favor. If she'd shown any interest in him, given him any sort of green light that emboldened him to press on with his attempts at seduction, the men with Medina would have probably taken it upon themselves to put the waiter in the hospital with shattered bones and broken teeth.

Bianca had learned over the past few years that the kindest turn she could do her fellow man was often to encourage them to just walk on by her without a passing glance.

Minutes later a new waiter, this one older, blander, and almost catatonic in his countenance, appeared with her entrée, coq au vin, with the sauce in a silver boat on the side. He put it in front of her with a quick and perfunctory "bon appétit," and then he was gone.

Bianca Medina reached for her fork and knife now; she put the handsome young waiter out of her mind and did not think of him again.

• • •

The Escalade pulled back in front of the archway at 7 Rue Tronchet at midnight, and Bianca Medina returned to her three-thousand-square-foot fifth-floor suite. While one of the dark-suited men remained in the lobby, the four others entered the suite with her. They took up their positions in the living area, kitchen, and guest rooms, while she entered the master bedroom alone without a word to anyone.

She'd fly home tomorrow, but not till early afternoon, and she knew her detail would not allow her to go anywhere other than to breakfast before heading to the airport. This meant she could sleep in, so she dawdled in her room for a while. She looked through the rest of her magazine while lying on the bed, then spent a few minutes standing on the balcony and looking out over the forecourt of the property. She regarded the single shot of brandy in the large lead crystal decanter on the nightstand by her bed, then poured the shot into the snifter left there for her. She drank the sweet liquid while she perused her magazine once more. And then, shortly after one a.m., she pulled an extra blanket from the linen closet next to the bathroom door, climbed into bed, and flipped off the light on the end table next to her.

Seconds later she began to cry.

• • •

Are you fucking serious?

Court Gentry knelt just twenty feet away, watching the woman through a slat between two louvers in the door of the linen closet, a thin sheen of sweat glistening in the thin shaft of moonlight running across his forehead. He'd removed the lower shelf in the closet so he could fit there on his knees, and then he'd pushed back tight into the small and dark space and covered his body with a pair of large pillows. And he was glad he'd done so, because when his target had opened the door to grab the extra blanket, he'd been able to remain tucked under the middle shelf and out of her view.

He looked forward to being able to stand again to straighten his legs, but his plan had been to give his target time to fall asleep before moving on her.

But now she was crying for some reason, and Court worried it would take her a while to nod off.

He looked down to his watch; its hour and minute hands were tipped with vials of tritium gas so they would show faintly, even in complete darkness. He told himself he could wait a half hour, but then he'd need to act, whether or not she was asleep.

33

Court was dressed head to toe in black, and he wore a small black pack on his back staged with rappelling gear, a suppressed Glock 19 snapped into an open-style molded polymer holster on his hip, and a pair of flash bang grenades on his Kevlar vest. A black Benchmade Infidel switchblade was hooked into his back pocket, smoke grenades and a fixed-blade knife hung in sheaths on his utility belt, and another blade was hooked into one of his black Merrell boots.

He had a plan tonight, and he'd prepped accordingly, perhaps even overpreparing with all the gear on his body, but Court had learned through hard experience that out here in the field he could rely on no one but himself, so everything he might possibly require on an operation he needed to have within reach before the onset of action.

Court had been trained by the CIA, specifically by a grizzled Vietnam veteran he knew as Maurice, and Maurice had a saying that played back in Court's brain at times like this. *Son . . . you can never have too much ammo unless you're drowning or on fire.*

Court had laughed the first time Maurice said it, but he quit laughing the first time the saying had saved his life.

Bianca Medina's crying intensified for a few minutes, then softened to sobs, and eventually even that drifted away. Court didn't know what she was upset about, and he didn't really care, except for the fact he wanted her to hurry up and fall asleep so he could get on with his night.

The last thing he needed was her calling out to her gorillas when he crossed the room towards her.

Soon Medina rolled onto her side, facing Court's direction. The blinds were open on the French doors out to the balcony, and faint moonlight from outside reached into the room and illuminated her face. Even from across the master bedroom, the man in the closet could see that the woman's eyes were open and wet.

Count sheep, lady. I don't have all damn night.

To his pleasure, soon her eyes closed and remained so. He watched the cadence of her breathing slow finally, and he knew she was out, or close to it.

After another check of his watch, he told himself he'd move in five minutes.

Just then, the shafts of moonlight on Bianca Medina's face altered, and

Court leaned to his left to try to get a look outside on the balcony. He didn't have much room to maneuver where he knelt, but by pressing his head all the way against the wall, he could see what had interrupted the light.

He blinked hard in surprise.

One of Medina's bodyguards stood on the balcony just outside the window, staring through the glass at the woman lying in bed.

Court knew the layout of this property because he'd had the run of the place for much of the time the entourage was out to dinner. He'd come down from the roof of an adjacent building full of retail spaces, and he'd dropped onto the balcony where the guard now stood. There was no real access from any other part of the building, which meant the bodyguard must have climbed out the window of the other bedroom in the suite and scooted along a foot-wide ledge to make his way to the balcony.

What the hell? Court wondered. *Does this guy really have orders to watch his protectee sleep?*

The woman seemed to have no idea he was there, or else she was so accustomed to being watched over like this that it no longer bothered her at all.

Or else, and Court imagined this to be a distinct possibility, it *did* bother her, and that was why she cried herself to sleep.

Court almost felt sorry for her for a moment.

Almost.

The arrival of the close-protection agent on the balcony complicated the situation exponentially. Court had a Gemtech suppressor on his Glock pistol, but shooting this asshole was still going to make a hell of a lot of noise. The men in other parts of the suite would all hear it, and they'd come hard and fast in the protection of their client.

He decided he'd watch the guard for a few minutes to see if he'd leave, or at least turn away. But if the man remained there, focused on Bianca Medina through the glass door of the balcony, Court would just have to deal with the sentry before carrying on with his mission, because it looked like there was no way he was getting to the girl without the man seeing him.

• • •

There was little automobile traffic in the 8th Arrondissement at this time of night; the area was all but deserted, but a single man on a bicycle rolled along the Rue Tronchet, passing the Madeleine church. A few seconds later a second bicycle appeared from the north, and a third turned onto the street from the west just after that. All three cyclists slowed when they came to a point just south of the big red double doors closing off the forecourt of the *hôtel particulier*.

Two of the men climbed off their bikes and stepped up to the wall just feet from the doorway, while the third dropped his kickstand and parked directly under the security camera pointing down to the pavement in front of the doorway. He deftly climbed up onto his bike, put one foot on the top tube and another on the seat, and used the wall of the building and his left hand to balance himself there. With his right hand he pulled a can of black spray paint from the pocket of his hoodie. He shook the can a couple of times, then sprayed up from below, coating the lens of the camera black in an instant.

The two others watched him work, and as soon as he was finished they rushed forward, knelt at the door latch, and pulled out their lock-picking tools. One man centered a flashlight's beam on the lock while the other worked, and while this was going on, the man on the bike jumped down, pulled out his phone, and speed-dialed a number. He stood there looking up and down the street, ready to warn the lock-picking team of any passersby on the sidewalks or vehicles on the road.

He did see one vehicle almost immediately, but he did not caution his mates. A black work van with its lights extinguished rolled slowly into view on the far side of the Madeleine church to the south, some hundred meters away, and it stopped there.

Into his phone the lookout whispered, *"Je te vois."* I see you.

Behind him, he heard a soft click as the lock picker finished his work. The man pushed down on the latch slowly and softly, so as to avoid any echoes in the cobblestoned forecourt on the other side of the arched passage just beyond the door.

Then the kneeling man whispered, "We're in."

With that, the lookout delivered an urgent whisper into the phone. *"Aller! Aller!"*

The van began racing forward, closing on 7 Rue Tronchet, as all three men at the door pulled submachine guns from inside their coats.

CHAPTER 5

Court decided he had to get on with it, because his legs were cramping, and he had a funny feeling he was going to need to be able to walk, or more likely to run, in order to survive the next few minutes. He'd aim for stealth for as long as possible, but he'd be ready to go loud the instant gunfire was required. He pulled his suppressed Glock with his right hand and slowly pushed the linen closet door open with his knee. He climbed out, stood on aching legs, then began sliding slowly to his left, along the farthest edges of the room, moving away from the balcony and away from the bed.

His first objective was the door that divided the master bedroom from the rest of the suite. As he inched along the wall in the dark, he kept one eye on the sentry, who was still facing the woman on the bed, slightly away from Court's position here at the man's nine o'clock. With his other eye Court kept checking Medina herself to make sure she did not awaken, because her eyes were pointed in his direction.

When he arrived at the bedroom door, Court stopped and leaned back against it, still facing the open room. He reached into the cargo pocket on his left leg and pulled a device from it. It was a TacWedge door jammer, a light plastic chock that could be slid under a door and forced into position, making the door nearly impossible to open from the other side. He knelt down slowly, still checking the two forms across the room, making sure the guard remained outside on the balcony and facing the woman, and the woman was still asleep, or at least unaware there was an armed man in black forty feet away.

As he reached out with the wedge, preparing to make it impossible for the four men in the suite to gain access to their protectee, he was surprised to hear a man's shout, somewhere downstairs outside the building.

It seemed to echo up from the cobblestoned forecourt. Court saw the bodyguard on the balcony spin away quickly and rush to the railing to look down.

And almost immediately Court heard the thundering boom of a rifle in the forecourt below.

The bodyguard ducked back away from the edge and pulled his weapon from inside his jacket.

What the fuck?

The first gunshot was followed one second later by a string of automatic gunfire; Court could hear shouts now in the living room of the suite, on the other side of the door behind him, as Bianca's bodyguards became aware of the threat. The American dropped the rest of the way to his knees, held his pistol up towards the balcony, and reached behind him to jam the TacWedge under the door. Then he stood and heel-kicked it hard into place.

The sound of his actions was drowned out by an explosion outside that set off car alarms and broke glass all over the neighborhood. As soon as the echoes of the boom died out, another intense volley of fire kicked off. The shouts of men—the rhythmic and repetitive cadence of *"Allahu akhbar"*—made it all the way four stories up and through the closed balcony doors of the bedroom.

Court was surprised that this attack was happening now, but he wasn't surprised it was happening, because he knew something about the threats his target faced. These assholes below were ISIS, they were coming for her at the same time he was, and he'd been assured by his client that they would *not* hit until tomorrow.

Courtland Gentry was a man trained against believing in coincidence, and he had a sinking impression that he had been set up, or at least willfully misinformed about his mission. And *this* pissed him off. Even in the chaos of this moment, the myriad new and imminent dangers he now faced at his objective, Court still had the presence of mind to tell himself that he was going to beat the living shit out of the people who'd hired him for this operation when this was all over.

But first he had to deal with the woman.

At the same instant that Bianca Medina spun out of bed in her warm-ups and sweatshirt, panic-stricken by the gunfire outside, the bodyguard on the balcony flung open the French doors, on his way to put his hands on his protectee and lead her to safety. The man hadn't yet seen Court, but since the American was in the middle of the large room and advancing on the same objective the guard was, Court knew he wasn't going to be invisible for much longer.

Behind Court someone tried to open the bedroom door, then shouted and slammed against it when he found it braced shut. The bodyguard looked up towards the sound, saw Court there in the darkness, and swung his weapon up to fire.

Court's weapon was already on target, so he fired first, sending a 9-millimeter hollow-point round across the room and into the Syrian's throat. The bodyguard lurched back with a cry of shock. He grabbed at his wound, but Court shot him again, this time through the solar plexus, and the man fell flat on his back, his arms wide, half inside and half outside the balcony doors.

Bianca Medina screamed in utter terror.

The sound of the suppressed gunshots had been all but hidden by the thunder of several weapons firing at once in the stone forecourt and the lobby of the property below, so the men slamming their shoulders into the door of the bedroom wouldn't have heard them, but Bianca Medina *did* hear the noise, and she saw the flash of the weapon held by the masked apparition running at her, just five meters from her bed. She dove back onto the king-sized bed and rolled over to the other side. Here she launched off and hoisted the lead crystal decanter that had held the brandy, swinging it over her head like a bat.

Court himself leapt onto the bed, in pursuit of his fleeing target. He holstered his weapon as he did so, and by the time he landed on the other side, both his hands were free.

"I'm on your side, Bianca."

She swung the lead crystal decanter at the man in black, but he ducked back and away easily.

39

In French she shouted, "Take my money! Don't hurt me!"

Court closed on her again, and the decanter whipped by his face once more, but this time Court swept it from her hand, knocking it across the bed and onto the floor. Then he took the woman by both wrists and spun her around and up to the wall. Leaning against her body with his own to control her, Court pinned her hands behind her back.

"Listen to me! Calm down! I won't hurt you, but everyone else around here will. We need to go, and I'll need your help."

In English she shouted into the wall, "What is happening?"

New gunfire snapped inside the building now. The attackers were clearly making progress on their way up the two sets of stairs on opposite sides of the property. For all Court knew, others were in the elevator and could be here on the top floor in seconds. Bianca's bodyguards in the suite banged on the door of the master bedroom and slammed into it with ferocious tenacity, desperate to get to their protectee.

"What is happening?" she shouted again.

Court said, "You and I are checking out. As for the rest of that racket, my guess is hotel security and your bodyguards are fighting it out with the Islamic State."

She looked back to him, eyes wide. "ISIS? What does ISIS want with *me*?"

Court didn't look at her now; he just spun her around as he held on to her arm. He looked around the room, trying to figure out how the hell to get both himself and the woman to safety. While doing this he said, "Lady, we *both* know the answer to that question."

Bianca *did* know the answer, but Court imagined she had been hoping her rescuer did not.

To her credit, Bianca Medina seemed to realize quickly that she was in serious trouble, and this man in black was her only lifeline. "What do you want me to do?"

Court looked around the big room. Men banged frantically on the door. "Give me a second."

With a panic-stricken voice she said, "You just told me we had to go *now*!"

His original plan had been to use the climbing rope and rappelling equipment stored in his pack to simply hook her onto him with a harness, and then use the harness on his own body to lower them one story down to the balcony below her suite before heading to the hotel stairs to make a stealthy escape through a back exit. But a gun battle of this magnitude raging in central Paris was going to bring a *lot* of law enforcement, and Court knew he didn't have time to make it down the stairs inside the hotel, through security and terrorists, before the police arrived and cordoned off the property at ground level.

He told himself he needed to somehow get all the way down into the forecourt and out an alleyway to a neighboring property, in the next minute or two, to have *any* chance of avoiding getting caught in a massive police cordon.

Court could climb down the outside of the building on his own in that amount of time, but he sure as *hell* couldn't do it while attached to this terrified woman. He looked around the suite a moment more, and formulated a hasty plan. His eyes darted to the dead body, then to the door of the room, and then to the balcony railing.

"Hey!" she shouted. "What are we going to—"

Court came up with a solution for the equation in front of him. He raced over to the body of the dead Syrian lying on the balcony threshold, grabbed the man by the underarms, then dragged him hurriedly across the hardwood floor, all the way to the door of the suite on the opposite side of the room. A gunfight had begun raging just outside; the men who, seconds earlier, had been banging on the door were now shooting it out with someone near the exterior door to the suite, and no one was trying to get into the bedroom for the time being.

Court pulled the end of a spooled climbing rope from his bag, wrapped it under the dead man's body at the underarms, then tied it off quickly and securely with a bowline knot that would tighten the more tension it was put under.

"What are you doing?" Medina asked.

He stepped up to her now, playing the rope out of the pack and tossing it in coils on the floor as he did so. "I need you to trust me."

"I . . . I don't trust you at all!"

"Then *fear* me, lady. That'll work." He drew his Benchmade Infidel; the blade fired out and glowed in the dim moonlight, and with it he cut the rope where it went into his bag. He took this end and tied it onto a clasp

41

already attached to a single-point nylon-and-elastic harness, which he also yanked from the bag.

Bianca's terror was giving in to confusion. "What is . . ."

Court reached behind Bianca's torso and wrapped the harness under her arms, brought both ends around and above her breasts, and fastened them together with the metal locking clasp.

She tried to pull away, but he was too strong, too fast. Too sure of himself.

"Why the *fuck* are you tying me to Mohammed?"

"I'm trying to make Mohammed useful." He turned the woman to the balcony, then pushed her along through the open French doors.

Bianca quickly figured out that the man in black wanted her to climb out over the railing to be lowered down, and this stopped her in her tracks. "No!"

The gunfire stopped in the suite so suddenly that both Court and Bianca spun back to the new quiet, but Court returned to his work quickly, and soon he tightened his hand on Bianca's shoulder, turning her back around to the railing. "We have to hurry. You'll be fine. I promise. Just close your eyes."

Someone banged on the door now, fifty feet away.

"I can't do it!"

Court snapped his switchblade closed and threaded the device's belt hook inside the harness around Bianca's torso. "I'm going to lower you down very gently. When you get to the ground, cut yourself loose. Find cover behind one of the stone planters in the forecourt. I'll free-climb down. Wait for me."

"No! I can*not*! I'm scared."

Court lifted the woman off the ground now, cradling her in his arms. He jerked his head towards the door to the suite. "Whatever is about to come through that door will be a lot scarier than this."

Court's plan was to use the dead guard as a counterweight and the friction of the body along the fifty feet of travertine bedroom floor and stone balcony tile as a means to control Bianca's descent more easily than lowering her himself. Since the dead bodyguard weighed more than the Spanish fashion model, Court knew he would have to assist her descent by pulling the rope along, but this would be easier and faster for him than slowly lowering the 110-pound woman four floors down to the cobble-stones.

Court stepped up to the balcony railing, and the woman squeezed her eyes shut.

"Please, monsieur . . . I just—"

"I'll be gentle, and I'll go as slow as I can. It will be a nice, smooth ride as long as you—"

An explosion behind caused them both to spin their heads around again. The door to the living room had been blown in with some sort of charge, and debris tore through the room. As the two on the balcony watched, a pair of figures began rushing into the bedroom through the smoke and dust. Behind them in the living room, three more apparitions appeared. All the men held weapons and wore black tactical gear, and they seemed to float around in the haze like danger itself.

Court stood with Bianca fifty feet away, directly in the line of fire of five submachine guns.

The Gray Man whirled back away from the danger, and with all the momentum of his spin, he heaved the woman over the balcony railing, throwing her out into the night air.

Court spun back and drew his Glock, while behind him Bianca Medina screamed as she dropped like a stone.

CHAPTER 6

The slack rope tightened, and in the bedroom by the shattered living room door the body of the Syrian guard lurched and began rocketing across the travertine floor, many times faster than Court had planned.

Court knew his only option had been to toss the girl and engage the attackers, but he also knew that throwing her over the side like that was going to give her too much momentum, more than enough to send her to her death if he couldn't arrest her descent before she hit the hard stone tiles of the forecourt.

But he couldn't even address that problem yet. The first burst of incoming rounds screamed high over Court's head, and he raced forward on the balcony, then dove headfirst, launching himself to the right of the French doors, rolling on his right shoulder under the spraying gunfire and up onto his kneepads in a firing stance. He came to a stop upright, still in view of the enemy through the sidelight next to the doors. His Glock was out in front of him, his front sight lining up on a target, a man moving laterally in the bedroom from right to left, trying to get his own sight picture on Court.

But the American saw the terrorist first, aimed his weapon first, and fired first, and he hit the man just under the right collarbone. A second shot sparked off the man's MP5 rifle, ricocheted up into his face, and sent him tumbling back against the far wall of the bedroom and down to the floor, covering his eyes and screaming.

Court felt the compression in the air from a shrieking round missing the left side of his head by less than a foot, and he saw the muzzle flash ahead, pinpointing his target kneeling near the linen closet, still obscured by smoke and darkness in the recesses of the bedroom. Court fired a string of four rounds in his target's direction, over the dead man tied to Bianca and sliding along facedown on the floor.

Behind Court on his left, the rope whined and burned as it ran over the iron railing.

He knew if he grabbed the thin rope with his bare hands it would rip his hands to shreds, and Bianca would continue falling too fast to survive the impact. And even if he grabbed the corpse as it passed he would probably dislocate an arm and still fail to stop Medina from hitting the cobblestones hard.

His only chance to prevent Bianca's impact with the ground was to dive flat on top of the dead-body counterweight before she hit.

Court fired three more rounds through the sidelight again, towards the doorway to the living room, then rolled out from behind concealment, launching himself to the left with all the power in his legs.

He landed on the bodyguard fifteen feet from the railing, then went flat, emptying his Glock at the terrorists in the doorway as he glided along on top of the corpse.

He stopped just six feet from the edge of the balcony as his pistol locked open.

Bianca would be dangling just a few feet off the alley pavement now . . . *if* Court's calculations had been correct. But if he had made an error in his math, then she would probably be lying dead on the cobblestones of the forecourt behind and below him.

A massive, sustained volley of gunfire erupted now, and the balcony was riddled with lead. Court rolled off the body, then again went to his right, outside the view of the shooters but not out of danger, as their bullets threatened to rip apart the stone masonry of the outer wall of the bedroom. All around him on the balcony, planters cracked and spilled their contents, glass shattered, and bullets ricocheted up into the night with a high-pitched whine.

This was not a sustainable fight for him, Court knew, but he also knew he could not simply climb down the outside of the building without these

45

men making their way to the balcony and easily picking off Medina as she hung there by the rope.

Either he had to defeat the attackers up here totally, or else he had to find a faster way down to the forecourt.

As he reloaded while lying flat on the balcony tile, an idea came to him. He fired half a dozen more 9-millimeter rounds to keep the heads of the men in the living room down, then reached for his vest and pulled a device from it with his left hand. It was a "nine-banger" flash bang grenade, and Court pulled the ring and side-armed the small can towards the enemy at the door.

After just one second, while it was still in the air soaring across the bedroom, the nine-banger began to detonate, and intense white bursts and extremely loud reports erupted, but the device continued to sail on, hitting the travertine floor at the doorway and bouncing into the living room, right in the middle of the men there.

Nine flashes and booms in all blasted from the device, and while it was still going off, stunning and blinding everyone in the area, Court unfastened a second canister from his belt. This was a single-detonation stun grenade. He pulled both pull rings and slung it towards the threats in the living room.

This one did not arc as high; it bounced along and then slid across the bedroom, but right at the doorway it, too, detonated, delivering an explosion of 180 decibels—30 decibels louder than a jet engine on takeoff. It gave off a burst of light rated at one million candelas, enough to cause flash blindness to anyone within close proximity.

Even before the device went off, Court was up off the balcony tile and running forward, towards the danger, as fast as he could, his eyes closed and face averted from the light and his brain anticipating the boom that would take the others by stunned surprise. He crossed the bedroom in less than three seconds, leapt through the air, landed and slid on his hip along the travertine through the doorway into the living room. Here he found himself in the midst of three utterly stunned attackers. None of the men could see or hear, and Court's plan had been to simply shoot each man with his suppressed Glock and end the threat completely. But just as he skidded to a stop on his back and leveled his weapon at the first dazed terrorist, gunfire cracked from the doorway between the big suite and the hallway that led to the stairs. Multiple flashes of light erupted, and Court realized there was at least one more gunman in the hall engaging him.

Court shifted his aim to the doorway, spreading his legs and pointing his weapon down between his feet, and fired his Glock until it emptied again, sending the shooter or shooters there to cover and buying himself an instant of mobility.

He didn't have time to reload the pistol and shoot the three men on their knees around him, so he slapped his empty weapon back into the polymer holster and reached into his pack with one hand to grab the second rope line that he stored there, while using his other hand to take hold of the ammo vest worn by the closest terrorist.

Court yanked the man to him, hooked the carabiner on the end of the line to the man's vest, then leapt to his feet and started back for the bedroom in a low sprint.

He'd made it just a couple of steps before booming gunfire from the hallway behind him began again, and just two more steps before he reached the other two men there at the doorway. Both were still down on their hands and knees, only now beginning to fight their way out of the several-seconds-long disorientation brought on by the two grenades.

As Court passed the second man he saw that the terrorist had a baseball-sized M67 hand grenade hooked in a pouch on his vest. Court reached out as he ran by, jammed his thumb inside the pull ring, and pressed on the safety lever with his hand. He raced on, yanking the pull ring along with him.

The still-dazed man recognized what had just happened, but his reaction was slowed by his concussion and his double vision. He just climbed up to his feet and reached out weakly towards the man rushing by, as if to stop him.

Court kept running, even faster now, letting the ring drop to the floor of the bedroom as rope spooled out from his backpack behind him. A round from an MP5 slammed into the bedpost ahead and on his left, splintering the hand-carved finial, but all Court could do was shift a little to the right, duck lower, and run faster.

And worry, because there was much to worry about just now. He knew he could be shot dead before he made it off the balcony, and he knew that if the man with the line hooked to his vest came to his senses and unfastened the carabiner in the next three or four seconds, Court would plummet to his death. Similarly he understood that if the guy with the grenade on his chest got his shit together and threw the device Court's way, he'd be riddled with steel shot before he even got over the railing.

He shifted back to his left as more rounds slammed the French door ahead on the right, and he listened to the sound of the Kevlar line that was quickly playing out of its spool in his pack. He knew he didn't have enough length to get him down to the ground, but the other end exited his pack at the bottom and connected to the body harness under his clothing, and the line was, at least, long enough to get him down a couple of floors.

Court dove headfirst over the balcony railing. Behind him the man on the other end of the Kevlar line had been in the process of trying to get his vest off, but just as he unhooked the first plastic buckle, he launched forward, landed on his knees, fell onto his face, and began sliding towards the doorway, closing on the terrorist with the live frag grenade on his assault vest. This man had himself recognized the danger he was in, and he was in the process of frantically trying to get the grenade off his body.

The grenade detonated, killing the man wearing it, plus another ISIS gunman, and wounding the stunned attacker tethered to Court, along with a fourth ISIS fighter who had entered the living room from the hallway.

And the wounded man on the line slid on towards the balcony.

CHAPTER 7

Court dropped two stories before his harness grabbed him around the crotch and the waist, and then he slowed as the human counterweight in the living room began jolting and sliding across the floor. When the man got caught on the wreckage of the French door, Court stopped completely, still far above the forecourt. He knew it would be faster to cut away the rope than to remove the harness under his clothing, so he pulled his boot knife, took a firm hold of the balcony next to him, and cut his own lifeline away. Court climbed down the rest of the way, using the line attached to Bianca and his feet pushing along the balconies of the lower-floor suites to help him descend.

As soon as he made it down to the forecourt he saw Bianca, only a few yards from him and facing away. She had managed to cut herself free of the rope, but now she just stood there in shock, unable to run for cover.

"Are you okay?" he asked, taking her by the arm and removing the switchblade from her hand. As he spoke he started to lead her out of the line of fire of anyone in the front lobby or above in her suite.

She spun around and punched Court in the chest. He took the blow, and then a second, but he caught her third swing. He yanked her now, pulling her roughly across the forecourt.

"You fucker!" she screamed.

Court looked back up to the balcony, then again at the woman. He pulled her into a side alleyway that led through a neighboring courtyard. "Believe me, I get it."

Still holding her close, he ran with her through the courtyard, but since she was barefoot and the light was bad they did not run fast. Court carried a tactical light but didn't want to use it to avoid the risk of being sighted by any high-stepping police who had managed to make it to the scene in the first couple minutes of the action.

He had a car waiting for him on the street that ran along the Square Louis XVI, three blocks northwest of the hotel, and by the time they made it there, the night was filled with sirens and squealing tires.

He checked her eyes as he put her in the car, and he thought she was suffering from shock, but she spoke clearly as he climbed into the driver's seat.

"Where are we going?"

Court didn't answer. He just started the dark blue four-door and took off towards the north.

A minute later she tried again. Through the tears that came inevitably after the stress and turmoil of the previous five minutes, she said, "Monsieur, where are we—"

"Seat belt."

"*What?*"

"Put on your seat belt. Safety first."

"Are you joking?"

He did not answer, so she did as she was told, fumbling the easy task for several seconds because of her shaking hands. When the lock clicked into place, she sniffed unglamorously. "Monsieur, will you please take me to Charles de Gaulle Airport? I have a flight this afternoon, but I can try to get an earlier—"

He interrupted her. "I'm taking you somewhere safe. You have friends in the city, people who will help you."

"*Friends?* From Zuhair Murad?"

Court turned to her as he drove, then looked away. "No, lady, you were not rescued from ISIS terrorists by a dressmaker."

"Who are these friends, then?"

The man in black pulled his phone from his pocket and tapped a button, placing a call. Bianca looked up to him, obviously hoping to learn something from his conversation about what the fuck was happening all around her, but after a ten-second wait the man simply said, *"En route. Quinze minutes."* On the way. Fifteen minutes.

This told her next to nothing other than the fact that, just as he had said, there were others involved in all this.

She wiped tears from her eyes with the sleeve of her sweatshirt now. "Listen. I need you to tell me—"

Court turned to her. "Look straight ahead, out the window, not at me. And stop talking. You are out of danger, for now. That is all you need to know."

Court could tell Bianca did not want to comply. But he could also tell she was scared. Not just scared because of what she had just survived, but scared of Court himself.

Bianca Medina knew dangerous men, and she would recognize that Court remained a threat to her.

Bianca looked down at the dashboard for nearly a minute before she said, "Thank you, monsieur."

Court turned to her again suddenly, startling her anew. "Don't thank me. I didn't do it because I like you. I did it because it was my job. Like I said, I know who you *really* are."

Bianca just stared ahead. After several sobs she got control over her emotions. "If you know who I really am, then you also know you are in a lot of trouble right now. Many people will come after you. Even here in Paris."

The man continued looking ahead. "Lady, I *really* wish they would try."

. . .

They drove along back streets until they reached the commune of Saint-Ouen, in the Seine-Saint-Denis district, some four miles north of the action on the Rue Tronchet.

The neighborhood was full of immigrants, mostly from North Africa and the Middle East, and in the last few years there had been a massive influx of Syrian refugees. It had little of the charm of the city center; more poverty, more crime. Saint-Ouen was also the home of the Paris flea market, the largest concentration of secondhand furniture dealers on Earth. Throughout a dozen massive buildings the market was open several days a week and brought in buyers from all over the world.

Court's vehicle was one of only a very few on the road this time of the morning as he turned onto the Rue Marie Curie, and his headlights provided the only illumination when he navigated down a tight alley running off it. Soon he turned through the open gate of a tiny parking lot that ran between two darkened warehouses full of unrestored antique furniture. The gate was pulled closed behind him by a man whom Court could just barely make out in the darkness, and then Court parked the car and turned off the ignition.

He went around the front of the vehicle, helped Bianca out, put a hand on her arm, and guided her through the misty artificial light of the parking lot. No one was watching, but if any spectators *had* been around, his actions would have appeared chivalrous. Nevertheless, he was certain the young model could feel the frostiness in his grip, because he pulled her along more roughly than he had back at the hotel on the Rue Tronchet. Out here, alone, there was no longer any question of the woman's compliance. She had overcome her shock, but she wasn't yet in a frame of mind to put up much resistance to what was going on. She'd do as he said, and she'd go where he pulled her.

Court led Bianca by the elbow through an open door in a warehouse and into a circular stairwell. Halfway up he saw a bearded man lean around from his position at the top of the stairs, looking down. Court drew his pistol and pointed it at the man's head.

Bianca shrieked with alarm.

Quickly the man raised his empty hands. Court continued climbing, keeping the barrel of his weapon pointed at the man's face.

"Are you armed?" Court asked in French.

The man pointed down to his waistband. Court let go of Bianca, shifted his pistol to his left hand, then frisked the man with his right. He pulled out a Czech-made handgun, ejected the magazine, and cleared the round in the chamber, racking the slide one-handed by striking the rear sight on his belt. The cartridge bounced down the stairs, and then Court tossed the weapon down behind it and listened to it clank along the steps as it fell.

Court turned the man towards a door and pushed him onwards. "Open it."

The bearded man did as instructed, and Court escorted both Bianca and the security man inside.

Court found himself in a small but well-appointed apartment full of crackling firelight. This space had been built in the 1950s for a wealthy antiques dealer, and the furnishings and feel were a striking departure from the simple masonry warehouse facade of the building. The fireplace warmed the living room, and a middle-aged woman in a sweater and slacks sat in front of it. Two young men wearing black jackets and jeans leaned on the wall by the draped windows, and an older man stood by the fire, his hand propped on the ornate mantel as if he were posing for a photo.

The middle-aged woman had attractive red hair and olive skin; she was clearly Middle Eastern. And the man standing at the fireplace, Court saw, was Dr. Tarek Halaby, the man he'd met in the cemetery that morning.

When Court saw Halaby, he said, "This clown was in the stairwell. My instructions were clear to the Frenchman I spoke with on the phone. I didn't want any armed men in my way when I arrived."

"I apologize for the miscommunication. This man is with us."

Court holstered his weapon. "And I almost turned his head into a canoe. You guys can't follow instructions?"

Halaby started to answer, but Bianca spoke up now, in English, to the middle-aged couple by the fire. "Who are you people? I don't know you."

The redheaded woman stood. Her manners were gentle and stately, and there was a calm smile on her face that belied the situation.

She answered Bianca in Arabic. "If you will follow me, daughter, all will be explained. We have tea prepared, some clothes for you to change into, and a private place for us to sit and talk awhile."

Bianca did not reply at first, and when she finally did, she said, "Speak English, French, or Spanish, or don't talk to me at all."

The redhead furrowed her eyebrows, then repeated herself in effortless English.

Bianca said, "I want you to tell me what is going on right now."

The woman by the fireplace smiled. "My name is Rima Halaby. This is my husband, Tarek Halaby."

Medina shrugged. "These names mean nothing to me."

"We are both medical doctors, surgeons, living here in Paris."

"And?"

"And we are Syrian exiles."

Bianca Medina blinked. Swallowed. After a moment's hesitation, she furrowed her thin eyebrows. *"So?"*

Rima smiled at her like she was dealing with a petulant child. "As I said . . . come this way. I will answer all your questions."

The raven-haired Spanish woman was a quarter century younger and nearly a full head taller than the redhead. Rima put a gentle hand on Bianca's arm and turned to usher her down a hallway that led to the rear of the apartment.

The man Court had pushed into the room had moved to a position between the windows, but he took a step forward now, as if to shepherd the model along if she did not comply. But Bianca didn't need the hint; without further protest she followed the redhead.

Bianca looked back over her shoulder to the American as she did so, but said nothing, and soon she disappeared in the darkness behind the older woman.

The bearded guard followed behind them, along with one of the other men who'd been standing near the windows. Court could see the print of a pistol on the man's hip under his jacket. The other man by the window—Court imagined he was armed, as well—just receded back against the wall, looking on.

Court took these men for security. Court knew what this organization was up against, and a few guys with guns loitering around this safe house didn't seem like much of a defensive setup.

He shook his head in disgust, and he glared at Tarek Halaby.

CHAPTER 8

The doctor standing by the fireplace surveyed the American he'd hired for tonight's work. The asset had some scratches on his face, but more notable than the superficial wounds was the man's unmistakable anger.

And Halaby was sure he knew why. Tarek's wife, Rima, had warned him against dealing in person with this dangerous man, and Rima, as usual, had been right. But Tarek had insisted on interacting directly with the asset.

Now Halaby could not help but wish the Frenchman who'd connected him with the American operator were here, in his shoes, instead of waiting in the back room of this apartment.

It had been the Frenchman's idea that he remain hidden from the asset. Tarek assumed the man had his reasons, because the Frenchman had experience in these matters, and he clearly knew what he was doing.

Halaby waited to hear the door close down the hall before addressing his new guest. "We are monitoring police channels. Through them we understand Daesh chose tonight to come for Mademoiselle Medina. Of course we were aware they had an operation planned against her, as we informed you, but our intelligence indicated it would happen tomorrow when she was on the way to the airport." He motioned to the chairs in front of the fireplace, but when the American did not move to sit, Halaby decided to remain standing next to the mantel.

The American replied, "Yeah, that's what you told me."

"I'm truly sorry. We were going on information we received from—"

"You said four gunners. Five, maybe."

"Correct. That's what I was told. How many did you encounter?"

"Seven, *minimum*. Could have been more."

Halaby considered this, then said, "We knew she would be a prime target for them. But this Islamic State cell was from Brussels, and we did not know for sure how many would come to Paris. I'm sorry the numbers were off from what we expected."

"You wanted that woman's help, and you wanted to save her life so she'd be more inclined to give you the help. The ISIS hitters showed up right when I was making my move, so I'd say everything worked out in your favor tonight." With an angry glare the American added, "I guess that just makes you one lucky son of a bitch?"

Tarek Halaby heard the sarcasm, and he saw the irritation, but he had no reply that would convince the American operative that he had not misled him. So he changed the subject. "Did anyone see you?"

The man seemed to take a few breaths to control his rage, then replied, "No one who is around to talk about it. I avoided hotel cameras. The car is clean." He looked around at the room. "But still . . . a little free advice, because you guys look like you could use it. Do your organization a favor. Consider this safe house burned. Move your operation as soon as you can. Triple your security, even if you have to hire goons paid by the hour."

"I'll take your suggestion under advisement."

The American rolled his eyes. "Or die. It's up to you. Seriously, dude. This isn't Band-Aids and biscuits anymore. You *do* realize you guys are fighting a war, don't you?"

"We are not soldiers. My wife and I . . . we are doctors. Healers. We spent the first six years of the war raising relief supplies. Twice a year we would go over the Turkish border into northern Syria with our son and daughter, also doctors, to run health clinics, to perform surgery on wounded civilians. We are not violent people. But we have been forced into a life we did not choose to lead, actions we are not comfortable with, because we know our nation requires—"

"Skip it. Forget I asked."

After a time, Halaby said, "Nevertheless . . . despite the difficulties to-night, you did exactly as you were told. Thank you."

The American moved towards the door. "I wanted to help, but now . . . this is just business. You will transfer the rest of the money into my account by dawn or I'll come looking for you." He looked at his watch. "You have three and a half hours."

"It will be done well within your time frame. Of course."

The American turned for the door again, but Halaby called out to him.

"Monsieur . . . I know you are angry. But remember. We have resources. Donations from all over the world. A man of your skills, of your discretion. There might be more work for you in the future. Opportunities on the horizon involving our struggle."

"You had *one* chance to show me how you operate. You kept key information from me, and you almost got me killed." He opened the door. "You guys are on your own."

Tarek Halaby watched the asset leave without another word.

• • •

"She's in the bathroom throwing up," Rima Halaby said as she entered the living room, startling her husband, who was still facing the door and thinking about what the American had said.

Tarek was embarrassed to be caught in a moment of self-doubt and reflection. He said, "To be expected. We'll give her a few minutes, but we don't have much time to make this work."

Rima herself looked to the doorway now. "The American. Any problems?"

"He's furious. He thinks we knew Daesh was coming tonight."

"Then he's crazy. Why would we lie about the danger? Our entire operation depended on the survival of Bianca Medina."

"Yes . . . but the information about Daesh attacking wasn't our intelligence, it was intelligence we were given. Do you think it's possible we're being manipulated in all this?"

"By *whom*?"

Tarek turned to his wife. "Who do you think?"

"You're talking about Monsieur Voland?" Rima looked back to the dark hallway, in the direction of the bedroom. "Of course not. Voland is on our side. He has led us this far. In fact, with the exception of that American, who is a simple mercenary, everyone working with us has the same objective."

"I don't know," Tarek said. "The American seemed to care about our cause for some reason."

She took her husband by the hand. "He cares about one point two million euros. Come. Enough talk of our shadow men. Let's move on to the next stage of our operation."

. . .

Tarek and Rima Halaby entered the back bedroom suite just as the Spanish model stepped out of the bathroom; Bianca had let her hair down and she was now dressed in clothes Rima had bought for her earlier in the day. Dark jeans, a brown cashmere sweater, simple flats. She sat down at a small wooden table across from the Syrian couple, giving off no hint she'd been vomiting just minutes before. She had stopped shaking, her back was straight, her hands were folded on the table in front of her, and she appeared as if she had come for a job interview.

A young man with a submachine gun hanging off his shoulder sat on the windowsill and looked down to the misty parking lot below, and another man, small and thin and wearing a dark blue suit, sat in a leather wingback chair in the corner. He had wavy silver hair, but his face was enshrouded in darkness because he'd positioned himself outside the spare lamplight in the room.

Rima Halaby spoke first. "You are certain you are not hurt, daughter?"

Instead of answering, Bianca motioned to the man in the blue suit. "And who is *that*, there in the shadows?"

"He is a friend," Rima replied.

Bianca looked at the man for a while, then turned back to the Halabys. "Tell me what happened tonight."

Rima said, "A cell of terrorists from the Islamic State tried to kill you. My organization has prevented this, and we delivered you here, to safety."

"*What* organization?" Bianca asked.

Now Tarek spoke. "Let's begin with you. You are Bianca Medina, daughter of Alex Medina, a hotelier in Barcelona."

"And for that I have been attacked by Daesh and kidnapped by you?"

"We *rescued* you. We did not kidnap you."

Bianca said, "I am starting to wonder about that."

"Your father," Rima said, "Alex Medina of Barcelona. He was born Ali Medina . . . of Damascus, was he not?"

Medina lifted her chin a little. "And if he was, is that a crime?"

"No crime," Rima said. "I'm just establishing your familial connection to Syria. I'll come back to it. You are twenty-six years old; you began modeling at thirteen. You must have been very good at it, because you were traveling the world within a year. Living between Barcelona, New York, and here in Paris."

"You read old magazines, I see."

Rima went on. "At age twenty-four, during the height of your fame and success, you were invited to Damascus to attend a party honoring your grandfather, a construction industry giant in the nation and closely tied to the government in power. There you met Shakira Azzam, the first lady of Syria. The two of you became close friends. Before long you were invited to the palace for a party, and via this invitation you met Ahmed Azzam, the president of Syria."

"That's ridiculous. I barely knew Shakira, through European friends in the fashion industry, and I've never met—"

Tarek leaned over the table now. "There is no use in lying to us. You are here tonight because of your own actions. You are here for the same reason Daesh targeted you."

"And what reason is that?"

"You are the lover . . . pardon my indelicacy . . . the mistress of Ahmed al-Azzam. The president of Syria. And *this* means you are having an affair with the most horrible man in the world."

. . .

Bianca felt the muscles in her face quiver uncontrollably, so she turned away from her interrogators and looked to the wall in the room until she felt she could regain enough manufactured poise to face them.

Eventually she turned back and looked into the woman's eyes. She chose the redhead as the target of her attention because she was softer than her husband, both in nature and in disposition, but Bianca Medina had no illusions that this woman would be kind to her. Medina constructed her facial expression to convey what she wanted it to convey, to play a role, just as if she were performing for a camera's lens. She hid her emotions and insecurity and projected a practiced air of confidence, something she had learned from many years of modeling.

She was an expert at hiding who she was, of masking what she felt.

"You two are insane. I am no one's mistress."

And, just like a camera lens, Rima Halaby did not blink. She said, "We know everything, daughter. You will only waste time denying what we know to be true." She put a hand out and rested it on Medina's folded hands gently. "But don't worry. No one here is judging you for your decisions."

"All right," Bianca said, and she pulled her hands a few inches closer to her, out from under Rima's. "I have been living in Damascus. But that is only because my father has a home there. I needed to get away from Paris and New York. I wanted to return to my roots, to my heritage. There is no law against living in Syria with a Spanish passport. In fact, I also have a flat in Barcelona, and an apartment in Brooklyn.

"But I have no relationship with Ahmed Azzam."

Rima surprised Bianca by reaching again for her hands, taking them in hers, and pulling them closer. "Listen to me, daughter. The information about your affair with Ahmed came from a well-placed source inside Syria. Someone who, frankly, knows *everything* about you and what's been going on."

Bianca forced a laugh. "A *source*? Who is this supposed source?"

Tarek leaned forward now. With a solemn tone he said, "The first lady of Syria. Shakira Azzam."

There was no more posturing for Bianca, no more contrived poise. The color drained from her face, her eyes widened, and the muscles in her neck fluttered. She muttered a hoarse reply. *"What?"*

Rima nodded solemnly. "It's true. Intelligence officials here in France intercepted a message out of Damascus to an ISIS operations commander in Belgium. It came from someone close to Shakira. The message mentioned that you would soon be taking a three-night trip to Paris to participate in Fashion Week, and it identified you as the mistress of the emir of Kuwait, who is a sworn enemy of ISIS. This is not true, of course. We assume Shakira wanted you targeted, but she did not want it made public that her husband was a philanderer. We have contacts in Syria, however, and they did some further digging on you. They determined you were the lover of Ahmed Azzam."

Rima smiled sympathetically now. "I'm sorry to have to tell you this, but it seems Shakira was trying very hard to entice the Islamic State to murder you for sleeping with her husband."

Bianca spun out of her chair and raced back into the bathroom. She slammed the door behind her, and the Halabys listened to her vomit again into the sink.

CHAPTER 9

The New Shaab Presidential Palace in Damascus sits on Mount Mezzeh, overlooking the Syrian capital, where the ultramodern, cubist complex looks more like a high-tech fortress from a science fiction film than any presidential residence. At 5.5 million square feet and constructed largely out of Carrara marble, it is a gargantuan display of dictatorial excess for everyone in Damascus to see, simply by looking up and to the west.

The New Shaab had been built in the midseventies, designed by a Japanese architect for Jamal al-Azzam, the father of the present leader of Syria, but Jamal never lived in the monstrosity himself; he deemed the palace too big and ostentatious for one family. And for the first dozen years of his son Ahmed's rule, Ahmed Azzam agreed. Before the war came to the city, the Azzam family had lived in a modern but relatively nondescript home in a residential district of the Mezzeh municipality, west of the city center. But when bombings, assassinations, and kidnappings kicked off in the capital city itself, the pretentious citadel on the hill became the only safe place for the Azzams. Ahmed fortified the complex with his most trusted guards, police, and intelligence officials, and he moved himself and his family inside.

The first family of Syria lives in a thirty-room guesthouse on the northern edge of the property, officially speaking, but Ahmed Azzam almost always spends the night in an apartment in his suite of offices a quarter mile away from his family in the palace proper. His wife also has an office suite at her disposal on the other side of the palace grounds, but with young children, she finds herself with the kids most nights in the guesthouse.

But not *this* night. This night the forty-seven-year-old first lady sat alone in a plush salon in her private apartment. At three a.m. she wore a sweater and a pair of designer jeans, her dyed blond hair was pinned up, and she sat on a white leather sofa with her legs curled under her.

She watched Al Jazeera World News with the volume low, and a satellite phone rested next to her.

She'd been like this for the past two hours.

Her half dozen personal assistants had been sent away for the night, so they were all back in their palace apartments, but they also knew they needed to keep their phones on. All six of them remained on call for the summons that often happened when Shakira was up late and scheming.

She might want food; she might want information; she might want someone to drive over and personally check on the nannies of the children to make sure they were watching over her two teenage daughters, Aaliyah and Kalila.

And if this happened, any one of her assistants would climb out of bed and do her bidding without hesitation, because the mercurial Shakira al-Azzam commanded just as much respect and fear among the staff as the president of Syria himself.

Shakira had not been raised to live in a palace. Born in London to Syrian parents, she had grown up in an upper-middle-class Western childhood. She studied business and graduated from the London School of Economics before taking a job at a bank in Switzerland. She worked hard and enjoyed the life of a successful young Western European. But on a trip home to London she met Ahmed al-Azzam, then a fledgling orthopedic resident working at a clinic in Fulham.

The two young and good-looking Syrians fell for each other quickly, and they were married within a year, and just a year after that they were forced to return to Syria when Ahmed's father died of liver disease.

Ahmed had had no desire to lead Syria, but his older brother, the real heir apparent, had died in a car crash in Damascus, and the al-Azzam family would not relinquish the power over the nation that Jamal Azzam had fought so hard to acquire and maintain. For Shakira's part, she'd had no aspirations to be first lady, but just like her husband, she fell into the job, and soon decided no one would ever take it from her as long as blood pumped through her veins.

Before the civil war that now ravaged her nation, Shakira had spent ten years cultivating an image. She was beautiful, brilliant, and unceasingly kind to everyday Syrians, and never more so than when the cameras were rolling. Despite ongoing accusations of atrocities attributed to her husband's government, even before the war, she was a fixture among the glitterati in London, Paris, and Milan.

A New York fashion magazine had referred to her as "the Rose of the Desert," and this moniker stuck with her for a decade. Another magazine had dubbed her the Lady Diana of the Middle East.

Ahmed was socially awkward, soft-spoken, and easily distracted. Shakira, on the other hand, was a master manipulator of her husband's message, and she managed his relationship with his people. She controlled how his image and voice made it to the citizens of Syria and the citizens of the world.

Her husband was an Alawi, but Shakira was a Sunni, and when the war came she helped broker deals between many of the Sunni groups in Syria that were now helping the Azzam government in its war against the Sunni majority.

Few knew that much of her husband's success, his power, his very survival, was due to Shakira.

The war had changed her husband. In the past three years the Russians had moved into Syria en masse to help Azzam, not because they liked him or believed him to be in the right in this struggle. No, they helped him because they wanted air and land bases in the Middle East, and access to a Mediterranean port. Along with the Iranians, the Russians had helped turn the tide against the rebels, and while Shakira had seen herself as invaluable to her husband for years, now she worried that his alliance with Russia was minimizing her importance to him.

Ahmed had grown into the scheming and brutal dictator that for fifteen years he'd only portrayed himself as while Shakira had served as the major power broker behind the scenes.

Though she, the Iranians, and the Russians had successfully bolstered her husband's regime, bringing it from the brink of destruction to where they were now, within a year of outright victory in the brutal civil war that had raged for over seven years, the public image Shakira had carefully cultivated for herself had been utterly destroyed. The wider world knew her husband for what he was, and the wider world was not buying what Shakira was selling anymore. The civil war that the Azzam regime prosecuted mercilessly had eroded any lingering goodwill that the jet set, the Western press, and anyone outside the loyalist enclaves in Syria had for Shakira. No longer was she flying off to Italian islands to meet with rock stars to talk about world hunger. The EU had banned her from traveling into its borders, and sanctions locked down all of her husband's personal bank accounts in Luxembourg and Switzerland, and more than half of hers.

The fawning media outlets of the world had long ago ceased fawning about Shakira.

Though her nickname before the war had been the Rose of the Desert, now people in the Western press had taken to referring to her as the First Lady of Hell.

. . .

And now, as Shakira sat watching television and glancing down to her satellite phone every minute or two, she thought about the last few years, what she had endured for her husband, and what he had put her through.

Shakira had introduced the enchanting young Spanish model Bianca Medina to Ahmed, and for that Shakira would forever be angry with herself. That Shakira did not know about the affair for the first year of it was her second major regret. She should have been watching her husband's actions closer, for the sake of both herself and Ahmed.

It wasn't the affair itself that bothered her. No, she didn't care about who her husband slept with. He was slow and simple, boring and unloving to her. Shakira was involved in an affair of her own, after all, although she was certain Ahmed had no idea. As long as she raised the children and continued to support the regime, she had always felt her place was secure for the rest of her life, or at least the life of her husband. She'd lived her days certain that their mutual survival remained important to them both.

And then something changed.

Shakira had recently learned details about her husband's relationship with his mistress, and now Shakira saw Bianca Medina as a threat, a threat that could destroy everything she'd worked so hard for.

So the bitch had to die.

A knock at the door was followed by the sound of footsteps in the entryway to her quarters. She had been expecting no guests, but she knew who it was, because no one else in her world would dare walk into her private salon without waiting to be acknowledged at any time of day or night, *especially* not at this rude hour.

The footsteps stopped as the late-night caller waited to be summoned, but before she called out, she glanced at her TV. Al Jazeera had just transitioned to a live cut-in on their programming; the screen changed from the TV studio to a shot of a darkened Parisian street, flashing lights and running police and medical personnel in the background.

Shakira smiled thinly, hopeful that the impeccable timing of the man at the door would fill in the details of the images on her huge television.

She spoke in French. "Come in, Sebastian."

A man stepped through the darkened salon quietly. When she heard him walking up behind where she sat on the sofa, Shakira lifted the sat phone and held it up. "I thought you'd call. Someday someone will see you coming into my flat in the middle of the night. They'll suspect you aren't here to discuss my holdings in Switzerland."

The man knelt in front of her, close. He leaned forward to kiss her, but she did not mirror the action. They did kiss, but she clearly had other things on her mind.

He said, "I was discreet. I thought it would be best if I delivered the news I have in person."

"Tell me."

He leaned in again, and she started to lean back and away. She was all business, and wanted this conveyed to the man. But as she tried to separate from him the second time, he brought a strong hand out, put it behind her head, pulled the face of the first lady of Syria to his, and kissed her hard on the lips.

Just as she started to kiss him back he let go, stood, and went to a chair on the other side of the coffee table.

Shakira quickly sat up and composed herself, hiding the fact that she'd even held a moment's interest in his affections.

Sebastian Drexler was forty-three and Swiss, with close-cropped white-blond hair and steel blue eyes. He was a thin but fit six feet, and his mature face bore no wrinkles to speak of. While he was unmistakably good-looking, his eyes conveyed danger along with intelligence.

Shakira knew Drexler well enough to see his guarded mannerisms. Something was clearly wrong. "Did you not call because you needed the walk from your office to think about how you would inform me that you failed?"

Sebastian Drexler was a supremely confident man, so he delivered his bad news with the same cool tone as if he'd told her he'd just won the lottery. "There is much we do not know yet, but I have been monitoring communications between Islamic State's foreign operations bureau and their cell in Paris. It appears ISIS has failed in their objective. The lone surviving operative who escaped the attack reported to his command that Bianca Medina was not in the suite, and the Syrian bodyguards killed five or six of the eight attackers. Others were captured by French authorities."

Shakira's face darkened. She spoke in a measured tone, fighting to control herself. "Where is Bianca now? With the police?"

"No. And that's the curious part. I've been listening in to police radio transmissions in Paris, as well. The police there think she's been kidnapped."

Now Shakira gasped in surprise. "*Kidnapped?* Kidnapped by whom?"

"Unknown. Certainly Daesh doesn't have her. The cell member who contacted the head of their foreign operations bureau was quite clear. He didn't take the woman, he didn't even *see* the woman, and his comrades are all either dead or in the hands of the police."

Shakira stood and began pacing the dimly lit room. "I didn't bring you into this to lose her! I will *not* accept failure!"

Drexler remained seated. An air of composure surrounded him. "We haven't failed, Shakira. We *will* find out what's going on, and we *will* fix it. I have people employed in Paris right now who are very well connected, and they will locate the woman and those responsible for taking her."

"Where the hell were these amazing men of yours when this all happened?"

"I had them perform reconnaissance of the hotel earlier today to make sure there was no extra security in the area that we would need to alert the

67

Daesh team to watch out for. But by necessity I moved them off target during the afternoon." He added, "These men know what they are doing; they *will* get me answers."

Shakira tossed the satellite phone across the sitting area towards the man facing her. He caught it deftly. She said, "Well then, call them and get me those answers! You know what's at stake here. We have to find out where she is. We have to get her before she tells whoever has her the dirty little secret that could destroy us."

Sebastian Drexler stood, dialed a number on the sat phone, and stepped back out of the private salon to talk with his people in Paris in privacy.

CHAPTER 10

In the apartment over the antique furniture warehouse in Saint-Ouen, 4,374 kilometers northwest of Damascus, Bianca Medina walked back into her interrogation after taking five minutes in the bathroom. The Halabys were still seated at the table in the bedroom, patiently waiting; the guard was still at the window; and the silver-haired man in the blue suit remained in the corner, outside the light.

The Spanish woman had composed herself during her break, and as soon as she sat, she asked her next question. "Who *are* you?"

Tarek answered now. "We are the opposition in exile."

"The opposition?" Medina laughed when she repeated it. "*What* opposition? The only opposition I've ever heard of stayed in Syria and fought. They aren't in Paris."

Tarek seemed wounded by the comment. He answered her defensively. "The entire world will soon know about the Free Syria Exile Union, and Ahmed Azzam himself will come to fear us."

Bianca Medina looked back and forth at the couple in front of her. "But . . . if you think I am involved with your enemy, why did you save me?"

Rima replied, "Because we know you can help us."

Bianca had seen this coming, but she played like she did not understand. "Help you? In what way?"

69

"We are here to solicit your assistance in ending this terrible war that has destroyed our nation. The nation of your father."

Bianca held on to the side of the table for support. "You think I have something to do with the war? That was not part of my life. I have been living like a prisoner in Damascus for two years. Prisoners don't end wars."

Tarek said, "Not so much of a prisoner. Ahmed Azzam let you come to Paris, didn't he?"

"With five of his best security officers controlling me at all times! Did you know he ordered one of his men to watch me sleep every night? Does that sound like any kind of freedom to you?"

"Why did he allow you to come at all, then?" Rima asked.

Bianca sniffed. "He *wanted* me to come. Ahmed likes the thought of his mistress working as a model in Europe. It makes him feel cosmopolitan, young and virile, I suppose. I didn't ask; I just took the opportunity."

Tarek said, "Obviously if he thought there was any chance you would run, he would not have let you go."

With a slow blink and a look of genuine surprise, the Spanish woman said, "*Run?* How could I possibly run?"

Bianca noticed the same quizzical look on the faces of the two at the table with her that she herself wore now, but in the back corner of the room, the man who sat alone in the dark did not react.

"And what is it you think I know that will help your cause?"

Rima motioned to the man in the corner. "This is Monsieur Voland. He is a former member of French intelligence, and he works with us now. He wants information about a trip you took with Ahmed last month to Tehran."

Bianca said nothing.

"You both met with the Supreme Leader of Iran, in complete secret. The French know about it because they have an agent in the Iranian government, but they have no way to prove the meeting took place."

Tarek spoke up. "You will be that proof, Bianca."

"What does it matter? I wasn't in the meeting itself, I don't know what was discussed."

"Ahmed conducted the trip in secret because he could not let his Russian masters know he was working with the highest levels in Iran. He wants to bring more Iranian military into his country, to give them permanent bases, to blunt the power the Russians have over him. Now that the war is winding down, Ahmed is negotiating with the Shiites in secret. If you go public with details of the trip to see the Supreme Leader, then the Russians will know of Ahmed's plan."

"And what will that do?"

Tarek said, "The French think this will cause discord between the Russians, the Iranians, and the Syrians, and this could lead to the end of the brutal regime in Syria. All we need is for you to speak publicly about the trip. This can help stop the bloodshed that, you *must* know, has killed half a million people in the last eight years."

Bianca rolled her eyes. "Half a million? Lies."

"Would you like me to show you films of children being killed by sarin gas, dropped in bombs from Azzam's air force bombers?"

Medina repeated herself. "Lies. Ahmed has been fighting terrorists and insurgents for seven years now, and fighting the lies of the West."

Tarek looked to Rima. "We'll need to deprogram her brainwashing."

Bianca shook her head. "No, you won't. I don't have time for any of this. My flight leaves at one p.m. I must go back."

Tarek replied, "To *Damascus*? Didn't you hear what we just said? One of the most powerful people in that nation just tried to have you killed. You *can't* go back."

Bianca's eyes widened now, a look of near panic. "I can, and I *will*. This afternoon I'll fly to Moscow, and tomorrow morning I'll fly home to Damascus."

Tarek spoke to her in a cruel tone now. "Other than the affections of a psychotic mass murderer, what are you missing so badly in Syria? What can you find there that you can't find here in Paris?"

She blinked thick teardrops now. "Is that a serious question? What kind of a person do you think I am?"

Neither Tarek or Rima spoke at first, thinking the answer to be obvious, but soon Rima's woman's intuition told her she was missing an important piece of the puzzle. She leaned forward. "What is it, Bianca? What is back in Syria that you can't leave behind?"

Bianca blinked slowly. Uncomprehending. But then it dawned on her. "You don't know, do you?"

"Don't know *what*?" Rima asked.

"My . . . my baby. My *baby* is in Syria."

Rima's and Tarek's heads swiveled to each other, and then they both turned to the silent man in the wingback chair in the corner. He gave them a look of concern, but to Medina the look did not give away much in terms of emotion.

Soon Rima turned back to Bianca. "You have a child?"

Bianca wept openly now. "You thought you knew so much about me, and yet you didn't know this. He is my life, the only thing that matters in this world."

A pronounced vein on Tarek Halaby's forehead pulsed. "When did this happen?"

"*Happen?* He didn't happen! He was born! His name is Jamal, and he turned four months old last week."

Rima cleared her throat. "Jamal." She looked at Tarek, then back to Bianca. "And . . . and the father?"

Bianca shouted through angry sobs. "Who do you think? Ahmed Azzam is the father!" Then she stood. "I've got to get out of here."

The guard by the window moved forward with a hand out, motioning for Medina to sit back down. Tarek stood, as well, and stepped around the table towards her. She made no move towards the door, but she did not sit down, either.

"Am I your hostage?" she croaked. "Am I a prisoner here, just like I was in Damascus?"

Rima stood, stepping around the table, but she moved behind Bianca. She led the woman gently back into her seat. "No, daughter. Of course not. We only want what's best for everyone. You will see. We are friends."

It took Tarek several seconds to recover from the bombshell news about the love child of the Syrian president. And when he did recover, his words were considerably less calming than those of his wife. "You are our guest, and you will remain so until you speak publicly about your trip to Tehran with Ahmed Azzam."

Medina shook her head. "I won't do *anything* for you as long as my child is in Damascus. Torture me if you want, but you will get nothing!"

Tarek asked, "How on earth are we supposed to get your child out of Syria?"

"I don't have any idea, but I didn't put you in this situation. *You* did. I am only thinking of Jamal. You either let me leave right now, or you kill me right now, because you're insane if you think I'm going to abandon my baby willingly."

The man in the dark blue suit stood, eyed the Halabys, and left through the door to the hall. The Syrian couple followed without a word to Bianca Medina, leaving the bearded guard to watch over her.

CHAPTER 11

Sebastian Drexler sat on a bench in a darkened vestibule outside Shakira Azzam's quarters in the presidential palace. He held his satellite phone to his ear and listened to it ring.

It would be difficult to explain himself if he was found by one of the palace guards right now: seated outside the first lady's private quarters in the middle of the night while the first lady was alone inside. But Drexler's confidence was born out of his intelligence, hard work, and meticulous study. He'd lived here at the palace for two years, and he had long since worked out all the security measures the guards employed. He knew the sentry rotations and patrol schedules, the individual proclivities of palace personnel, the camera angles of the CCTV system . . . even the direction of the motion sensor lighting in the gardens and pathways outside. The former Swiss intelligence officer could walk through virtually all the corridors in the main building and avoid being caught on security cameras or encountering sentries by now, and he'd made a game out of besting the palace guards.

Drexler had spoken boldly to Shakira about his "people" in Paris, and he had every right to do so. He'd hired four members of the Paris Police Prefecture, well-placed law enforcement personnel working there in the capital, to feed him intelligence and monitor the movements of Bianca Medina for the three days she was in France, and so far they had done a fine job. But the truth was that Drexler had not told the captain in charge of his small cell of dirty police the full extent of his interest in Medina, and now that there had been a terrorist attack in Paris involving the woman, he did not know if the man would balk if ordered to hunt Bianca Medina down and kill her.

ISIS was supposed to handle that end of the operation, and ISIS had made a mess of it.

Henri Sauvage was the leader of Drexler's cell in Paris. In the past two years Henri and his crew had tracked down and surveilled Syrian dissidents, agitators, and expatriates in Paris via the French police database, over French police CCTV networks, or by using actual shoe leather.

The four French cops had proved themselves reliable and discreet, which was good, and they'd proved themselves insatiably greedy, which, as far as Drexler was concerned, was excellent.

The phone rang so many times that Drexler worried Sauvage had stopped taking his calls after the dramatic gun battle, so he was relieved to finally hear a click and an "'Allo?"

Drexler spoke in French, and he adopted the code name he used when working with his Paris cell. "Sauvage? It's Eric. What have you learned?"

The man shouted into the phone. "What the *fuck* happened tonight, Eric?"

"Calm down, man," Drexler said. "I told you there might be an event at seven Rue Tronchet. I wanted you to be ready to check it out immediately if something happened."

"It was ISIS! It was a major *fucking* ISIS operation! Are you with ISIS? *Mon dieu*, am *I* with ISIS?"

"Get a hold of yourself. Don't be so dramatic. Of *course* I'm not with ISIS, and neither are you. You and I have worked together for some time, you know that. I'm just someone who hears things, and I heard something. I didn't know if it was true or not. Just relax, and tell me what you know."

"I'm outside the hotel now, but I went in as soon as I got here. Man, it was a *fucking* bloodbath in that suite. Bodies everywhere. Blood. Scorched walls, bullet holes, broken glass. It looked like a damned—"

"But the girl? I heard she is missing."

Sauvage said nothing at first, then replied softly. "I'm out, man. We all are. We didn't sign up for any of—"

Drexler butted in. "No, Henri, you aren't out. You and your boys are in, and you're in thick. Give me what I want, or this goes bad for you very quickly."

"Are you threatening me?"

"Only because you are making me do so. We can resolve all this quickly, you can earn more money than your sad government job will pay you in years, and then we can all move on."

When Sauvage hesitated, Drexler said, "Or I go to your employers and reveal the other operations you've been a part of over the past two years."

Sauvage hesitated a little more, but he finally did give Drexler the information he wanted. "The girl is gone. Nobody knows where she is."

"Who took her?"

"One man. All alone."

Drexler looked down at the satellite phone in his hand, a look of shock on his face. "One of her bodyguards?"

"*Non.* They are all dead at the scene. Whoever took her was someone not associated with her trip, or with the hotel. Everyone else—dead or alive—is accounted for."

"What about CCTV?"

"The kidnapper was a pro. He avoided the hotel cameras; we figure he must have come in from the roof. We checked neighborhood traffic cameras, and that's how we know we are dealing with a single man. We see the girl being walked along at a fast pace by a lone individual. This guy didn't look like an ISIS terrorist. White, about one meter eighty in height, with a beard and dark clothing. They were heading north on foot, but we haven't determined where they went yet."

Drexler thought a moment. "Whoever did this has been following her during her trip to Paris."

"We didn't see anyone, but we are considering this possibility and are looking into it. We've reviewed recordings of cameras here at seven Rue Tronchet and nothing has turned up, but I have Foss and Allard checking with restaurants, clothing stores, and other venues she visited while in town. We're tapping into CCTV networks now, and I'm hoping we'll get something in the next hour."

Drexler said, "Check for traffic tickets around venues she's visited."

Sauvage replied coolly. "I don't know who you *really* are, Eric, but you know I'm a cop. No need to tell me my job."

The Swiss asset working for the Syrian first lady replied, "You know enough about who I am. I'm the man paying your wage. Do as I *fucking* say."

A pause, then, *"Oui, monsieur."*

"The ISIS man who was captured. Is he talking?"

"No. He's got grenade fragments in him; he probably won't survive the night."

Drexler hoped he didn't. He was no use to the operation any longer, and he had failed in his task.

The French captain added, "Like I said, we'll try to have something within the hour."

"Call me back in fifteen. Find me intel about the man who took her!"

"But—"

"Fifteen," Drexler repeated, then hung up the phone.

CHAPTER 12

After Bianca Medina revealed the existence of her son, Tarek and Rima Halaby left the bedroom where the interrogation was taking place, following Vincent Voland back up the hall to the living room of the warehouse apartment. They did not speak during the walk up the hall, not until they had shut the door to the living room and locked it, and not until Rima sat at the kitchen table and placed her head in her hands, rubbing her eyes as she spoke.

"How did we not know about the child?"

Tarek was angry, defensive. He paced the room. "*No one* knew. In fact, she could be lying because she doesn't want to help us. Just a ruse to get her back to Syria."

Rima looked up at her husband. "You saw her, same as me. Was that woman lying to us?"

Tarek stopped. His shoulders sagged. "No."

"She was absolutely panicked," Rima said. "The baby is real. Her predicament is real."

Tarek looked to Voland, now seated at the kitchen table across from Rima. "Monsieur Voland, this is something your contacts should have known."

The Frenchman shook his head. "I am your man in Europe. Yes, we identified Bianca as being Ahmed's mistress, but that was from electronic eavesdropping. I told you from the beginning that we do not have an agent in place in Damascus. Your organization has more contacts inside Syria than I do."

Rima said, "The question is, what do we do now?"

Tarek replied, "Assuming this is true, it's going to be difficult to get this woman to work for our cause. She will see anything she does against Azzam as a direct threat to her child. He knows, presumably, where his baby is, after all. She goes public to reveal the Tehran meeting, and Ahmed could harm the baby as retribution."

Voland said, "Certainly as long as her baby is in Syria, she will not willingly give us information. But the one thing we must *not* do is let that woman return to Damascus. Our operation to take her worked beautifully. We have come too far to turn back now. We *will* find a way to exploit this."

Rima's forehead furrowed. "How?"

The Frenchman held his hands up on the table. "The baby changes nothing. We encourage Mademoiselle Medina to go public with details of her Tehran trip."

"And by 'encourage,' you mean . . . torture?"

Voland shrugged in a uniquely French way, shoulders high to his ears with his head dropping into his neck like a turtle. "Not at first. Yes, of course we must consider enhanced interrogation techniques, methods that will be uncomfortable to her, mostly psychologically, but somewhat physically, as well. But we begin gently, and only adopt the more extreme measures if forced to do so."

Rima stood up from the table and paced the living room now. "We want her help. We *need* her help."

"And we will get it." Voland said it coolly, as if his enhanced interrogation techniques caused him no personal stress at all.

"But . . . we aren't torturers," the redheaded woman replied.

Voland motioned to the back bedroom. "Madame, let us not forget who that is sitting in there. Medina is having an affair with Ahmed al-Azzam. A man responsible for five hundred thousand deaths in seven years. While your nation was burning to the ground, while your friends . . . your . . . your *family members* were dying, she was living the high life in Damascus, enjoying the finest foods, and sleeping with the Monster of the Middle East."

Rima snapped back. "Don't you dare lecture me on the crimes of Ahmed Azzam! Tarek and I are well aware. No one here in Paris needs to remind me of the situation on the ground there."

"But of course," Voland said with an apologetic bow. "I merely state that no measure that will happen to Medina by my hand will approach the misery faced by the dead, wounded, and displaced. We can't squander this opportunity because we don't have the stomachs to go forward." And then he shrugged again. "Neither of you needs to be around when my people and I interrogate Mademoiselle Medina."

Tarek said, "If you torture her, you will get lies, obfuscations. She won't comply."

"I can see through lies. We make her tell us things we know as if we do not know them. When I am satisfied we are getting the truth, we reach for that which we do not have." When neither of the Halabys spoke, Voland asked, "What other choice is there?"

Rima was adamant. "I will not allow you to torture that woman. No matter who she is sleeping with. I don't believe that's the best option."

"Then tell me another!" Voland shouted. When she did not answer, he turned to her husband. "Clearly, Doctor, your wife does not have the fortitude for our mission. We have one opportunity to exploit the president's mistress, and Rima will not allow us to adopt the measures we need to—"

"My wife and I speak with one voice, Monsieur Voland. The woman is not to be harmed."

Rima and Tarek reached for each other's hands and held them across the table.

Voland leaned forward. "Well, then. I suppose we should just let her go. Call her a taxi. Wish her a bon voyage on her flight back home to the arms of Azzam."

Rima repeated herself: "We will not turn into the monsters we are fighting against!"

Tarek interrupted. "Maybe if we show her evidence about Azzam's crimes, perhaps over time, this will help persuade her."

Rima shook her head. "Impossible. She cares only for her child, as any mother would. Look. We have connections to the rebels in Damascus. They can retrieve the child and bring him up here."

Voland shook his head. "The rebels won't get within a kilometer of the president's son, wherever he is. These men you speak of haven't even been able to attack a two-man guard post outside the city library without suffering losses. Sending them for the child would be a disaster."

Tarek thought for a moment. "There *is* another way. We can send someone with real skill to get the baby. To bring him up here. Then we will earn her compliance. With both Medina and her son here, she will be motivated to speak out against Azzam."

Vincent Voland and Rima Halaby both looked at Tarek in confusion. Voland asked, "And whom do you suggest we ask to go to Syria?"

"The American asset. You told us he was one of the best in the world at this sort of thing. Obviously the work he did tonight proved you to be correct."

The Frenchman shook his head. "My dear doctor. The American asset is brilliant, true, but that's the problem. What you need to find is a fool, because what you are proposing, going into Syria to take the child of the president, is a fool's errand."

Tarek countered, "Rima and I have other contacts in Damascus, inside the medical community mostly, who would assist him if we asked."

Voland wasn't buying it. "*Untrained* contacts. Listen to me. As I told you before, this American is at the top of his trade. He knows what he is doing. His work tonight was stellar, but one man cannot possibly accomplish what we would need in order to bring that child out of Syria. Plus, the American will have already destroyed the phone he used in tonight's operation. I found him via a special secret clearinghouse for people of his . . . talents, and I could reach out in the same manner as before, but there is no guarantee he will be checking in with the middleman for days, weeks, or months. I have no other way to get in contact with him in the meantime."

Rima added, "Tarek, you said he told you he would not work with us again after what happened tonight. That bridge is burned."

Tarek replied, "Perhaps he won't work with us, but we can ask."

The silver-haired Frenchman took a few slow breaths. He did not hide the fact that he thought he was dealing with fools. "Again, we have no way of reaching him."

"I have a way," said Tarek.

Voland cocked his head and turned in his chair to the older man. "How?"

"We owe him a lot of money. He said if we didn't pay by dawn, he'd come find us." With a little shrug he said, "We simply do not pay him."

Voland raised an eyebrow. "This plan of yours will ensure that *he* sees *you* again . . . not that *you* will see *him*."

Rima let go of her husband's hand now and grasped him by the arm as the implications of what Voland was saying sank in.

Tarek said, "If we don't pay, I'm sure he'll reach out."

Voland spoke with authority. "I'm sure he will, too. In fact, I've seen numerous crime scene photos showing what it looks like when this man 'reaches out.' Your plan to provoke a violent contract killer is disapproved."

Halaby put his hand on his wife's hand and pulled on it so she eased off the viselike hold on his arm. "We do not work for you. You work for us."

"And I have provided you no greater service since our collaboration began than by suggesting you leave this American asset alone. Trust me and my interrogations of Bianca Medina. I will not use any measures that are violent. Only gently psychological pressure." He smiled a little. "Give me time, and I will get you the results you seek."

CHAPTER 13

At the New Shaab Presidential Palace on the hill overlooking western Damascus, the first lady sat in the near darkness of her private apartment, still watching the news from Paris, even though she knew the violence described by the reporters and the images of flashing lights did not translate to a successful conclusion to her mission there.

She looked at the clock and saw that Drexler had been gone for a half hour, but just then a gentle rap at her door announced his return. He let himself in again and sat down across from her in the sitting area. He didn't bother trying to kiss her, and one look at him and the expression on his face made her even more certain that this evening that she had been so looking forward to had turned into a disaster.

"What is it?"

"My men in Paris tell me Bianca Medina was rescued from the attack this evening by a lone individual. Local traffic cameras recorded them running through the street north of the hotel. So far there is no information on where they might have gone."

"This was one of her security team?"

Drexler shook his head. "The bodies of all five of the bodyguards accompanying Medina have been identified at the scene. No one knows who escaped with her from the suite . . . but we are already developing a working theory."

"Tell me."

"The day before yesterday, Medina and her bodyguards went to a fitting at a boutique on the Champs Élysées. A scooter was given a parking ticket across the street from the shop. The vehicle belongs to a Syrian immigrant, and by looking at traffic cameras my people have found this scooter, and the man on it, outside two more locations Medina visited during her time in Paris. We have determined, with a high degree of reliability, that he was conducting surveillance on Medina."

"Who is he?" Shakira asked.

"The man who owns the scooter is a member of the Free Syria Exile Union. Are you familiar with them?"

Shakira cocked her head. "It's an expatriate Sunni medical aid group allied with the insurgents. Why would a group of doctors and nurses be following Bianca?"

"The only conclusion I can make is they have transitioned into a more violent organization."

Shakira rolled her eyes. "All the real rebels are dead, so now anyone thinks they can pick up the banner. Do you think this Syrian was the man who took Bianca Medina?"

Drexler shook his head. "Nothing in this twenty-two-year-old's history makes me think he could have done all he would have had to do to get her out of that hotel. But his presence the other day near Medina lends credibility to the theory that the Free Syria Exile Union was involved. I have my people looking into the organization hard right now to see if we can learn anything actionable."

Shakira Azzam lay back on the sofa and closed her eyes. After several seconds' silence, her voice broke the stillness. "The failure of your plan has created new dangers. What am I to make of your competence?"

Drexler remained calm. "You can release me from my duties whenever you wish, but just be aware what your options are. You wanted Medina killed by Daesh while she was in Europe. Not by my people. I merely complied with your wishes and passed on the information about her trip to the operational commanders of the Islamic State in Belgium. The information I gave them, that Bianca was the mistress of the emir of Kuwait, ensured that they'd make their attack. I don't know what else I could have done other than gone up there to shoot her myself."

Shakira said, "It had to be a group unaffiliated with us. If Ahmed had somehow found out she was assassinated by contract killers, he would have had his intelligence services investigate. There would be a chance the assets could be tracked back to you, or to me, and that would not do. We *had* to proceed in this manner."

Drexler said, "Well, apparently someone else found out about the Belgian ISIS cell's plan. And whoever it is who has her now might be learning things from her that we don't want getting out to Western intelligence agencies."

Shakira walked to the window. She looked out over the plains north of Damascus for a time. "Will she tell them about the child?"

Drexler replied. "Perhaps. Perhaps they already knew."

The first lady of Syria spun back to her Swiss intelligence chief. "If the West finds out about her baby, and publicizes it, it won't hurt Ahmed. It will hurt *me*. He'll find a way to get her back to Syria, and then he will move me and my children out of the palace and move his Spaniard and his son in."

Drexler looked at the floor. They'd had this conversation before. "I don't know."

"Well, I do. As long as she is alive she is a threat to me, and a threat to me is a threat to you. You must go to France and locate her. You must kill her, even if you have to do it yourself."

Drexler ran a hand along the crease of his suit coat while he thought. "We've been through this already. My people in Paris can do the legwork there. As you are aware, there are reasons I am not at liberty to travel freely throughout Europe myself."

"I know. But I also know you are a crafty man. I am sure you have a plan to get back into Europe. False papers, identities."

"The problem is the fingerprint scanners at immigration controls. They are damn difficult to defeat."

Shakira rolled her eyes. "You can lie to others, Sebastian, but I know men like you. You have a plan to run from Syria if your fortunes should change for you here. There is a way around the scanners, and you know it. If you want more money, we can talk about more money."

"It's not a question of money." He stood and crossed the room to her, standing closer than any other man would dare. "I would never run from you."

She looked away, an expression of indifference or insecurity, he could not tell.

He suspected it was the latter, disguised to look like the former.

Drexler said, "There is a way into Europe. Yes. But it will be dangerous."

"Then that means you and I *both* have been endangered by the failure of your operation tonight."

Drexler ignored the comment and stayed on mission. "The team in Paris will continue to work to find out what happened tonight, and I'll look into the possibility of going to France myself."

"When you do, when you find her . . . torture her," Shakira demanded. "For me. There should be a price above death for her treachery."

Sebastian smiled a little. "Of course."

Shakira glared at Drexler for several seconds, still furious about the evening's turn of events, then looked back out at the moonlit landscape. Far in the distance, easily fifteen kilometers to the east, two flashes of light erupted near each other, just seconds apart. Shakira presumed she was watching an aerial bombardment, perhaps Russian fighters targeting the rebel stronghold of Misraba, just outside the city. She said, "My husband can't know that I know about the boy, and he can't know I am involved in Paris."

Drexler said, "That goes without saying. And if he thought for an instant I was involved in any of this, I'd be shot without a moment's hesitation."

She said, "Ever since we met, our fates have rested in each other's hands. If I go down, you go down. And if you fail in your tasks"—she looked back over her shoulder—"you know I'll have you killed."

Drexler bowed to her. "Then I should begin preparations immediately."

Shakira put a gentle hand on his arm now. "I don't want anything bad to happen to you." She kissed him, and he kissed her back. "How will you get into Europe?"

Drexler smiled at her in the dark apartment now. "I will wait for your husband to ask me to go on his behalf."

He left Shakira standing there, alone, convinced she must have misheard him.

Shakira stayed at the window, watched another pair of bombs strike targets too far away to identify, then returned to the plush sitting area near the TV.

Soon she leaned back on the sofa and stared at the ceiling, tears formed in her eyes, and the wrath in her heart burned like acid.

. . .

In the first ten years of their marriage, Shakira and Ahmed al-Azzam had two children, both daughters. Azzam had demanded a son from his wife, so it was to Shakira's great relief when she bore her husband a male heir shortly before her fortieth birthday. Ahmed Azzam could have chosen any woman in his nation to replace Shakira as first lady, and only when her son, Hosni, came into the picture did she finally feel secure in her place.

Having a male heir was paramount for Ahmed Azzam. There would be an election someday for Ahmed's successor, but just as had been the case when Ahmed took the reins from his deceased father, the election would have only one candidate. When Shakira presented her husband with a son, everyone in the nation knew the palace would belong to the al-Azzams for another fifty years at the very least.

Shakira had felt secure for the first years after her son's birth, but when he was five years old a routine medical checkup revealed an inoperable brain tumor, and Hosni died before his sixth birthday.

Ahmed was inconsolable about his son, but beyond mere grief was the realization that his wife was now forty-five, and even for the elite of the nation, five years of war had depleted the medical capabilities inside Syria.

They tried for another year to have a baby, and when they did conceive, the Azzams' happiness was short-lived. Doctors confirmed she was pregnant with a baby girl, and the pregnancy was terminated soon after.

Ahmed was only fifty-two, so Shakira felt they would remain in the palace for decades to come. The two of them had decided that Ahmed's thirteen-year-old nephew, the son of his younger sister, would someday carry on the Azzam dynasty, but neither the boy nor the parents of the heir apparent had any notion of this.

Shakira had been a crucial colleague to Ahmed in the palace, if not a true emotional partner, and she'd been the backbone of the Sunni coalition that fought on the regime's behalf in the war, so Shakira felt safe in her place there. But all the security she felt faded away when Shakira found out that the woman her husband was bedding here in Damascus had secretly produced a male offspring, and he had given the boy the name Jamal, the name of Ahmed's own father, the former leader of Syria.

Shakira did not begrudge Ahmed the affair itself. She'd been sleeping with the Swiss intelligence officer who worked in the palace since shortly after they met. But the anger that welled in her the instant she'd learned Ahmed had a son with Bianca Medina had only grown in the last few months, and she'd been plotting her next move for all this time. Shakira did not think for a moment that her cold and calculating husband would have allowed his mistress to become pregnant, much less to bring a child to term, unless he had plans for the woman and the child. Children were inconvenient, especially when born out of wedlock to national leaders in the Middle East, and Shakira knew her husband would have had Bianca killed the second he found out she was with child unless his goal had been to replace his wife and make his own child the third generation of Azzam to rule the nation.

Shakira could not let this happen, and the only way she could stop this, to save herself and her children from being cast from power, was to kill Bianca Medina. She didn't believe Ahmed would throw his wife out of the palace if there was not both a mother and child to bring into the palace to replace her, so with Bianca dead, the baby would cease to be a threat to Shakira.

Then Shakira felt she could reassert herself by reminding Ahmed who *truly* ruled the presidential palace.

. . .

Sebastian Drexler was back in his office and thinking about his dangerous predicament at eight a.m. when his satellite phone rang. He snatched it up, hoping the caller was someone from his team working in Paris, and further hoping the caller had some actionable intelligence for him.

"Yes?"

"It's Sauvage."

"What have you learned?"

"We picked up the individual performing surveillance on Medina the day before yesterday."

"Any resistance?"

"He came along. The kid's name is Ali Safra. As I told you before, he's a Syrian immigrant, a member of the Free Syria Exile Union."

"Where is he now?"

"He's in the trunk of Clement's car. He confirms he was tailing Bianca Medina in the city, but he doesn't know anything about a larger mission other than surveillance and reporting. He did say there was a meeting yesterday morning at Père Lachaise Cemetery, where the head of the Free Syria Exile Union met with a foreign asset, but Safra says he wasn't anywhere near that meeting. I think he's telling the truth; he doesn't strike me as the type of guy you'd involve in the center of your plans."

"He's an idiot?"

"Just an immigrant with a menial job. No connections to anyone other than those in the FSEU."

"Who is the leader of the Free Syria Exile Union?"

"According to the kid, it's a husband and wife running it. They are surgeons here in Paris. Tarek and Rima Halaby. Mean anything to you?"

"Never heard of them. Have you run into them up there?"

"Negative, but we pulled their records from the EU crime database. They both have one arrest in Turkey for unlawful entry. Seems they got picked up crossing the border from Syria about three years ago."

Drexler thought about this. "So they snuck over into Syria to help the rebels, and were grabbed coming back into Turkey."

"Looks like it. What do you want me to do?"

"Find out where they are."

"We have an address already. Here in Paris, on the Left Bank."

"Do you think Medina might be held at their flat?"

"Doubt it," Sauvage said. "It's a nice place, right in the city center. And it's their home address. They might be armed, they might have security, but this is no place to hold a captive."

Drexler paused. He was about to up the ante in his relationship with his agents in the Paris police. "Hit it."

A pause on Sauvage's side now. Then, "What does that mean? 'Hit it'?"

"Raid the location, be prepared for violence."

"This is something you've never asked us to do."

"You're a cop. Isn't that what cops do every day?"

Sauvage took his time, then said, "We can find a ruse to enter some other flat. Bring in some patrol officers to stand outside; make it look legitimate."

"Send two of your men. Don't go yourself. And this can't be a straight police operation. We need to know where Medina is, and we won't find out if the Halabys are in custody where we can't get to them."

"*Pas problem, Monsieur.* I'll send Allard and Foss; they will question the Halabys on the premises. The other cops won't know what they're up to." After a beat, Sauvage said, "We have not discussed compensation."

Drexler replied, "All four of you will be paid double the agreed-upon amount."

"*Tres bien*, for the raid on the Halabys. But what about the kid in the trunk?"

Drexler decided to push his luck, to see how far these men would go on this operation. "Make it where anyone looking for him never finds him." After a pause, he said, "I'll triple your compensation."

"We aren't assassins."

Drexler decided he wouldn't push harder. Not yet. The eyes and ears of Henri Sauvage in Paris were too crucial to this operation in light of last night's disaster. He said, "Do you have a place you can keep him out of sight for a couple of days?"

"I have property outside the city. I can have Clement take him there and watch over him." And then, "But I still demand triple for the operation. I'm no fool. I know you will be sending someone to eliminate him."

"Fine. Have your men call me as soon as they have the Halabys. I can help with the interrogation of them over the phone." He hung up and drummed his fingers on the desk. It was all the more crucial that he get to Paris now, considering it was obvious he did not have men there he could rely on to kill on his behalf.

CHAPTER 14

Drs. Tarek and Rima Halaby spent most of the early morning after the attack on Rue Tronchet with Bianca Medina at the Saint-Ouen safe house of the Free Syria Exile Union, but the young woman gave them no more useful information, and the interview brought a frustrated Vincent Voland no closer to his goal of convincing Bianca to go public with details of Azzam's trip to Tehran to negotiate with the Iranians behind the backs of the Russians.

Voland agreed with the American's assessment that Bianca Medina should be moved. There had been a lot of activity at the warehouse during the early-morning hours, and there was always a chance a local security camera or a busybody neighbor had picked up something that could lead police to the location. The Halabys had no doubt about the morality of their actions, but they were both well aware they were breaking a huge number of French laws in their virtuous pursuit of the overthrow of the leadership in Syria.

After taking several hours to arrange the transfer, Voland and five of the security men of the Free Syria Exile Union headed to a second location, a country estate southwest of the city, while Tarek and Rima took a trusted forty-five-year-old former Syrian Army sergeant named Mustafa as personal protection and headed home, south through Paris towards their 6th Arrondissement apartment. Mustafa drove and kept his eye on the roads, and he insisted on escorting them into a shop as they stopped off for groceries.

At eleven fifteen a.m. they pulled into their busy central Paris neighborhood. Mustafa was vigilant, well aware of all the dangers, but along the last few blocks the Halabys themselves eyed passersby, looked at rooftops, and even flinched when a motorcycle raced closely by their Mercedes. They were on edge, but neither of them mentioned it to the other.

Both Tarek and Rima were ready to get home and get a few hours' sleep. It looked like there would be days, if not weeks, of stresses ahead for them, but for the time being there wasn't much the two surgeons and opposition organization leaders could do other than try to rest.

The Mercedes pulled up to the sidewalk outside their building. Tarek and Rima climbed out with their groceries, keyed in an electronic code by the door, then passed through a narrow entryway towards the stairs. Only when the door clicked shut did Mustafa pull back into traffic to park the car in the garage two blocks away, and only then did the Halabys breathe a sigh of relief.

They climbed one flight of stairs in their twenty-unit building, then walked down a long hall with windows overlooking a pedestrian-only passage below. The hallway made a right turn, then continued a few meters without windows, and here Tarek put the key in his door lock. They entered their second-floor apartment, shut and deadbolted the door behind them, then flipped on the lights in the entryway. He and Rima peeled themselves out of their raincoats, hung their umbrellas in a stand just inside the door, and headed together into the living room on their way to the kitchen.

And as one they stopped in the middle of the room. Rima dropped her plastic bag of groceries, and an apple rolled across the floor.

A man sat in the chair by the window in the corner, facing the entryway. A black pistol with a silencer attached rested on the side table next to him.

The large grandfather clock in the living room ticked off a pair of hollow seconds before Rima let out a soft gasp.

Tarek Halaby recognized the American. He wore a simple dark green cotton pullover and black jeans. His hands were folded in his lap, nowhere near the handgun on the table, but both of the Halabys recognized that the

American's confidence was born out of skill, not arrogance. He could get to that pistol before they could do a thing to stop him.

Rima spoke softly to her husband in Arabic now. "Well . . . *That* sure didn't take long."

The Halabys had expected to see the American, but not this soon. They'd gone against Vincent Voland's wishes, and they had not sent the final payment to the numbered account maintained by the handler of their contract killer. It had been a gamble, but they'd wanted a face-to-face meeting with him.

Tarek cleared his throat to hide his nerves. In English he said, "I am thankful my plan to meet with you again has worked."

"Some might call it your plan to commit suicide."

"We just wanted to talk to you. I will, of course, forward the money to the account right away, while you watch. The funds are yours, regardless of the result of our conversation. Please just give us ten minutes to speak with you first. It is an absolute emergency."

"I told you I wasn't interested in anything you had to offer."

"Five minutes," Rima implored. "*I beg of you.* It's a matter of utmost importance."

The American sighed, then looked at his watch. "I'll give you one minute. If I am interested in the conversation, I'll give you another minute. If you are *really fucking* entertaining, you'll get a third minute." He motioned to the sofa in front of him. "Then I'm gone for good."

Rima spoke as she and her husband sat down. "That's just fine. Thank you."

The man said, "Your driver . . . is he coming up here after he parks?"

Tarek nodded.

"Does he want to catch a bullet in the eye?"

Now Tarek winced. "No. Certainly not. We will tell him you are our guest. He will wait outside."

Now the asset motioned to a pair of large framed photographs on the wall across the room. They were portraits, one of a man, one of a woman, and they both appeared to be in their mid- or late twenties. "Children?"

Rima nodded.

"Any chance they will pop in on Mom and Dad while I'm here?"

Tarek answered brusquely. "No. No chance at all."

The American in the chair said, "All right. First, make the transfer."

Tarek pulled his laptop from his bag and opened it, and within three minutes he had transferred the money into the account. While this was going on, Mustafa returned to the flat after parking the car and was surprised to see the stranger sitting with his principals. His left hand slipped inside his jacket, but Tarek held a hand up and assured the former Syrian soldier that everything was fine, and they sent him to wait in the hallway.

The American confirmed the wire transfer with his smartphone, then looked up at the couple. "The clock is ticking."

Rima had sat still and quiet during the transfer, but now she smiled at the stranger in her living room. "What is your name, sir?"

The American chuckled now as he rolled his eyes. "You guys are too much."

"I'm sorry," she said. "Is that not a question asked of men like you?"

"Call me whatever you want, doc, but you've got forty-five seconds to do it."

Tarek spoke quickly. "There has been a complication."

Another little eye roll. "Sorry, folks. No refunds."

"You misunderstand. It is not a complication with you. You were magnificent. Just as advertised. No, the problem is with Mademoiselle Medina."

The man in the chair reached for the pistol and scooped it off the table, startling both Syrians. Then he leaned forward and slid it into his waistband in the small of his back. "You're losing me already. If I snatched the wrong lady, then it's the fault of whoever you've got acquiring your intel. Not me."

"She *was* the right woman," Rima said.

The American cocked his head. "So . . . she's not his mistress?"

Tarek answered now. "She is. But . . . she is also something else. Something we didn't know about when we sent you to rescue her." He looked down at his hands, and then back up.

Rima leaned in. "She is a mother. Her four-month-old son is back in Syria."

The grandfather clock ticked off a few seconds more before the American just said, "Oops."

"Her child is currently under the care of a nanny, guarded by security officers at her home in Damascus."

The American blew out a sigh, clearly understanding where the conversation was going. "And this is the part where you tell me who the daddy is."

Tarek said, "According to Mademoiselle Medina, Ahmed Azzam is the father."

The visitor looked off into space now. "That throws a wrench into the works, doesn't it?"

The Halabys struggled to understand the colloquialism, but Tarek responded, "Azzam is aware of this love child of his. In fact, he is the one protecting his son with members of his own security detail."

Now the American sat up straighter in the chair. Tarek could tell he was genuinely curious, which meant he likely had another minute to convince the man to help his cause.

He asked, "Protecting him from . . . *who*?"

Rima answered. "From his wife, Shakira Azzam. She knew about the affair; of that we are certain. We do not know if she is aware of the child."

"So . . . your whole plan was to flip Bianca so she would give up Ahmed's plan against the Russians, hoping that might weaken the regime. But Medina left a baby back in Syria, a baby Ahmed has access to. She'd have to be a pretty shitty mother to turn on Azzam now."

Tarek nodded. "She refuses to help us. Needless to say, she wants to return to Damascus to be with her son. And needless to say, we can't let her do that."

The American asset said, "I hate to state the obvious, but you two don't know what the hell you are doing. I'm not just talking about the fact that you were clueless to the compromises of your target. Compromises that make her worthless as an intelligence asset. I'm also talking about the stunt you just pulled: neglecting to pay a freelance asset because you wanted to talk to him . . . two times out of three, that will get you killed in this game. Your ploy to get me to listen to you worked this time, but you try that next time with another contract asset, and he will shoot you at stand-off distance and be done with it."

"With your help, sir," Rima said, "there won't be a next time, and there won't be another contract asset."

The American whistled softly. "Oh . . . I get it. You coaxed me here so you could ask me to go into Syria and kidnap the son of the president."

Tarek shook his head. "No. Not a kidnapping. It would be a rescue mission."

"Right. All I have to do is find a way to explain that to the bodyguards, the cops, the intelligence officials, and the military forces in my way." When neither Tarek nor Rima spoke, the man just leaned back in the chair. "You two are out of your damn minds. No fucking way you'll get me to go to Syria."

Tarek said, "We can get you in, and we can get you out. We have people there who will help you."

"Doc, three fourths of the shit that goes wrong in my life starts with some asshole feeding me that *exact* same line." He stood up to leave.

Rima and Tarek stood, as well, and Rima said, "Sir, I wouldn't ask you to go if I didn't believe you could do it. A Westerner can get in via a weekly charter flight carrying surgeons into the capital to work at Syrian regime hospitals. We can put you in with them, with all the documents you need to be safe.

"Our documents are good. Just look at yesterday, for example. We provided you with the intelligence and papers that you needed to succeed in your mission."

"That's a lousy example, whether you know it or not. Either you are lying to me, or someone else is lying to you. Last night wasn't what it looked like. It was a setup."

"A *setup*?" Rima was stunned.

"Someone in your organization purposefully sent me into that address at the same time ISIS was planning to make their attempt on Medina."

"Ridiculous." But then she asked, "Why would someone working for us do that?"

"It's all about earning the trust and allegiance of the woman. If I snuck her away from her bodyguards, she might have been thankful, or she might still have looked at it like it was an abduction. But if I pulled her out of there in the middle of a terrorist attack, she would have been more appreciative, even more beholden to those who rescued her."

Rima said, "But everyone in our organization who knows about this operation is committed to overthrowing Ahmed Azzam. Sending you in when we knew the terrorists would attack only increases the chances you would be killed and fail, or Bianca would be killed, which means *we all* would fail."

The American had an answer to this. "Someone in your organization knew my reputation. They knew I could succeed when others could not. Very few people know this, and nobody who did *not* know this would dare roll those dice."

Tarek and Rima stole a glance at each other.

The American said, "And you both know *exactly* who I am talking about." When neither of them spoke, he asked, "Who is he? The Frenchman I spoke with? Is he the one pulling your strings?"

There was more pained silence in the room, until Tarek said, "I am sorry to put it this way, sir, but you are hired help. I am not giving you information about our organization. Only what you need in order to do the job."

Court looked at the refined middle-aged couple, and he could not see any hint at all that they ran a rebel group. "Why do you do this?"

Rima looked at Tarek, then back at Court. Her eyes misted over. "We did not want war with Ahmed Azzam. It was the young who thought it could be won. Those of us in the older generation, we told the young people . . . 'You don't know the Azzam family. They will drown the nation in blood before they relinquish power.' But the young would not listen, and now they are dead.

"All the dancing, the singing they did when the protests began. The pride of fighting for something they believed in.

"All those beautiful young people, all those beautiful memories, all that hope, is buried under the stone now. All that remains is Ahmed and Shakira Azzam. They are smiling over the corpses of the rebellion."

Tarek added to his wife's thoughts. "Personally I wish the rebellion would end, but you'll never hear me saying that publicly. Not because I support Azzam. Just because I know he will kill every living thing that opposes him now."

"Then why do you run a rebel movement?"

Tarek answered for them both. "We have our reasons. Now we have to do whatever we can to bring him down, and Bianca Medina is the key."

Court said, "You act like you are in control of what's going on. You two are just puppets." And with that, he headed past them towards the entryway. He put his hand on the door latch; he was steps away from disappearing again.

Rima said, "If you leave, what will happen with the war in Syria?"

"I didn't start it, and I sure as hell can't end it." He looked back and forth between the two of them. "Look . . . like you said, I'm just the hired gun here, but I can see the problem with your entire op. Your reach exceeded your grasp. If you flipped Bianca, you might have been able to get Azzam in hot water with the Russians. But this plan of yours wasn't ever going to lead to his ouster. This was a harassing action. Nothing more." He shrugged. "You tried, and you failed."

He opened the door now, looked out into the hall, but turned back before departing. "What will you do with Bianca?"

Rima said, "That is no concern of yours, clearly. You are leaving her, and us, behind."

The man said nothing, but neither did he make any move to walk through the door.

Tarek heaved his chest. "She will be taken care of here. She will not be harmed. But we can't let her return to Syria. She knows too much about us and our organization now."

The asset looked at the floor now. "The kid? What will happen to the baby when his mom doesn't come back?"

To this Tarek said, "Ahmed has never acknowledged the son's existence, so *anything* could happen. But if he has any decency, then I suppose—"

The American looked up. "Jesus Christ, do you realize what you just said?"

Tarek stared blankly at the man at the door. "The baby will not survive long. If Azzam thinks Bianca is dead, he won't bring the child into the palace. Shakira would not stand for it. Azzam will be looking for Bianca now, but when he does not find her, he will have to remove the compromise." Tarek frowned. "Kill the child, most likely. But you can't expect us to just send Bianca home to Azzam after what she knows. We *must* keep her here, and try to persuade her to help us."

The American did nothing to hide the disdain from his face. He just turned into the hall. Mustafa pushed off from where he was leaning against the wall and looked at the Western stranger.

Rima called out from behind. "We know we aren't in control of all this. We aren't trained as revolutionaries."

"No shit," snapped the American.

"We are doctors," she continued. "And we are desperate for our people back in Syria, for the future of our nation. We thought this was a perfect opportunity to find important information about Azzam that could be used against him to end the war. It *was*." Rima's eyes teared. "We just didn't know about the baby."

The American said, "You are playing a dangerous game you don't understand. Please, take my advice. Free the girl. And then go back to aid and comfort . . . something you're good at."

And with that he left the couple alone in their second-floor apartment, pushing past Mustafa in the narrow hallway.

CHAPTER 15

Court walked down the long hallway towards the stairwell. He descended one flight, moved through a narrow and dark passageway to the door to the street, then stepped out onto the Rue Mazarine.

A pair of motorcycle cops wearing the uniform of Public Order and Traffic Control rolled in his direction from the north, slowing to a stop not far from the Halabys' large apartment building. They showed no interest in him, and there were two dozen other pedestrians around, so Court simply turned to the south, then made a quick right on a small winding avenue with outdoor cafés on both sides of the street.

The two helmeted cops never saw him.

Court's personal security was at the forefront of his thinking now. All the pedestrians around him, the people he could see through the shop windows, in the vehicles passing by: they all had to be assessed as a potential threat. His eyes scanned and his brain spun as he evaluated individuals, looking for pre-assault indicators, the flash of a camera lens striking sunlight, any odd mannerisms that could indicate someone taking interest in his presence.

And cops. Court *always* had an eye open for cops, but especially in Paris, because he had something of a history here.

He'd been to Paris more than two dozen times in his life, which meant he knew these streets, and that helped him both assimilate and keep a keen eye for anyone acting out of phase. He spoke the language and he had the feel and rhythm of the city down cold. Not all of his experiences had been good; he'd nearly been stabbed to death just a few blocks south of here a couple of years earlier in an alleyway that ran off the Rue de l'Ancienne Comedie, and then he nearly bled out along the Left Bank of the Seine just a few blocks to the north.

But despite his close calls, he was comfortable here in the French capital; his tradecraft normally kept him safe, and he had every confidence it would do so today, at least long enough for him to get out of town.

And getting out of town was on his mind now. He told himself he had to go someplace far away from the neophytes who had hired him into this sloppy train wreck of an operation. But as he walked, he couldn't help but feel something tugging at him, something telling him he shouldn't leave the Halabys to swing in the wind alone.

He had no doubt they'd be killed before this was all over. There was danger in Paris, even from threats borne out of Syria. The Halabys were running the group holding the Syrian president's mistress, and that would send a lot more bad actors into the area, sooner and not later. Azzam would either want her back or he'd want to silence her. Either way, people would die. Court knew he had no business in the middle of that madness, but he still felt like shit about leaving a lot of nearly defenseless people to deal with the fallout.

The naïve and foolish young mother. The middle-aged couple working for the peace and health of their people, only to find themselves at the heart of a high-stakes, life-and-death operation.

And a four-month-old child. Son to the devil incarnate, true, but a baby whose only crime was having a shitty dad.

It was a cruel, sick, heartless world; this Court told himself not for the first time, and as he turned onto the Rue Saint-André-des-Arts, his eyes still wary for threats, his mind began wondering just why he gave a damn about some random baby in some faraway land. Twenty-four hours ago he was trying to keep his head in the game because of his feelings for a woman on the other side of the world he might never see again, and now he found himself on the verge of getting caught up in a multifaction civil war in the Middle East, a quagmire that looked more and more like a never-ending meat grinder.

Why the hell did he even care?

It didn't take him long to come up with the answer. Even though nothing that had gone wrong for the Halabys in the past twenty-four hours was, in any way, his fault, Court knew that his own actions now would determine if these people lived or died.

And it wasn't impossible to imagine that getting that child in Damascus to safety could also play a small but important part in bringing one of the most brutal dictatorships on Earth to a close.

Court sure as hell didn't want to go to Syria, but he weighed it against the alternative: sitting around in some European café, sipping coffee with the knowledge that right then a baby was being hunted, a mother was helpless twenty-five hundred miles away from her son, a well-meaning husband and wife were in imminent peril of assassination, and a savage dictator was winning his war.

Court's moral compass was trying to steer his body to get involved, but his brain was fighting back, because Court's brain had long ago concluded that this moral compass of his was an unrelenting pain in the ass.

"No . . ." he said aloud. "No fucking way."

Just then, Court's attention cycled back to the present. His PERSEC radar pinged when he saw another pair of motorcycle cops pull to a stop on the Rue André-Mazet, blocking the narrow road. But just as quickly as he alerted to them, the two young officers pushed their bikes up on the pavement and took their time removing their helmets. They showed no interest in Court as he approached their position across the little street, and as he passed them he saw no hint of trouble.

As he stepped by the pair, the radio on one man's shoulder chirped, a voice asked the officer where he was, and the bike cop relayed the street corner. Court thought little of this, until the voice on the radio ordered the two bike officers to maintain their positions until further notice.

Court kept walking, but he understood now that this duo was holding some sort of a soft perimeter, right in the center of Paris. They were clearly waiting for someone or something. Neither of the young cops looked in any way anxious; Court thought they might have been set up for a passing march or something similar.

But he thought back to the other pair of cops he saw. They had been pulling up right in front of the Halabys' apartment building. Were they part of this perimeter as well, or were the Halabys at the center of this police action?

Court turned left and then he stepped into a restaurant crowded with lunchtime diners, picked his way through the throngs of businesspeople and tourists, and continued walking all the way to the rear of the establishment. Something told him to double back to the Halabys' apartment building, to check on them just on the chance the police were there, arresting the couple for their involvement in the action the night before.

For their own good, Court realized, the best thing that could happen to Rima and Tarek would be to get picked up by the cops for questioning. Their life expectancy would go up surrounded by locks and bars, because the clock was sure as hell ticking on their survival out here in the wild.

Court told himself he'd feel better about this whole thing if they were arrested and confessed to snatching Bianca Medina, and the Spanish woman was released to go home to her child. He just wanted to see if this was, in fact, what was going on.

He pushed through the back of the restaurant, turned left in a tiny alleyway, then made it out on the street a half block beyond where the two motorcycle cops on the Rue de Buci could see him. He was just two short blocks from the Halabys' building now, and his only plan was to be a spectator if the cops had come calling on Tarek and Rima.

Court arrived back on the Rue Mazarine, a half block south and across the street from the building, and now he saw a total of four motorcycle police officers from Public Order and Traffic Control, all parked in front of the door to the apartment.

He turned to his left and kept walking, keeping his eyes on the action but affecting the cadence and bearing of just another lunchtime pedestrian.

So . . . the Halabys got themselves flagged by the local police. He wasn't surprised, and he wasn't feeling especially guilty about it. He knew that nothing he had done at the scene the evening before had anything to do with them being tied to the event at 7 Rue Tronchet. No . . . One of their surveillance guys talked, or one of their men holding Bianca got cold feet and dropped the dime on them.

Court wondered what this meant for Medina, and for the baby. Perhaps when Bianca was released she'd race back to Syria, into Ahmed's arms, and all would be quickly forgotten.

A four-door Renault Mégane pulled up in front of the house, and two men climbed out. Court recognized the emblem of the DRPJ on the door of the vehicle, the Direction Régionale de Police Judiciaire de Paris. These were Paris criminal police, local investigators. They pulled badge lanyards from their shirts and waved them at the four motorcycle officers. The four uniformed and helmeted men stepped to the side, the glass door was opened with a code entered into a keypad on the wall, and the two detectives headed inside.

Suddenly Court realized he'd seen these two detectives before. These were the men who'd been hanging around outside 7 Rue Tronchet on civilian motorcycles, and they'd taken off not long after Bianca was dropped off at her hotel.

At the time Court had wondered if they'd been involved in surveillance on Bianca Medina, but since they left within minutes of her arrival, he'd pushed his concerns aside. But seeing them again here, now, was confusing to him.

Court turned into the doorway of a small grocery store and entered. Here he immediately began pretending to look over a display of wine by the front window, giving him a covert vantage point on the building across the street.

Something was very wrong about this situation. These plainclothes guys were investigators for the Paris Police Prefecture, and this didn't make sense to Court. Of course there were twenty apartments in the building, and these guys could have been conducting an investigation at any one of them. But this was the 6th Arrondissement. Surely there were a hundred crimes going on in Paris right now, but the 6th Arrondissement was about the least likely of any of the twenty in the city to see this kind of action.

No . . . a half dozen police on the scene of the exact building where the couple at the center of the high-profile kidnapping the night before lived. Court wasn't one to believe in coincidence. These cops were definitely here for the Halabys.

But if the authorities thought there was one chance in a hundred that Bianca Medina was being held here, or if they thought the people involved with her abduction were right here in the city center in an upper-class apartment building, surely they wouldn't have just parked bike cops from Public Order and Traffic Control out front and sent a pair of local detectives upstairs for a chat. No, terrorism was a federal crime here in France; federal investigators would have brought tactical officers with armored assault vehicles, and they would have hit this building hard.

This whole thing looked fishy as hell, and Court suddenly had a bad feeling about what was going on in front of him.

He stood there in the grocery store across the street, watching the four motorcycle cops standing at the front door, talking to one another. They had been ordered there, obviously, but they weren't on any sort of anti-terror mission. The cops carried SIG Pro 9-millimeter pistols, telescoping batons, and Mace on their belts, and they were four fit enough men, but these dudes were just window dressing. They'd been planted here by the two cops who'd gone upstairs.

The same two guys who'd conducted recon out in front of the Rue Tronchet a few hours before the ISIS attack yesterday.

Court made a judgment quickly, using all the evidence before him. Those two cops were dirty. Working for the interests of Ahmed or Shakira Azzam, was his best guess.

He told himself he could not stand here across the street while the Halabys were detained or assassinated by Azzam's proxies. He had to stop them, and to do this he'd need to get past the bike cops. He could take another route into the building, but that would take time. He'd gained access via the roof of an adjoining building earlier in the day, and there were second-floor windows that he could possibly scale up to, but whatever the hell was going on over there was going on *right now.* And if they were planning on bundling the Halabys up to take them to a secondary location, then at least six armed men would be out in the street at the same time when the couple came out the door. For all Court knew, a paddy wagon was en route, or another dozen motorcycle cops would be here any minute.

Court wasn't going to shoot it out with French cops, most of whom would be completely innocent.

Shit, shit, shit! Court thought. He looked up and down the street, trying to decide what to do.

Part of him wished he'd just kept walking five minutes earlier, but part of him knew this was *exactly* why he had come back to check on the situation. If the Halabys had one shot in hell, that shot was the Gray Man.

He blew out a long sigh, looked up and down the narrow winding street, and realized he was probably about to beat the shit out of four innocent policemen who hadn't done anything wrong.

CHAPTER 16

The gentle knock on the door of the Halabys' apartment came as Mustafa was dealing with the whistling teakettle in the kitchen, so only Rima heard it at first. She was alone in the living room, with Tarek back in the master bedroom, changing out of the clothes he'd been wearing for the last thirty hours. When she heard the rapping she immediately thought of her upstairs neighbor, Mrs. Rousseau, who often called unannounced. Perhaps she'd heard the talking and had come to see if she could pick up any gossip as to the identity of the Halabys' English-speaking visitor.

Rima went to the door and looked through the peephole, and was surprised to see a police badge being held up by a clean-shaven man in his thirties. Behind him, a bald man had a badge of his own, hanging from a lanyard around his neck.

The man closest to the door clearly saw someone looking through the hole, because he said, "Monsieur and Madame Doctors Halaby, I am Lieutenant Michael Allard of the PJ. I have Intern Lieutenant Anton Foss with me. Open the door so we can speak for a moment, *s'il vous plaît.*"

Rima knew the Police Judiciaire were local criminal investigators. She also knew this was not good, but she saw no way to avoid a conversation. She turned to the kitchen and whispered to Mustafa, telling him to hide the pistol he kept inside his jacket, but she had no idea if he heard her.

Unsure, she left the chain on the door but unlocked it. The idea was to talk to the men, to make some noise doing so, and to buy some time.

"Bonjour, monsieur, how can I help you?"

Lieutenant Allard smiled. *"Comme ça." Like this.* Without hesitation he brought his leg up and kicked hard against the door, breaking the chain and knocking Rima back two meters into the entryway.

The second man rushed past the first; Rima saw a black gun with a long silencer in his hand, and as they moved into the living room, the bald man shouldered into Rima as he passed, knocking her back several meters more.

Lieutenant Allard kicked the door shut as he entered, then raced across the entryway, took a stunned Rima by the arm, and pulled her deeper into the apartment.

Mustafa spun into the living room from the kitchen with his pistol just coming out of his jacket, a look of alarm on his face. The bald Parisian police officer was only three steps away, and he was raising his own weapon. Both men were committed to action; their proximity and mutual surprise meant there was no opportunity for de-escalation. Foss fired before his silencer was level with the Syrian's chest, hitting the Syrian in the shin and causing him to jerk his body in reaction to the pain and noise. A second loud snap came from the cop's gun as a round hit Mustafa in the stomach, and a third caught him in the top of the head as he fell forward, face-first onto the floor.

Expended cartridges from Foss's SIG bounced around the room. Blood drained freely from the dead man's skull, creating a halo in red on the brown tile flooring.

Lieutenant Allard pushed Rima hard, deeper into the living room, shoving her onto the sofa she'd been sitting on minutes earlier while talking to the American. Allard's own gun was out, but it wasn't pointed at Rima. Instead it was pointed at the hallway leading to the rest of the apartment.

Dr. Tarek Halaby raced out of the hall, straight into the line of fire. He wore his undershirt and his suit pants, and he pulled up immediately, raised his empty hands, and stood there, looking down to his wife, who lay on the sofa on Tarek's right.

"Non!" he shouted. "Don't hurt her! We'll give you whatever you want!"

Lieutenant Allard lowered his weapon, then twitched it towards Rima, motioning for Tarek to join his wife. The second police officer stepped over to Mustafa, picked up his gun, and slipped it into the small of his back.

Allard now pointed with his free hand to the dead body in the kitchen doorway with the halo of blood around the head. "That man, I am *sure* we will find, had no license to carry a firearm in France. We had no alternative but to shoot him."

Tarek and Rima just stared back at him. Tarek asked, "What do you want?"

Allard pulled a chair out of the seating area, spun it around, and sat down on it backwards. "We want Bianca Medina, and before you tell me that you don't know who or what I am talking about, you need to understand one thing. We arrested Ali Safra, your underling at the Free Syria Exile Union. He informed us about his surveillance of Bianca. We also have video of her being led away from her hotel last night by a man, obviously hired by you. You have broken dozens of French laws in your kidnapping operation, and you both could spend the rest of your lives in prison for your actions, but we would be willing to work with you on the charges if you tell us where Medina is being held."

Tarek said, "Only two of you? You think we have kidnapped a woman at gunpoint, killed five bodyguards and at least as many terrorists, and you and your colleague here are the only ones to come to look into the matter? Do you take us for fools?"

Rima's voice cracked when she spoke. "You are not policemen. You are agents of Ahmed Azzam."

The Frenchman made a face of disgust at the name. "I assure you my badge is legitimate. I am merely here making an inquiry."

Allard pulled his badge lanyard from around his neck and tossed it to Tarek, now sitting on the couch next to his wife. "Trust me, monsieur. I have more officers at the front door, and several more holding a perimeter around the neighborhood. And inspect my badge, if you must. Ask yourself . . . if I were not a real policeman, why would I keep up the ruse? Why wouldn't I just shoot you in the knee, or your wife in the forehead, and force you to give me information?"

Tarek looked at the badge, then up at the man standing over him and his wife. The second man was closer to the kitchen, his pistol low in his hand. "I know people at PJ. Let me contact them, see if you are who you say you are."

Allard chuckled. "You are in no position to make counterdemands."

"Then we will say nothing until you take us to the Thirty-Six," Tarek said. The massive headquarters of the PJ was at the famous address of 36 Quai des Orfèvres, and Parisians referred to the building simply as "the 36."

Allard shrugged. "We could go to the station . . . but time is of the essence. The life of the Spanish national who was taken last evening is all we care about."

Tarek repeated himself. "We will say nothing until we are at the station."

The Frenchman did not move a muscle for nearly ten seconds. Then he slowly smiled and shook his head. "*Non.* I think we will do this right here."

He pulled out his phone, dialed a number, and actuated the speaker function.

. . .

Court stepped out of the grocery store and walked purposefully across the street and directly towards the four police officers. The door to the Halabys' apartment building had been propped open with a planter by one of the policemen, and Court hoped like hell the four men standing there would let him enter unchecked.

But he had no such luck. As soon as it became apparent where he was going, one of the men spoke to him in French, asking if he lived in the building.

Court stopped ten feet from the door, in front of the four officers. "Sorry, do you speak English?"

One of the other police officers took over. "Do you live here?"

"Yes . . . what's going on?"

"Investigation upstairs. What is your flat number?"

Court couldn't see the address cards on the wall by the entryway, but when he'd been inside before, he'd gotten a handle on the organization of the building. "Five oh two." He smiled. "Hope it's not me you're investigating."

The cop shook his head. "Three zero one. Still . . . you'll need to remain outside. Only for a few minutes."

Court knew the Halabys lived in 102, but he didn't believe they were off

110

the hook in this. No . . . these guys down here had been given the wrong apartment number by the shady cops upstairs to disguise their real operation.

Court ignored the cop's request and continued up to the door by stepping between the policemen, but he kept smiling. The English-speaking cop spoke louder now. "Hey . . . can you hear?"

Now there were two men on each side of him, all on the street or the narrow sidewalk. Court's hand was extended towards the propped-open door, still eight feet away. He kept moving and took another step on the sidewalk until the closest motorcycle cop reached out with a hand and put it on Court's right bicep to stop him.

And that was all Court needed.

He locked the cop's grasp down on his arm with his left hand, then spun hard to the right, taking the young man by surprise, yanking him off balance, and sending him stumbling helmet-first into his motorcycle. Behind him, Court heard the snap of a telescoping baton firing out to its full length, and in front of him Court saw a second officer reaching for his baton, an instant away from bringing the steel shaft into the fight.

Court spun around and charged; he took the wrist of the first officer who had his baton out and controlled the weapon with his left hand. The other officer flicked his own baton, telescoping it into a two-foot-long pipe that he moved to swing at Court's forehead, but Court yanked the baton arm of the man in front of him forward and used this man's weapon to block the strike from the second officer. After the blow bounced off, Court stripped the weapon in the hand he held by twisting it hard and down, and he body-checked the man over the top of the same motorcycle the first man had crashed into.

Pedestrians on the Rue Mazarine all around shouted and screamed in alarm.

The fourth cop snapped open his baton with one hand while he keyed the radio on his shoulder with his other, preparing either to call in reinforcements or to alert the pair upstairs, but Court swung his baton and smashed the radio and the officer's hand, sending the man to the ground clutching his wounded fingers.

Two cops swung at him nearly simultaneously with their blunt weapons, he blocked the first blow, then jabbed the butt of his baton forward,

111

striking the attacker in the mouth and knocking him backwards. As soon as his hit was achieved, he moved his body low and into the man swinging from behind, closing the distance and halving the efficiency of the man's blow. Court took this weak baton strike off his shoulder, absorbing the pain to process it later, and he swept around the man's backswing with his right hand, bringing his baton around and slamming it hard into the officer's helmet at the left temple.

The first man who'd fallen was back up; he readied his own baton, but Court targeted his hand, picked it up with his own, and closed his body into the threat. Their batons both swung and struck each other, first low, then high over their heads.

The second officer Court struck was now pulling himself up to a standing position with the aid of his motorcycle, and Court saw him reaching for his pistol. Court looked back to his present adversary, and on his next swing, Court caught the inside of the man's elbow with his hand and did something no cop was trained to defend against in baton class. Court let go of his baton, fired his hand straight forward at the officer's face, and rammed his fingers under the cop's sunglasses and into his eyes.

The man dropped with a shout. His eyes would be bruised and burning and swollen. He'd be out of the fight for the rest of the day, if not the week, but Court hadn't done to this man a tenth of what this man was trying to do to him.

As the cop fell, he released his baton. Court grabbed it by the telescoped end, swung it in a full-power 180-degree arc, and cracked the handle of the weapon against the slide of the SIG handgun that had been rising behind him.

The pistol flew from the officer's hand, spun through the air across the street, and clanged along the sidewalk there.

This man realized he didn't have a gun or a baton now, so he charged in desperation, but Court sidestepped him, took him in a headlock, and reached down to the man's utility belt. He pulled off the can of chemical spray attached there, thumbed open the safety tab, and shoved the man away. As the uniformed officer spun back around to face his attacker, Court fired the thick gel across the man's face, sending him to his knees screaming, clawing at the chemical irritant in his eyes.

All four officers lay in the narrow street now. Two were unconscious, one rolled around grabbing at his face, and the fourth moaned in the fetal position clutching his broken fingers. And around the scene, twenty or so passersby, men and women of all ages, stood and stared in disbelief at what they'd just witnessed.

Court now pulled his own pistol from his belt and held it over his head. In French he said, "Anybody who points a camera at me is getting shot."

No one reached for their camera phones.

Court ran to the door to the apartment building and moved the planter holding it open as he entered. He pulled an item that looked like a silver key from his pocket and pushed the device into the deadbolt lock on the outside. The item was an instrument used to slow down any pursuers—a generic metal key that fit in most any lock, but where the bow met the shaft of the little instrument the metal had been filed down. Court snapped off the bow, leaving the shaft all the way in the lock and making it difficult if not impossible to open the door without either removing the lock or carefully digging in and picking out the metal of the shaft with a pair of needle-nose pliers.

He pulled the door closed, the lock engaged, and Court knew he'd removed this door as an entry point for the police, at least for the time being. Still, there was a side entrance to the building on a pedestrian passage on the north side, so he knew he had to hurry to both stop the dirty cops from kidnapping or killing the Halabys and avoid getting gunned down by furious police reinforcements.

• • •

While the fight raged downstairs, in the Halabys' apartment a man's voice came over the speaker phone. *"Allo?"*

Allard placed the phone down on the coffee table in front of him and said, "Monsieur Eric? I have them here. You are on the speaker."

A man spoke in French. "Bonjour, Drs. Halaby . . . My name is Eric, and it is a pleasure to speak with you, even if we must just do it over the mobile phone."

The Halabys did not respond.

"I'll cut to the chase. We are in a predicament, and you can help us."

"Who . . . who are you?"

"I work for a party with an interest in locating Bianca Medina. It is our understanding she is in your care and, I must tell you, I will do whatever it takes to achieve my objective."

Tarek said, "We will tell you nothing."

"*We?* How wonderful to hear your harmony and cohesion with your spouse. But you see, Tarek, the truth is, I only need one of you alive to tell me where Medina has been taken. Lieutenant Allard? Will you do me a favor and put the barrel of your pistol against Rima's head?"

Allard looked at the phone, and then at Foss. Slowly he lifted his weapon and followed the instructions of the voice on the phone.

When the weapon was flush with Rima's forehead, the middle-aged Syrian woman shut her eyes and tears dripped out.

"Please!" Tarek said.

Just then, the radio in Allard's back pocket chirped. A broken transmission came through, first of a man coughing, then words. "Lieutenant? This is Belin . . . downstairs. An armed man is inside the building!"

The two police officers in the Halabys' apartment looked at each other, and then they spun their heads to the door.

Into his walkie-talkie Allard said, "Who is he, and why the *fuck* did you let him in?"

"He . . . I don't know who he is. And we did not *let* him do anything."

"Get up here, now!" Allard ordered.

"We are . . . we are all wounded! We've called for backup."

"Shit!" Allard said.

Eric spoke up now over the mobile phone. "What's going on?"

The policemen ignored him; they were focused on this new danger. Allard put down the radio, because he could hear someone sprinting up the hallway outside.

114

CHAPTER 17

Court raced up the creaky wooden-floored second-story hallway, closing on a right turn that led to the door to the Halabys' apartment. His right shoulder was sore from the blow he took from the baton in the street, even more so now because his suppressed Glock 19 was in his right hand and out in front of him, causing the muscles in his rear deltoid to flex right where he'd been hit by the weapon. On his left as he ran was a row of windows that looked down on the Passage Dauphine, a cobblestoned pedestrian alley that led back to the east, away from the front of the building. The windows went down the length of the hall—the last one was right there at the turn, and Court knew that just beyond that was a window into the Halabys' living room, on the other side of the wall ahead of him.

And this gave him an idea.

He continued running forward with his weapon raised in front of him, carefully aimed it high on the wall between the hall and the Halabys' apartment, and pressed his finger against the trigger.

. . .

Allard and Foss listened to the sound of the approaching runner and kept their pistols trained on the door, but as the footsteps neared the turn in the hallway ahead and to the right on the far side of the wall of the living room, the footsteps were replaced by the snaps of gunfire. Holes appeared high in the wall ahead of them, a framed painting fell to the ground and crashed, and the two men dove to the floor.

"Who's shooting?" called out the man they knew as Eric on the speaker-phone, but neither man was interested in providing a running commen-tary of what was going on. They heard the crash of broken glass an instant later; they tried to train their weapons on the origin of the sound, some-where on the other side of the wall, but just as their focus turned back to the door, a much louder explosion of glass on their right grabbed their attention.

A figure came crashing through the living room window, fewer than ten meters from where they knelt. A man fell to the floor and rolled in front of the television, shattered glass still flying through the air all around him.

Both cops swiveled their aim to the movement across the room, but the man rolling up into a crouch by the TV fired first. Foss's head snapped back before he could sight on the target, and his weapon spilled from his hand. Allard got a shot off, high and off the right shoulder of the figure, and as he made to squeeze his trigger again, he just had slight recognition of a flash of light emanating from the silencer of the man's pistol before his world went black.

. . .

Court rose to his feet, crossed the living room, and fired an additional round into the heads of both men. Rima Halaby screamed in shock at the sight of even more blood splattering across her living room. He trained his weapon on the Halabys quickly, and Rima covered her eyes.

Now he spun his weapon towards the dead Syrian security man in the doorway to the kitchen, then swiveled it down the hallway to the back of the apartment.

Still covering the unknown space down the hall, Court shouted at the couple. "Anyone else?"

"No," Tarek said. "No one."

Court lowered his pistol. "Are you hurt?"

Tarek checked on his wife; she was sobbing in near panic but he felt over her body, and then he checked himself out. Neither of them appeared to be bleeding. "We're . . . I think we are okay."

Court jerked his head towards the two dead cops. "They were working for the Syrians."

"We know," Tarek replied, staring at the three dead bodies on the floor of his apartment. Next to him, Rima brought her hands from her eyes. She was still sobbing, but Court could see that she'd handled the terror and chaos of the past few moments better than most, be they male or female.

Court holstered his weapon in his waistband, ignored the hot suppressor touching his thigh, then helped the couple up to their feet. "Listen to me carefully."

"Wait!" Tarek said. He looked down at the phone on the table and pointed to it.

Court looked at it, picked it up, and saw that there was an active call. He put his finger over the microphone. "Who the hell is this?"

"A man's voice," Rima said. "He said he is working for someone trying to find Bianca. He sent these men."

Court still had the mic covered when the voice spoke. "From the sound of things, I might need to hire some new men in Paris."

Court nodded to Tarek.

The doctor leaned closer to the phone. "Your men are dead. You will never find Bianca now."

"Your new guest, the American. Is he too shy to talk?"

It was silent in the room for seconds, except for the sound of police sirens coming outside the broken window.

"Who are you?" Court finally said.

The man on the other end of the line replied, "Who are *you*? Of course I can work out on my own that you are the mystery man who abducted Bianca last night, but beyond that, I admit that I'm at a loss."

Court studied the man's voice. Court thought French was probably this man's native tongue, so he suspected he, too, might be a local police officer, just like the dead men on the floor.

Rima Halaby was still panic stricken, but she was a strong woman, and it was clear to Court she knew the importance of this moment. She shouted into the phone. "You are working for a monster! A man who has ordered the wholesale genocide of my people."

"He is fighting a rebellion," the voice replied calmly. "But I'm not going

117

to get into a political discussion with you. It sounds to me like you all need to get out of there before the police arrive. Frankly I hope you make it."

"You are helping us now?" Tarek asked.

Court answered for the man on the phone. "He can't get his hands on you if you're locked up."

"Smart man," the voice said. "Mr. American, why don't you take this phone so you and I can discuss this further when you are somewhere safe from the police?"

Court replied, "Sure, asshole. Why don't I stick this tracking device in my pocket? Why don't *you* go fuck yourself?"

There was a short, perfunctory chuckle. "Very well. But know this. Whoever you are, your involvement has ensured that a lot of people are going to die, including the Halabys, including yourself. I have more men in France, and they will be seeing you soon. I have a funny feeling you and I have not heard the last from each other."

"You can count on that." Court hung up the phone, then wiped off the keypad.

As soon as he did so, Tarek said, "He claimed his name was Eric, and he didn't say it, but he is definitely Swiss."

"How do you know that?" asked Court.

Rima answered. "We were speaking French with him before you arrived. The word for 'mobile phone' in France is *portable*. But he said *natal*. Only the Swiss call a mobile a *natal*."

Court wondered why a Swiss would be involved in this, but he didn't have time to think it over. He said, "Fifty cops are going to be flooding through this building in a few seconds. But the police downstairs think the detectives were going up to the third floor. You need to leave now, out the side door, and just keep on going."

Rima nodded. "Okay . . . just let me pack some—"

"No packing! Just go! March right through the cops, they aren't looking for you."

"But . . ." Tarek said, "they'll find the bodies in our flat."

"At which point the police *will* start looking for you. You'll be able to prove these two cops were working for Syrian interests, that this was an assassination attempt, and then you will be in the clear. But for now, you'll have to run."

The couple stood and put on their overcoats as they headed for the front door. "Thank you," Rima muttered, but in her hurry and shock she did not even look Court's way.

"Wait," Court said. "You have to do one thing for me now."

Tarek turned back to him. "What is that?"

Court told him what he needed, Tarek Halaby complied, and then the Halabys left their apartment, heading for the elevator and the side exit. The sounds of sirens echoed off every building in the Left Bank now; the police were already covering the front and back streets, but Court just closed and locked the apartment door, then headed back to the smashed window, leaving all the bodies as they were. Climbing through the window, he looked down towards the Passage Dauphine and saw a pair of cops standing at the side door, almost directly under Court's position. They weren't looking up, so Court swung out silently and moved along from window ledge to window ledge. Once he was out of view of their position he descended via a drainpipe and ran off to the east, ducking into a travel agency for a brochure as a cavalcade of police cars rolled by.

CHAPTER 18

Sebastian Drexler sat in his office, thinking over his conversation with the Halabys and this mysterious American working for them. He'd told the man he expected they would have more dealings with one another, and he fully anticipated this to be the case. He hoped he'd see him at the end of a gun barrel, and on the streets of Paris, for two reasons.

One, Drexler saw himself as more than capable in a fight, and taking down this American who was making so much trouble for his operation would be supremely satisfying. And two . . . More than anything on this Earth, Sebastian Drexler wanted to go home to Europe.

Here in Damascus he had money, power, women, and respect, but he dreamed of seeing his home continent again, of being around Westerners and Western food, customs, and ideals.

But he knew he had to be careful in Europe, because if the police in any nation on the continent picked him up, he'd never set foot outside a prison as long as he lived.

Drexler was born in the picturesque Swiss mountain village of Lauterbrunnen to parents who owned a climbing-expedition tour company, and he became a top-ranked youth alpinist before leaving the nation of his birth for university. Educated in international relations at the London School of Economics and Political Science, he then spent a few years in his nation's foreign intelligence service. But the slow pace of Switzerland bored him, so he left his home country and took a job for a private risk management firm specializing in helping large corporations navigate their business interests in dangerous African conflict zones.

Drexler was bright, cunning, ruthless when he needed to be, and ambitious. After a couple years working for multinationals, he went out on his own, peddling his expertise as a veteran intelligence operative with third-world experience to well-heeled African warlords. He spent two years working under Gaddafi but got out before the fall of Libya. Then he spent two more years in Europe doing the remote bidding of Nigeria's corrupt leader Julius Abubaker, and then he did stints supporting the aims of the leadership in Egypt under Mubarak, in Zimbabwe under Mugabe, and in Sudan under Bakri Ali Abboud.

He was a field man who could think, not a mindless gunman but a well-versed and broadly trained operative. He could protect, he could investigate, he could surveil his clients' opposition and assess his clients' threats. And yes . . . he could assassinate.

Hell, Sebastian Drexler could raise armies and sack nations.

But he grew tired of the Third World and sought employment back on his home continent. It took Sebastian Drexler years to make his way back to Europe, but finally he left Africa and was discreetly hired by one of the oldest family-owned banks on Earth, Meier Privatbank of Gstaad. The institution employed him as a "consultant" for ultra-affluent private clients, assigning him to those who needed Drexler's discreet physical and mental abilities to help keep their funds right where they belonged: at Meier Privatbank.

He broke up family squabbles that threatened accounts with all manner of subterfuge and silenced his clients' legal problems with intrigue and violence. In rural Denmark, a wealthy family patriarch with cancer decided he wanted to remove all his holdings at Meier, some thirty million euros, and donate them to medical research. The younger members of the family were livid, but legally, there was nothing they could do.

The children consulted the bank; Sebastian Drexler arrived at the family estate outside Silkeborg and poisoned the patriarch to death with tainted meds before he could complete the transaction.

The patriarch's kids were pleased, as were Drexler's employers at Meier.

Drexler did not have a conscience; he had a code. He served the wishes of his employer without question or hesitation. He would cheat, intimidate, maim, kill; he would fund an insurgent attack on a factory in Morocco, contract and sanction a street criminal to stab a lawyer over his wallet in Athens to get him off a case—do *anything* that would further the wishes of his bank's clients to keep his bank's balance sheet large and risks to his clients' assets small.

Life was going well for Drexler, but eventually his crimes caught up with him. Interpol identified him as a criminal and a killer for his actions in Africa, the Middle East, and Europe, and they began investigating his rumored ties to the Swiss banking industry.

His employers could have washed their hands of him, but instead they made him an offer. He was told there was work for him, lucrative work, in a place Interpol would never persuade the local police to arrest and extradite him.

One of his bank's largest clients had a need for a personal agent, someone to help her navigate a tricky political and criminal climate both at home and abroad, and a well-rounded, well-connected operative like Herr Drexler might be able to succeed in this mission quite handily.

He was offered the job as the personal action arm of Shakira al-Azzam. He would not be stationed in Europe—which was good news, because Drexler was now persona non grata in Europe—but in Syria itself. If he moved to Damascus to work for the beautiful and powerful first lady, she would win, the bank would win, and Drexler would win.

Well . . . that was how it was all sold to him, and he leapt at the chance to get out of his dangerous predicament in Switzerland. But he had no idea of the dangers in which he'd find himself in Damascus. Even as a personal agent of a member of the first family, it was a perilous environment.

Syrian president Ahmed al-Azzam himself had to sign off on the plan, and he was agreeable to the idea, for the very simple reason that the hundred million euros in Switzerland at Meier Privatbank was essentially the last of the money he and his wife had socked away abroad as a hedge against being overthrown at home. If the Swiss bankers who'd managed to hide his loot this long wanted to send a European spy to work full-time keeping their financial interests protected, then Ahmed knew this would work better than his own intelligence service trying to do the same.

Of course as soon as Drexler arrived, he was thoroughly vetted by

Syria's notorious Mukhabarat, their General Intelligence Service, but he was cleared, and then he began doing the bidding of both Shakira and Ahmed, and he began working with the Mukhabarat on operations that involved keeping the foreign assets of the first family secure.

There were a great number of threats to the Azzams' offshore finances. Government entities searching for them, reporters inquiring about them, third-party banks with questions about the legitimacy of the nominees on the trusts. Over time Drexler developed a large network of European employees to further the Azzams' aims on the continent: cops in Paris, intelligence officials in the UK, corrupt lawyers in Luxembourg, computer hackers in Ukraine.

Shakira's accounts stayed safe, and more money was funneled into them from time to time from the Azzams' corruption schemes in Damascus.

This relationship between Drexler and the Azzams had been working well for all parties involved, and the Swiss contract agent had been fully busy with his tasks, when an affair between the first lady and Drexler developed. From Shakira's side it was easy to see what fueled the desire. She was a woman locked away in a palace with few around her other than sycophants who were completely beholden to her loveless husband. When dangerous but exotic Drexler came into the picture, he met her gaze and showed his interest in her, and unlike other men, he was allowed confidential meetings with her in her private apartment.

It took no time for her to make a move on the attractive European.

Drexler, on the other hand, was motivated by a combination of two simple drugs: adrenaline and lust. He'd slept with a warlord's mistress, a concubine of the Egyptian president, the wife of a Nigerian general, and even the daughter of the chief Interpol inspector in Greece in charge of his case. Sebastian Drexler was a hunter of pelts, and Shakira was suitable for hanging over his mantel.

There was nothing special about their affair to him. He'd had better, but over time he had come to worry that the cold and cruel woman might actually think she was in love with him, and in the dead of night he found this more terrifying than the prospect that Ahmed Azzam could find out about the affair and have him killed.

Sleeping with the first lady had been the riskiest thing in Sebastian

Drexler's life of danger a year earlier, when Shakira summoned him to her offices and asked him for discreet help on a delicate personal matter. Drexler, only too glad to ingratiate himself even further to the first lady and thereby solidify himself as a fixture in the Syrian regime, heeded the strange request to track down a Spanish woman living in Damascus and find out just what she was up to.

It seemed like it would be easy work. Shakira had made an enemy of some woman here in her country, she did not want to go through official channels to pursue what Drexler assumed was nothing more than a catfight, and he figured he'd have the matter taken care of in a couple of days.

He could not have been more wrong.

Drexler conducted a tail on Bianca Medina, doing most of the legwork himself, and he slowly came to the realization that this squabble between two women was, in fact, something much more.

The first tip-off was the high-level security protection. Medina never went anywhere without a special group of Alawi close protection officers ringing her. For a civilian this was unheard of in Damascus. His research into the detail showed him they were being paid for out of a special fund at a bank owned by high-ranking members of the ruling Ba'ath Party, and this worried Drexler even more than the security itself.

But he continued because the first lady was not one to piss off, and if his employers at Meier Privatbank ever heard that he wasn't doing as instructed by their client, there would be hell to pay in Gstaad as well as in Damascus.

His surveillance of the woman's home in the Mezzeh 86 neighborhood told him she didn't seem to leave the house for work, and although she was single and she loved the nightlife, she definitely wasn't connected to a large group of friends or acquaintances. She frequented the best clubs and restaurants in the city, but she always returned home alone, surrounded by her guards.

Drexler determined that unless she was sleeping with one of her protection detail, she was celibate.

And then, on the eighth day of his coverage, his worries that this operation might turn into something delicate were confirmed. Around midnight he noticed three nondescript vehicles rolling along Zaid bin al-Khattab Avenue in Bianca Medina's neighborhood. Through his night vision binoculars he saw that they bore plates indicating they were owned by the presidential security force.

When the detail turned into the circular drive in front of Medina's property, Drexler's apprehension grew. And when the Alawi private security force left the house minutes later, the Swiss agent began to have grave concerns that he knew what was going on.

His fears were proven right when two more vehicles pulled into the property just after. President Ahmed al-Azzam himself climbed out and entered the home.

So . . . there it was. The president of Syria was clearly having an affair with this twenty-five-year-old Spanish model, and Drexler's client in this matter was the president's wife.

He knew instantly he had found himself between the biggest rock and the hardest place of his entire, exceptionally dangerous career. He could lie to the first lady: say he learned nothing about Bianca Medina. Or he could inform on the president of Syria, a man who could have him shot and dumped in a ditch whenever he wanted.

Drexler immediately went back to the first lady and told her that because of his obligation to his mission working to protect the assets held in Meier Privatbank, he no longer had the time he needed to devote to this personal side mission. This ruse lasted about five seconds. He'd known Shakira was an intelligent woman, but he'd not been prepared for how quickly she saw through his bullshit.

"Ahmed showed up at her house, didn't he?" she asked.

"Ahmed? You mean your husband?" was Drexler's too-casual reply, and he cursed himself for being so transparent.

To his shock, though, Shakira just smiled a little.

"I knew about the affair. I won't tell you how I knew. Nothing scientific. Woman's intuition, I guess. I thought perhaps you could bring me proof of the extent of it."

There was no way Drexler was going to continue spying on Bianca Medina, not even for the second most powerful person in his patron nation. He replied, "I do not feel comfortable doing that. You understand, I'm certain, that President Azzam could make serious trouble for me."

Shakira shrugged, then kissed her lover. "You're sleeping with his wife. You think this is worse?"

Drexler said, "Here, in your apartment . . . your husband isn't going to find out what I'm doing unless you tell him. But out there? Running surveillance on his mistress? I will be detected, and that will be seen as a hostile act."

Shakira sighed and shrugged. "No matter. What you have done has been more than enough."

This confused Drexler, and he pulled back out of her grasp angrily. "What have I done? I have no photographs. No information of what, exactly, is taking place."

Now Shakira's smile was genuine. "You try telling Ahmed that. I won't tell him that I know of his affair with Bianca, but if he does ever find out I know, he'll probably assume my own personal intelligence agent was the one who informed on him."

It was a chilling comment, and Drexler did not know how to process it, but Shakira released Drexler from his duties regarding Medina that very night, and this relaxed him greatly.

He returned to his work for the General Intelligence Service and the interests of Shakira's accounts at Meier Privatbank, and he considered himself lucky to be clear of the danger of reporting against one of his benefactors to his other.

But it was just months later when he was with Shakira in her private quarters. They were both nude and covered in a thin sheen of sweat; around them the Egyptian cotton bedsheets were twisted and balled and damp, pillows strewn about the floor.

Drexler was deep in the aftereffects of postcoital calm, and not in the mood for a serious talk, but while Drexler had been in charge during their lovemaking, the second the sex was over, she reacquired her air of authority and detachment.

As a complete non sequitur Shakira sat up in the bed. "I've heard a rumor, Sebastian, and I need you to find out if it's true."

"Any chance I can take a shower first?"

When Shakira told him that she had learned Bianca was pregnant, Drexler was incredulous. He could envision no scenario where Ahmed would allow a mistress to have his baby.

But Shakira felt differently. She worried that a boy was on the way, and a boy was a threat to her children, to her own power in the nation.

If Drexler had been uncomfortable earlier with the prospect of inform-

126

ing on the president to his wife about an affair, now he was out of his mind with the quandary he found himself in.

He was in a corner, but he went to work. He began digging, hoping like hell there was no pregnancy, no child, but after a time he found, to his horror, that the mistress had indeed given Azzam a son. And, in the worst news of all, the boy was named after Ahmed's father, the man who'd ruled Syria for thirty-five years. Instantly Drexler knew for certain he had information that Ahmed al-Azzam would kill to keep under wraps.

He worried about telling Shakira, but she demanded information, and he knew she could make things difficult at Meier if he did *not* reveal what he knew.

Drexler found himself once again in the center of a very dangerous game, so he did what he had to do. He picked a side. He knew that telling Shakira about baby Jamal would not give her reason to kill him, but if he told Ahmed Azzam about his discovery, the Syrian president might just kill him for finding out.

When he told her the news, she took it stoically, then said, "The only reason Ahmed has kept me around is because of my relationship in the Sunni community. When the war is over, when the Russians and Iranians have pushed out all the foreign threats, then he won't need the help of the Sunni groups any longer. Think about it, Sebastian. If he starts a new family with his young Alawi concubine and his new child . . . what do you suppose he will do with me? And if something happens to me, what will happen to you? You know too much."

Only because you made me an accessory after the fact, Drexler raged inside.

Shakira continued, thinking about all aspects of her and Drexler's shared predicament. "And what of the money at Meier Privatbank? After all, it was you—their agent—who found out about the affair. Do you think Ahmed will leave the hundred million euros in Switzerland, knowing that they have this information about him? He will kill me, take the money from your bank, and you will be here in Syria with no benefactor at home or abroad. You will be a loose end."

It occurred to Drexler that if he could only get away with strangling Shakira Azzam to death right then and there, it would solve a lot of his problems.

127

But it wouldn't solve all of them and he would not get far, certainly not out of Syria. Drexler understood that for now, at least, his own personal fortunes were inexorably tied to the continued good health and good standing of the first lady.

"What do you propose we do?" he asked.

"Stopping this woman is the only way to safeguard the account at Meier, and that is your job, is it not?"

He shrugged. Despondent now.

She leaned forward to him with a conspiratorial look. "We're in this together, Sebastian. We need to find a way to get rid of Bianca."

The Swiss man looked at her like she was crazy. "How does that help you? If you kill his lover, you think that will make you safe?"

"He can't know I did it, but once she's gone, then I'll be secure. You don't know Ahmed. He is in love with this girl. Foolish, reckless love. He is too insulated now to ever find anyone else. The Russians want stability in his regime, and that means me in the palace, smoothing things over with the Sunnis. Ahmed will fight the Russians over his infatuation with that Spanish bitch, but he won't go back to the drawing board if something happens to her."

Drexler, resigned to his fate, began working for Shakira Azzam. But try as he might, he was not able to discover the location of the child. Bianca owned a home in Mezzeh 86, directly south of the palace, but it was locked and darkened now. Wherever she and her child were being kept, it was likely someplace ultra secret Azzam had set up for her.

And for Shakira's part, she knew she could never kill Medina in Syria. Ahmed would learn of her involvement, and that would spell disaster for her. But when Drexler found out that Ahmed Azzam's lover would be traveling to France, he helped Shakira concoct a scheme to co-opt ISIS into killing her, by framing her as the concubine of the emir of Kuwait, sworn enemies of the Islamic State.

• • •

Drexler had been sitting in his palace office, brooding over the events of the past two years, when the encrypted voice app on his mobile phone rang. He snatched it up, although he knew what he would hear.

"Oui?"

As expected, it was Henri Sauvage on the other line. "Eric? Something's happened."

Drexler listened to the police captain for several minutes without reply as he reported the deaths of Allard and Foss.

Sauvage closed his report by saying, "No video of the incident, but the police officers on the scene say this man, this American . . . he's something else."

"Keep working on finding Medina," Drexler instructed.

"Dammit, man! This is big. Two of my men are dead, and French intelligence is working with the FSEU!"

"Wait. French intelligence? What do you mean by that?"

"A guy was rooting around the Thirty-Six this afternoon, asking questions about Foss and Allard. I didn't know who he was, but my superiors gave him the run of the place. After he left I found out he was a recently retired internal security spook."

"Name?" Drexler asked.

"Guys like that don't drop names, Eric."

Drexler thought a moment. "Answer me this. Was he midsixties, short with wavy silver hair, a faux highborn act but chewed fingernails?"

A pause. "You know him?"

"His name is Vincent Voland. I've never met him . . . but I know him well."

"Listen," Sauvage replied. "I didn't sign on for street battles and dead cops and old spymasters rooting around my office. I don't want any part of any of this anymore."

Neither did Drexler. But although he found himself sympathetic to Sauvage's sentiment, he knew he needed the man's compliance.

"You aren't going anywhere, Henri, and we both know why." Just as Shakira had something on Drexler that she could use to doom him, Drexler had something on Sauvage. Evidence of all the crimes he'd committed on Syria's behalf. The little stuff at first, the bigger stuff in the middle . . . and then the events of the past twenty-four hours.

No . . . Drexler knew Sauvage was in his back pocket. The Swiss agent said, "I'm coming up. Find Bianca Medina before I get there."

"But—"

Drexler hung up the phone. Just then his assistant spoke over the speakerphone on his desk.

"Mr. Drexler?"

"Yes?"

"Sir . . . the president's office called. President Azzam would like to speak with you privately this evening. Eleven p.m. in his office."

Although his heart began hammering inside his chest, for the first time that day, Sebastian Drexler smiled.

CHAPTER 19

Sixty-five-year-old Vincent Voland breathed the vapor of the rainy evening, walking alone along the wet cobblestones as he approached the lighted sign of Tentazioni, an intimate Italian restaurant at the top of a steep and narrow lane in Montmartre. The restaurant was nearly empty at ten p.m., but tonight's meeting was set for this venue, at this time.

Tarek Halaby had called Voland just after his and his wife's encounter with the two Police Judiciaire officers working for Syrian interests. He'd explained how the American had shown up minutes before the attack, then again during the attack, and about how he'd saved them both. Tarek then demanded a face-to-face meeting tonight, leaving it to Voland to determine the time and the place, and the Frenchman had picked this restaurant because of its small size, the visibility afforded by its windows, and its intimate atmosphere.

Voland knew Tentazioni well; he would sense immediately if anyone here did not belong, and he could then simply snake off down one of the nearby side streets and alleys and disappear.

The Halabys themselves weren't particularly safe in Paris now, but Voland felt this locale would be quiet enough where they could get in and get out without encountering police or other interested parties.

The silver-haired Frenchman stopped in a wide patch of misty darkness, just down the Rue Lepic from the restaurant, far enough from the lights and tourists of the Sacré-Coeur up the hill to the east. As he stood there he looked into the windows of the little Italian eatery. There were just a few tables occupied, but Voland did not see either of the Halabys yet.

This surprised him. The Syrian couple knew next to nothing about tradecraft, so he didn't give them credit for the play of showing up late for a meet to scout the location from afar.

He backed into the darkness along the sidewalk next to a simple storefront undergoing construction and looked down to his phone to dial Tarek on a secure voice app. But just as he lit up the screen, he felt the cold tip of a pistol's suppressor touch him at the base of his skull. He flinched, then immediately froze, afraid to make any movement that would cause the person at the other end of the weapon to pull the trigger.

He spoke softly in the dark, still afraid to alarm whoever had a gun to his neck. Softly he said, "*D'ou vien-vous?*" *Where did you come from?*

The reply was delivered in English. "From somewhere in your past."

Voland closed his eyes in an attempt to block out the fear, because he understood instantly what was happening. The Gray Man had him at gunpoint and, perhaps even more importantly, the Gray Man had him figured out.

He responded softly, lest he excite the man who held his life in his hands. "The Halabys told you how to find me?"

"They owed me a favor."

"*Oui* . . . they certainly did. I heard about what you did to earn that favor. Two dead PJ investigators. By your hand, I assume?"

"My hand? No. By the weapon pressed against your spine."

"Ah. I see."

"Let's go."

"Where are we go—"

A rough hand grabbed Voland by the shoulder and yanked him backwards.

. . .

Court directed the man off the street and into the old building undergoing remodeling. Here he pushed Voland up to a wall that smelled like fresh plaster and stale rainwater, and he fished through the man's raincoat. He pulled out his wallet while keeping the man pinned to the wall with the pistol pressed hard against his forehead.

As he fumbled with the wallet, he said, "I probably don't need to tell you that I can pull the trigger before you can grab the gun."

"*Non*, monsieur, you do not need to tell me a thing about your abilities."

Court looked into the man's eyes at this, then went back to his work. He one-handed the wallet open and held it close to his face so he could read it in the golden glow of filtered streetlight. "Vincent Voland. That's your real name?"

"It is. I thought you knew who I was."

"Only in the general sense. You are French intelligence, you think you know something about me, and you hired me through my cutout in Monte Carlo because, in your estimation, I was the only guy out there who could have pulled off last night while those ISIS shitheads were attacking."

"I am not French intelligence, currently. But I was."

"And what do you do now, Monsieur Voland?"

"I am a private consultant."

"Yeah?" Court leaned close, menacing. "Well, I'd say I'm in need of some consultation right about now."

The older man was nervous—Court could see the tells even in the low light—but Voland affected a little smile. "I am not currently seeking new clients."

"Too busy leading Rima and Tarek to their deaths?"

"That is unfair," Voland replied. The Gray Man was talking, not shooting, so Court could see the Frenchman's fear about his predicament fading away, and he was growing a little less terrified, even though there was still a pistol pointed at his head.

"What do you know about me?" Court asked.

Voland's eyes narrowed now. He knew something but didn't seem certain how he should answer. Finally he said, "I know you used to be an American intelligence asset. And I know that the CIA has disavowed you."

His information was old and incomplete, Court realized, but he had no intention of bringing him up to date. "Anything else?"

"Yes. I know about Normandy."

Court chewed the inside of his lip. "What do you know about Normandy?"

"Two years ago I was an executive with DGSI."

Court knew this was French domestic intelligence. "Go on."

"I was involved in the investigation of a series of murders here in Paris, and then a massacre at a chateau in Normandy. It was determined that the man at the center of it all was the rogue American intelligence asset known informally as the Gray Man."

When Court did not reply, Voland added, "And all that killing, of course, was done by you."

Still Court said nothing.

Voland nodded and smiled. "Nicely done, by the way. The bodies recovered were a wide array of criminals and scum. Businessmen with nefarious connections, and foreign paramilitaries involved in all manner of illegal activity on French soil." He shrugged. "The police here would still love to get their hands on you, even before what you did last night, and again today. But as for our intelligence services . . . let's just say we've moved on to more pressing matters than Normandy."

Court knew he should have denied all involvement in the incident Voland spoke of, but his thoughts were on the present, not the past. "I'm not here to talk about two years ago."

The Frenchman nodded. "I understand. And I must thank you for what you did today for the Halabys. As their consultant, I suppose we should talk about you getting a hefty bonus for your work."

Court lowered his pistol finally, and holstered it inside the waistband at his right hip. "And I'm not here because I want money."

"Then you have me at a loss. Why *are* you here?"

"I'm here to figure you out. It's obvious the Halabys are being manipulated by someone in all this. My guess is that someone is you. My survival depends on me having an understanding of who knows what about me. The Halabys don't know anything, but you seem to know it all."

"Why do you care about the Halabys and their objective?"

Court looked off out the window into the night. "I'll be damned if I know." Turning back to Voland, he said, "How about you? What's your interest in all this?"

"The Syrian exiles are my clients. Can't it be as simple as that?"

"Nope. If that were the case, you'd do what they told you to do. But I've seen enough to know that *you* are using *them* for your own agenda. I want to know what that agenda is, and who is pulling your strings."

Voland gave an exaggerated shrug. "My nation is very energized to bring al-Azzam down. As is yours, by the way. Both of our countries have troops in Syria."

"Fighting the Islamic State, not the Syrian Army."

"Very true. It is a complicated situation. My nation has no official policy supporting the decapitation of the Syrian regime. We can't be involved in making a bad situation even worse. There are enough refugees in Europe as things stand. If a new flood came in, our current government would fall in the next elections. But behind the scenes? In a deniable fashion? France wants an end to the refugee crisis, and creating a rift between the Iranians, the Russians, and the Azzam regime would be a good beginning."

Court shook his head. "There is more. What are you *really* trying to accomplish?"

Voland nodded softly, as if giving himself permission to reveal more information. "There is someone close to the first lady of Syria, Shakira al-Azzam. A Westerner. He is the one who communicated secretly with ISIS in Belgium about Bianca Medina. The Halabys know nothing about him, but he is a secondary objective for me in this operation."

Court leaned closer to Voland. "The man I spoke with on the phone. Rima said he used the name Eric."

"A pseudonym."

"Who is he?"

"Does the name Sebastian Drexler mean anything to you?"

Court turned away and began slowly pacing the dark and unfinished room. "Holy hell."

The Frenchman said, "Ah . . . I thought it just might."

"I guess it stands to reason Drexler would be involved with Azzam. He's worked for every other son-of-a-bitch dictator around."

"*Exactement.* He is a very dangerous man, and he is wanted for crimes in many countries, but no one wants him more than me."

"Why?"

"The last four years of my time in DGSI, my job was to find and arrest

Sebastian Drexler. I got close multiple times in Africa. But I failed. I am not one who gives up easily, so I continue to hunt the man, even while no longer employed by the French government."

"What sort of crimes has he committed here?"

"I am not cleared to tell you, but suffice it to say, crimes that were costly, embarrassing, and damaging to the French people."

Instantly Court could think of a half dozen major imbroglios the French government had been caught up in during the last decade. With Iraq, with Libya, with Egypt. Knowing what the infamous Sebastian Drexler was capable of, Court imagined the Swiss national could have quite possibly been the culprit for one or all of these.

"So, you are using this operation with the Halabys to draw Drexler back into France?"

"With Shakira Azzam as his benefactor in Damascus, I think it likely that her desperation over this operation will entice her to force Drexler to come here in person to locate Medina."

Court said, "If it were anyone else, I'd have to ask why you were going through all this for one guy. But Drexler . . . I get it."

"I feel confident Drexler will come."

Court looked Voland over. "It's just you working with the Halabys? No one else from French intelligence? No one to support them if Drexler comes up here with fifty assholes?"

Voland chuckled. "First . . . As I said, I'm no longer officially with French intelligence. I am just helping them with this objective. And second . . . Drexler can't get fifty . . . as you say . . . *assholes* into France."

"No offense, dude, but there are a lot more than fifty assholes already *in* France. I'm looking at one of them right now, as a matter of fact. You double-crossed me yesterday when you didn't tell me ISIS was planning to hit that night, and you are double-crossing the Free Syria Exile Union now for France's own self-interests."

That sank in a moment, till Voland said, "It is only me. French intelligence has been hands-off with the Halabys and their organization because of the delicacy of the situation with the rebel groups in Syria. We can't be discovered assisting an extremist movement."

Court fired back, "I'd say Tarek and Rima are about as far from extreme as you can get and still be involved in a civil war."

"Yes . . . but politics being what it is in this country, the government's opposition could frame this poorly if word got out. The FSEU has a half dozen former Syrian rebels guarding Bianca in a safe house right now, and they will remain in place until she talks. That should do, as long as they keep their location hidden. Really, the FSEU are a fine group when it comes to getting money together for food, weapons, logistics, and such, but they aren't a fighting force, and they aren't an intelligence organization."

"Which is why they got tricked by the ex-employee of an intelligence organization."

Voland shook his head. "No one tricked them. I was told in confidence by an associate in DGSI that Drexler had notified the ISIS cell in Belgium about Medina's travels here. ISIS doesn't know she is Ahmed's mistress . . . they were told she was having an affair with the emir of Kuwait."

"But French intelligence knew about the affair."

"Correct. My contact at DGSI knew I was consulting for the Free Syria Exile Union, and he knew the Halabys had the resources and zeal to transform their group into something more . . . *effective* than a relief organization, so I used them as cover to hire you to rescue Medina."

"Why did Tarek and Rima transform from a relief organization to a direct-action arm of the rebels? What is it they aren't telling me?"

Voland nodded now in the dim light. "You are a very perceptive man."

"I get lied to a lot. I'm used to looking for ulterior motives."

The elder Frenchman himself began pacing the room. "The Halabys' two children, a son and a daughter, were young doctors here in Paris. They began going on medical aid missions to Syria for the FSEU. They spent a lot of time treating civilians wounded in the fighting." He heaved his chest and sighed. "They were killed last fall when the hospital in Aleppo where they were working was flattened by Russian bombs."

"Jesus," Court muttered.

"When Tarek and Rima's children were killed, they could no longer avoid involvement in the war itself. They started raising money for weapons and other equipment in the West, sneaking it over the border with their relief supplies." And then he added, "I was hired to facilitate this operation, and then along the way I learned about Medina, Drexler, and the ISIS plan. I arranged to bring you in to help with that."

"And here we are," Court said.

"Here we are," Voland confirmed.

"Now they want me to go in and get the baby."

Voland cracked a smile now, as if this were the most ridiculous notion he'd ever heard. "Of course they do. The operation to compromise Azzam's secret talks with the Iranians will only go forward with Medina's help, and they will not allow me to use enhanced techniques on the woman. It would be a boon to the Halabys' operation if you'd go to Syria and rescue this child, but personally, I think it utter madness."

"I want to talk to Bianca," Court declared flatly.

"For what purpose?"

"For the purpose of determining my level of madness."

Voland was gobsmacked. "So, there *is* a chance you will go to Damascus?"

"There's a greater chance I'll get on the next bus leaving town."

"Monsieur . . . if you go to Syria, you *will* die."

Court repeated himself. "I want to talk to Bianca."

"Very well. I can arrange this."

It was silent in the unfinished room for several seconds. Then Voland said, "Ah . . . you mean *now*."

"I *do* mean now."

CHAPTER 20

President of the Syrian Arab Republic Ahmed al-Azzam was a tall and thin man, always impeccably dressed, but his fashion acumen did little for him, because he had yellowish skin and a seemingly constant five-o'clock shadow. Even as he sat behind the massive walnut desk in his expansive office, amid art and antiquities and bodyguards in tailored business suits, he still did not look the part of the leader of his nation.

Sebastian Drexler had met him a few times before and he was always left with the same impression. Whereas Shakira Azzam was a beautiful, mature woman, classically featured, and with an air of brightness about her, Ahmed Azzam looked grim and disengaged, even when he smiled.

He looked less like Shakira's husband and more like her uncle the undertaker.

But today he appeared even more drawn and anxious than usual. Drexler knew why, but he pretended like he did not.

The Swiss operative fought the undertaker imagery now as he sat in Ahmed Azzam's large palace office, facing the man with the too-narrow eyes and the too-thin chin. Drexler was here on a mission, and the mission required him to be taken into Ahmed's confidence.

So Drexler merely smiled back.

Azzam motioned to the tea service on the corner of his desk, and then

139

he reached for one of the empty cups. Holding his hand around it, he said, "You are well, Mr. Drexler?"

Four male attendants stood close by, and one poured for both men, while the other three kept their eyes on the foreigner and their hands near the pistols inside their jackets.

When the tea was poured, Azzam ignored it, so Drexler did, as well. He said, "I am very well, sir. Thank you for inquiring."

"Our lovely weather is to your liking, I assume?"

The daily highs in Damascus this time of year were in the low eighties, and the lows in the midfifties. It was, indeed, beautiful weather, Drexler had to admit, although he would have given it up in a heartbeat to stand in a snowstorm in his homeland.

"Damascus is an oasis, Mr. President."

Azzam's little mouth stretched into a forced smile. "I am hearing interesting things about you from my people in the Mukhabarat."

Drexler's chest tightened. No one likes to hear that a nation's intelligence service is saying *anything* about them to the president of the nation. But even less so when the person in question is targeting the president's mistress and sleeping with his wife. He wondered if Azzam had brought him here only to tell him he was to be executed.

Drexler managed to force out a neutral enough "Is that so?"

"Yes. My people in GIS tell me you have been helping them out on some operations in Europe with your contacts there. Work that is above and beyond your duties on the finance side. You have my personal gratitude for your assistance. As you are well aware, this is a difficult time for our nation. Your connections overseas are crucial to our operations to keep Syria strong."

Drexler relaxed somewhat. It didn't sound like he was to be trucked off to the notorious Saydnaya Prison for execution after all. "It has been an honor to serve Syria, and to live in this amazing city and nation. I owe you a personal debt of gratitude for that."

Azzam bit at an unruly fingernail, then took a sip of tea that proved to be clearly too hot, so he put it down. He nodded distractedly. "I have a new operation for you and your contacts . . . it takes place in Europe, and it needs to be done quickly and with discretion."

"Mr. President, I will do my best, but it is difficult for me to travel in

Europe. Nevertheless, as you know, I have people all over the continent. My best efforts and my best contacts are at your disposal."

Azzam kept biting at his nail. "I wonder if there might be a way you could possibly go yourself?"

Drexler pretended to think on the question, but in truth, he was marveling on the fact that this was going even better than he'd hoped. "Yes, sir. As a matter of fact, there *is* a way. I have discussed with your Mukhabarat what I would need if I were ever called upon by your government for a personal mission into one of the nations where Interpol has impeded my safe travel."

"Tell me the procedure you would use."

Sebastian Drexler did so, giving Azzam a quick layman's explanation for a complicated operation, and the Syrian president actually smiled and even gasped once while listening to the details.

"You seem to know all about this," Azzam said when Drexler was finished, and this unnerved Drexler a little. The procedure he outlined was a means to get into Europe, and for Drexler to know it so well, he wondered if Azzam suspected he might have been preparing to flee Damascus and return home at some point. But Drexler sold his knowledge of the method as more professional necessity than an actual plan of action.

"Mr. President, if there were a book written on this procedure, I would have been the one to write it. I have been working on this with doctors and scientists for five and a half years, beginning back when I was living in Sudan."

"But it's untested?"

"We've tested it. We sent agents to Europe two times using this method, and both times we were successful."

Now Azzam nodded enthusiastically. "Oh . . . then we shall use this procedure to move you into Europe."

"Thank you, sir. Obviously it will require some significant resources to accomplish, so I assume it is something that would only be approved in the case of a national emergency."

"Approved," Azzam said with a hand wave. "How quickly can you go?"

Drexler feigned surprise. "Well . . . depending on the nature of your operational necessities, I can begin preparing the resources immediately. It will take several hours to get the equipment and people in place and brief them, but I could be on a plane leaving Damascus within twenty-four to thirty-six hours of you authorizing the mission."

Azzam gave a squirrelly, awkward smile. "Then the day after tomorrow you will leave. Time is critical, you see."

Drexler nodded, and then he hesitated before asking the next question. "What can you tell me about the operation, sir?" He was worried about where this would lead, but it would have been inauthentic and suspicious if he did not inquire.

Azzam looked out his window. From there he had a good view of the southern districts of Damascus, though they were mostly obscured by darkness. "There is a young woman in Paris who has been kidnapped. Did you hear about the attack there last night?"

"Yes, of course. It's all over the news. ISIS raided a private hotel, kidnapped a young Spanish fashion model. A very beautiful woman, from the pictures on Al Jazeera."

Azzam smiled again. Drexler knew him to be an oddball, so he was no longer creeped out by his mannerisms. The Syrian president said, "The media says she was the lover of the emir of Kuwait, but they have it wrong. That woman is my lover."

Shit, Drexler thought. He'd hoped the president would send him off with some ruse, but the man seemed unabashedly proud of the truth.

Drexler feigned shock for a moment, then said, "My condolences, Mr. President, but I understand the gravity of the situation. I and my team in Europe will find her, and we will bring her back to you."

"I know you will, Sebastian. When you get to Paris, of course you will have access to all the resources at our embassy there, and that includes all the men from GIS that you require."

"Excellent," Drexler said, but he didn't like hearing this. Men from the General Intelligence Service working in the French embassy would be tasked with rescuing Medina from her captors, whereas Drexler wanted her killed. Still . . . there was no way he could decline the assistance.

Azzam leaned forward. "I am watching you carefully to make certain you have everything you need to take care of this. She is a good woman. I fear for her safety. Bring her back to me."

"I will do my very best." Drexler was going to kill Bianca Medina, but he'd be damn certain that the man sitting across the desk from him would never suspect that for an instant.

"And breathe not a word of your true mission to anyone."

"Certainly not, Mr. President."

"I really *do* mean anyone. I know you work closely with my wife. I also know you understand discretion, and you understand my reach if you let me down."

"Of course I do. You can count on me."

Drexler looked across the desk at Azzam's thin, awkward smile, and he thought he would be having a lot of nightmares about that face in the days and weeks to come.

· · ·

Drexler left the president's office a minute later with carte blanche to do whatever he wanted in Europe. There wasn't much further left to fall for Azzam, reputation-wise or sanction-wise, so if Syrian intelligence agents were caught on a street in France, it would hardly make much difference, diplomatically speaking.

Drexler was pleased that the president had done just exactly what he wanted him to do, and his plan was already meeting with success. The one snag was the fact that he would have Syrian intelligence officers with him in Paris every step of the way, but, he told himself, he'd find a way around this problem. Things would have been so much easier if the damn ISIS gunmen had simply managed to shoot Bianca Medina the previous evening, and there was no denying that the next few days would be dangerous for Drexler, but he was a man who was accustomed to adversity, and accustomed to surviving, and even thriving, in danger.

He left the president's wing of the palace and began walking to the first lady's wing. She'd be there, waiting for him, wanting to know what her husband had told him. He told himself he'd fuck her before he said a word, to demonstrate that he retained some power in the relationship outside the bedroom, even if it was just making her wait to hear his news.

CHAPTER 21

Vincent Voland himself drove Court to the safe house outside the city, leaving first the traffic and lights of Paris and then the modern highway to the south before taking a side road through the countryside.

At eleven p.m. they passed by the tiny hamlet of Vaumurier, and soon afterward Court saw a road sign for La Brosse. Before they reached the village, however, Voland turned the Citroën into a narrow gravel drive all but hidden by thick woods.

The driveway wound through the trees for a quarter mile before it passed a long greenhouse illuminated only by the vehicle's headlights. Court tried to peer into the black beyond the illumination, but he didn't see any hint of the main house until they were within a hundred feet of it. It seemed to be a large structure, but there was no electric lighting outside, and either the windows were all covered or there was no power running to the property at all.

As Voland slowed the vehicle over loose stones, a single light flipped on at a side door of the house, next to the gravel parking circle. Under it a man in a brown leather jacket stood with a pump shotgun hanging from a sling over his shoulder. The wall behind him was covered in ivy, and the stone building looked like a large and well-built farmhouse.

A motion light flipped on, and Court saw two other security men standing around in the dark outside. One had an old Uzi, and the other wore a pistol in a shoulder holster.

As Voland parked the Citroën, Court looked over what he could see of the grounds and the farmhouse. "This is too big to be private property owned by the FSEU. This looks like some kind of government safe house."

Voland pulled the parking brake and turned off the ignition. "Government property, but not government run. My consulting firm rented it from DGSI through a front company, and we, in turn, have loaned it out to the Halabys' organization."

"French intel is all over this op. When are you going to tell me that you've been lying and this whole thing is government sanctioned?"

Voland surprised Court by laughing at this. "Perhaps you have forgotten, but less than twenty-four hours ago a large cell of ISIS terrorists from Belgium perpetrated an attack in France that led to a great number of deaths. If you think the French government knew about the ISIS attack in advance and then simply allowed it to take place in central Paris, then you've been watching too many bad movies. No, monsieur, that was me alone, and one of the most difficult decisions I've had to make in my career."

Voland sounded sure of himself, but Court harbored suspicions nonetheless.

He followed the older man through the side door, past the bearded man with the shotgun. Once inside, Court found the building to be a well-kept, medium-sized farmhouse, stately but certainly not garish. The lights were on, but every window had thick blackout curtains drawn.

Rima and Tarek Halaby stood in the kitchen by the stove, but the middle-aged couple approached Court warmly as soon as he entered. Court could still see the strain on Rima's face, but she had some of the color back she'd lost earlier in the day when three men died right in front of her. She hugged Court, a Western act that turned into a somewhat awkward gesture considering the fact that Court just stood there with his hands to his sides and his eyebrows so furrowed they almost touched. Both of the Halabys thanked him again for saving their lives earlier in the day, and Rima poured him tea.

Court ignored the tea. "I'd like to talk to Bianca, in private."

"Why privately?" Rima asked, suddenly on guard.

"Because I want her to tell me where her kid is. And I think she might do it if I can get her to trust me."

"Does this mean you will go and rescue the child?" There was obvious hopefulness in Tarek's voice.

"Let's not get ahead of ourselves."

. . .

Rima led Court into the kitchen, then through a doorway off it. Down a flight of wooden stairs adorned with a tattered red rug that looked like it predated the reign of Napoleon, Court found himself in a large and well-stocked wine cellar. Rima nodded to a young guard with a beard and a ponytail sitting at a table between two heavy wooden doors. The man looked at Court suspiciously, then stood and produced an old brass key on a big ring. The young man said something to Rima in Arabic, but Court's command of the language was rudimentary, so he didn't understand.

Rima turned to him. "He wants to know if you have a gun or a mobile phone. We can't let Bianca have access to either for the obvious reasons."

Court wanted to tell her that Bianca wasn't going to get his gun or his phone off him, but instead he obliged. He pulled out his Glock and laid it on the table next to the door, then pulled out his phone and put it down next to the gun.

Both the guard and the co-director of the resistance organization were satisfied, so the key went into the lock.

Court cleared his throat, and both Syrians looked back to him.

The American lifted his right foot and rested it on the table's edge, reached down to his ankle, and pulled a stainless steel snub-nosed .38 pistol out of its holster. This he put on the table next to his primary weapon. Then he reached into his jacket and pulled out a second, and then a third phone. These he put on the table, as well.

A folding knife came out of his waistband, and he tossed this next to the phones.

Court eyed the man in the ponytail. "On the first day of sentry school they teach you not to use the honor system."

Rima said, "This is my nephew, Firas. He's a schoolteacher by trade."

"Tell him he shouldn't quit his day job," Court said, but Rima did not translate.

Court turned back to the heavy wooden door and Firas opened it.

. . .

He was shocked by how much Bianca Medina had changed in the twenty-two hours since he'd last seen her. She wore jeans and a beige sweater that was too short for her five-foot-ten-inch frame, and she lay sprawled across a small bed in the small room. She looked tired, drawn. She wore no makeup, and he could see the dark circles under her eyes that told him she hadn't slept in nearly two days.

The wall behind her was the stone outer wall of the farmhouse, and the floors were cold tile. The room smelled like damp stone. A private bathroom looked well kept, and there was an uneaten plate of fish and rice that had been brought down for Bianca from the kitchen. An empty bottle of champagne sat on the table, and not a brand a top European fashion model would normally drink, Court determined. Someone, Court presumed it was Bianca herself, had meticulously picked at the label until it lay torn in little bits on the table.

She clearly wasn't being mistreated here, but it wasn't much of an existence for someone who was accustomed to living well.

Upon recognizing the American who fought her away from the Syrian guards and the Islamic State attackers the evening before, she pushed herself up to a sitting position and spoke in English. "I didn't expect to see you again."

Court slid a simple wooden chair closer to her and sat down. "Did you hear what happened today?"

"I haven't heard *anything*. No one will talk to me."

"A pair of local police detectives, working on behalf of either Ahmed or Shakira Azzam, attacked the Halabys. They were looking for you."

Bianca rubbed her red eyes, although no tears drained from them. "Ahmed won't rest until I am found. I guess Shakira won't rest until I'm dead." She asked the next question in a matter-of-fact tone. "How are the Halabys?"

"They survived . . . this time. The two Paris police detectives were killed."

147

"Let me take a guess. You killed them, right?"

Court did not answer.

She reached over into a plastic cooler next to her bed, and from it she pulled out a fresh bottle of champagne. Water dripped from the bottle, but she ignored the mess as it collected on the floor and on her jeans. While Court looked on, she expertly removed the foil, the wire, and the cork.

Off his look, Bianca said, "I wanted something to help me relax. I meant Xanax, Valium. They brought me scotch." She sniffed wet congestion. "I put up a fight and got this. Haven't drunk anything so cheap since I was fifteen years old." She gulped from the bottle, then held it out to Court. He just shook his head.

Bianca swigged again, then nodded. "I'm an alcoholic, I guess. Have been since I was a kid. Ahmed used that to his advantage. Among other things. I stayed off booze during the pregnancy . . . and I was good after Jamal was born . . . till I came up here." She shrugged. "Now look at me." She put the bottle on the floor between her knees. "The contaminating influence of the West, I suppose."

"People drink in Syria. It's not exactly Saudi Arabia."

Bianca shrugged. "Yeah . . . and I was one of them." She looked up to Court. "Hey, can you ask them to get me a phone? I want to call Jamal's au pair. My son needs me. I've been gone too long."

Court didn't answer her; there was zero chance this prisoner was going to get a phone to call home, but he wasn't going to tell her that right now.

Instead he said, "Help me understand . . . How did you get caught up with Azzam in the first place?"

Bianca smiled a little. She was sad, stressed, tired, but Court saw that she could still look beautiful with only a smile. "My grandfather on my father's side was from Tartus, Syria, on the Mediterranean coast. I'd visited twice as a child, then four years ago I was invited to a party in Damascus. It meant a lot to my parents for me to go, so I went, and I met Shakira. We became friends, and she introduced me to Ahmed. They were very kind to me, treated me like I belonged in their nation. I decided to stay for a season, to show my solidarity for Syria and the Alawis . . . I am an Alawi, if you did not know."

Court said, "I knew."

Bianca raised her eyebrows. "You researched me?"

"I wanted to know if you would put up a fight in the hotel. I thought any religious or tribal affiliations might be relevant. Of course, that was before I was let in on the joke."

"The joke?"

"That I'd be grabbing you at the exact moment the terrorists attacked."

"Ah," she said. "That made everything easy, didn't it?"

"Not everything. Just you."

A look of anger flashed across her face, but it dissipated, and she kept talking. "I bought a home in Damascus. I wanted to stand against the lies perpetrated by the West against my people. Shakira thanked me personally for my actions. We would have lunch every week, and we went on shopping trips in the city together, if you can believe such a thing now."

She gulped another swig of champagne.

"Then Ahmed asked to see me privately. Of course I knew what was going on, but I was flattered. He is one of the most important men in the world, obviously."

He's a psycho, Court wanted to say, but he held his tongue. He needed this woman on his side right now.

"Our relationship developed quickly. I'm convinced Shakira knew all along and did not mind."

"Apparently she minds now," Court said.

"Only because of my son. My son is a threat to the future of her children, or at least she thinks he is. Ahmed wants to leave her and bring me into the palace, but it's complicated because of the war. Shakira is Sunni, and she has power with the Sunni groups helping the Alawi government. But when the war is over . . . when it is safe, he will send Shakira out of the country with some money and her kids, and . . ."

Her voice trailed off oddly.

"You all right?"

Her eyes went distant. "I think that's what I wanted once. I don't want that anymore."

Court sat there, patiently waiting for her.

She said, "I thought I loved Ahmed. I became his mistress, and then . . . slowly, I began to feel like a prisoner. I thought it was just because of the war, and the Western lies . . . but when I became pregnant, I thought maybe I should kill myself."

"Why didn't you?"

"I was afraid, I suppose. Then I had Jamal." Her eyes fixed again and beamed; she stared into Court's eyes and their brilliance made him uneasy. "When I saw Jamal I realized I had never felt love before that moment. I had *finally* done something right. I *finally* had a purpose to my life." She kept looking at Court. "I am wondering. Does a man like you even know what it feels like to love?" She drank some more champagne from the bottle while she waited for an answer, never taking her eyes from his.

Court looked away and changed the subject. "You still live in your house?"

"No. Ahmed bought me a new home in Damascus, in a neighborhood he can get to quickly and quietly from the palace. Neither his name nor my name were used in the purchase."

"Your baby. He stays with you?"

She cocked her head. "Of course he stays with me. What kind of question is—"

"Will Ahmed move him now that you've disappeared?"

"He can't. He is careful about Jamal. He uses special guards who work for him directly, so there is no connection back to the presidential palace. It would hurt him with the Sunnis if word got out about his other family, because it would hurt Shakira's standing, and she's the one thing keeping the Sunni militias from rising up against him."

"How many security officers at your house?"

"Why do you ask?"

"How many?"

"It . . . it depends. About five or so."

"I want to know everything about your home."

She seemed surprised by the change in the conversation, and she lowered the bottle, held it between her knees. "Why?"

"Because the Halabys need your help, and the only way you'll give it to them is if some idiot goes to Syria to get your kid."

She regarded him for a long time, then snorted out an angry laugh. "What . . . you will just fly into Damascus, knock on the gate to my house, and ask the guards if you can take my baby for a drive?"

"Think that would work?"

Bianca did not smile, but her chin rose, her eyes widened. "Do you really think you can do this?"

"I have a plan."

"It had better be a good one."

"Well, the quality of it will improve the moment I get some idea where I'm going."

Now she wiped her face, brought her hair back behind her ears, and sat up even more. Court saw that the woman felt she was being teased with a lifeline, but she felt her own actions now were the only way to encourage the man across from her to toss it her way.

"Sir . . . I am begging you to do this. What do you want from me?"

They talked in general about the layout of her house and the habits of the guards there, but Bianca did not tell Court the exact location, only the district of the city she lived in. Court suspected he understood why, but when he asked her outright for her address, his suspicion was confirmed.

Medina looked down to the floor for nearly a minute. Finally she said, "I will tell you where Jamal is being kept once you get to Damascus. If you are caught at the border you might give up information under torture. I can't let Ahmed know I'm helping the people who've kidnapped me. If he knew that, he would *definitely* kill my son."

Court realized this would make his job more difficult, but he also realized this was the right move for Bianca to make. It made Jamal a little bit safer, and it put Court at more risk.

If he had been the boy's parent, he would have done exactly the same thing.

"I understand."

Court stood, but Bianca said, "How do you plan on traveling with a four-month-old?"

Court cocked his head. He didn't really understand the question. "I'll just carry him, I guess. How much can he possibly weigh?"

Bianca closed her eyes. Suddenly Court could see disappointment on her face. "You haven't even thought about this, have you?"

"Full disclosure . . . I've never snatched a baby before. This will be a first."

"Do you have children?" When she didn't get an answer, she said, "No . . . you wouldn't, would you?" She sighed. "Well, I can tell you one thing. You can't do this alone. He needs food, care. You don't look like someone who can take care of a baby."

Court just stared back at her.

"His au pair is there. She is with him all the time, and she can take care of him until you bring him to me. Her name is Yasmin. She will help you."

"Why would she help me?"

Bianca said, "She will have no choice. Azzam would have her killed in an instant if Jamal disappeared while she was with him, and she knows that. If you take my baby, Yasmin *will* come with you."

"Okay."

"Sir . . . you hold Jamal's life in your hands. As you do Yasmin's. As you do mine."

No pressure, thought Court.

He began to stand, but she reached out and put a hand on his leg.

"I lied to the Halabys."

Court sat back down. "Lied?"

"I told them I knew nothing about Ahmed's movements. It's not true. I know things."

"Why are you telling me this? I didn't ask you any—"

"I know about a trip he will be taking soon."

"A trip? Out of Syria?"

She shook her head quickly. "No. Other than our trip to Tehran, he hasn't left Syria in years. He rarely even leaves Damascus. But he will leave the capital this time. He is going to review his troops at some bases, then he is going to a new Russian base somewhere."

"Why?"

"The crown prince of Jordan spends time in the field with his troops. Shakira told Ahmed this makes him look strong, so Ahmed will do it, too. And this new Russian base . . . I think something is special about it; he said he wanted to be there to bask in the glory, but I don't really know what he meant by that. This is all top secret, but Ahmed told me about it to impress me, and to tell me he wouldn't be by to see his child for a few days."

"So you don't know where he's going?" Court asked.

She shook her head. "No. But he did tell me when. He leaves next Monday. He will be gone until Tuesday."

"Any chance he'll cancel his trip now that all this is going on with you?"

"No chance. He would have to explain himself to the Russians, and he won't do that. No . . . he *will* go."

"Thank you," Court said. "I'll talk to you again when I'm in theater and in play."

She climbed off the little bed and went to her knees, then hugged Court tightly while he sat on the chair. Tears dripped from her long lashes now. "Please don't forget. My son is counting on you."

Court took her by the upper arms and separated the two of them a little. He looked into her eyes. "He's counting on you, too, Bianca, because when I *do* get back here with the kid, you better start singing to the Halabys. They've seen their country destroyed, a half million killed, their own two children blown to bits, chemical weapons used on their friends. They are desperate. For your sake and theirs, you need to give them what they want."

"Monsieur, if you bring me back my Jamal, I will do anything I can possibly do to help them end Ahmed and Shakira's rule."

CHAPTER 22

Court climbed the stairs and stepped back into the living room, and there he saw the Halabys sitting and drinking tea with Vincent Voland. All three looked up to him. While Voland's face was as impassive as only a veteran intelligence operative could make it, the Halabys could not hide their hopes and expectations.

Court said, "Surely you are all aware that Shakira Azzam is going to send people up here to try to find and kill Bianca."

Voland said, "I've told the Halabys about Sebastian Drexler. The man who called himself Eric. Obviously he controls members of the local police force. I think it likely he will come himself now that his earlier attempts have failed."

"What about Ahmed Azzam's men?"

Voland said, "French intelligence is watching the Syrian embassy here in Paris closely. We know who the GIS people are. Of course they have non-official cover operatives, not working at the embassies, and those men we can't track."

"Are they any good?"

"They aren't bad. One of their number, an operative who used the code name Malik, killed four federal police officers in Belgium last year. There have been assassinations in Paris, but only of Syrians in exile. We don't see them being able to put any numbers of non-official cover operatives together, and if they did, there is no way they could find us here at this safe house.

"A man like Drexler . . . perhaps he could find us. He is well connected throughout Europe, intelligent, and deeply cunning." Voland smiled a little. "The good news is we know Drexler won't be working with Syrian government assassins. He's essentially on the opposite mission as they are."

Court said, "But if Drexler comes to this house, he won't come alone."

Voland nodded. "He'll put together some sort of force, yes. And the Syrians here protecting Bianca, while committed to the cause, aren't particularly skilled. I am reaching out to an old friend who can help with security."

Tarek said, "We'll keep the woman safe, but our operation will only succeed if she talks."

Court knew what he was suggesting. "Yes, Tarek. I will go to Syria to get the kid and his nanny."

Rima said, "This is wonderful news. I can talk to our connections immediately. It will take them up to a week to get you the papers you need to pose as medical staff."

"I'm not waiting a week, I'm not posing as a doctor, and I'm not using your connections. I'll make my own way in."

"Your own way?" Tarek almost shouted it. "Are you crazy?"

Vincent Voland looked stunned. "You speak fluent Arabic?"

"Just enough to get myself into trouble, actually."

Tarek asked, "But then how are you—"

"I am going to leave here, and then in a few days I will contact you from Damascus. That's all you need to know. When I call, you will put Bianca on the phone, and she will give me directions to where I need to go to get her kid. Once I have the kid and the nanny, I will make a run for the border."

Rima and Tarek looked at each other. Tarek said, "Lebanon is to the west. Lebanon is Hezbollah, which means it's almost as dangerous for you as Syria."

"Right," Court said. "Scratch that."

Rima added, "To the north is Turkey, and the border is easy to cross, but that's a long way away from Damascus. Plus, ISIS owns five times the territory the Americans, Kurds, and Free Syrians do, and it's a fluid battlefield."

"I'll pass."

Tarek said, "To the east is Iraq, three hundred kilometers distant, inhospitable terrain, and the war is being fought there, as well. Eastern Syria is populated with ISIS fighters, and then, if you *did* make it into Iraq, it's another five hundred kilometers of desert to civilization."

"Where I would find *more* people who probably wouldn't mind killing me."

"It's very possible."

"Yeah. No."

Voland said, "That's why south is your best option. It's a five-hour drive to the Jordanian border from Damascus. There will be checkpoints along the way, which you'll have to avoid on your own, but once at the border, I have contacts in the Jordanian intelligence services who can get all three of you across."

Court asked, "Why would they do that?"

"They don't know who you are, and they don't know who Bianca is. But they know who *I* am, and they trust me. When they learn that getting three people over the border is the way to cause a split in the relationship between Russia, Syria, and Iran, they will be willing to help without question."

Court nodded. "Jordan it is."

Tarek stood up now, put his arm on Court's shoulder. Court wished people would just stop touching him. The Syrian said, "If I were younger, stronger, faster. If I were trained." He gave Court a little smile. "If I were you. If I were you I'd go in there, and I wouldn't return until I was dead, or until Azzam himself was dead."

"Let's not get carried away. I go in for the baby and the nanny. I get them, find a way south down to the Jordanian border, and get out of the country. That's it."

Tarek reached a hand out now. "We thank you for what you are going to do."

Court shook Tarek's hand and said, "Save your gratitude for when I get back. I might get popped at the border, at a roadside checkpoint. My cover might get compromised and I could get tortured to death in a prison before I get within twenty klicks of that kid."

Rima stood and put her hand on Court's face, looking up at him with warm eyes. "Most people just don't care. The fact that you care enough to try makes you someone worthy of my respect. My nation needs your help, monsieur. I've seen so many people die in my hands in the past seven years."

Me, too, Court thought, but while she was thinking about those she'd lost on the operating table, he was thinking about those he'd killed.

. . .

In the car on the way back to Paris, Vincent Voland drove in silence. Court could tell something was on his mind.

"What is it?" he asked.

The Frenchman said, "The Halabys might not be battle-worn resistance leaders, but they *do* have contacts in Damascus, and you are making a mistake by not using them to get into the country and get around."

Court said, "You think I'm going to trust a network of theirs? No . . . if I go in, I go in with my own resources."

"Again . . . I must ask. What resources do you have in Damascus?"

Court didn't answer. There was no need to tell Voland anything else about his plan to get in. Instead he pivoted. "You need to help them with Bianca and the safe house. With guys and guns, yes, but they also need training. Their tradecraft is nonexistent, and you can be damn sure that if Sebastian Drexler comes here, he'll be ready for a bloody fight."

Voland said, "We will be prepared for him if he finds us here. I have four men joining us. All ex–Foreign Legion, masters in weapons and tactics. These four, along with the six armed Syrians here on the property, mean we will be ready for anything."

Court hadn't liked the layout of the property at all from a defensive standpoint. The woods all around would make it easy for infiltrators to get close to the farmhouse, and he had only noticed the one way into Bianca's room in the basement; this made retreat impossible. But all he could do was hope the men Voland said he was bringing in would take steps to minimize the problems with the location.

Something else was bothering Court, so he changed gears. "What aren't you telling me?"

"What do you mean?" asked Voland.

"There are parts of your story I'm not buying. The handler in Monte

Carlo, for instance. You went to him to find someone to grab Bianca, and he told you he just happened to have access to the Gray Man?"

Voland shrugged his shoulders. "Not exactly. When you first contacted him and established your bona fides, he came to French intelligence. They notified me."

"French intelligence again," Court said. "They seem to be more involved in all this than even the Halabys."

Voland simply said, "As I have told you many times, I am not directly affiliated with *any* agency of *any* nation. But my contacts have been very helpful in my work with the Halabys. Remember, if Sebastian Drexler comes up here looking for Bianca, a lot of agencies around the world will be happy."

"They'll be happy only if you kill him," Court corrected.

Voland made a face of displeasure. "We do not have the death penalty here, like you do in America. If he comes up here, our intelligence services will pass the information on to the Police Nationale, who will simply try to arrest him."

Court said, "From what I know of the guy, he won't go down without a fight."

"D'accord." Agreed, said Voland.

"Too bad I'll be out of town."

To this Voland smiled gravely. "Yes . . . too bad, indeed." After a few seconds Voland added, "Maybe you should stay here. Not go to Syria."

"What are you talking about?"

"I can pressure Bianca to work with us. We can tell her you have gone, and are working on getting her son back. We can salvage something out of the Medina operation, and you can help us with Drexler."

"You sound concerned suddenly about how much trouble Drexler can cause here."

"It's not that. I am concerned about your chances in Syria. I know your reputation, but still . . . you are going into a war with many sides, and you have no side of your own."

Court said, "I have to see this through. For all their failures in this operation, the Halabys are good people, and their cause is honorable. And from what I can tell, I'm the only good guy in the Halabys' corner."

Voland made an annoyed face. "Present company excluded?"

"Hardly."

The Frenchman sighed. "Then let me talk to my former counterparts at DGSE, foreign intelligence. If you don't trust the Free Syria Exile Union to support your operation, perhaps you will let someone with more experience provide you with assistance while you are down there."

Court just stared out the window. "You're forgetting one thing."

"What is that?"

"I don't like you, Voland. You're the asshole who sent me in on top of an ISIS operation. And I don't even trust people I *do* like, so there is no way I'm going to have you, or the DGSE, working as my handler on my operation down in Syria."

"So you are just going to Syria on your own?"

"I'll be on my own, no matter what anyone promises me. Better for me if I go in with that knowledge than thinking you're up here holding on to my lifeline."

"*Mon ami*, it is clear that you *do*, in fact, have serious trust issues."

"Yeah. I wonder why."

CHAPTER 23

Police Judiciaire Captain Henri Sauvage had gotten cold feet about all this shit. He hadn't said anything to his partner yet, but he had decided to walk away from all the money he'd been promised, to settle for the money he'd already been paid, and to get the *fuck* out of Paris.

As far as Sauvage was concerned, Eric, the shadowy voice on the phone who'd hired him to find and stalk men and women on behalf of Syrian interests here in Paris, could go to hell.

Sauvage's division of the Police Judiciaire was the Criminal Brigade, known around Paris as La Crim, and they did have a counterespionage group, but Sauvage wasn't on it. He worked instead in the homicide division. But even though he wasn't a spy or a spy hunter, he understood the concept of MICE. MICE was the acronym for the four principal forms of compromise used by intelligence officers—money, ideology, compromise, and ego. And even though Sauvage wasn't trained professionally on the techniques, he recognized that the man he only knew as Eric had roped him into this mess by using three of the four on him to great effect.

Henri Sauvage had no ideology whatsoever—he was in it for the dough—but the other three motivations had brought him to where he found himself today. Money was easy to see; this was why he had agreed to work for Eric in the first place. But looking back on it now, he realized the man had played on his ego, as well, by making him feel important enough to recruit three other men in the force to help him. After this was done, Sauvage, Clement, Allard, and Foss continued taking payoffs to provide information to help the Syrians in Paris, first providing information out of Criminal Brigade databases. Eventually Eric upped the ante with footwork, having Henri and his boys tail men and women, Syrian expatriates, rebels, and reporters speaking out against the Azzam regime.

It was not long before the stakes were raised for the cell of police officers, when one of the Syrian immigrants they had been tailing simply disappeared.

Sauvage and his group knew good and well the man they'd surveilled had likely been assassinated, and by this time they had worked out that they were proxy operatives of the Syrian regime. But the four kept at it. Their standards of living had risen, and with this rise came the need for more and more money to fuel their lifestyles. Plus, the missing man had not been a French citizen or well connected, so no real attention was paid to the event, and Sauvage and his team got away with it scot-free.

Over the next year they were involved in two other operations that appeared to have led to assassinations, but Sauvage's cell was still only involved in hands-off work on the fringes of the operations, so the four men remained compartmentalized from any real danger to themselves, their liberty, or even their careers.

But then the ante was upped again when the mysterious Eric ordered them to follow a Spanish model named Bianca Medina while she visited the city to work at Fashion Week and to report on the security around her.

This, Sauvage had known instantly, was a very different animal from all their other work for the Syrians.

Every fiber of the captain's being had been against this, and his three partners in crime pushed back, as well, but by then the compromise was in play. Eric had enough dirt on the French cops to put them all in prison, so there was no way they would not comply. Plus Eric insisted that, as always, their input in the operation would be relatively minor.

So they did as ordered, followed the Spanish model, surveilled the location where she was staying, and passed on the information to Eric.

And in the process they became fully involved in the high-profile terrorist massacre that took place in central Paris three nights earlier.

Now the four police officers were in it up to their necks, and when Foss and Allard had been gunned down two days earlier in the apartment of Syrian expatriates, who *themselves* were now missing, the tension on the two remaining members of the cell of dirty cops was ratcheted up to ten.

And that tension had become unbearable for Henri Sauvage.

He'd decided to take his family and run, at least for a while. He knew that when he did leave town, Eric would probably go through with his threat to reveal his involvement in the ISIS attack, but Sauvage told himself Eric had no direct proof, and Sauvage could explain the accusation away by constructing an elaborate explanation that Eric was a confidential informant he'd been running off book, who had now turned against him because of an unrelated disagreement.

It was a gamble, but less so, Sauvage determined, than continuing the hunt for Bianca Medina and standing by while more people were slaughtered across the city.

So Sauvage decided to hit the bricks, but he could not just leave his partner behind to deal with this alone. To make his escape from his problem, he needed to sell Andre Clement on the idea of running out on Eric, as well. To this end he'd asked Clement to meet him at a location where they often met confidential informants for clandestine meetings: the Car Park Stalingrad garage next to the Gare du Nord train station.

. . .

Five minutes before one a.m., an exhausted and on-edge Henri Sauvage drove down the ramp and into the underground garage, parked his little but speedy Renault 308 with the front grille facing the exit ramp, and sat there in the nearly full but perfectly quiet garage while he texted Clement.

Ou est vous? *Where are you?*

Sauvage had smoked half a cigarette before the reply came.

Deux minutes. *Two minutes.*

Soon Clement's four-door Citroën rolled down the ramp, and Sauvage flashed his lights. The Citroën turned his way and began rolling forward. Behind it, a pair of sedans also rolled down the ramp. One turned to the left and one to the right, and they disappeared in the massive garage.

The Citroën parked in the closest space, just a few spots from Sauvage, so the captain and cell leader got out of his car, left the door open, and strolled over with his walkie-talkie in his hand. He tossed his cigarette, stepped to the driver's-side window of the vehicle as it slid down, and leaned down to talk to his old friend.

And that was when he realized something was very wrong.

Thirty-three-year-old Andre Clement faced forward, his hands gripping the wheel so tightly his fingers were white . . . and only then did Sauvage see the man in the backseat with a pistol pressed against the back of Clement's head.

Andre Clement looked up at his partner with eyes filled with dread now. "I am sorry, Henri. I couldn't take it, so I tried to run out on this shit. I was going to leave it behind, pack up the kids and just—"

Without warning, an earsplitting crack battered Sauvage's senses; Clement's head snapped forward inside an arc of flame. Blood splattered the inside of the windshield and the steering wheel, but Sauvage did not wait to check on his partner's condition. Instead he spun away, ducked down as low as he could, and sprinted back around to his Renault.

He dove through the open door and fired up his engine, not quite sure what the hell was going on but *damn* sure he needed to get the hell out of there. But just as he shifted gears to race from his space, a Ford van that had been parked in the garage shot in front of him on his left to cut him off. The van had no lights on, but Sauvage could see a man in the front passenger seat spin towards him with a short-barreled submachine gun.

The two sedans that had entered the garage a minute earlier appeared with squealing tires, shooting forward towards Sauvage.

The captain only now went for the weapon he kept in a shoulder holster, palmed the grip of the HK pistol, and started to yank it free. But looking around he could see a half dozen guns either pointing at him already or moving into position to do so.

Henri Sauvage released his grip on the weapon and raised his hands. His car door flew open and he was yanked out by a man with olive skin wearing a gray denim jacket and jeans, and the man pushed Sauvage forward and through the sliding door of the van, onto a floor covered in plastic tarp.

Other men jumped into the van with him; he could hear and feel them more than see them while facing down on the plastic.

The vehicle squealed its tires again as it headed off.

Sauvage had a knife in his left boot, but it was found by one of the men on top of him now. He wondered at first if they were federal police or intelligence officials; that would make sense, of course, considering his peripheral involvement in an ISIS operation in Paris, but it certainly did *not* explain why they'd just executed Andre in cold blood.

But when he was pulled up into a seated position, pushed against the side wall of the van, he got a better look at the four men in the back with him.

"Who the fuck are you?" Sauvage asked, but he was pretty certain he knew now. They were all Arab. He assumed they were Syrian nationals, living in Europe but serving as either intelligence operatives or contract operatives for the Azzam regime.

These men had been sent by Eric, and they'd be killers, each and every one.

When he and his partners in his "side job" for the Syrians followed someone who soon disappeared, *these* were likely the boys who did the disappearing.

But there was a modicum of good news for Sauvage. These men hadn't killed him yet, so even though he was sitting on a tarp that looked like it had been put there to catch his flying brain matter, he felt like he retained some ability to affect events.

All he had to do was talk to these guys and say *exactly* the right things, and he would be able to save his life.

The man closest to the front of the van wore a black turtleneck, and his black hair was curly, longer than the others. He was somewhere in his late thirties, and he wore a Beretta pistol in a black leather shoulder holster.

Sauvage could see a confidence and authority in the man's face, and he decided *this* was the man to talk to. "Do you speak French?"

"Yes, you may call me Malik." He said it in a commanding tone that convinced Sauvage he'd made the right decision to address him.

"All right, Malik. I take it you're in charge?"

"*Oui.*"

"Why did you kill Andre?"

"He was planning on leaving town. We worried you were thinking about doing the same. We could not let either of you go."

Sauvage leaned closer to the man and pushed some outrage into his voice, even though fear was the predominant emotion going through him right now. "I'll ask it again. Why did you kill Andre?"

"Eric ordered us to sacrifice your partner to teach you a lesson." Now Malik leaned in towards Sauvage and adopted a similar angry tone. "Have you learned that lesson, Captain Sauvage?"

The Frenchman leaned back against the wall of the van. They were driving around, making left and right turns, and Sauvage had no idea where they were heading.

"What the fuck do you guys want?"

"We want you to fulfill your responsibilities to us. Your work with the police will be crucial in the next days as we hunt for Bianca Medina. We need her alive, unharmed, and we need your help for this."

"I can't help you, man. She's probably long gone from France."

Malik shook his head. "No. The group that has her, the Free Syria Exile Union, is based here. They are being supported by a former French intelligence officer named Voland, who also lives here and has worked here much of his professional life. All signs point to the fact that they are still in the area."

Sauvage said, "If you have all this information, what the hell do you need me for?"

Malik surprised Sauvage with a shrug. "I do not know. Eric has demanded we take you alive, encourage you not to try to run away, and give you something to do before he comes here himself."

"Wait . . . Eric is coming *here*?"

"Tomorrow."

"From . . . Syria?"

"I do not know where he is now."

"And what is it I'm supposed to do?"

"Simple. Find the girl."

Sauvage sighed. "Clement was holding a low-level operative in the FSEU at his farm near Versailles. This man, Ali Safra, didn't seem to know anything when we questioned him the other day, but perhaps we could talk to him again."

"No," Malik said. "We just came from there. He knew nothing about where they are now."

"How can you be sure?"

"Because he died without telling us, and it did not appear that he much wanted to die."

That sank in for a moment. Sauvage slammed the back of his head against the wall of the van in frustration. He knew there would be no getting away from these men, and they wouldn't leave till they had Bianca Medina in hand. He decided he'd better work with them to get this done fast so they could get out of his life of treason against his nation. "How many men do you have here in Paris?"

Malik did not answer, and when he did he equivocated. "I have enough."

"Come on," Sauvage said. "I need to know your manpower. We will have people to tail, locations to monitor. I have all the intel from the Police Judiciaire, but it's only me now. I need help to cover known FSEU locations to find the woman."

Still Malik did not speak. Sauvage could tell he wasn't used to handing over information about his force. "Look, man. I don't want to have to go to Eric and put you in the crosshairs—"

That did the trick. Even though Malik was in charge, it didn't seem like he wanted to cross swords with Eric. "There are fourteen of us. All paramilitary and intel operations trained. We've been pulled from work all over the continent. This includes a three-man unit of communications specialists, with equipment capable of jamming mobile phones and Internet."

"Fourteen." Sauvage nodded. "That's a lot of guns."

"What is your plan to find the woman?" Malik asked.

Sauvage's actual plan had been to run for his life, but he wasn't going to tell Malik that. Instead he said, "I have gone back to images we have of Free Syria Exile Union personnel for the last few years. Public events, photos on social media, images captured by police or other cameras around the Halabys. From this we are identifying members who were associated with them back before they were involved with the rebellion itself. We can put tails on all the main players to see where they go, who they meet with."

Malik said, "That could take time. We need to know where to go by the time Eric gets here."

Sauvage cocked his head a little. "This guy, Eric. What's his connection to Syria?"

"I do not know. What I *do* know is that he has the power to order assassinations on behalf of the regime. That's enough for me to know to do what I'm told. If you are smart, this will be enough for you, too."

The van began to slow; the door was opened on Sauvage's right. Malik cocked his head towards the door. "That is all." The vehicle jolted to a stop now. "We are giving you one chance to survive this, unlike your three associates. Find the woman, or find us someone who can lead us to the woman. Do it quickly, or Ahmed Azzam himself will order your death."

Sauvage's knees went weak, but he fought through the sensation, and he climbed out of the van. He found himself back in the parking garage, next to his Renault, and as the van rolled off, he saw that both Clement's body and his vehicle had disappeared without a trace.

CHAPTER 24

Lars Klossner didn't go anywhere without his bodyguards. It wasn't that he was particularly paranoid by nature—no, it was that people actually *were* trying to kill him.

Munich is a statistically safe city—safe for most everyone *not* named Lars Klossner. But the forty-seven-year-old German had spent two decades cultivating a reputation that necessitated the four German and Austrian ex–special forces close-protection detail who moved in box formation around him whenever he was in public, and the armored Mercedes G65 utility vehicle that rolled along nearby, driven by an armed driver in constant radio contact with the detail.

It was past midnight now, and Klossner had spent Friday evening at his regular table at Zum Durnbrau, a traditional German restaurant that began its life as an inn in the fifteenth century. After dinner and drinks he enjoyed an evening walk through the city center, and he pretended that he was just one of the crowd, even though his "mates" were actually his bodyguards and his silver Mercedes rolled along behind, ready to swoop in and cocoon the big German within two inches of steel armor, then race him out of the area.

The list of people wanting to end Klossner remained fluid. Right now he was aware of two contracts on his life, but his feelings would be hurt to learn there weren't at least two or three more.

As he walked through the crowded Marienplatz in the city center this cool and clear Friday evening, he certainly didn't appear to be a man who needed any more security than anyone else in the square. He had a Santa-like beard and a massive, Santa-like belly, and though he was obviously a middle-aged man he was dressed like a German hipster: a designer hoodie and a 2,500-euro puffy jacket, 1,600-euro eyeglasses, and a red knit cap that made him look like he was posing for a catalog that sold adventure wear to those who had never sniffed a whiff of adventure in their lives.

Although he didn't stand out as a dangerous individual, Klossner was a man who had forged great success in the industry of violence. He ran a network of security experts that performed all manner of military training on four continents. From Bolivia to Gabon, from Guyana to Niger, from Indonesia to Yemen, Klossner Welt Ausbildungs, GMBH, provided top-flight private military instruction to anyone who could pay.

With training on anything from basic firearms handling all the way up to battalion-sized field tactics, KWA mercenaries stood ready to train the armies, rebel groups, and private security forces of the world.

Klossner's company did not field hit men or spies, per se; his was not, on the surface anyway, a cloak-and-dagger outfit, but his specialty was dealing with nations and organizations that had difficulty securing high-quality instruction cadres from abroad because of issues of politics, corruption, or human rights abuses.

And there was an especially shadowy side to Klossner's operation that did not show up in the accounting books. It was known by all who hired KWA to train or lead their troops that the foreign mercs they employed could be offered off-hours work in a covert direct-action realm.

If one worked as an employee of KWA, one knew that his contract might have him training or organizing paramilitary forces in El Salvador or cold-blooded rebel marauders in South Sumatra, but he also knew he might also "moonlight" running black ops in these war zones himself.

KWA's stable of talent was well paid, but most people who worked for the German security firm didn't do so because it was their first choice. Instead, most KWA employees worked there because they were encumbered by something that kept them from being employed at one of the upper-tier security companies around the world. They had criminal convictions, they had been tossed out of other organizations for violating rules of engagement, or they fought drug or alcohol addictions.

Or else they were just evil.

Boiled down to its essence: Lars Klossner was a bad guy who contracted bad guys to go fight for and train bad guys. His was a closed loop of dirty.

. . .

After his walk through the center of Munich, Lars Klossner and his security turned onto Max-Joseph Strasse and then entered the vestibule of an ornate apartment building. They were buzzed in by the lobby guard, and then the entourage headed for the elevator. Outside on their right, the silver Mercedes rolled into a large lighted garage, and the garage door closed quickly behind it.

While the driver parked and shut down his vehicle, a private elevator took Klossner and his detail up to his vast third-floor penthouse, and here the protectee waited in the hallway with a pair of his men while the other two checked out his living quarters to make sure it was safe to leave their boss alone for the night.

After the all clear, Klossner stepped into his private quarters, while his security men retired to their end of the penthouse, took off their leather coats, and unslung their weapons. They pulled earpieces out of their ears, and only then did they relax. The chatting came instantly and easy, and when the driver of the Mercedes arrived a few minutes later, all five of them grabbed beers, called their wives and girlfriends, and began watching an FC Bayern soccer match they'd recorded during the week.

In his quarters, Klossner turned on his stereo, undressed, and took a hot shower. Afterwards, he toweled off and wrapped his rotund frame in his robe. He'd just begun brushing his teeth when he looked up into the mirror over the vanity.

Something moved in the low-lit bedroom behind him.

Lars Klossner looked harder into the mirror, the toothbrush hanging from his mouth, and he saw a figure in black leaning against the far wall of the bedroom. The man held a suppressed pistol in his right hand against his thigh, business end down.

The man's left hand rose; he held something in it. Suddenly the music stopped. The man by the wall tossed the stereo remote onto the bed.

The toothbrush came out, the German spit and washed his mouth out with bottled water, and he spit that out, too. He looked back into the mirror at the man standing there in the dim light.

Klossner turned around slowly, facing the figure in the darkness. *"Wer sind Sie?"* Who are you?

"Speak English, Lars."

The German flicked his eyes to the door. "I have bodyguards, you know."

"Yeah? Is that what you call them?"

Klossner's face twitched a little. The door remained closed; there was no sound of footsteps rushing up the hall.

"Dead?" he asked.

"Nah," the figure replied. "Just oblivious. You can call out to them if you want to . . . but you *really* don't want to."

The man with the American accent stood by a light switch. To Klossner's surprise, he reached over and flicked the switch with the tip of the suppressor of his pistol.

Several lamps in the room turned on simultaneously.

The German blinked hard again. *"Mein Gott.* Violator? Is that you?"

. . .

Court Gentry used the tip of his Gemtech suppressor to flip the lights back off, enshrouding himself and Klossner again in the dim.

"No one calls me that anymore."

"Ah, yes. Now you are the Gray Man." The skin on the heavy German's face suddenly looked almost as white as his beard. "How did you get in?"

Court had slipped in through the garage behind the Mercedes, then knelt behind the vehicle, removed his shoes, and crammed them in his backpack while the driver turned off the engine and climbed out. He'd followed the driver up the three flights of stairs, staying one floor behind him on the ascent, and timing his soft footfalls so he'd remain undetected.

When the driver unlocked the back door to Klossner's penthouse, Court began racing up the stairs on his stocking feet, pulling a folded envelope from his back pocket as he went. The driver entered the hallway, and the hydraulic closer began pushing the door closed behind him. Court was rushing to the other side of the door, still silent but taking the stairs three at a time now. Just as the door met the door frame, Court slid down onto his knees on the landing and shoved the envelope forward between the latch in the door and the strike plate in the doorjamb. The thick folded paper impeded the automatic latch from slipping into the strike plate mortise and locking the door, and this prevented the door from locking when it closed.

Court breathed a sigh of relief; he'd made it with barely a tenth of a second to spare.

A latch clicking into place makes a distinctive sound, and this door had not clicked, so Court knew there was a chance the driver on the other side of the door might return to investigate. He reached across his body with his left hand, drew his pistol upside down, and held it that way towards the door right in front of his face.

He waited for a minute, but the door he held unlocked did not open, and the driver did not return, so eventually he stood slowly and quietly, and he opened the door just enough to look into the hall.

The hall was clear, and Court was inside Klossner's penthouse.

. . .

But he didn't tell Klossner any of this now. When he did not answer the question of how he got in, Klossner said, "Ah . . . yes. A magician never reveals his secrets." After a pause the German spoke in a grave tone. "There are only two reasons you would show up in my house. Either you have come looking for work . . . or . . ."

Court replied, "I'm not here for the other reason."

Klossner let his relief be known with a heave and a long sigh. He put his hand on his heart for a second. Court thought he was joking, feigning a heart attack, but from the look of the big man he didn't know if the man might, in fact, have been having some sort of cardiac episode. Klossner lowered his hand with a smile, however, then stepped into the bedroom with his hands away from his body. He moved laterally along the wall and lowered himself down onto a settee. "How long has it been? Four or five years? It was Ankara. You were a burned Agency asset, working freelance, if memory serves. You didn't have your nickname yet."

"A simpler time," Court joked without smiling.

"For you, maybe. A team I sent to Turkey had just lost a contract because the man they were protecting was assassinated right under their noses." Klossner looked around. "Circumstances not unlike this, actually. I found out who did it, and offered you a job, because I saw what you were capable of. I actually thought I might dip a toe into the contract killer industry."

Court did not reply.

Klossner waved his hand. "You took one look at my operation . . ." Klossner laughed now. "And you kept on walking. Not your cup of tea, as the English say. You found me immoral. Dishonorable."

"Like I said . . . A simpler time."

The German considered this, then bobbed his head towards a stocked mirrored bar along the wall. "Care for a drink?"

"Nein, danke."

"If you aren't here to kill me, we can party all night."

"I'm looking for work. Something to get me out of Europe, quickly and quietly. Something that pays."

"I've never had a job applicant show up in my bedroom with a suppressed Glock in his hand."

"I couldn't be sure if you still held a grudge about Ankara."

"I'm a businessman, Violator. That was business." He shrugged. "And if you want to work for me now, that's business, too."

"Any openings?"

Klossner raised an eyebrow. "As much as I'd love to employ you, I must admit the fact that you killed your last employer in St. Petersburg gives me a moment's pause."

"Not true."

"Not true that you killed him, not true that it was in St. Petersburg, or not true he was your last employer?" When Court said nothing, Klossner shrugged. "Whatever, no harm done. Gregor Sidorenko was a madman. Bad for the security industry at large. I'm glad you slotted him." He added, "I just hope killing the boss isn't your new trademark."

Court holstered his suppressed pistol under his jacket.

"And they also say everything that happened in Washington, D.C., a couple of months ago was you. All the attacks and killings there."

173

"Sounds like someone is giving me too much credit."

The German smiled again, and this time it did not fade. "That's a good line, but the problem is, I *do* know some of the things you've done in the past, so I know you are one of the few out there who actually lives up to his hype."

"I'm here looking for work, so far be it from me to discourage you from your belief that I am a superhero."

The German laughed harder than before. "It's nice to see you again. Wasn't at first, I must say. Who wants to meet the Grim Reaper in their bathrobe?"

"I've got to get off the continent," Court stressed. "I'm willing to go anywhere, as long as I can get out of here."

Lars Klossner looked at the American with a curious eye now. "What have you gotten yourself into?"

Court stood silently against the wall.

"Right. None of my business. Let me think . . . A job in Caracas just fell into my lap. It's not your speed, really, a little simplistic for you, small-arms training for a rebel outfit that's in need of some—"

Court interrupted him. "Think bigger."

The German did so. "Ukraine?"

"I said *out* of Europe. Ukraine is in Europe, Lars."

"That it is . . . just thought you might want to see Kiev again."

Court didn't blink at this reference to his past, and Klossner let it go. The German rubbed his thick cheeks. "Well . . . there *is* something else, but you'd have to get your hands dirty. *Very* dirty. The Violator I knew four years ago wouldn't have touched this, but if the news can be trusted, you might have changed, if you don't mind my saying so."

"Where?"

Klossner hesitated. "The job is in Syria."

Court faked a little chuckle. "No thanks. The Free Syrian Army rebels are floundering. I'm not going to be the last rat to jump onto that ship before it goes down."

Klossner waved a hand in the air. "No. Not the FSA. Not the Kurds or the Turks or the Americans or the Iraqis." He shrugged. "This is work for the other guys."

Court nodded slowly. "I see."

"I've heard all about your moral code. I'm sure that's cost your handlers a mint in the past. If you do the job in Caracas, it might align more with your sense of right and—"

"I'll work for the Syrian regime. I don't give a shit. Not anymore."

Klossner scratched his snow-white hair. "I'd love to hear the story about what turned you into a black hat."

The room remained silent, and Klossner took the hint quickly. He said, "Never mind, then."

"Tell me about the job."

"You'd be working with a militia."

"A militia?"

"Conventional wisdom in the West is that Azzam runs his military. That's a fable. The Syrian regime is no longer a true centralized state; it's a union of warlords, with a warlord politician at its center. In fact, it is very fractured, very tribal down there. A lot of different militias, offshoots of the military, all under the Azzam regime coalition. And they fight among themselves, as well. One of the most corrupt nations on Earth, because Azzam has to let all these warlords and chieftains rape the nation economically so they will continue to give him their support. I've been there three times in the past three years, and I can tell you, it's a crazy place full of crazy people. Militias aligned with the regime but also affiliated with organized crime, and now you add in the Iranians and the Russians running around like they own the place." He sniffed. "Regular civilians are caught in the middle."

"If the Russians are there, why are the militias hiring labor from you?"

"The Russians are in the air, conducting special operations in the countryside, that sort of thing. They have Chechen and Ingush Muslim Special Forces down there, as well. But they are on their own, not folded in with the locals that support Azzam. The militias are all trying to professionalize so they can retain some power when the war ends. The Sunnis are helping Azzam now, but the fight will really be on when the rebels die off and ISIS dies off and the foreign enemies of Azzam give up."

Court feigned casualness in his next question. "Who's the client?"

"You'd be working for one of the roughest of all the regime-aligned units down there. They are called Liwa Suqur al Sahara. Heard of them?"

175

Acid fired into Court's stomach now, but he didn't even blink. "The Desert Hawks Brigade."

The German grinned yet again. "You are a pro, Violator. Of course you know all the players, even in *that* quagmire. I have forty-three contractors positioned there right now at different bases for the Hawks and there's something like a dozen different PMCs plying their trade down there with other groups. Most of what my boys do is training . . . but . . . there *is* extra-curricular work that comes up. What the Desert Hawks Brigade have my guys doing after hours . . . it's shit the fucking Chechens wouldn't even touch."

Court felt unease in the pit of his stomach, but he didn't let on. He feigned thinking it over, then said, "This will do. I need to get to a place where I won't be tracked."

"Well . . . you can't get much more off-grid than a free-fire zone in the Middle East. You want the job, it's yours."

Court breathed slowly, careful to not give off any cues as to his true feelings.

"I'm in."

"*Sehr gut,*" Klossner said with a nod. "An Aussie guy working at the Hawks Brigade base in Babbila near Damascus just got a kneecap shot off in an ISIS attack on his convoy on Monday, and I had a guy ready to re-place him going down tomorrow. I can bump him and send you instead, if you like. Or we have a couple of openings at other bases around the coun-try, but I figured you'd rather be near civilization."

"Damascus will do fine. I appreciate it." It was better than fine. Court had been prepared to ask point-blank to be stationed near the capital in the event he was being sent to some backwater. He couldn't believe his good fortune.

Klossner looked at his watch. "*Gut* . . . I have to get my people to work on your papers all night, but we can do it. You'll fly from Munich to Beirut in the morning. There we have an arrangement with a charter airline that will do the short hop up to Latakia. It's on the Syrian coast, and the air base there is controlled by the Russian air force, so we don't violate the no-fly zones in the interior." Klossner winked now. "Hate to have you blown out of the sky on the way in. Anyway, the bad news about the Da-mascus base is that to get there you'll have to truck across country . . . and it's not exactly the most peaceful drive these days. Another military company lost a couple guys on the highway recently, but it's nothing a man like you hasn't seen before."

"I'll be fine," Court said, but he was already second-guessing this sure-fire way of his to infiltrate Syria.

Klossner shrugged. "I'd be a son of a bitch if I didn't fill you in about the loss rates. They are high, but I guess you've experienced worse in other theaters."

"Tell me."

"Let me put it this way. I've been sending operators into Damascus for three years, and in that time, eight out of ten of my guys have made it out in one piece."

Terrific, Court thought. His *cover* identity had a built-in twenty percent casualty rate. He was even less optimistic about the chances of his actual operation, which would no doubt be several orders of magnitude more dangerous.

Klossner stood and crossed the room over to Court now. The big man kept his hands away from his body, and Court was sure this was to keep his dangerous visitor at ease, but it made Court worry that Klossner was going to try to get him in a bear hug. Instead he stopped a few steps away from Court by the wall. "Normally there would be a physical, but you look pretty good to me. Have to ask, though . . . you aren't doing drugs, are you?"

"No drugs."

Klossner scanned Court up and down like he was livestock at a sale. After a few seconds, he said, "You're different. Not physically. I just mean . . . taking this job, knowing you'll be working for the Azzam regime. You're *sure* you're not on something?"

Court said, "Look me over like a mule, but you aren't getting blood or DNA."

"*God* no. Of course not. I understand you are a different case, a damned celebrity, and you will be treated as such." He raised his eyebrows as a new thought came to him. "I'd like to exploit this, financially. Tell the Syrians you are special, require special rates."

"No," Court said with authority. "I don't want to stick out. Especially not down there."

Klossner waved a hand through the air. "The Gray Man. I get it. Forget

I mentioned it. The guy I'm bumping to send you down. He's Canadian. You'll take his documents, assume his identity." Klossner shrugged again. "It's a fake name, anyway. All my guys use pseudonyms on their ops. Safer for everybody. I'll have my people come here tonight and get your picture to match it to the docs. I'll get more papers for my Canadian contractor and send him to Caracas." Klossner shrugged. "He was a coward anyway, didn't want to go to Syria."

"Works for me."

Klossner reached out and shook Court's hand. "The *motherfucking* Gray Man," he said, still marveling over the fact that the legend was here in his presence.

• • •

Court lay folded in a small closet in a guest room of Klossner's penthouse apartment, the door cracked and his pistol by his side. He'd unmade the bed, then turned on the light in the bathroom and closed the door. If anyone came into his room tonight they'd think they'd caught him up and taking a piss, and this would buy him some time to mount a counterattack.

He stared at the dark ceiling, thinking about the operation to come. He'd have to be in a car on the way to the airport in less than four hours, but for right now his nerves kept him awake.

So far, everything was proceeding according to plan. He'd known for a long time that Lars Klossner was running mercs into Syria, and making a small fortune doing it. He'd also been reasonably sure Lars wouldn't pass up the opportunity to send him down if given the chance to do so. Court had hoped he'd be on his way in two or three days but was astonished to find out he'd be getting on a plane within eight hours. It didn't give him much time to study maps, but the quick infiltration into Syria was one of the first good things that had happened for the chances of little Jamal Medina in the past three days, so he told himself he should just try to relax and go with the flow, up until the moment when he had to break his cover legend and make a run for the kid.

Court wondered about the job ahead. Not the kidnapping of the child; instead he speculated about what he might have to do as a contracted member of a Syrian regime militia.

He hadn't known Klossner was working with the Desert Hawks Brigade, and this sucked, because he knew all about them and what they were doing in Syria.

At the darkest portion of the war for Azzam, he signed a decree that allowed businessmen to raise their own militias to defend their capital assets. This action, in one fell swoop, turned the smugglers, con men, and kleptocrats of the nation into warlords.

The Desert Hawks Brigade became one of the most successful and violent pro-regime armies in the conflict. Independent of the Syrian military chain of command, they helped the regime by fighting its enemies, but they were also able to spend their time stealing and smuggling, assassinating their rivals in the underworld.

Working for the Hawks in Syria was a little like working for both the Nazis and the mafia at the same time.

The Desert Hawks Brigade was infamous. They regularly tortured and killed men, women, and children, and now Court would be shoulder to shoulder with these monsters. Suiting up for the Desert Hawks meant Court would probably be asked to do some horrible things, but if he wanted to maintain his cover, he'd have to comply.

And there was another downside to using this means to get into Syria. As soon as he broke away from the Desert Hawks and went for the baby, Court knew the affable but imposing German sleeping nearby in the master bedroom would probably become a sworn enemy. But that was a problem for another day. Pissing off the president of a company that rented out mercenaries to train and kill for third-world death squads didn't seem like a great idea, but Court figured getting into Syria on his own, with a good cover legend about what he was doing there, was worth the risk.

This was going to be a tricky operation, to say the least, and the fact that he did not know how much time he had before Ahmed Azzam decided to remove the compromise of his child and simply move him or kill him only made Court's operation to come more unsure.

He closed his eyes and willed himself to catch a couple of hours' rest, because he knew one thing— right here, right now, lying in a closet in Munich, there wasn't a *fucking* thing he could do about what would happen tomorrow in Syria.

CHAPTER 25

Jamal Medina began to cry.

The house had been quiet since the four-month-old baby finally went to sleep two hours earlier, but Jamal was letting all within earshot know that it was time for a late-night feeding.

The au pair had been dozing on a mat near the crib—the baby had the more luxurious arrangement—but she sat up quickly and checked the clock. It was eleven fifteen p.m., a little earlier than usual for Jamal to want to eat again, but the only thing the au pair found consistent with the baby was inconsistency, so she was not surprised in the least.

Yasmin was the only person in the home allowed to handle the baby, but she was not the only person in the home. She was surrounded by five security men: all Alawis, and all members of a specially vetted Ba'ath Party unit, chosen for their skill and their support for the Azzam regime.

Yasmin Samara was a twenty-four-year-old Sunni Syrian and the granddaughter of the former speaker of the Syrian People's Council, a Ba'ath Party official who served both Ahmed al-Azzam and his father before him. She had worked as an au pair in France for three years, then returned home to take a job as the nanny of a wealthy expatriate woman who lived in Mezzeh.

It wasn't until she was brought in to meet a very pregnant Bianca and garnered her approval that she was told the father of the baby she would be looking out for was the president of the nation. Bianca stressed that she could not mention this to a soul, but it wasn't until Ahmed Azzam himself dropped in on his new child that she understood the full scope of the danger she was in. Azzam was kind to her, but when he left, he left one of his security officers behind a moment to remind her to keep her silence, and that any failure to do so would be a criminal act.

Yasmin was the right girl for the job because she was an excellent nanny, and she hadn't breathed a word to anyone, not even her family.

Bianca had been due back earlier in the day, but Yasmin had not heard any news from her. She wondered if the beautiful Spanish model had found some excuse to stay in Europe a little longer, but she doubted this, because Bianca had confided in her that Ahmed Azzam barely let her go in the first place, and sticking around overseas was a surefire way to make him angry.

Yasmin was deathly afraid of Ahmed Azzam, although he'd been in her life for all of her life. Bianca, on the other hand, didn't seem to be afraid at all. The married man was obviously in love with his Spaniard; Bianca would tell Yasmin stories about his awkward romantic acts that made the young au pair blush.

As she carried Jamal into the kitchen tonight for yet another feeding, she rubbed the dark hair on the top of his head and sang him a little song with a tired voice. At the bottom of the stairs she saw lights appear in the circular driveway out front. Yasmin felt sure it would be Bianca, finally home from her trip, and she was glad she'd bathed Jamal just before bedtime.

As Yasmin stood in the living room a security man climbed off the sofa, slipped his suit coat back on to cover the pistol in a shoulder holster, and looked out the window in the entryway.

But only for a second. Then, with wide eyes, he spun around and looked at Yasmin.

"It's him!"

"Him" could only mean one thing. The president of Syria was making an unannounced visit to the home where his mistress and his son lived.

Now Yasmin was doubly glad she'd bathed the boy.

. . .

Ahmed Azzam looked positively drained when he marched through the door behind the four bodyguards.

He stepped past the security men already working here in the house and up to Yasmin. He didn't look at his son at all as he stared her down. "Have you heard from her?"

Yasmin shook her head. *"La, sayidi."* No, sir.

"She said nothing to you about her trip?"

Yasmin did not meet her employer's gaze. She only stared at the floor. "She said she was nervous."

"Nervous?"

"About being back on the runway. It had been so long. She was worried about her looks after the baby. Getting back in shape . . . things like that."

"Had she been acting strangely before she left? Any calls to the home from people you did not recognize?"

Yasmin's huge wide eyes darted up to Azzam, then back down to the floor. *What is going on? "La, sayidi."* No, sir.

"She is missing," Azzam said. "I do not know when she will return. While she is away I will place more security here around you. You are not to leave the house. You are not to talk on the phone."

"Nem, sayidi." Yes, sir.

He put his hand on his boy's head, stroked it for a moment, and again Yasmin stole a look at her employer. An expression of frustration, anger, and . . . was it fear?

Ahmed looked away from his son and back to Yasmin. "If she contacts you in any way, I will know it."

"Of course, Mr. President."

Azzam reached out and put his hand on the side of Yasmin's face. "Your grandfather was a great man, daughter. He was a friend to my family for a long time. I miss him every day."

She started to thank him, but her voice caught in her throat as his hand lowered from her face, traced down the side of her neck, over her shoulder, down again, and then onto her chest. He stopped there, opened her robe a little, and slid a cold hand inside and around one of her breasts.

She worried he could feel her heartbeat; worried that her high heart rate from her near panicked state would anger him or make him think she was lying.

Yasmin said, "The Samara family has always been honored to serve the Azzam family."

Azzam looked at her a moment more, then drew his hand away, like a snake slipping back into the tall grass. He turned away without another word.

Yasmin watched him step over to the head of the guard force of the house. "How many men do you have here?"

"Five, sir. Around the clock."

"Make it ten. And find a way to double the security throughout the neighborhood."

"Of course, Mr. President. Is there any specific threat I should know about, sir?"

Azzam turned for the door. "Yes. *Me*, if you fail to protect my child."

. . .

As Ahmed al-Azzam climbed back into his SUV, he thought again of just ordering Yasmin and Jamal shot and disposed of. He had great plans for the boy, true, but if his son was exposed, if Bianca talked and compromised the child, then the plans for his son's future as the male heir would become null and void.

But he did not give the order for his men to kill the two. He told himself he'd give Sebastian Drexler time to get to France, to find his lover, and to determine what the hell had happened. If she could prove that she had nothing to do with her disappearance and that she had been careful about what she had said to those who took her, then his plan for the future—new wife, new son, new heir, new relationship with Russia and Iran, and new strength at home with the total conquest of his domestic enemies—would remain intact.

If not . . . if he was left with any doubts at all about Bianca's culpability in all this . . . then he would not allow his weakness to show. He would, instead, simply erase any evidence that Jamal had ever happened.

CHAPTER 26

Saydnaya Prison was lodged in the mountains twenty miles north of Damascus, near the hillside town of the same name. It was a massive walled complex with two main structures: the large, square White Building, and the even larger, tri-winged Red Building.

The prison had originally been built to process and hold a few thousand inmates, but since the war began, the population had soared. Now more than fifteen thousand prisoners were locked in cramped, foul, and cruel conditions inside, mostly in appalling cells along the echoing hallways that ran down the long wings of the Red Building. Windowless chambers originally built for solitary confinement in both the Red and White Buildings now held nine at a time, and the group cells were used to house many times that number.

Deaths from beatings, malnutrition, dehydration, and denial of medical care were common, but these were not the main causes of death here at Saydnaya. No, most people who died here were killed during the mass executions carried out in the dead of night in the basement of the White Building, where groups of twenty to fifty blindfolded men convicted in kangaroo courts were hanged by the neck simultaneously, their bodies then loaded into trucks like bags of flour to be dumped in unmarked mass graves in the nearby hills.

Killing enemies of the regime, be they combatant, protester, journalist, or others, was the regime's only real answer to any threats to the rule of Ahmed Azzam. Tens of thousands had been hanged since the beginning of the war, mostly here at Saydnaya, and Amnesty International referred to the complex as a human slaughterhouse.

. . .

Sebastian Drexler pulled up to the lower gate of the prison at eight a.m. and shifted his white Mercedes E-Class into park at the guard shack. This wasn't his first time at the facility, so he knew the routine. He handed his identity badge and government credentials over to the guards, received a grounds visitor's badge, waited for a Jeep to meet him, then followed the Jeep up the hill. Together the two vehicles drove the long winding road across brown earth towards the complex. Here Drexler parked in a tree-lined lot located between the Red and White Buildings, pulled out a wheeled suitcase and a leather portfolio, climbed into the Jeep with his luggage, and rode with three intelligence officers from the Political Security Directorate into the main gate of the Red Building.

The Jeep parked by the main door and four men got out and showed their credentials through bulletproof glass, and then they were buzzed in and allowed to move freely around the main portion of the facility. On all his previous visits to the Red Building, Drexler had gone into the main entrance, then taken the hall to the right towards the interrogation section, where he would either question prisoners or meet with interrogators to pick up intelligence; today he and his chaperones made a left at visitor processing and headed towards the infirmary.

By eight thirty he and the three intelligence officers were drinking tea in a conference room, and here Drexler was introduced to a dark-bearded man in his fifties and a taller man with white hair in his sixties. They were both vascular surgeons from Tishreen Military Hospital in Damascus, and the senior of the two, Dr. Qureshi, had been brought up to Saydnaya the day before to take charge of today's procedure.

"Is everything ready?" an anxious Drexler asked the white-haired surgeon.

Qureshi turned to the director of the prison for an answer.

The director said, "Yes. The prisoner has been held in the White Building, which is primarily for short-term housing of political prisoners. But the medical facilities here at the Red Building are superior, so we are having him brought over here to us."

"Fine," Drexler replied. "We must not begin the procedure until the helicopter has landed. Everything is dependent on timing. I cannot waste one moment once we start."

"Understood," Dr. Qureshi said. "I have eight other doctors and nurses with me. They all know their roles. I was the lead surgeon on the test cases that were done last year. We will be fast, as you have requested."

The other surgeon said, "We have trained on the process. The notes you provided us and the research you have done on the process were very helpful. But this will be my first implementation in the field. We spent yesterday afternoon practicing the operation. We are ready."

Drexler sniffed. "I'll hold my applause until I make it through immigration in Europe."

The dark-haired surgeon said, "Of course, sir."

• • •

Thirty minutes later a Soviet-era Mi-8 helicopter landed at the heliport outside the Red Building and Drexler's luggage was loaded on board. Shortly thereafter, he was called into a windowless room just down the hall from the main operating suite of the infirmary.

Two prison guards stood against the far wall, bracketing a man in a prison uniform standing there, shackled to the wall.

Drexler looked him up and down. He was a healthy man, of average height and with very light brown hair, just a few shades darker than Drexler's. The prisoner just stared back at him silently, unsure who this non-Arab man was or what language he spoke.

Drexler addressed him in English. "Your name is Veeti Takala. You are thirty-six years old, and you are from Finland."

The man nodded his head vigorously. "Yes, that's right. I am a videographer, working for ITN. I was taken from my hotel room last night. All my papers are in order."

"I know they are, and I appreciate that."

"I am not a spy!"

"I know that, too. If you were, you wouldn't be here."

"Who . . . who are you?"

186

"Well, I'll tell you who I'm not. I'm not the lifeline you were hoping for."

The prisoner's eyebrows furrowed. "I don't understand. I demand to speak to my embassy."

"Afraid that won't be possible. The locals here don't have the best consular system around, I can tell you that. And, unfortunately, there is no Finnish consulate outstation here in Saydnaya Prison." Drexler chuckled at his joke and looked at the guards, but they did not speak English, so the humor was lost on them.

The prisoner just cocked his head, regarding Drexler as if he were mad.

"The problem is," the Swiss man continued, "that you have something that I desperately need."

"What do I have? I had a backpack with me in my hotel room. Check it out. You can have anything. Cameras, computer . . . money. Anything you—"

"What I *really* need, actually, is your identity. I must make my way into Europe, and that is a problem. You see . . . I was a very bad boy once." He held up a hand and corrected his last statement. "More than once, to be perfectly frank, so the Europeans don't like me. In fact, they are hunting me down. I had a little plastic surgery on my face two years ago, so it is difficult for their cameras and computers to recognize me. But to get into Europe . . . it is more difficult. With your identity, however, I can travel freely."

The Finn nodded slowly, thinking he understood. "I get it. You need my passport." He was conspiratorial now. "It's true. You and I look similar. We're about the same size, same age. You can use it. Just let me go."

Drexler nodded along with the Finn for a moment, they both smiled, and then Drexler continued smiling, but his up-and-down head bob suddenly turned into a left-and-right shake of the head.

Still smiling, still happy as he could be, Drexler said, "But you *don't* get it, man. You *don't* understand."

Veeti Takala stopped smiling. "Don't understand *what*?"

"A passport alone won't work."

"What do you want, then?"

"It's not what I want, friend; it's what I *need*. I need . . ." Drexler reached inside his jacket, drew his FN pistol from his shoulder holster, and flipped off the safety. "I need your fingerprints, and there's just no pleasant way to

187

take them from you while you're alive, so I'll do you the kind gesture of making this easy for you."

The Finn's face went white, and his eyes locked on the gun.

Sebastian Drexler leveled the gun at the man's heart. "I don't know if you are curious, but I've been told by the doctors that the moment this gun goes bang, I will have fewer than thirty-six hours to get into Europe before the prints begin to decay."

The Finn started to hyperventilate. Through it, though, he was able to croak out, "Sir . . . I beg of you—"

"Don't beg. I am you now, and you are me, and I would never lower myself to begging." Drexler took a step back and fired one round into the man's chest.

The blast in the small room was earsplitting. The 5.7-millimeter projectile tore through the Finn's heart at a range of less than three meters. The guards standing next to the prisoner held him by the shoulders as he crumpled forward, then pushed him back up against the wall as Drexler himself helped to unhook Takala's wrists from his shackles. Drexler then stepped to the side, two male medical attendants wheeled a gurney straight into the room, and together with the others they laid the prisoner down. The victim was on his back and being rolled out of the holding room before his eyes flitted and rolled up and the last breath escaped his lungs. As they pushed him up the hallway towards the operating room, Drexler shouted out in Arabic, "The clock is ticking! Watch the hands! Take care of the fingers! Those are mine now."

Drexler could not watch the procedure on the body; he had to get himself prepped, so while the surgeon and his team worked in the operating room, Drexler undressed and took a quick shower. After this, he entered another operating room, sat on a chair waiting for him there, and reached his hands over a table covered with blue surgical draping. Nurses positioned his arms so his hands faced up, and leather bindings were wrapped around his wrists so he could not move them.

Some time later Dr. Qureshi entered the room, carrying stacks of interlocking metal pans. Everything was arrayed on tray tables near Drexler, and while he watched the clock, Qureshi and his team went to work.

The surgical team began with the pinky finger on Drexler's left hand. They applied a caustic solvent on the fingertip to roughen it up, and the patient grunted with pain, but he urged the surgeon to continue. A silicone gum was spread in a thin sheet on the skin to protect it, and then Qureshi took a soggy wet piece of live natural sponge out of a dish of salt water with a pair of forceps. This the surgeon cut to the size of Drexler's fingertip, taking his time to make a precise little oval.

Some high-end fingerprint readers have a feature designed to ensure that the prints are not silicone imprints or harvested from cadavers by using software to compare the spatial moisture pattern of a finger's pores to detect natural secretions. But Drexler knew a spoof for this. The small organic sponge, saturated with salt water and a little glycerin and placed carefully under the cadaver print, kept the dead skin moist longer, and it allowed just enough dampness to register on the surface.

Once the sponge was glued in place with a latex adhesive that bonded with the skin, the surgeon lowered surgical eye loupes over his eyes to magnify Drexler's fingers. He very carefully reached a set of straight-blade forceps into a dish marked "L-Hand, 5" in Arabic to indicate the pinky finger, and he retrieved Veeti Takala's pink flesh.

Drexler was surprised how thick the dead skin was; he had pictured something translucent, like an onion peel, but the surgeon held up a dense and opaque chunk of human tissue.

Drexler asked, "How are you going to make that look natural on my finger?"

The surgeon did not look up from his magnifier. "The cement I will use on the sides will be tinted to your skin tone." He shrugged a little, though he kept working. "A close examination of your hand will reveal that these fingerprints are not your own, but it will still be difficult to detect."

"The Mukhabarat will hold you personally accountable if I fail, Doctor. If that was not clear before, let me stress it now."

Looking through his magnifying loupes, the surgeon put cement on the sides of the dead flesh, very carefully, as if he were painting a tiny figurine. As he did this he said, "I am the best vascular surgeon in Damascus. I am not, however, a cosmetic surgeon. You have my full capabilities at your disposal, and you will not leave here until I am certain I cannot provide you with better results. If that is not good enough, then I suppose we will both suffer. Brow wipe!"

Drexler cocked his head at the exclamation, but understood when a nurse stepped in and blotted the surgeon's forehead.

Qureshi continued. "In the meantime, sir. I must ask you to stop talking. You will have your job to do wherever it is you need these new fingerprints to take you. But for now, allow me to do *my* job. It would be a pity if your threats caused me to perspire all over my masterpiece."

Drexler wondered if Qureshi knew he could have him thrown into a cell here at Saydnaya for his attitude even if he did a perfect job on his hands.

But he let the surgeon slide, for now.

Qureshi placed Takala's fingertip over Drexler's finger and pressed it into place. He added more cement around the sides, tinted it with a paintbrush and a natural coloring, and placed a piece of plastic over the finger. Then his assisting surgeon used padded tissue forceps to hold the fingertip in place while Qureshi went on to the pinky finger on the right hand.

Back and forth they went on like this, left hand to right and then back to left, one finger at a time. It was a slow and meticulous process, and the surgeon weathered the periodic admonitions of his patient throughout. Drexler kept an eye on the clock across the room and watched it tick away, and he took out his frustrations on Dr. Qureshi, but the surgeon remained steadfast, and he got the job done.

Just after the two-hour point the white-haired Syrian gently clamped the padded forceps onto the last finger, the thumb on the right hand. He looked up at his patient. "I am aware you understand the protocol, but I will remind you. You will need to keep these moist. A lotion will travel in your Dopp kit; it is marked as a store brand, but in actuality it is made for use in cadaver labs in Europe and America to keep necrotic tissue fresh. Use it every two hours.

"Even so . . . the flesh will begin to deteriorate in thirty-six hours, and the sponge secretions will have dried out by then, as well."

• • •

Sebastian Drexler wore oversized gloves to protect his fingers as he walked out to the waiting helicopter, already spooling up on the launch pad behind the Red Building. His three intelligence officer escorts climbed into the Mi-8 with him, and within seconds they had lifted off towards the airport in Damascus.

As they flew high over the green landscape, Drexler had one of the Mukhabarat men place a call to a phone number he gave him from memory. A headset was placed on Drexler's head, and he waited to hear a woman's voice answer on the other line.

"Yes?" It was Shakira Azzam.

"It's me. I'm leaving now. I'll be on the ground there late this evening." The U.S. and Europeans had massive amounts of electronic intelligence assets pointed at Syria, and even though it was difficult to grab a satellite call, Drexler knew he needed to stay vague when speaking on an open line.

Shakira Azzam replied, "And my husband knows you are going?"

"Yes. He asked me personally to go and attend to the issue."

"Well . . . he and I both want you to have a successful journey, but he and I are after a different outcome."

"You can rely on me."

"I want updates." A pause. "And I look forward to your safe return. If something should delay you, I will reach out to my own contacts abroad to try to find you . . . in case you need some help."

Drexler knew this was a not-so-veiled threat against him trying to run from Syria.

"I will be home within days, my darling."

"And we will celebrate." Shakira hung up the phone, and Drexler nodded to one of the officers in the back of the Mi-8, who then removed the headset.

The Swiss intelligence agent looked out the window now as the hills below gave way to the northern suburbs of Damascus, anxious but supremely confident about the mission ahead of him.

CHAPTER 27

Court Gentry sat in the back of a twenty-five-year-old Saab 340 turboprop, his mind full of worry about the mission ahead of him.

He was winging it, he knew, and until he got on the ground and took in the lay of the land, he would have no way of planning his next move.

The vibration of the landing gear lowering into place below his feet brought him back into awareness of his surroundings. He looked out the window over his right shoulder; all he could see from this vantage point was the endless green sea. The aircraft seemed like it couldn't have been more than a thousand feet in the air, but just then the plane entered a hard bank to the north, tipping Court forward in his side-facing seat, and when it leveled off he looked out the window again and saw whitewashed buildings on the coastline, then terraced olive fields on a hillside.

It looked utterly peaceful, but he knew that the area around Latakia was anything but. It was in the hands of the Syrian regime and its proxies, but insurgent attacks were not uncommon.

Here in the cabin with him were a dozen other men. He hadn't spoken to any of them, nor they to him, but he took them all for security contractors of some sort. A couple were Hispanic-looking, a couple more had to have been Japanese, one was black, and the rest were fit-looking bearded white guys. Just like Court himself.

They all sat in silence, their packs in their laps or by their sides.

Over the airfield Court had a moment of deep unease about his decision to come to Syria. Latakia's only airport, Martyr Abdul al-Azzam, had been divided into two separate entities with two separate names. The Russians had erected Hmeymim air base virtually on top of the commercial airport, and they effectively ran the vast majority of the place now, so much so that even before he touched down he could see evidence of their presence everywhere. The first three aircraft Court saw upon landing all bore Russian military markings. A pair of Su-27 fighters and a massive Ilyushin Il-76 cargo jet were all taxiing to the parallel runway, and a long row of new and massive bombproof hangars to the east showed him that the Russians were dug in and planning on staying awhile.

Court had read that this was Russia's only fixed air base outside its borders anywhere on Earth, which told him something about their commitment to maintaining influence over Syria. A Russian admiral had bragged that Hmeymim was its newest "unsinkable aircraft carrier" in the Med, a boast Court understood better now as he looked around at the incredible amount of military aviation hardware on display.

As his plane touched down and raced along the runway, it shot past a couple of Syrian Arab Air Force MiG-25 Foxbats, then a Russian Mi-8 helicopter, a pair of Russian MiG-29s, and more Russian and Syrian cargo and transport aircraft.

The Saab turboprop taxied to the only nonmilitary apron on the entire airfield and parked next to an Iranian commercial Airbus A320, and here Court followed the other passengers and a member of the flight crew to the exit.

He stepped through the hatch with just a small bag holding a small amount of clothing and gear, his orders from KWA, a wallet stuffed with euros, and his forged documents for Syrian immigration; Lars Klossner had assured him the KWA men working with the Desert Hawks would provide him everything he needed and, since he'd be thoroughly searched by Syrian immigration officials on his arrival, there was no point taking anything he didn't need that might get confiscated.

As he deplaned on the warm, sunny tarmac, a cluster of three armed Syrian officials greeted him and the others with bored nods, and together they walked up a metal stairway and into the terminal. Here, Syrian Arab Army forces stood around acting as security, wearing camouflage uniforms. Court saw that most were outfitted with AK-103 rifles, and a few carried pistols. Several armed Russian soldiers were sitting around, as well, which was an odd sight in an airport terminal, especially considering the fact that the men were armed but didn't seem to be providing any security or other function.

As Court followed the immigration men down a long hall, he saw the flag of the regime—green, white, and black stripes with two green stars— hanging everywhere, along with photographs and paintings of Ahmed Azzam. In some the thin ruler of Syria wore business suits and smiled, and in others he wore various military uniforms and scowled, but he was always there, always looming large over the airport terminal.

Court figured he'd be seeing a lot of Ahmed's face in the coming days.

The American posing as a Canadian was X-rayed, wanded, and frisked; his satchel of gear was perfunctorily inspected by unsmiling men who seemed more interested in their next smoke break than capturing an assassin entering their nation by private aircraft. Probably, Court surmised, since there were hundreds of private security contractors in the country, and they were constantly coming and going via this same route.

But when his Inmarsat satellite phone was pulled out of his bag and looked over, the customs inspector confiscated it.

"No phone," the man said.

Court was next separated from the other contractors and led to a desk in the immigration office, where they took his documents, looked them over, then looked Court himself over. An official there made a call and soon a middle-aged mustachioed man in a gray suit appeared, and he took the passport and checked both it and Court over even more carefully than the immigration officer had. Court took the man to be from Syria's Mukhabarat.

The man with the mustache finally handed the passport back to the immigration officer, and he leaned over his shoulder while he checked it against a computer in front of him. As he did he addressed Court in accented English. "You are Graham Wade from Canada."

Court nodded. "That's right."

"You are KWA. Contracted to Liwa Suqur al Sahara."

"The Desert Hawks Brigade. Right again."

The immigration officer began typing on his computer. Soon a printer behind him fired out several pages, and the official stamped them with three different embossing tools, folded them, and placed them in a plastic jacket. He stamped the passport and handed it all back to Court. The Mukhabarat man said, "You are permitted to enter the Syrian Arab Republic. You are not permitted to travel off your military base unless escorted by an officer of the Desert Hawks, the Mukhabarat, or the Ministry of the Interior. Failure to comply means you will be subject to arrest and expulsion, or arrest and a prison term."

Court said, "No wandering around. Got it."

"Photography, audio recordings, mapmaking, telephones for personal use, and GPS devices are prohibited."

"Okay." Court was allowed to pass, and when he stepped out into the arrivals hall, he saw more uniformed Russians, as well as a large group of men in business suits pulling along hand luggage. These men, Court assumed, were Iranians: either diplomats, businessmen, or a mixture of both, getting ready to leave on the Airbus he'd seen on the tarmac.

The other mercs from his flight all found their rides, and they trickled out of the terminal. Court, on the other hand, stood there in the middle of the small arrivals hall for a few minutes, and then, when he saw no one there to greet him, he walked out the front of the building and into the sunshine.

Across the parking lot he saw a beige pickup with a machine gun mounted in the back and four men standing around it. They wore Western-looking desert-print military uniforms, but they were all clearly Arab men. They didn't look his way, so Court kept hunting for the KWA man he had been told he would meet here at the airport.

He noticed a bald man in cargo pants leaning against a newer-looking white Toyota pickup truck. He was just a couple of spaces away from the four men in desert camo, but he didn't seem to be associating with them at all. The man gazed in Court's direction, standing with his hands on his hips and a pair of wraparound sunglasses hanging out of his mouth by one of the arms. He was stocky, with a thick chest and forearms covered in tattoos, and he wore a black T-shirt.

The man made no move in Court's direction, but he kept looking right at him.

It was no big trick for Court to identify the person he was here to meet.

Court would be interacting with some hard men on this operation, so he'd not expected balloons and a banner. He walked over to the man and extended his hand. "I'm Wade."

The bald man put on his shades, pushed off the vehicle, and ignored the handshake. He replied with a Cockney accent. "Remains to be seen."

"What's that?"

"You are whoever your KWA deployment orders say you are."

"Yes, sir." Court was in cover now, and he knew he needed to act and talk like a private security officer on a high-threat contract. He'd worked around such men on different assignments around the world, and he'd trained with some of the more high-speed contractors stateside.

He fished out his KWA folio from his backpack and handed it over to the Brit.

The man took the papers, looked them over, then returned his gaze to Court. He spoke softly, even though there was no one in earshot. "First things first, mate. I'm Saunders. I'm not 'sir.' I'm labor, not management, and I don't need some terrorist sapper thinking differently. We straight on that?"

Court doubted there were any insurgents sneaking around here at a Russian/Syrian regime air base, and if there were, he felt confident they would have higher-priority targets around here than a couple of guys in T-shirts standing in a parking lot. But he didn't argue. "Saunders. Got it."

Court could tell Saunders had been around. He had an impossibly hard, weathered air about him. Even though this guy might have been labor, he was clearly a veteran employee of Klossner's organization, and since he was British, this probably meant he could well have been former Royal Marines or SAS, Special Air Service, the UK's elite special operations unit.

Court couldn't help but wonder what had befallen the man to where he now found himself working as a mercenary, employed on a contract with a militia of cold-blooded murderers in Syria.

But he didn't ask.

Saunders said, "All right, 'ere's what's gonna happen. Those blokes are with us." He nodded to the four men in camo uniforms standing around the technical. They were all looking Court's way now. "They are Desert Hawks Brigade, and they go where we go, just to make sure we get there.

"We've got a long drive ahead, all the way to our base just east of Damascus in Babbila. It's three hundred klicks, and it's not gonna be a joy-ride, so we're gonna tag along with a convoy that's forming up in Jableh, just fifteen minutes from here."

Saunders led Court to the passenger side of the white Toyota, and Court opened the door. A set of body armor and an SA80 bullpup rifle lay on the floorboard.

"Is this for me?" Court asked as he sat down and put his feet on the gear.

Saunders climbed in on his side. "No, mate. That's *my* kit. You'll get your kit once we get down to Babbila, but we'll find a surplus weapon and armor for you to take along on the convoy."

Both men had to show their credos twice before leaving the airport, but once outside, the bald man stomped on the gas and raced to the south. Behind them the Desert Hawk technical followed, with one man standing in the bed holding on to the machine gun.

They rode in silence for a moment, but just when Court thought Saunders wasn't going to do any talking, the man said, "Today's your lucky day, Wade. That is, assuming you came down here to see some action. You and me are gonna get shot at this afternoon."

"On the road to Damascus?"

As they made the turn off the highway that led towards Jableh, the Brit nodded. "It's been a bloody shooting gallery for the past few weeks. I came up here in a convoy the day before yesterday on the same road we'll be taking back. We got hit twice in the hills. Small arms, nothing coordinated. Still, two SAA blokes traveling with us were hit. One of the poor sods didn't make it through the night. Shot in the bum, he was, which would be a laugh if it hadn't clipped his femoral." He looked over to Court. "And last week Daesh cut off the highway for ninety minutes. Killed seven civilians and two Syrian cops. FSA, Daesh, Al Nusra . . . that highway goes right through the middle of the territory of a lot of enemy groups."

Court nodded, in a casual manner. "How are we supposed to know who is who?"

The question seemed to surprise Saunders, and he thought about it for a moment. "Sometimes you see blokes wavin' flags, sometimes you see kit or clothing that tells you who you're up against, but you usually only have time to ID the colors on the bodies after you kill the buggers. Does it

197

matter? If some bloke is shooting at you, shoot back at them. We gotta hard job down here, Wade, but *that* part's dead easy."

"Right." Except it *wasn't* so easy for Court. Jabhat al Nusra was the local brand of Al Qaeda, and Daesh was ISIS. He'd pour lead at either of those groups if he ran into them, no questions asked. But FSA was the Free Syrian Army. While it was a loose coalition made up of a lot of different disparate elements, in theory, at least, they were the good guys in this fight. Court, on the other hand, was most assuredly working on the side of the villains down here. Would he really open fire on an FSA unit attacking the Russian and Syrian regime forces?

He told himself all he could do was hope he didn't come into contact with FSA fighters, and sort out what he would do if the time came.

As they drove along in silence, Court realized Saunders wasn't going through the typical security contractor process of asking who he knew and where he'd been. It was commonly referred to in the industry as "butt sniffing," a way of sizing up others in the field to establish one another's bona fides. Court had answers ready if Saunders asked, and he'd expected a grilling. "Wade" was a pseudonym, but Court was here in place of a real man, with a real background Court had studied on the flight from Munich to Beirut.

But Saunders hadn't asked a thing about his past or his experience.

Court appreciated the silence, but on top of this it only made him more certain of his assumption that the guys he'd come into contact with down here would be cut from a different cloth than the private military contractors he'd worked around in the past. These men were straight-up mercs, and they were *not* here for the camaraderie or any belief in the righteousness of their mission.

• • •

They arrived at a small Syrian Arab Army base just after one. Both men climbed out of the pickup, headed into a guard shack, and handed over their embossed KWA badges and travel papers. Still, they were frisked for explosive vests and the pickup was checked over thoroughly for bombs.

Back in the truck they waited for the Desert Hawks traveling behind them to make it through security, and then they all drove to a row of low buildings within sight of the ocean to the west. A group of four light-duty military trucks of various makes and models sat single file in a lot out front. Court saw two trucks with Russian military markings, and two older and larger trucks with the markings of the Syrian Arab Army.

Saunders said, "This 'ere's our convoy. We don't leave till thirteen twenty, so we've got a little time to find you a weapon."

Court followed Saunders into a warehouse, where the British contractor spoke with some Syrian Arab Army soldiers. After yet another show of badges and some signing of some forms Court couldn't read, a squeaky padlock was removed from a squeaky door and they were let into a room full of weaponry: AKs stacked on tables and shelves, along with ammunition, cases of big green helmets, and stacks of steel body armor in chest rigs.

Court could see dust hanging in the air; the smell of gunpowder and gun oil was thick in Court's nostrils.

The American said, "Let me guess. You want me to take one of *these* pieces of shit."

"Like I said, you'll get a proper weapon when we get down to our base, but we want you ready for today's run. You can borrow what you need here for the drive down. This is what they hand out to the civilian regime-backed militias."

The equipment was decidedly low tech, but Court had trained on, and implemented in the field, weapons of all types and quality.

He pulled on a heavy olive-drab vest that held armor plates, and then he stepped over to choose a rifle.

If given any choice for a weapon to take on a mission such as today, he would have chosen an HK416 A6 rifle with an eleven-inch barrel and a Gemtech suppressor and a second, twenty-inch barrel that he could exchange with the eleven-inch if he found himself pinned down by shooters at long range, along with a holographic weapons sight and a quick-detach three-power scope. His rifle would have a laser acquisition device, a high-lumen flashlight with a pressure switch, a six-position adjustable stock with an adjustable cheek weld, and a horizontal forward grip.

Yeah, that would have been his dream choice for a vehicle operation through a high-threat area.

But this grungy and small armory had probably never seen anything like that.

Instead he pulled a worn-out and worm-holed wooden-stocked AK-47 with simple iron sights off a rack. It was virtually identical to the model invented by wounded tank crewman Mikhail Kalashnikov back in 1947, but Court knew AKs, and he could use the weapon with deadly effect out to five hundred yards.

He checked its function and deemed it in proper working order. As he adjusted the weapon's old nylon sling for his height and preference, Saunders loaded a big canvas satchel with rusty thirty-round magazines. He handed the satchel over to the man he knew as Wade, who immediately put the heavy sack down on a table and began counting the magazines.

"Fourteen mags. Four hundred twenty rounds," Court said. "That's more than I've ever carried in my life." Even though he was in character, it was the truth, at least when carrying a weapon that fired a big 7.62 round like the Kalashnikov. He picked up the magazines one at a time, loaded them into his chest rig, locked one into his new rifle, and racked a round into the chamber. He flipped the safety up, then pushed the five remaining magazines away on the table. "I'll go with two hundred seventy, just in case we get attacked by Godzilla."

The Brit looked at him like he was an idiot. "Right. So you've made the Latakia-Damascus run before, have you now?"

"You *know* I have not."

"Well *I* have, so listen to me. Through the hills east of Latakia, through Masyaf, across Hama, down around Homs, and south through the northern suburbs of Damascus, blown to rubble by the regime but still full of rebels. The entire route could be crawling with roving terrorists and marauders, popping out at every turn. You probably won't need all this ammo, but if you do, you'll bloody well wish you had it."

Court thought the guy was exaggerating, but the voice of his former CIA trainer slipped into his mind again, telling him there was virtually never such a thing as too much ammunition. Court scooped up three of the five mags, crammed them into pockets in his cargo pants, then lumbered for the door.

. . .

The convoy prepping to make the run to Damascus was a multinational affair. Court and Saunders were the only Westerners and the only foreign mercs in the group, but there were two nearly new GAZ light military transport trucks containing a dozen or so armed Russian soldiers, two Russian-made ZIL-131 Syrian Arab Army trucks with what appeared to be about twenty young infantrymen, and the four Desert Hawks Brigade soldiers who'd been caravanning along with Court and Saunders.

There was also a black Land Rover with three Arabs in civilian clothes. Court nodded towards the men and asked Saunders who they were.

Saunders himself gave them a curious eye. "Probably Mook."

"Mook?" Court asked, although he knew.

"Mukhabarat. Syrian intel. I have a meeting with the Russians and Syrians at the lead vehicle. Maybe I'll find out, but I'm not gonna ask about them. You stay here with the Hawks."

Saunders went forward to talk to the leaders of each group represented, and he returned a few minutes later. "Right. Those blokes in suits are definitely Mook; they'll be riding right in front of us in the middle of the formation. The SAA will take the front and the rear of the convoy. The two Russian trucks will travel together behind the lead vehicle. We leave in five mikes."

Even though he wasn't a security contractor, Court knew vehicle operations in high-threat areas better than most. "What's our plan? If we come upon a downed vehicle, or a firefight going on in the road, do we assist?"

"Negative. You and me are being paid by the Hawks, so our job is to get down to the base in Babbila and do what we're told. We aren't being paid to fight it out with rebels along the highway. We'll let some other poor bugger do that. If the Russians and the SAA don't stop, *we* don't stop. If they *do* stop . . . well, I will make the decision on whether we keep going or stick with the convoy."

Court said, "Seven light vehicles, forty-five men, and one mounted machine gun might scare off a small unit of adversaries, but anything larger might see us as an opportunity."

Saunders rolled his eyes. "Off the bleedin' bird less than an hour and you're tellin' me how to roll, is that it, Wade?"

"Hey," Court said. "You're labor, just like me. Remember?"

Saunders spit on the dusty asphalt. "We won't be the only vehicles on the road, so the trick is just to make ourselves a harder target than the other sons of bitches out there, so the bad guys shoot somebody else."

"*That's* our plan?"

Saunders donned his body armor, pulled his rifle out of the floorboard of the pickup, racked a round into the chamber, then checked to make sure the safety was engaged. "I told you, Wade. We're *gonna* get shot at today. Might as well sit back and enjoy the lovely weather till it 'appens." He headed around to the driver's seat.

There was nothing Court could do but slip on his sunglasses, climb into the passenger side of the pickup, hold his old Kalashnikov at the ready, and begin scanning his sector.

It was going to be a long afternoon, he could feel it.

CHAPTER 28

French Judicial Police Captain Henri Sauvage drove south out of Paris in an early-afternoon rain shower. He had a lot on his mind, but he pushed it away as much as possible to focus on the task of the moment.

Ahead on his right, halfway through a wooded area that covered a square kilometer, a gravel driveway wound back into the woods. Sauvage didn't slow his two-door Renault as he approached it, but he peered intently up the drive while passing, doing his best to take in every detail.

And when it was behind him he kept driving. Traffic was steady, and it occurred to him he might not find a place to turn around to head back for a while. Still, his job was not to go back; at least it wasn't yet.

And he hoped like hell he wouldn't be given that order by the Syrians who controlled him.

He took out his phone and placed a call. As soon as he heard the call go through, he spoke. "The gate is closed at the entrance. No one is in sight."

"Good," came the reply. A kilometer behind him, the Syrian asset he knew as Malik sat in the passenger seat of a Volkswagen Touran van, and he drove down the same road Sauvage drove on. Sauvage could hear him relay his message to the men in the vehicle with him in Arabic.

"What do I do now?" Sauvage asked into the phone.

"We'll pass by the property in thirty seconds. Then we'll meet you in Saint-Forget on the Rue de la Motte."

Sauvage thought Malik's French pronunciation was horrendous, but he didn't say so. Still, he had done what was asked of him today, so the Frenchman did push back a little into the phone. "Why do you need me? I told you what I found out about the property, I led you here. Just let me go home."

"Rue de la Motte. Ten minutes." The phone call ended.

Henri Sauvage tossed his phone down into the passenger seat and shouted curses to himself. He had gone to Foss's funeral two hours earlier and would be attending Allard's the following day. Andre Clement's body had not yet turned up, but since Sauvage saw him die, he knew it wouldn't be long at all before he'd be going to his partner's funeral, as well. And as bad as Sauvage's mood was now, he figured by the time he hugged Clement's children at his graveside, he'd be ready to kill himself for everything he'd gotten his friend involved with.

The thought of saying to hell with it all and killing himself, thereby outsmarting Eric and the Syrians manipulating him, did have a moment's appeal to him. But then he thought better of it. No . . . he wasn't going to kill himself. He was going to be a good little bitch for Eric; he would do what he was told, make his money, and then take his family and get the fuck out of here.

The best revenge was a life well lived, and he told himself he owed it to his dead friends to enjoy himself on their behalf. He was being paid a lot of money to find Bianca Medina, and he was reasonably certain he had done just that.

He'd spend it well.

. . .

Ten minutes later, Sauvage leaned against the hood of his car parked at a flower market in the town of Saint-Forget. The Volkswagen van pulled up and the sliding back door opened.

Sauvage just stood there. "*Non.* I'm not getting back in that van."

Malik rolled his eyes. "Of course you are, man, because if you don't, we shoot you right now."

He heard the *shick-shick* sound of a pistol's slide being racked in the darkness of the van, and his fantasy of retaining some control over his life melted away in an instant.

Sauvage climbed into the vehicle.

The van pulled out of the flower market parking lot and Sauvage sat on the bare floor against the wall, facing two of Malik's men. The plastic tarp had been removed, which should have made Sauvage feel better, but he figured these men would shoot him and just hose out the back if it came down to it.

Malik himself climbed out of the passenger seat and into the back, squatting down in front of the French police captain. "Tell me how you know the woman is being held at that property."

"Everyone has been looking for the Halabys since my colleagues were found dead in their flat. A team at La Crim has spent a hundred man-hours watching videos of the Free Syria Exile Union, and they have identified thirteen key members of the outfit. They tracked the phones of all these men and women, and physically surveilled some of them, but so far they haven't found any connection to here."

"So?"

"I *did* find a connection. I expanded my search to family members of the Halabys. A nephew of Rima was geotracked to this estate last night, and he is still inside. I arrived here at five thirty this morning, and shortly after seven a.m., a European man in his sixties pulled in. I took a photo of him, blew it up so I could see it, and determined I was looking at Vincent Voland, former intelligence official and currently employed by the Halabys."

Malik was impressed. "So . . . he's in there right now?"

"Yes. Along with two men who look very much like Syrians. Not the nephew I'd originally targeted, so apparently there are more people in that house."

"What do you know about the residence?"

"I know nothing, which means I know a lot."

"Elaborate."

"The property is registered to a shell corporation in the Cook Islands. Any research into the ownership, who is living there, what goes on there, just dead-ends."

"And to you this means . . ."

"It means it's either owned by a business with an interest in hiding its physical property, or it's some sort of a DGSE or DGSI safe house. The fact that Voland is here leads me to the latter assumption. He's officially retired from the government, but my assumption is he's working with the FSEU while retaining contacts in French intelligence."

Sauvage could see the worry in Malik's eyes, and this relaxed him. Thank God the Syrian realized they were all in over their heads. Sauvage pressed. "That's right. The French government might be involved. Are you guys really going to roll into that estate with your guns out, ready to make off with that woman?"

Malik did not answer. Instead he asked, "How long until the police find this place?"

"How the hell should I know?"

"Eric will not like that response."

Sauvage sighed. *"Je ne sais pas." I don't know.* "There's no surveillance on the place by us, yet, no chatter about it around La Crim, but it's just a matter of time before someone connects the dots. If there are other members of FSEU here, and the federal police are investigating them, then either my people at La Crim or the federal police will find their way here, sooner or later."

Malik said, "Eric has communicated with us. He will be here tonight."

Sauvage said, "And then what will you do?"

"I'll do whatever Eric orders me to do. Same as you, if you are smart."

"I was brought into this for intelligence, surveillance."

Malik said, "And I'm sure that will remain your main role. But we will need you close by."

Sauvage shrugged. "Just call me when he gets here and I will—"

"No." The van stopped. The door opened. As before, the driver had gone in a circle, and they were now back at Sauvage's car in the parking lot of the flower market. "One of my men will accompany you until Eric arrives."

"For what purpose?"

"I see how scared you are. Your attendance this evening is required. We would not want you running off."

"Of course I'm scared! I'm not a killer. Not an accessory to murder, either."

"Interesting. Eric tells me you are one of his best."

Sauvage closed his eyes. "I didn't want any of this."

"Did you want this?"

Sauvage opened his eyes. Malik held a rolled-up wad of euros the size of a grapefruit.

"The fuck is that? I have an account in Cyprus where I—"

"Walking-around money. From Eric. A way to show our gratitude, and perhaps an easier way to help you get out of town when this is over. To-night."

Sauvage took the money. He always took the money.

CHAPTER 29

Saunders and Gentry drove in the center of the small convoy to the southeast, first through zones of unquestioned regime control, rolling through checkpoints that parted for the Russians and did not close back up until the SAA truck at the rear of the procession passed. Court remained vigilant every second of the way by keeping his eyes on the sector Saunders instructed him to cover, but also by listening in to radio traffic. Saunders had a handheld radio tuned to the convoy's channel, but most of the transmissions were between the SAA units, in Arabic, and Court only picked up words here and there. Still, he figured he would be able to tell from the tone of the other men speaking if someone saw real danger ahead.

Court spoke reasonably good Russian, though he didn't want Saunders to know. He hoped the Russians would be the first to spot any trouble, because that way he knew he'd have more of a heads-up and better intel about any threat.

He found himself surprised by the quality of the highway they rolled along, even out here in the sticks of Syria. It was as good as most he'd seen in the United States, and although the traffic was extremely light, the vehicles that were on the road were making good speed.

Saunders wasn't a chatty man, but neither was Court, so for the first hour barely any words were exchanged between the pair. Court just rolled

208

with the silence, establishing his cover legend as a grizzled and stoic mercenary. But eventually he decided he needed to mine this guy for any information he could get about what he could expect after they made it down to the Desert Hawks' base, and he wanted to feel the man out to see about options for getting *off* base once he got there.

While still eyeing the roadside, farmland, rural buildings, and the distant hills, Court said, "I've been working in Southeast Asia, mostly."

"Heard me ask, did you?"

"No."

"That's right. Ya didn't."

"I was just mentioning it to say I don't know much about what's going on around here."

"You'll learn. Everybody learns. Or else you die."

"Wouldn't mind avoiding the 'or else.' Anything you can tell me that might help?"

"You were hired to train the Hawks. I *wasn't* hired to train you."

"I know we're training Desert Hawks . . . but I also heard we're deploying with them."

Saunders glanced across the cab of the pickup at Court for an instant, then looked back to the windshield. "Where'd ya hear that?"

"From Lars Klossner himself."

Saunders shrugged now. "Almost every bleedin' night they send us out with Desert Hawks special forces units."

"To do what, exactly?"

"No-knock raids, arrests, and good old-fashioned hits."

"In Damascus?"

"Sometimes. Sometimes not." He looked at Court again. "Does it matter?"

"No . . . just curious." Court pressed his luck. "Who's the oppo?"

Saunders repeated himself. "Does it matter?"

"Only to avoid blue on blue." Court couldn't let on that he had misgivings about targeting certain opposition groups in this conflict, but he needed information about just what, in fact, the Hawks had the KWA men involved with.

When Saunders didn't respond to this, Court turned to the man. "Look. I'll be a hell of a lot better at this if I get some kind of a sitrep on what we're dealing with. You might even persuade me to watch your back in the process."

"I didn't ask you to watch my back."

"No . . . but would it hurt?"

Saunders looked like he'd rather just sit and drive, to be alone with his thoughts. But after a moment he sighed. "Blimey. All right, just to shut you up, I'll give you a two-minute lesson on who's who around here."

"That would be helpful."

"But keep scanning your sector. If you get killed before we get to Damascus, I will have just wasted my breath."

"Copy that."

The Brit rolled down the window and spit, then rolled it back up. "All right, school's in session. First let's talk about our side, the regime and its loyalist supporters. Russia's 'ere in country, they are the patrons to the regime, helping to prop it up, but Russia hates most of the militias fighting for Azzam, especially the Sunni militias. *Especially* the Desert Hawks Brigade. They think the Hawks are too big and too powerful now, so they figure it's just a matter of time before the Hawks turn their guns around and start fighting the regime itself. Russia has a stake in Azzam; they are here in the country by his order and they have him by the bollocks, so any potential threat to him is seen as a threat to Russian interests here."

"Makes sense."

"Most of the Christians here support Azzam, because even though he's an Alawi, which is a Shiite tribe, he belongs to a minority and runs a secular government. He doesn't persecute other religious minorities as long as they support him. If the Sunni jihadists took over, it would be bad for the Christians, just like what's happened everywhere else the jihadists took over. The Christians might not love the Alawites, but they know that without them in power, they're fucked."

"Got it."

"It's short-sighted, of course. Azzam will kill Christians the same as he'll kill anyone else if they so much as complain about the weather, but that's the way it is."

"Right."

"The Russians do like the Syrian Arab Army, Azzam's regular troops, and they work with the Desert Hawks from time to time, but there isn't any love between the groups.

"Then you've got your foreign Shiites. Hezbollah is fighting here, blokes from Lebanon, and they support Azzam, but they stick to themselves. Ditto Iran. They have battalions of fighters here, and they use Russian air in their attacks, but they don't fight alongside the Syrian Arab Army or the Sunni militias like the Hawks."

"Why are the Shiites fighting for Azzam?"

"Because he's an Alawi, which is a Shia sect. Iran knows Shias are outnumbered in the Middle East by Sunnis, so even though Azzam isn't much of a Shiite, he's closer to them than any other national leader around here, so they help him out. It helps that the Iranians are in bed with the Russians, too, but that might all change soon."

"What do you mean?"

"There's rumors floating about that Azzam is trying to get Iran to expand into Syria in a permanent presence. The Russians won't take kindly to that, since they are trying to use the nation as their Middle Eastern outpost, so if Iran moves in and stakes a claim to bases and territory, the three-way love fest of the past four years will turn into a right bloody mess."

This tracked with what Court had learned from Voland about Azzam sneaking into Tehran to negotiate with the Supreme Leader.

Saunders adjusted his rearview as he drove. The convoy was rising into some steeper hills now, and the British mercenary seemed to tighten up his focus on his surroundings. Court turned away from his lesson and began scanning the thick pines on the hills on his side of the highway.

Saunders continued, "So, that's the friendly forces. Now on to the rebels and terrorists. The rebels are ten times more fractured than the loyalists, which is the only reason the regime is still around. You have the FSA, the Free Syrian Army, but really it's just dozens of groups and clans, most of which aren't anything like an army, and many of which aren't even remotely free. Then there's ISIS, who used to be just in the east and north, but now they're in little pockets around Damascus, too. And there's Al Nusra . . . that's Al Qaeda. They are in the north mostly but tend to pop up wherever you don't want them. They've been active around here, too."

Court just muttered, "Jesus."

"The Americans are way up north and way out east, fighting ISIS, which is good, but they are supporting the Kurds, which is not good."

"And what about the Kurds?"

"Yeah, they are up north, mostly fighting ISIS, but also the Azzam regime, and they also have their own section carved out of the country. And when you talk about the Kurds, you have to split them up into tribes, factions, political groups, and the like. They aren't just one entity, either. The Kurds fight in the SDF, the Syrian Democratic Forces, which is a group of Kurds, Sunnis, Assyrians, and Turkmen."

"And the foreign mercs? Us. Does anybody like us?"

Saunders looked at Court and laughed. "That's a good one, Wade. Yeah, all the militias like their own foreign contractors, but nobody likes anybody else's. The Desert Hawks like us, because we train their special operations forces, and they use us to help fight their little denied battles."

"Like these raids you mentioned?"

The convoy raced past a row of slower-moving cars also heading southeast; Court and Saunders looked over each vehicle as it passed.

Saunders said, "The Hawks have a particular beef with a Syrian Army unit called the Tiger Forces."

"What kind of beef?"

"Regular old mob shite. Remember, they ain't fightin' a war down here."

Court furrowed his eyebrows. "They're not?"

"No, it's a gang fight. The Hawks are run by a criminal overboss, and so are the Tigers. They fight over oil smuggling routes; they get into it over turf wars. In a country as mad as this, with twenty-five groups trying to kill one another, the Desert Hawks Brigade still finds time to pick fights with would-be allies. It's bloody mad."

Court knew all he could do was pray he would be able to get the hell out of his cover identity and on with his real job, otherwise he might get himself killed in some arcane Syrian mafia turf war that he didn't even understand.

Before Court could speak, Saunders leaned over the wheel and looked through the windshield intently. "Have you noticed any buses on the highway in the past couple of miles?"

Court cocked his head. "Buses? I don't remember seeing any. Why?"

"Bus drivers are the best intelligence agents on the highway. They know what's going on. If you see buses, you know the road is considered safe enough. If you *don't* see buses . . ." Saunders began scanning his mirrors. "Well . . . you tighten up your chin strap and flip off your safety."

Saunders looked back to Court. "I don't see buses."

It was true. Court realized he'd seen small sedans and hatchbacks, plus a few commercial trucks, but he didn't remember passing a bus in the past several minutes.

Just then a large, white tractor-trailer approached in the opposite lane. The vehicle was on Saunders's side, so Court wasn't focused on it. He was in the process of checking his rifle again when the radio came alive with animated Arabic. Court turned back around, understanding from the tone of the transmissions that something was going on.

Saunders said, "Look at the lorry."

Court did so. The big vehicle was riddled with bullet holes. It had clearly been attacked up the road, and even though it had managed to survive, it was heavily damaged.

"Eyes open, Wade. We're heading into it."

After an order given over the radio, first in Russian and then in Arabic, all the vehicles in the convoy began racing faster along the road, including Saunders's pickup. Court thought it to be a wise move, to accelerate through any potential kill zone. The enemy would be dug into fighting positions that they had chosen, whereas Court and the others in the convoy had no choice in the matter, and if fighting came, they would be fighting at a distinct disadvantage.

Court looked through the windshield to the Desert Hawks technical, just ahead. The gunner stood behind his belt-fed machine gun, and he pulled the charging handle back on the weapon to rack a round. He began swiveling the barrel left and right, ready for a fight.

Court jammed his own rifle barrel outside the open window of his vehicle and aimed it on the terrain to the south. The high rolling hills were completely covered in green trees and shrubs; Court couldn't see a man-made structure in any direction. It seemed like the right place for an ambush, and all he could do was hope that whatever force was waiting up there in the trees would take one look at the line of Russians, Syrian soldiers, militiamen, and machine guns and decide to hold their fire till some helpless vehicle passed.

The convoy had to slow for a turn and cross a twenty-foot-long bridge that went over a small drainage culvert, and Court's hope that the attackers passed on his convoy died when puffs of dust pocked the highway ahead of the Desert Hawks technical. An instant later he heard the unmistakable cracks and zings of incoming rifle fire.

"Contact left!" Saunders shouted, and he one-handed his bullpup rifle out the driver's-side window and began squeezing off rounds with his right hand while he controlled the steering wheel with his left.

Court had no targets on his right, but he'd told himself he would fire if he saw anyone armed. Yes, there could be FSA men up there shooting at him, but he wasn't just going to sit back and let them kill him.

Court was firmly engaged on the side of the bad guys now. He'd feel bad about it later, but for the moment he was going to concentrate on survival.

Just then an explosion on the highway fifty yards ahead of the pickup sent a fireball into the sky; an instant later the Russian GAZ truck that was second in the convoy slammed on its brakes. The next Russian truck locked its brakes as well, and behind it, the Syrian Mukhabarat Land Rover swerved to try to avoid the stopped vehicles in front of it.

The Land Rover slammed into the rear of the Russian GAZ.

Saunders shouted out a curse as he slowed, steering his pickup to the left, into the opposite lane, to avoid hitting the scrum himself.

Court could see what had happened now. A massive IED had been placed in the drainage culvert under the highway and detonated just in front of the first Syrian vehicle. It appeared that the explosion had gone off just a couple seconds too early, so the lead vehicle had avoided outright destruction, and it had also avoided crashing down into the crater, but now the Syrian ZIL truck lay on its left side to the left of the crater, and it blocked the westbound lane.

There was no room to continue on the road to the east because of the massive crater and the debris around it; the only way forward was to leave the highway and slowly move over brush, down through the sloped drainage ditch, and up on the other side.

Court knew this would take a minute at least, and attempting this while under fire from the hills would be madness if there was any other option.

Syrian soldiers who had survived the rollover began crawling out of the downed truck, and small bits of rock, dirt, and highway asphalt rained down on Court's pickup.

Saunders yelled into the radio. "Reverse! Reverse!"

Court's head was on a swivel now. He didn't believe the objective of the attackers had been only to fire a few rounds, take out the lead vehicle with an explosive, and then melt away. No, knocking out the front of the convoy was the enemy's way of trying to block or slow the others in the convoy so they could be picked off.

Court leaned out his window and waved frantically to the Syrian truck behind him, trying to motion them back so the surviving vehicles could all egress out of the kill zone to the west, but to his horror he saw that the truck had stopped, and the occupants were dismounting.

"They're bailing!" he shouted to Saunders.

By now gunfire was outgoing as well as incoming. The men in the Russian trucks and in the Desert Hawk technicals were firing at faint puffs of smoke on the hillside to both the north and south.

A voice came over the walkie-talkie in Arabic, and Saunders said, "The tail vehicle is disabled! Fuck it! I'm going around them!"

Saunders tried to back around the Syrians jumping from the damaged truck, but as he accelerated in reverse, machine-gun fire raked the hood of his white pickup. The noise in the cab where Court sat was cataclysmic. Heavy chunks of lead traveling well above the sound barrier tore through the hood and engine. Oil, radiator fluid, and steam sprayed the windshield.

The pickup jolted to a halt. Saunders ground the gears for just a second before shouting, "It's dead! Bail out!"

CHAPTER 30

Court Gentry opened his door, fell out onto the highway, and then hustled in a low crouch with his rifle in his hand to the back of the pickup. Here he knelt behind the right rear tire for a moment, just long enough to wait for Saunders to join him. The Brit might not have been any kind of real ally, but in this fight Saunders was Court's battle buddy, and both men knew that they needed each other to increase their chances of survival.

In battle Court played second fiddle to no one, but he had the presence of mind to maintain his cover. He was a merc in the field working with a more senior employee of his company, so he'd operate as the second man in a two-man team.

Saunders appeared at the back of the truck, then he peered over it to the east, scanning the hills to both the north and the south. He shouted over the ungodly fire, "We've got shooters on both sides of the highway!"

Court popped his own head over the concealment of the truck bed. He saw gun smoke in the trees to both the north and the south, and most of the fire seemed to be at least forty yards to the east of where he knelt. Off to his right, he noticed a small rocky depression just off the highway, almost hidden because it was overgrown with weeds. He looked back at the puffs of smoke. "They're set up wrong! The ambush is centered on where the IED went off, so it's still to our east. If we can get in this runoff ditch on the south side we might find a little cover from both hillsides!"

Saunders couldn't see what Court was talking about from his position at the opposite end of the tailgate, but he apparently didn't have any other options near him. "Go!" Saunders ordered, and Court took off across the wide-open highway, across the shoulder, and towards the low brush and grass.

All the while the roar of gunfire continued in all directions.

He covered fifty feet of open ground, a few bullet strikes tore through asphalt and dirt around him, and then he dropped and rolled onto his chest in low brush and rocks in the slight depression by the side of the road. Stones cut into his knees and forearms as he slammed into the ground. Here he shouldered his rifle again, scanned the hill above him, and called out to Saunders, still at the truck. "Move!"

Court kept his cheek tight on the stock of his AK, searching for targets through the old iron sights. Saunders tumbled on top of him a few seconds later, rolled into a prone firing position, then immediately began scanning up the hill right next to Court.

Court looked back to the highway now. The Desert Hawks were still on their technical, but no one was on the machine gun, and one of the four militiamen hung halfway out of the truck bed behind the weapon. In front of the Desert Hawks' technical, the sedan with the Mukhabarat officers was burning and smoking, smashed against the back of the second Russian vehicle. The first Russian truck had turned around on the highway and was in the process of moving back to the west, but the driver seemed to be waiting for orders before taking off. Court was glad they were still around, because the half dozen soldiers in the open back were all firing their weapons up towards the wooded hills.

But there still seemed to be more fire coming in than going out. From the bullet strikes on the highway, Court estimated that more than a dozen weapons were raking the convoy from high ground.

Saunders rose and fired a burst up the hill, more to Court's right and less to the east. "They're tryin' to flank us to the south!" he said as his weapon emptied.

Court himself saw movement in the trees almost directly in line with their position, and he knew they'd be exposed here in the gully once the enemy repositioned on the hill above them.

He realized the entire convoy was in danger of being wiped out, himself included.

And back to the west, from the direction the small loyalist cavalcade had come from, civilian cars began rolling up the highway, unaware of the gun battle happening around the turn. Some tried to reverse out of danger, and others tried to race on past the fight, a disastrous decision because through the smoke and chaos the civilian drivers found that the road was blocked by a blown-out bridge. As Court watched, two civilian vehicles slammed on their brakes at the IED crater and got caught behind the indecisive Russian soldier behind the wheel of the GAZ.

Court scanned back up to the southeast and saw his first enemy now, as the smoke trail from an RPG revealed a man a hundred yards up the hill. He lined up his rifle's front post on the bearded man, who immediately began reloading the weapon.

Court shot the man through the chest, with absolutely no consideration as to what side of the civil war he fought on.

Three Syrians from the truck that had been disabled just behind the white pickup made a run for the gully where the two mercenaries lay. They ran too close together, and they left no one behind to cover for them. Court saw their mistake when they were almost to the shoulder of the highway, and he shouted to Saunders, "Covering fire!"

Court sent bursts from his AK to the northern hillside, while next to him Saunders emptied a magazine into the trees on the southern hillside. When Court's weapon emptied he reloaded with blinding speed, using his fresh magazine to flip out the spent mag before snapping the fresh mag into the magazine well. While he did this he looked back to the Syrian soldiers in the road.

None of the three had made it into the gully. One lay dead on the shoulder; a second rolled around wounded in the tall grasses by the highway, lying in plain view of all the shooters on the hill. And the third man had turned around and run back to the poor cover of the unarmored Syrian ZIL truck in the center of the road.

When Saunders stopped firing to reload, Court could hear that he'd taken his handheld radio with him, because excited Arabic transmissions crackled from inside a pocket in the British mercenary's load-bearing vest.

As Court dumped rounds into the trees at puffs of smoke, the shouting through the radio switched from Arabic to Russian.

Court translated the broadcasts for Saunders. "Two enemy technicals inbound from the east."

Saunders looked over to Court. "You speak Russian?"

Normally he wouldn't have let on about the languages he spoke while adopting a cover legend, but there was no denying this. "Just enough to know to pull my head down."

Saunders leveled his weapon on the north side of the hill and fired off a short burst. "Well, I bloody well knew *that* without an interpreter!"

A torrent of rifle fire tore up brush just a few feet from where Court and Saunders lay. "Shit!" Court said, firing at a flash deep in the trees to the southeast.

Men in Arabic spoke over the net now. Saunders was occupied with a target, but Court asked, "Anyone saying who these assholes are?" So far none of the Russians had identified the adversary over the radio.

Saunders fired again. "Nobody around here gives a toss but you, Wade!"

Court squinted into the distance through smoke to the east, and he could just make out the approaching pickup trucks now. They weren't on the highway but moving along thick brush on the steep hillside just below the tree line. They advanced on the wrecked convoy at a reckless clip. To his horror, Court saw what looked like two long and fat barrels protruding from the beds of each of them, larger and thicker than the barrel of a machine gun.

He had a feeling he knew what he was looking at. To Saunders he said, "ZU-23s on those technicals!"

"Bloody hell," Saunders muttered, and then he scanned to the east with his scoped rifle to confirm.

The ZU-23 was a 23-millimeter Russian twin-barrel antiaircraft cannon, but many insurgent groups around the world mounted them on technicals to make an extremely powerful and effective weapon that could be used for both air and ground targets. A couple of hits from a ZU-23 into a heavy truck could easily destroy it and all inside.

Saunders confirmed Court's suspicion. He used the three-power scope on his rifle for a better view, ignoring supersonic rounds that cracked over his head and struck the rocks just feet behind him while he looked. He ducked back down to relative cover. "You're right. We have to take those out before they rip us all to shreds."

219

The trucks were still some six hundred yards distant, a long shot with a rifle, but this was all but point-blank range for the ZU-23.

The gunfire all around was unreal. It seemed that all the other regime forces in the fight were engaging individual fighters on the northern and southern hills, and even though a Russian had been the one to call out the approaching technicals, the fire was too heavy at closer distances for anyone to be able to take the time to engage the new threats effectively.

But Court had enough cover to pick his targets, so he rose to his knees again, aimed the simple blade sight of his weapon, and tried to get a bead on the operator sitting behind the closest gun. Through the smoke in the air from the rockets and the massive IED that had gone off a minute and a half earlier, and aiming at such a small target picture that was on the move, it was an impossible shot.

"I can't get the gunners from here."

Saunders spun to engage something up the hill to the south. His rifle fired three fully automatic bursts.

Court remained focused on the pickups; he shifted his aim to the windshield of the closest one. The vehicle moved in and out of thick brush now, so he could only see it an instant at a time. He gave up and resighted on the gun and the gunner behind it. Saunders sprayed another long volley of automatic fire on Court's right, but Court maintained his concentration.

He squeezed off a single round, and it pinged off the firing mechanism of the ZU-23. His round showered the weapon with a spray of sparks, inches from the gunner's head.

Saunders stopped firing and tracked over with his rifle just as Court fired again. Again Court hit the antiaircraft gun within inches of the operator. "Bloody close!" Saunders said, and then, "Right! Take mine!" He unslung his weapon, knowing the enhanced optic would give Court a better chance of making a shot that Saunders himself knew he had no chance of making. Court traded rifles, didn't even bother slinging the SA80, and lined up the holographic red dot above the tiny exposed spot at the top of the ZU-23 operator's head.

With a three-power scope the operator's head was still one hell of a difficult target. Court fired a round, and the man tumbled backwards out of the pickup.

"He's down," Court said calmly.

"Fuck me!" Saunders shouted over the gunfire of the battle. "Shoot the other one!"

Just then, the second ZU-23 opened up. The twin cannons each flashed two times, and almost instantly the crashing sounds of cannon fire and shell impacts made it to Court and Saunders's position. Four shells exploded right in front of the first Russian truck, sending fragments through the vehicle and knocking men down all over the length of the convoy.

Court fired at the second gunner, missed, then fired once more. This time he hit the man in the neck, spinning him from his seat, but he also drew an ungodly amount of fire from several directions. The entire weedy and rocky area in front of and behind him and Saunders began kicking up as bullets struck, so the two of them flattened in the depression next to each other.

The men made eye contact while they lay there, inches away from the line of fire. Saunders shouted over the noise, "I told ya!" He laughed maniacally and handed Court a fresh magazine for his rifle. "We're gonna burn through all our ammo!"

Freak, Court thought. Saunders reloaded the AK from a magazine he pulled off Court's vest, then held the weapon up over the side of the ditch and fired the entire thirty rounds blindly up the hill. Court reached up himself with the SA80, held it over the side of the depression in the direction of a cluster of distant attackers he'd spotted just as he'd dropped, and fired the entire magazine in short bursts.

He lowered the weapon and turned to Saunders to grab more ammo, and he was just reaching to the man's load-bearing vest to pull out a magazine when he saw movement close in the ditch, just fifty feet away. Two figures stepped through the trees and onto the rocks higher on the hill. They wore black beards, carried wire-stocked Kalashnikovs, and approached the highway cautiously with their guns raised. Court could tell they were trying to flank whoever had managed to find a fighting position down here, and the only reason they hadn't pinpointed his and Saunders's location was that both he and Saunders had flattened lower and paused in their firing to reload.

Court knew he'd be spotted in a second, so his hand let go of the magazine on his battle buddy's chest and slid down to the HK pistol holstered on Saunders's belt. Court drew the weapon as he shot forward on his knees, flinging himself on top of Saunders to use him as a firing platform. He extended the pistol out in front of him as both gunmen ahead reacted to the movement, swinging their rifles in his direction.

Court opened fire. Two quick shots at the first man, two at the second, two more at the first, and another at the second. Both men crumpled as they fell back into the trees, ending up one on top of the other.

Neither of the two managed to squeeze off a single round from their AKs.

Saunders looked back over his right shoulder just in time to see the two men disappear in the brush as they fell.

The Brit said nothing; he just finished his reload, rose up a bit, and opened fire up the hillside.

The sound of one of the ZU-23s firing another four-round burst told both men a new gunner had taken position behind one of the big weapons, and Court dropped the pistol and reloaded the SA80 quickly with one of Saunders's magazines, ready to try another long shot.

But just then he heard a new sound through the persistent gunfire.

Saunders heard it, too. "Helo inbound!"

"One of ours?" Court asked.

"This is Russian and Syrian airspace. The rebels and the jihadists don't have any air." He pulled his rifle away from Court, handed the AK back, and pointed to a spot in the sky to the west. There, a Russian Mi-28 attack helicopter bore down on the highway from fifteen hundred feet away. Almost as soon as Court noticed the aircraft, black streaks emanated from its pylons, racing towards the site of the ambush.

"Get down!" Court shouted, but Saunders was firing up the hill again and did not hear. Court reached out and grabbed the man by his body armor, then pulled him down flat in the gully, just as rockets streaked over the two men.

The Russian rockets exploded well clear of the depression, midway between Court's position and the technical. The helo fired again, and this time Court could hear explosions farther to the east.

When the Mi-28 passed low overhead, Court climbed back up to his knees. Even without the scope of the SA80 he could see that both technicals were scattered and burning along the southern hillside.

As every surviving member of the convoy sprayed rifle fire up onto the two hills, the Russian helicopter circled above, using its machine gun and rocket pods to destroy enemy targets of opportunity.

Minutes later an Arabic speaker on the radio called a cease-fire, and the order was repeated in Russian. Court and Saunders loaded fresh magazines into their weapons, then rolled onto their backs, exhausted by the effort and adrenaline flow of the previous ten minutes.

Saunders reached out a bloody gloved hand. "Cheers, mate. Good shootin'."

"Got lucky." Court shook Saunders's hand, and he saw the blood. "You're hit."

"Nah." The Brit lifted his arm to show it to the man he knew as Wade. "Cut me elbow on the rocks. It's nothing." It was bleeding from shallow scrapes. His T-shirt was torn at the shoulder, as well. He kept looking Court's way. "Done a lot of this sort of thing, have you?"

"Once or twice," Court said as he climbed laboriously to his feet.

"Southeast Asia, did you say? Can't say I've seen much in the news in the past fifty years that looks this intense coming from bloody Southeast Asia, and you don't look like you were even a sparkle in your daddy's eye back in the Tet Offensive."

Court knew his cover was being challenged. He just said, "I've been other places, too." He left it there, and Saunders did not pursue, but Court could feel the man's eyes on him behind his dark sunglasses. To change the subject Court added, "For the record, I didn't use all my AK ammo."

Saunders sniffed. "We aren't even halfway to Babbila, are we?"

The man had a point. "No. We're not." Court added, "That was a large attack, but they did a lot wrong, which is the only reason we're alive."

"I'll take a bit of good luck, though; God knows I've had my share of bad."

As they walked back to the truck the Englishman said, "And since you were so bloody curious about it, I can tell you who we were fighting. The only force around here that's got technicals with ZU-23s on them is Jabhat al Nusra."

"The local branch of AQ?"

"That's right."

Court made no outward reaction, but a weight was lifted off him knowing he hadn't just flown into Syria and killed a group of democratic forces fighting against Ahmed Azzam.

...

Minutes after the firefight, five Syrian Arab Army two-ton trucks, carrying some forty infantrymen in all, rolled slowly through the traffic jam of civilian vehicles, then made their way between the broken vehicles and scattered bodies to take up security positions. The dead and wounded were attended to, and Saunders was told equipment trucks were on the way to move the wrecked vehicles and to create a path in the brush to bypass the massive hole in the highway.

The wreckage of the convoy was horrific: vehicles smoking and burning, bodies and blood everywhere, thousands of spent shell casings and dozens of empty magazines lying on broken asphalt. The wounded moaned and men shouted orders to keep eyes on the hills in case the attackers decided to brave the helicopter circling overhead and return for more.

Three of the four Desert Hawks soldiers survived, although one of the survivors had taken an AK round through a hand. Court himself expertly bandaged the man's wound, and he helped the other two Hawks load their injured comrade, as well as the dead one, into the back of the SAA truck.

Two of the Russians had died in the fighting, and five more were wounded, including the platoon's medic. Three Syrian Arab Army soldiers were dead, with six more injured.

Six dead, twelve wounded, but Court knew that number could have been a hell of a lot higher.

While Court was bandaging an eighteen-year-old Syrian private's shredded but intact leg, word got around the area about the Western security contractor who shot both ZU-23 gunners, possibly saving the lives of everyone in the convoy. The three Mukhabarat men, who all managed to survive unscathed by finding a ditch to hide in on the north side of the highway, all came over to shake Court's hand.

Men that Court would gain great pleasure from killing in other circumstances smiled at him, tried to give him cigarettes, and patted him on the back.

Court found it surreal.

CHAPTER 31

Sebastian Drexler had spent the day traveling, and while doing so he did everything in his power to keep from touching anything with his new fingertips. In this endeavor he had been mostly successful. He'd touched little other than his mobile phone and his luggage while leaving Syria on his four-hour chartered flight to Moscow. In the bathroom of the aircraft he'd donned gloves to gently handle the zipper of his slacks.

Russia was the easiest way into Europe from Damascus, so he chose that route. He found it unfortunate that he had to fly hours out of his way to get to France, but sanctions against Syria meant only certain nations were allowing airline transport into and out of the Middle Eastern nation.

In Moscow's Sheremetyevo airport he went through a VIP line for customs and immigration, out into the Arrivals hall, and then he immediately walked over to Departures and checked in for his flight to Paris. He took care to keep his new fingerprints as shielded as possible, even when hurrying through the airport to board his 3:10 p.m. Air France flight to Charles de Gaulle.

In the first-class cabin he drank a vodka on the rocks, carefully holding the drink away from his fingertips, but he'd declined anything to eat, knowing that the most important part of his return to Western Europe was fast approaching, and the less he did that involved his hands, the better.

His flight landed at 6:15 in the evening; he was one of the first passengers to arrive at the immigration kiosks, and here he slid his passport across the desk to the official with a tired smile. He was asked to put his fingers on the reader, and he did so carefully, making certain to place them straight down so none of the glued areas would be recorded.

The immigration officer looked at the clean-shaven Drexler, then at the bearded man on the Finnish passport of Veeti Takala, and he made a little face, but he did not react with any noticeable suspicion. Then he looked over to his screen, presumably to make sure the fingerprints matched.

"How long will you be staying in France?" the officer asked.

"Three days. Then a train home to Helsinki."

The sound of the stamping of Takala's passport almost filled Drexler with ecstasy. He was home . . . or at least close enough for now.

. . .

Sebastian Drexler had told Malik he'd contact him the second he arrived in Paris, but his plane had landed forty-five minutes earlier, and he'd yet to make that call. Instead he sat in a plush living room in a suite at the Hilton Hotel Paris Charles de Gaulle, smoothing out the wrinkles of his navy Tom Ford sharkskin suit. A cup of coffee sat in front of him, but he ignored it and instead concentrated on what he was about to say.

The door to the suite's small dining room opened, and an attractive blonde in a business suit stepped out. Drexler detected an Austrian accent in her German. "The principals will see you now, Herr Drexler."

"Vielen Dank." He stood and stepped by the woman on his way through the door.

There were four sitting at the table, all stern-faced men. He made the rounds with officious handshakes, though he worried that his borrowed fingertips might be damaged with all the touching. But after the greetings he realized he needn't have worried; he found these four to be in possession of the weak handshakes of weak men.

He knew all these men by name, although he just thought of them as "The Bankers." They were with Meier Privatbank, Drexler's employer, and they had flown in to Paris Charles de Gaulle on this Saturday evening at his request. It was not a small thing to summon the directors of one of

Switzerland's oldest and most secretive banks to travel some six hundred kilometers for a meeting, and as Drexler sat down at the mirror-polished table, he couldn't help but revel in the thought that he commanded that level of respect from these men.

The revelry faded as he thought about it. No . . . *he* didn't command their respect. *She* did. These men were here because of Shakira Azzam. They thought of Drexler as a necessary evil. A cutout between her dirty money and their sanitized and perfect lives in Switzerland.

The man at the head of the table was forty-year-old Stefan Meier, the great-grandson of Aldous Meier, the bank's founder. Stefan was vice president, behind his older brother, Rolf, in the company and familial pecking order, but he was the only Meier who ever got his hands remotely dirty, which meant he was the only family member involved with the institution Drexler had ever met.

Meier said, "We know you are here on an important assignment for our client in Damascus. Is everything on track with that?"

Drexler assumed Meier didn't want to know any details about the work he was here to do. The vice president would only know that Shakira had demanded he fulfill an obligation to her, and if he completed the obligation to her satisfaction, she would reward the bank with more deposits and more business. If he failed to do the work, she could pull her accounts from the bank.

Drexler said, "I expect to have the job completed this evening."

"Excellent," Meier replied. "I know our client is rewarding you handsomely for going above and beyond your duties to her accounts, and our client's husband has been pleased with your work in maintaining his foreign interests, as well."

"I'm gratified to hear that."

Stefan Meier said, "The bank is more than satisfied with your work."

The words coming from the vice president were flattering, but none of the four men across the table were smiling. Drexler knew they were all here waiting for the other shoe to drop, to learn why their agent in Syria had demanded a meeting with them right in the middle of an operation.

Enough of the bullshit, Drexler thought. He'd just tell them. "I asked you all here because I would like to request immediate reassignment."

In the silence that ensued he scanned all four faces. There was no surprise, no alarm, no discernible emotion.

Drexler continued. "I've spent over two years in Syria. I've done everything asked of me. It's time for me to move on."

"I don't understand," Meier said. "We positioned you in Syria because it was the safest place for you due to your . . . legal troubles. I am certain Interpol hasn't lost interest in you in two years, and there aren't many locales like Syria that offer both freedom of movement for you and a crucial business need for us."

"Syria has simply become too dangerous an environment for me."

"Hogwash," said Ian Pleasance, the thick-jowled English director of bank operations. "The civil war is being won by the regime, and won handily. ISIS is on its last legs, ditto the Kurds and the FSA. Russia will protect Azzam, and by extension, it will protect you."

Drexler acknowledged Pleasance with a nod but said, "I'm not worried about ISIS or the FSA. I'm worried about Shakira and Ahmed. My work has positioned me directly between them."

Meier pursed his lips. "In what way?"

"It's about the job I am here to do in Paris. If I do it correctly, and Ahmed finds out . . . I will be killed when I return to Syria."

Stefan Meier flashed a glance to the director of operations. A look of annoyance that something so crass as murder would come up in this meeting. Stefan leaned back in his chair now, and Ian leaned forward.

"Perhaps this is something you and I should discuss in—"

"I have protected billions of dollars of assets at Meier in the past several years, and the bank knew of my, as you call them, *legal troubles*, the day I was hired. I only ask to be brought in from the cold, taken out of imminent danger, and set up somewhere secure. I will continue to work ceaselessly for the bank, just not in between the president and first lady of Syria."

The oldest man in the room, Bruno Olvetti, was the vice director of finance. He was there only because he served as the older Meier brother's eyes and ears. Bruno came to meetings like this to watch over Stefan and to report back to Rolf. He said, "This perilous position you speak of, how much of it is your own doing?"

"What do you mean by that?"

"Are you having an affair with Shakira Azzam?"

Drexler could not possibly imagine how Bruno could know about that. He thought it possible, likely even, that the old man was just bluffing. Assuming a relationship because he knew Drexler worked closely with Shakira on discreet matters. Shakira was an attractive woman, and Drexler considered himself a very desirable man.

He said, "Nice try, Bruno, but there is no affair."

To his surprise, Stefan Meier spoke up now. "You wouldn't be calling our client's word into question, would you?"

Drexler said nothing.

"She told my brother herself that the two of you are involved." Stefan laughed a little. "According to Rolf, she genuinely seems fond of you. Well done. You've somehow melted the heart of the First Lady of Hell."

Drexler recovered quickly. "All the more reason, gentlemen, to pull me out. There has been certain . . . pressure . . . placed on me by the first lady over the past year or so. It has put me at odds with the president and—"

Ian Pleasance took off his glasses and rubbed his drooping eyes. "Oh, come now, man. Are you here to tell us you are being sexually harassed by your client?"

Stefan and the others chuckled now.

The muscles in Sebastian Drexler's neck flexed, but he kept his composure. "I have told you what I've come to tell you. If I return to Syria, it is likely I will be killed, and it is likely the president will hold my employers . . . *yourselves*, that is, responsible for actions taken against him and his interests. He does still hold sway over his wife, you know. He could simply coerce her into moving assets from your bank."

Meier replied, "Shakira is free to remove her assets at any time, irrespective of what her husband knows, or suspects, or insists upon. Even if we comply with your request. If we simply recall you from Damascus, or never send you back there, then what is to keep her from getting angry with us and making other arrangements with her money?"

"That is a fair question. The bank will be safe when I don't return, because Shakira will be convinced that I died here in France. I don't need your help to do that; I just need your help after the fact. Shakira will learn of my demise only after learning of the success of my operation, and she will be indebted to Meier Privatbank."

"Such subterfuge," Stefan said with a smile. "You certainly have a flair for the dramatic, don't you? Sleeping with the Syrian president's wife, and devising a plan to simulate your own death."

Drexler did not bat an eyelash. "Herr Meier, in the employ of your firm I have killed or ordered the deaths of more than two dozen men and women. There is drama here that is not of my doing, as well."

Meier glowered at Drexler, but he made no immediate reply. Pleasance was about to speak when Drexler held up a hand.

"Gentlemen, I only ask for a way out of this posting. You need someone to do the work I do. Allow me to do it in Hong Kong, in Rio, in the Caymans. Just don't send me back to Damascus."

Stefan Meier continued his hard stare for several seconds, then nodded slowly. He said, "All right, Sebastian. You are a key element of the success of our bank. Accomplish your mission in France. Save Shakira's place in the palace. Then . . . *only* then, we will get you out of there."

"So I don't have to go back to Damascus?"

Stefan said, "You don't want to go and wish your lover *adieu* and *bon chance*?"

Drexler knew the bankers were toying with him. He was a fascinating character in their boring lives, exactly the man any one of these fat, weak men would love to be for just one day, so of course they would mock him, pretend his actions were beneath their station.

Drexler said, "I have no need to see her ever again."

Stefan shrugged. "Very well. Your plan to fake your death in Paris is approved. We will hide you in Switzerland until such a time as we find a posting for you that is to your liking."

Bruno Olvetti pointed a finger across the table. "Don't ever forget, Drexler. You may be our best fixer and hatchet man, but Shakira Azzam is more important to us than you are. As long as she is happy, we are happy. And as long as we are happy, you are safe. If you don't succeed in your mission here, or if you don't pull off your subterfuge with your little trick in faking your death, then we send you back to Syria."

Drexler stood, gave a courteous bow to the bankers, and headed for the door. He was motivated now like he had not been in years. A lifeline had been thrown to him, and all he had to do in order to take it and pull himself to safety was kill a fashion model being hidden by a pair of doctors and an over-the-hill ex–French intelligence official.

He thought about the American who'd caused him so much trouble, but he told himself Malik and his boys had enough men and guns to handle him.

Tonight he'd link up with Malik, the Mukhabarat assassin sent by Ahmed Azzam to help find and rescue Bianca, and the bent French police captain, and together they'd get their hands on Bianca Medina. He'd be threading a very small needle with his operation after that, but when he finally managed to kill Medina, and Shakira was both satisfied with Drexler's work and convinced he'd died in the execution of it, then he'd be able to be rid of Syria once and for all.

But first things first. He wasn't leaving Europe, not any time soon, at least. As soon as he climbed into his rental car, he would rip the dead flesh off his fingertips and say good-bye to poor Veeti Takala.

CHAPTER 32

Vincent Voland stood on the parking circle in front of the country estate near the village of La Brosse as the last of the day's light faded. In front of him, just rolling up the driveway by the greenhouse, a black Lincoln Navigator flashed its headlights.

Dr. Tarek Halaby stepped outside through the side door to the property and shouldered up to Voland. He, too, watched the vehicle approach.

"I take it these are the security men you ordered up?"

Voland nodded. "The very best."

"That money can buy," Tarek added.

"*Oui*. We must face the facts. After seven years of war, many have tired of your cause. The men and women still alive who will fight for you without charge are, in large part, men and women who know little about fighting." As the Navigator rolled to a stop, he added, "The men with the skills to fight this battle do not hold an ideological attachment to your particular fight. Nevertheless, these are men of principle. They will protect this property from anyone who threatens it."

Tarek Halaby's hand reached under his safari jacket and touched something unfamiliar there, and it occurred to him, not for the first time today, that he had never fired a gun in his life. All his time in Syria, surrounded by armed rebels and more than once within shouting distance of regime forces or ISIS terrorists, and he'd never taken to arming himself. He was a doctor, not a soldier.

But now he had a Walther P99 jammed into his corduroy pants, and an extra magazine in the pocket of the safari coat. Vincent Voland had offered the weapon a few hours earlier as they waited for the cavalry to arrive in the form of the four ex-members of the French Foreign Legion, and when Tarek at first demurred, Voland countered that the only thing between Syrian assassins and Bianca Medina were five over-the-hill ex–Syrian soldiers, none of whom had any special forces or advanced combat training; a nephew of his wife who taught high school physics; and a sixty-five-year-old former French spook who'd only used a weapon in anger once in his life, over thirty-five years earlier in Lebanon.

And, Voland had added, he'd missed that target in Lebanon.

When this realization sank in, Tarek took the pistol from Voland, along with five minutes' instruction on how to shoot it and reload it and a promise from the Frenchman that he wouldn't mention anything about the weapon to Rima Halaby, because Tarek doubted his wife would approve of him carrying a firearm as a matter of safety.

Now that the security men were here, Tarek wondered if he should hand the gun back, but only for a moment, and then he changed his mind. He didn't know these men any better than he knew this man Sebastian Drexler that Voland kept mentioning with a bizarre combination of revulsion and awe.

Tarek would keep an eye on these men just the same as he would anyone else with the potential to put this operation in jeopardy.

The SUV doors opened and four men climbed out. They carried short-barreled submachine guns, already slung on their shoulders, and large packs on their backs. To Tarek they all appeared to be in their fifties, and two of the four men were quite obviously overweight.

They looked nothing like the American contract killer he'd been working with, and Tarek found himself disappointed.

Voland spoke softly to Tarek as the men hefted bags out of the rear of the SUV. Clearly he recognized what Tarek was thinking. "It's been a few years since I've seen them, but they are a team that works together all over the world. They have quite a good reputation. Don't worry . . . they will handle themselves."

From his comment Tarek thought Voland seemed worried about the men's appearance himself.

Voland stepped forward and met the men in the middle of the parking circle, greeting them with warm and familiar handshakes, and with pats on the back he walked one of the men back over to the Syrian. The Frenchman said, "Dr. Halaby, I present to you Monsieur Paul Boyer." Tarek shook the hand of a heavy-set man with a trim gray beard and thin combed-over hair.

Boyer spoke with a French accent. "I and my men are at your service, Doctor. We'd like to be set up by nightfall, so perhaps we can do our formal introductions later."

"Bien sûr, Monsieur Boyer."

All four men passed into the house; the three associates of Boyer never even looked up as they walked by Tarek.

Halaby turned again to Voland, but the Frenchman spoke before the Syrian doctor could air his concerns. "Boyer is French, a former major in the French Foreign Legion. The others are Campbell from Scotland, Laghari from India, and Novak from Hungary. All Legionnaires."

Tarek said, "Four men, Vincent? I hope it's enough."

Voland smiled. "If Drexler finds this house, he'll have backup, for sure. But remember, he's working for Shakira, not Ahmed, so he can't use resources from the Syrian government. He'll have some local cops, like the two you met in your apartment, and they'll be cut down before they get within one hundred meters of Mademoiselle Medina."

Tarek felt a little better with this reminder.

Voland said, "Now, let's see where Boyer positions his men, so we can move your men to provide the best additional coverage."

The men returned to the house to speak with the FSEU security staff. Another night was coming, and despite Voland's confidence, with the darkness came danger.

. . .

On the far side of the house, Rima Halaby descended the stairs that led to the wine cellar. She'd taken to checking on Bianca twice a day, spending

234

an hour with her, gently reminding the beautiful model that all was not lost, since the American was surely somewhere right now looking to get himself into Syria.

At the bottom of the stairs she looked across the length of the large wine cellar and saw Firas, and when she did, she sighed. He had been down here all the previous night, and all day long, so when she saw him slumped over the tiny wine table she did not get angry. As long as the door to Bianca's room was closed and locked, Rima saw no problem with her nephew taking brief naps throughout the day.

As she walked across the concrete floor, her footfalls echoed in the room, and she expected Firas to stir. When he did not, she called to him.

"I brought a sleeping bag down here yesterday, Firas. Why don't you use it and get some rest?"

The young schoolteacher did not move.

"Firas? How is our guest?"

The young man did stir now, but he just moved his arm a little on the table, and in so doing, he knocked a wineglass onto the floor, shattering it. Rima was surprised by this, but doubly so when she saw a second glass, half filled with red wine, on the table.

She raced the rest of the way across the small room, and now she saw the two empty bottles on the floor.

"Firas!" she shouted, and her nephew sat up, ramrod straight, but he was disoriented, confused.

Clearly, he was drunk.

Now she moved to the door to the guest quarters, put her hand on the latch, and tested it.

To her dismay, the door opened, and to her horror, the room was empty. She ran through the narrow room to the bathroom; the door was open and it was unoccupied.

Now she ran back into the wine cellar, over to the storeroom adjacent to Medina's quarters. She threw this door open, hoping against hope she'd see the model in here, but instead she just saw racks of cleaning solvents, mops, furniture polish, and other housekeeping supplies.

"Firas!" she shouted again. "Where did she go?"

Back in the wine cellar, Firas was standing now on wobbly legs, but he wasn't responsive to his aunt's question.

Rima didn't have her phone on her, nor did she have a radio. It occurred to her that she wouldn't know the code to use Firas's iPhone, and this was something they should have organized before an emergency. She ran over to her nephew, opened up his jacket, and checked to see if his gun was still there.

To her relief Bianca had not disarmed him. Rima yanked the weapon from his pants, spun away, and raced up the wooden steps as fast as she could. She didn't know if the gun had a safety on it, though it hardly mattered because she wasn't going to shoot Bianca. It was a tool for bluffing, but she knew it would only work for that if she found her prisoner.

. . .

Bianca Medina opened the door from the hearth room that led out to the stone patio at the back of the home. Beyond the manicured lawn, a forest of hard woods looked dark and foreboding now as dusk set in, but she knew she had a much better chance of disappearing out there in the dark, so she fought against her fear and steeled herself to make a run for it.

She had grown more and more worried with each passing hour that Ahmed would simply kill Jamal back in Damascus, even if the American did his best to get there before he could do it. Bianca had spent the last three days thinking of nothing but her son, his predicament, and her utter inability to do anything to help him. She was his mother, and she found it unacceptable to just sit there in a tiny room off a wine cellar thousands of miles away from where her baby was in mortal danger.

So she'd decided to act with the tools available to her. Beauty, charm, intelligence, and a mother's ceaseless tenacity to protect her child.

And one more thing . . . the ability to drink most men under the table, assisted by the fact she'd been drinking wine heavily since her midteens.

She'd knocked on the door to ask Firas for a glass of wine from the cellar, and within ten minutes of him obliging her, they were drinking Bordeaux together. She'd asked him about his life and his family, and she'd learned that he was the nephew of Rima and Tarek, and he'd lost two cousins in the war: the Halabys' adult children.

They talked for an hour and drank two bottles of wine. Every now and then Firas would receive a text from upstairs checking on him, and he'd confirm all was well, but Bianca worried the entire time someone would come downstairs to relieve him, in which case she'd have to start all over with another guard, another life story, and more red wine.

But soon enough, the young schoolteacher's eyes went fuzzy and he put his head down on the table, and even though he wasn't unconscious, he was disoriented enough to where Bianca just told him she was going to the bathroom in her little cell, but instead she stepped around a rack of brut champagnes. When she felt sure his attention was not on the situation around him but instead on trying not to puke, she darted up the stairs.

She'd made it through the kitchen and the hearth room, and now it was time to flee the house entirely. She felt that if she could get to a road she could find a ride, and if she could find a ride she could get a phone. Her plan was to contact Jamal's au pair, Yasmin, and have her get a message to Ahmed that she had been kidnapped by Syrian expat insurgents, and this would ensure the safety of Jamal.

She stood up now, took a deep breath, and started to run.

"Take one more step and I'll shoot one of those long legs of yours!"

The sound of Rima Halaby's voice behind her, more stern now than Bianca had ever heard it, stopped her in her tracks. She raised her hands but did not turn back around at first.

Bianca said, "Madame, I am begging you. Please just let me go. It's the only chance for my son."

"The only chance for your son is the American who promised to put his life on the line for him, so the least you could do is fulfill your end of the deal and stay here."

Bianca turned around and lowered her hands.

"You and I are different, Doctor."

"This is true."

"I mean that you are able to trust men. I am not so trusting."

"I don't trust all men. But *that* man, I believed that *he* believed he could do it, and that was enough for me."

"But you have no idea what it's like down there in Damascus now. There is no way he'll survive, and by failing, he will reveal to Ahmed that I told you about Jamal."

"Believe, daughter. Allah sent him to help us."

"If that American is an angel, Rima, then he is an angel of death."

Rima's face hardened, "Perhaps that's just what my country needs right now," She looked at Bianca. "A man is risking his life for your child. He owes you nothing, your child nothing, me nothing. But he's doing it. Believe in him. And believe *me*, daughter, if you try to run away again, I will kill you with my own two hands."

. . .

Rima led Bianca through the hearth room on their way back down to the cellar stairs off the kitchen. The gun was low in her hand; she didn't need it, but it was there in case Bianca decided again to run.

As the women entered the kitchen, they passed by Vincent Voland and Boyer, the leader of the new team of security men. Rima gave a slight embarrassed nod, Bianca just looked to the floor, and soon they both disappeared down the stairs.

Boyer shook his head and turned to Voland. "Vincent, if you are having trouble keeping the prisoner in, you might find it doubly so keeping a motivated enemy out."

"Well then, I'm glad I hired you all. Whatever just happened, we will be certain it doesn't happen again. You just worry about the threats from outside, and we'll get things straightened out on the inside."

Boyer said, "Put your people around the house, in the windows. My team and I will split. Two of us at the front, two of us in back. We'll cover ninety degrees per man during the evenings." Boyer pulled the cocking handle back on the MP5 submachine gun hanging from a sling over his shoulder. "We'll be ready if they come, *mon amie*."

CHAPTER 33

Gentry, Saunders, and the two remaining militiamen had spent the entire afternoon driving south towards the Desert Hawks Brigade base near Damascus, stopping at loyalist checkpoints along the way. After the ambush up north, the men all but expected another engagement by hostile forces, but no attacks came. Even so, on two occasions between Homs and Damascus they passed wrecked-out and burned-out vehicles and evidence of other assaults on the highway, and twice more loyalist checkpoints had been hastily erected because of insurgent activity near the highway.

Originally Saunders had planned on completing the drive from the air base near Latakia to the camp near Damascus by five p.m., but it was almost eight thirty when he, Court, and the two militiamen rolled up the Damascus Airport Motorway and turned into the Babbila district to the southeast of the city. After another few minutes of driving, they pulled into a short line of vehicles waiting to enter the base of Liwa Suqur al Sahara, the Desert Hawks Brigade.

Court had been to Syria a few times before in his career, both with the CIA as a member of a hunter/killer team known as the Goon Squad and as a private assassin. He'd once assassinated the Nigerian minister of energy in the northeastern Syrian town of al Hasakah. But this was his first time in the capital. Driving around the city to get to the southeastern edge, he'd been impressed by the urban sprawl. It was well developed and modern, and from what he could tell from the highway, the city didn't seem to have any trouble with electricity or much trouble with infrastructure, although he imagined once you got into any remaining rebel strongholds, suddenly the lights would stop working and the roads would be a disaster.

But he was in the geographical heart of the regime now, and the regime seemed to have things, more or less, in working order.

They stopped at the front gates, made it through security, passed through the concrete-and-razor-wire barricade, and rolled up to a large, long barracks building. Here the four men climbed out, all tired from their eventful day. The two Desert Hawks soldiers headed off in one direction, and Court followed Saunders through the night in the other.

Saunders took Court into the administrative building, where he was processed into the base, given a badge as a member of KWA employed by the Desert Hawks, introduced to a few officers working on this Saturday evening, and then the two men headed back into the night.

After a ten-minute walk through rows of barracks and warehouses, they stepped into the KWA team room positioned in a building near the center of the base. Saunders nodded at ten or so men sitting in the dark around a TV playing a DVD of a superhero film. "Lads," he said, "meet Wade."

There were a few nods and a couple of grunts. Half the men didn't even look up.

It wasn't really much of a welcome.

A muscular man in his forties wearing shorts and a tank top sat at a table and spoke up in a South African accent. "Heard you got hit."

Saunders said, "Bloody full-on Al Nusra ambush. Twenty-five oppo personnel, minimum, and two technicals with bleedin' cannons on 'em."

"Friendly losses?"

"Six KIA, twelve WIA. It took an Mi-28 to end the bloody thing."

"Jesus," muttered a bearded and tatted American lying in his underwear on a sofa along the wall. "And all we did today was show ragheads how to throw frags through doors without them bouncing back in their faces."

Another man—Court thought he detected a Dutch accent from him—said, "You boys murder any of the fuckers?"

Saunders slapped Court on the back. "We've got us a real shooter here.

Our new Canuck Wade took out two ZU-23 gunners at five hundred meters."

"Sweet," the American said, but there were no more questions about the attack.

The South African stood up and walked over to shake Court's hand. "I'm Van Wyk. Team leader. Got an e-mail from Klossner himself about you this morning. He told me to fold you into the unit and you'd fit in like you've been workin' with us for years. High praise from a man who doesn't deal it out."

Court would have appreciated Klossner not saying a thing about him to the men he'd be with down here, but that cat was out of the bag now.

Court said, "I'll give you my best."

"From the sound of it, you already have."

Saunders asked, "We rolling out on a raid tonight, boss?"

"Good news," said the South African. "We've got the night free. Bad news. Tomorrow at oh six hundred we're heading northeast. Looks like a multiday deployment, working with the spearhead company of the brigade's First Battalion."

Court could tell by his expression that Saunders seemed surprised by this. "Why the hell are we doing that?" the British mercenary asked.

"New security sweep east of Palmyra. Big op, by the sound of it. Russians and SAA at the heart of it, Iranians to the west, militia to the east. That's all I really know, other than we'll be helping pacify opposition centers both in desert and urban terrain."

Saunders looked at Court. "These days the desert east of Palmyra is FSA to the north, ISIS to the south, split by the M20 highway. We could be fighting anybody and everybody on this run."

"Terrific." Court's mind was racing. He'd considered himself immensely lucky to be sent by Klossner to live on and work at a base in a Damascus suburb, considering how his target here in Syria was also in a Damascus suburb, albeit on the other side of the city. But now he had just learned that first thing tomorrow morning he would be saddling up and moving out somewhere else in the country entirely.

On top of this, he desperately needed to communicate with Voland and Bianca to find the location of Jamal's home, and for that he needed a phone or a computer. But phones and computers were off-limits for mercs.

Klossner had told him the KWA team leader here was only allowed to use commo equipment in the Desert Hawks Brigade communications room, and even then, only under watch by an English-speaking intelligence officer from the militia group. Court had no expectations he'd be seeing the inside of the communications room himself, so he knew he had one night to think of how to reach out to Voland, because it didn't sound like he'd get much opportunity to buy a mobile phone and an international calling card in the combat zone where they were heading.

He didn't know if Jamal had that kind of time, or if Bianca did, for that matter, because Court imagined Drexler would be working hard to locate her in France.

Saunders had peeled his body armor off and tossed it on the floor by the door. He looked over the cuts and bruises he'd picked up during the gunfight earlier in the day. "I promised the new bloke I'd buy him a pint for savin' me arse. Rally back here in thirty minutes for all who fancy coming with us." To Court, Saunders said, "Tomorrow morning at oh five hundred we'll get you kitted up like a proper operator. But tonight . . . let's celebrate our victory against Al Nusra."

Court cocked his head at this. "So . . . we can just leave and go out to a bar whenever we want? By ourselves?" The Mukhabarat officer at the airport had told him he was not allowed to travel anywhere without an officer of the Desert Hawks.

"Not exactly, but we've sussed out a way to slip off base, and we've got a Desert Hawks major complicit in our scheme. He'll go with us as long as we keep a drink in his hand. And it's not a proper pub. Sadly, you won't find too many of those here. It's a disco, and it's utter shit, but it's got booze. Better we go get pissed than sittin' 'ere all bleedin' night."

Court didn't feel like going to a disco, because he was tired, and also because he didn't like discos, but the opportunity to learn a tried and tested way to sneak out of the base was just too good to pass up.

"I've only got euros."

Saunders said, "They'll gladly take euros, so you can buy the first round."

. . .

Van Wyk, the team leader, showed Court to an empty bunk in the back, and here he dumped his armor, his rifle, and his ruck. He went to the bathroom, took a one-minute shower, and changed into fresh clothes: gray cargo pants, Merrell boots, and a plain black T-shirt. Once he was dressed he grabbed a bottle of water from the little kitchen and headed back into the team room.

Court was surprised to see that Saunders was dressed in casual civilian attire: blue jeans, a polo shirt, even a gold chain around his neck and a bracelet on his wrist. A couple of the other men looked like they were ready for a night on the town themselves.

. . .

Fifteen minutes later Court crouched in the dark behind Saunders and three other KWA contractors next to a building in the motor pool, staring at the fence line of the base just across a gravel road and a small lot full of trucks and cars. A pair of sand-colored Ural-4320 armored trucks lumbered by towards the main gate, well illuminated a hundred meters off to Court's right.

He was still surprised to be doing this; he felt like he was in the middle of one of those World War II escape films he used to watch with his dad and his brother when he was a kid.

A clean-shaven and thickly built Arab man in uniform stepped around the side of the metal building, just feet from where the men knelt. At first Court thought he and the other men had been busted by base security, but when the man raised a hand up to the group of men in the dark, Saunders called out to him. *"Keef halik, habbibi?"* How are you, friend?

Court was told the man's name was Walid, which was a first name, but no one mentioned his surname. He was a major in the Desert Hawks Brigade, and it appeared to Court he was a more than willing participant in all this. He knelt down with the KWA contractors, watched the front gate, and waited to make his move along with the others.

An outbuilding at the edge of the motor pool was only twenty feet from the fence, and this shielded a small portion of the fence from the main guardhouse. Saunders explained that this was their target, and together they waited for the trucks to arrive at the gate. When they did, the drivers each stopped to speak with the guards as they left the base.

The men moved out one at a time; Saunders led the way, sprinting across the road, through the motor pool, to the darkened fence line. Then he ran along the wire before disappearing behind the small outbuilding.

The Dutchman went next, then a Croatian, the Syrian militia major, and then Court. As he crossed the road, a light from a distant Jeep glowed in Court's direction, but he made it to the lot of the motor pool and ducked down behind an old two-ton truck as the vehicle passed, thus remaining undetected.

A minute later Court was behind the outbuilding with the others, and seconds after that they were joined by a KWA contractor from Argentina. The others waited while Saunders and Walid worked together on a small part of the fence, unfastening links that had previously been cut, then twisted back together individually to make it appear undamaged.

In just a couple minutes' work they opened a section large enough to crawl through.

It occurred to Court that if any enemy knew about this weak link in the base's security, they could just as easily exploit it as the men using it to go barhopping. Even though he knew this weakness was good news for him and his mission here in Damascus, he was curious about it.

As Saunders stood back so Walid could crawl through first, Court leaned over to him. "You don't worry about somebody coming through that hole in the middle of the night?"

"We came down here to fight, and anybody around here with the tactical muscle to find and exploit that tiny compromise would have to be one ballsy fighter. We all keep our rifles and our kit close by." He shrugged. "What can I say? If you work for KWA, booze is more important than safety. You'll learn."

They piled into Walid's personal vehicle, a new and well-equipped Hyundai Elantra. Court didn't think a militia soldier, even a midgrade officer, would normally make much money in the Middle East, but since he'd been told the Desert Hawks Brigade was a criminal organization at its core, it came as no great surprise to him that the man had some money.

With six men in the sedan it was a tight fit, but Court was more comfortable now than he'd been on much of the day's ride in the back of a hot truck. As they headed back towards the Damascus Airport Motorway with Walid behind the wheel, the Syrian tuned his stereo to 107.5, an English-language station, and the DJ played hits from the UK and the United States. Court found it hard to accept the fact that he was in Damascus with West Coast rap blasting on the radio.

Over the next half hour Court was treated to a master class by Walid on avoiding checkpoints in Damascus. He seemed to know where they were all set up, because he'd drive along the main drags for a few minutes, then pull off, roll through back streets, alleyways, or even parking lots, then slip back onto the main drags with his headlights off. He would pick up speed and turn his lights back on, then repeat the process again and again.

The major explained he had no fear of the checkpoints; he wasn't doing anything wrong that the National Defence Forces personnel that manned them would care about, since they couldn't give a damn about a Desert Hawks officer sneaking off his base. He simply didn't want the delay and hassle of the traffic stops and ID checks.

. . .

Court imagined they'd only traveled three or four miles by the time they hit the rustic Old Town Damascus section, but it had taken them nearly thirty minutes of driving. They found a place to park in a lot near the bar on Al Keshleh Avenue in the Bab Touma neighborhood, and the men stepped out of the car and stretched their legs.

Walid changed into civilian clothing in the parking lot, then crammed his uniform in a backpack in his trunk, and the six men began heading towards the bar.

A pair of what appeared to be eighteen-year-old boys wearing the uniform of the Syrian Arab Army and carrying polymer-stocked AK-47s stepped up to the men on the sidewalk. Court proffered his papers along with all the other men, and the two privates scanned each person's documents with a flashlight. The Desert Hawks major exchanged pleasantries with the soldiers, but Court noticed that Walid had to show his papers as well, and the SAA soldiers didn't treat his much-higher rank with much deference at all.

He was militia, and they were part of the conventional forces, so he wasn't an officer as far as they were concerned.

Court and his crew for the evening left the soldiers to their foot patrol and stepped into Bar 80, a two-level disco mostly full at eleven p.m. on a Saturday night. They were frisked by an armed bouncer at the front door, then wound their way to a bar on the second level, passing armed security men dressed in polos and jeans.

The six men sat at a table in the middle of the dark room. Court offered to buy a round for everyone, and then he and Saunders went to the bar to order.

After returning with the drinks, Court sat and sipped his Irish whiskey and focused on the men at the table with him. He quickly got the impression this wasn't going to be much of a party. Most of the men ordered scotch or whiskey, and they sat quietly drinking and smoking while looking around, not talking to the other men at the table. Walid was clearly the only one seriously enjoying himself, because he began to look buzzed by the end of his first drink.

At the table with Court were Saunders, Major Walid, the Croatian, the Argentine, and the Dutchman. The Croatian introduced himself as Broz, though Court didn't know if that was a first or last name. He was a big man with a crew cut and a flat nose that made him look like a boxer. The Argentine went by Brunetti. He was dark complected with a beard and mustache. A handsome face but dark, angry eyes.

The Dutchman was Anders. He was tall and blond, with a mustache and goatee that told Court the man desperately wanted to grow a beard but his face wouldn't accommodate his desires.

As Brunetti brought back a second round of drinks, Court began looking around the room, marveling at the revelry going on. There was a group of a dozen or more Russian military men—from their look and grooming standards Court figured they were probably air force, and from their burly bodies he took them for ground crew and not pilots. The nucleus of the group sat in a corner, mostly keeping to themselves, but a few of the men had ventured out on solo missions around the bar, hitting on attractive Arab girls or moving to the stairwell to head downstairs to the dance floor.

But the vast majority of the crowd in this room was clearly Syrian. Court found himself confused and fascinated by this. Here they were, within miles of rebel resistance pockets, and it appeared like life was going on without a care for these people. Around him a hundred people drank, smoked from hookahs, laughed and talked and flirted and joked, in the geographical center of so much horror.

Men, women, children were being bombed and starved and uprooted and slaughtered throughout the country—more than a half million dead in this nation in the past seven years—but in Old Town Damascus it was just another freewheeling Saturday night.

There was another surreal aspect of the moment for Court. This wasn't Afghanistan or Saudi Arabia or Pakistan, with strict moral codes enforced; this looked like a bar in Vegas or Chicago or Boston. There were no hijabs on the women here at Bar 80, and none of the men in view had long beards. There was a lot of jewelry and hair product on male and female alike, and the average age was below thirty.

Most of the places Court had visited in the Middle East had been a lot more conservative, but the vibe here in Damascus did remind him of the time he spent in Beirut, Lebanon, just seventy miles to the west.

But that was before Hezbollah took over and the party lights dimmed somewhat.

Saunders leaned over to him. "Right bunch of sorry bastards, we are."

Court cocked his head. "What do you mean?"

"Look around. Most of these Syrian blokes are soldiers, but they're havin' a laugh. Us mercs? We come to pound down drinks to keep the demons at bay. Warning you, Wade. You won't get much conversation around us."

"I'm not in Syria to make friends."

"Well then, you've come to the right place."

Saunders returned to his drink, and Court began scanning the crowd, slowly and carefully, with a new sense of purpose. To anyone paying attention to him, it would have looked like he was just another single guy looking for a girl to talk to, dance with, or take home.

But Court wasn't looking to hook up tonight. He was looking for a cell phone.

While he did this, Brunetti asked Saunders, the only fluent Arabic speaker at the table who also spoke English, to question Walid about the deployment to the north the following morning. Court could hear in Walid's voice that the alcohol was having an effect, even though he had just finished his second drink. The slurred Arabic was even harder to decipher than normal, but Saunders helpfully translated.

"He says something big's going on at a Russian special forces base near Palmyra in a couple days, so SAA is setting up a protective cordon. We're going to fill in gaps of the outer security ring to the east of the city . . . total

247

shit part of the country. Desert and rocks, is all, but there are some small towns along the M20 highway."

Court said, "Russian Spetsnaz can't protect themselves?"

Saunders relayed this to Walid, who answered back. Saunders said, "He thinks some generals or government officials are going to be visiting the base. No other reason the SAA would insist on installing a security cordon themselves around a Russian base."

Walid said something else, and Court could hear displeasure, almost despondence, in the militia captain's voice. Saunders said, "This fucker got out of goin' himself. He's staying back with brigade command in Babbila."

Court said, "He doesn't seem happy about it."

Saunders shook his head in disgust. "It's not because he likes to fight. No, he's pissed he'll miss out on what the Hawks will do when they take a town. They come back to base like they've spent the weekend at a bleedin' shopping mall."

Court made a face like he didn't understand, and off this look Saunders said, "Looting. The Desert Hawks are top-flight pillagers, but first they wait for blokes like us to clear the area."

Saunders said something to Walid, then drank the rest of the whiskey in his glass. He stood and turned to Court. "I told him not to worry. I'll bring him back some gold fillings, because everyone knows the Hawks send us KWA chaps in to commit the *real* atrocities." His face flashed a quick smile Court's way, but Court saw through it. Saunders was a haunted man.

He turned away and headed for the bar to get another drink, but called out as he walked, "I'm bringing back a bottle of Jack Daniel's."

CHAPTER 34

The five nondescript sedans were already running with drivers behind the wheels when Sebastian Drexler drove his rented Mercedes out of the evening rain and through the open doors of the large warehouse just off the grounds of Toussus-le-Noble Airport.

The airfield was just southwest of Paris, but more importantly it was only three kilometers northeast of where Henri Sauvage had determined that Bianca Medina was being kept, so Malik had rented the off-field storage facility to use as a safe house. His men had already outfitted it as a location where they could bring and hold Medina after the raid. If all went smoothly in Malik's plan, once Medina was in pocket they would fly a private aircraft into the airport; Malik would load Medina, Drexler, and some men for security aboard; and then they would all fly out. From there they would head to Serbia, far from where anyone was looking for the Spanish model. They would hold her in a safe house while they worked on getting documentation for Drexler and Bianca to go to Russia so they could finally travel back to Syria.

Malik had offered his plan to Drexler, and Drexler had agreed, although he had no desire to fly to Syria, Russia, or Serbia, or even to bring a living, breathing woman back to the warehouse by Toussus-le-Noble Airport.

But he'd go along with the plan tonight, and continue with the plan until Malik and his men left the operation behind so that Drexler could be alone with Bianca. At that point he would kill her and fake his own death at the same time, thereby slipping out of Shakira's grasp.

He anticipated sitting in a secluded cabin in the Swiss Alps within two or three days with a bottle of schnapps, his operation complete and his ties to Syria behind him, and he found it humorous that the dangerous assassin Malik would be left to answer for everything that went wrong on this entire operation.

Drexler climbed out of his Mercedes and saw Malik standing apart from his men and the five sedans, ready for a quick private meeting with the Swiss intelligence agent. As Drexler began walking over to the Syrian operative, it occurred to him that perhaps he should be worried that he and Malik were operating at cross purposes. He knew all about Malik's background. A former special forces soldier, he'd been recruited into the military intelligence service, then trained in assassination and demolitions in Iran by Iranian Quds Force commandos. After this he was sent to live in Europe under non-official cover, but he was handled by a senior Mukhabarat officer at the Syrian embassy in Paris. He and the thirteen men he commanded—all former military intelligence paramilitary officers trained in spycraft—were used by the Syrian regime, either here in France or anywhere in Europe where there was a need for dangerous covert operations.

Drexler himself had employed Malik's talents to assassinate men and women in Paris, Berlin, and Brussels over the past two years.

This op in Paris put Drexler in a precarious position, to be sure. He'd love to terminate Bianca Medina the second he saw her, but he imagined it would be difficult if not impossible to kill her during the raid; he couldn't let Malik or one of his men catch him in the act.

But even though bringing along the raid team of Syrian commandos hadn't been Drexler's idea—Ahmed Azzam himself had ordered the deployment of the European-based Syrian paramilitary assets—he assumed it would have been impossible to get to the woman at all without the added guns.

Drexler walked up to the Syrian commando team leader, the man who knew him only by his code name Eric. They did not shake hands. Instead, Malik held out a Beretta PT92 pistol encased in a leather holster. The Swiss operative took it, checked to make certain it was loaded and there was a round in the chamber, then tucked it into his waistband. He extended his hand again, and Malik gave him a silver snub-nosed revolver in an ankle holster. Drexler checked to make certain this weapon was loaded as well, and strapped it on his ankle. He also took the three extra loaded magazines for the Beretta and slipped them in the back pocket of his dark jeans.

Malik also gave Drexler a soft-armor Kevlar vest, capable of stopping handgun and submachine-gun rounds. The Swiss man had requested all these items from the Syrian, and Malik had come through.

As Drexler took off his jacket and donned his body armor, he saw the front passenger side of the white sedan open and a man unfold from the seat. He recognized Henri Sauvage instantly, because although they had never met in person, Drexler had been at first cultivating and then employing the police captain for two full years now, and the man's image, as well as his CV, were well known to him.

As Sauvage began walking towards them through the warehouse, with one of Malik's operatives close behind him, Drexler whispered to Malik, lest his voice echo, "He's been disarmed, I assume."

"Of course. And I've had a man with him constantly since this morning. He's told no one about tonight."

Malik had briefed Drexler by phone earlier about Sauvage's actions over the past few days. The man clearly wasn't in this for the money anymore. He was in this because of the fourteen men with guns standing around. It was a suboptimal influence mechanism for an intelligence officer to use over an agent, but Drexler hoped he wouldn't need the man's compliance for much longer. He figured he only needed to keep Sauvage around until they had the woman in pocket, and then he would be just as expendable as his three dead confederates.

Sauvage stopped in front of Drexler and Malik, but his focus was on the new man at the warehouse. "You're Eric, I take it."

Drexler extended a hand. "At your service."

Drexler could see the rage on the Frenchman's face, so he withdrew the hand.

Sauvage said, "To hell with you. To hell with every last one of you. You killed my partner. I'm not doing anything else for your fucked up cause."

251

Drexler noted that Henri Sauvage had grown a spine since Malik had told him he was surly but utterly docile. "This is a difficult time and I understand your anger. Let's just get through this evening and, as long as we achieve our objective, your obligation to us will be fulfilled."

Sauvage lit a cigarette now. "You don't hear so well, do you?"

Drexler sighed. "I hear the words. But I see into your soul. You want to live through this. Listen, *mon amie*. Your only job tonight is to stay behind the action, in case we don't get the woman. Tonight you will be safe, and sequestered from both danger and compromise. But I *will* require your presence."

Sauvage stared the man down for a long moment, then looked away with resignation. "Do I have a choice?"

"Everyone has a choice, but I think you would prefer doing what we ask rather than choosing what's behind the other door."

The Frenchman blew smoke into the night. "Tell me what's going to happen."

"Of course," Drexler said. "We will raid that property, but you will remain on the perimeter. In the event Mademoiselle Medina is not on the premises, we'll have to start back at square one, and we will need a high-ranking police officer here in the city for that. But if she's there, and if we get her, tomorrow you can wake up wealthy and safe, knowing you're finished working for me."

Sauvage shrugged. Drexler had obviously appeased him somewhat by his words. He said, "She's there. Along with at least five or six men."

Drexler smiled and looked at Malik. "Then my colleague and his associates should have no problems. Malik . . . consider this your show now."

The curly-haired Syrian waved to the five vehicles running their engines nearby. "We will board the cars and move to the predeployment locations. A member of the communications team will be dropped off on the north side of the FSEU safe house to disable the landline, and the other communications men will go to the west side, along with you, Monsieur Sauvage, for jamming operations. The assault team will infiltrate the woods on the south and western sides of the property by means of a private farmland access road that runs through it."

He looked at his watch. "It's eleven p.m. We will leave now to be in position to raid the home at midnight. Let's go."

Drexler, Sauvage, and Malik, along with the commandos standing around, climbed into the sedans, and all sixteen men rolled out of the warehouse and into the rain moments later. Other than Henri Sauvage, they were all armed, and other than Sebastian Drexler, they all thought they were on their way to rescue a woman for the purpose of returning her to Syria.

CHAPTER 35

In the center of the upbeat and raucous second floor of Bar 80 in Old Town Damascus, Court Gentry sat at a table made up of silent and dour men with a half-empty bottle of Jack Daniel's and a half-empty bottle of Old Bushmills in the center of it. Court wasn't drinking much himself; instead he focused his attention on a group of a half dozen young local men chatting up a gaggle of beautiful girls in their twenties at a table near the stairwell. The girls were only mildly amused by the attention, but the men seemed sure they were striking gold with their conversational skills.

Court had been on the hunt for a cell phone that would suit his needs for the last twenty minutes, which was why he had homed in on this particular group. He saw phones in the purses, hands, or pockets of everyone there, or on the table itself, and he recognized that if one of the men or women let their guard down, the table was close enough to the door to the stairwell that he thought he could push by, palm a device into his hand, and then slip away undetected.

But for now, he saw no obvious easy marks, so he kept scanning.

• • •

The evening wore on, the crowd thickened, and the men at Court's table kept drinking, though still, other than the Desert Hawks major, none of them appeared to be much affected by the alcohol. Walid was completely smashed now, and clearly he was an angry drunk, because he was telling Saunders a story in Arabic that involved the vast majority of curses Court knew in the language. The tale involved some battle he claimed to have taken part in, Court could tell, but he ignored the conversation and instead kept his head on a swivel, monitoring the actions of more than twenty people in the room. He looked at each person when they checked their phones, and he registered what kind of device they had. Court knew he could employ any phone in a pinch, simply by speaking in cached terms to Vincent Voland, but Bianca was going to have to pass over her physical home address, and Court would rather she didn't do that in the clear. No, he'd much prefer that the phone he grabbed had some sort of encrypted service on board so he could communicate freely. He knew all about the pros and cons of different common voice and text services, and he tried to profile the men and women in the bar to focus on those he deemed most likely to have such a service on their phone.

Court knew he also needed to know if the phone had an automatic lock screen. If so, he'd need one that had a passcode and not a thumbprint reader, and he'd need to determine the passcode, and this had led to more than one near miss in the past half hour.

Looking again at the table near the stairwell, he noticed a physically fit Arab man in his midtwenties in the group, and not only did he have a phone in a back pocket, but Court also noticed the unmistakable printing of a handgun slipped in his waistband in the small of his back under his formfitting shirt.

As Court looked on, the young man pulled out his phone and tapped in a four-digit code to unlock it. Court had long ago made a parlor game out of deciphering keypad entries by others through the process of their finger or thumb movements, and through this acquired skill he determined that the code on the iPhone was either 9191 or 8181.

He couldn't be certain till he tapped it out himself on the lock screen, but he was sure enough to give it a shot if the opportunity came.

The man looked at his phone for a few seconds, holding it with one hand while he drank a beer with the other, then locked the screen and put it down on the table.

One of the young Syrian's friends called him over to the bar to help him carry drinks back for the ladies. He stood up and began making his way through the crowd of people there, leaving his phone near the corner of the table.

Court knew this was the best opportunity he was going to get. He stood up and walked across the room, blading himself to get through the crowd quickly, and slid the phone off the table with one hand without breaking stride.

The dozen others sitting or standing close by never even noticed him pass.

. . .

Court had planned on going down to the downstairs bathroom to look over the phone, but he saw that the stairwell led up as well as down, so he headed upstairs. Seconds later he found himself on the roof of the two-story building, standing alone next to a large water tank. He figured he had no more than one or two minutes tops before the owner missed his phone, so he knew he had to work quickly.

The first thing he noticed about the device was that the owner was a member of a military unit. The screensaver was a photo of the young man in fatigues carrying an RPK machine gun and standing in front of a T-72 tank. The symbol on the man's uniform in the photo was a tiger, which told Court he was probably a member of the Tiger Forces, the regime special forces unit. This also explained the pistol under the man's shirt.

Court tapped 9191 onto the screen, and then he breathed a sigh of relief when the phone unlocked.

Court quickly scrolled through the apps on the smartphone, hoping there was no phone tracker software that could easily ping his location. To his relief he didn't find anything that could easily pinpoint him once the man realized his phone had been lifted, but to be extra thorough he went into the settings and disabled all the geolocating services. This added another barrier between anyone looking for this cell phone and its current location.

Then he scrolled through the apps on board the phone and was pleased to see he'd chosen his target wisely. The young soldier had installed a common app called TextSecure. This, Court knew, would work for his needs. It allowed encrypted voice and texts, so he'd be able to call Voland without too much concern about the communications being intercepted.

Court locked the screen, then stepped to the edge of the roof at the back of the building and looked down. A dingy cobblestone alleyway ran east and west, and a row of garbage cans sat just across the lane. The second-to-last can was open, and it was full of garbage.

Court tossed the phone underhanded; it sailed down through the dark and landed in the open can.

When Court returned to the second-story bar area, he saw he'd not given the Syrian soldier enough credit. It was clear the militiaman was already looking around for his cell phone. Further, it was obvious he was pissed off about his loss, and already suspicious that the device had been stolen.

A large group moved around the room together searching for the phone, the young girls all but forgotten. The men looked under chairs and on the bar, but they also began stopping people walking near their table or confronting bar patrons at other tables.

Court knew how to read a crowd, and he saw that this situation could quickly take a dark turn.

Within seconds the Tiger Forces soldier missing his device began upping his aggression, yelling at the girls at a nearby table, grabbing a passing server by the arm, and sticking an accusatory finger in the face of a man smoking a hookah at a couch against the back wall.

Court had slipped by the action unnoticed and was back at his table as if nothing was going on around him.

Another man in the Syrian soldier's group shouted at people over by the bar itself now, and another confronted both men and women at a table just next to where Court sat. The conversation was in Arabic and Court did not understand, but the tone was clearly hostile. The men spoke with the authority of military personnel, even though they were dressed for picking up girls and having an evening out with the guys, not in their uniforms.

The KWA men at Court's table noticed the commotion going on around the loud nightclub, and they all watched passively. Walid was too drunk to notice at all, still telling a story to the table, although it seemed only Saunders spoke Arabic well enough to understand him, and Saunders clearly was not listening now.

Court tracked the owner of the missing mobile phone as he made his way around the room for five more minutes, treating each patron he spoke with more harshly than the last. Finally a woman near the stairwell pointed over in Court's direction. She alone must have noticed him leave the room and then return. Immediately the soldier turned Court's way and stormed over, grabbing two of his friends as he approached the table of mercenaries.

He loomed over Court and said something; Court understood Arabic well enough to pick out the words "phone" and "take," but he pretended like he didn't understand a word.

Walid stood up on slightly wobbly legs and talked to the man a moment, then turned and spoke to Saunders. Saunders, in turn, looked to Court. "This asshole wants to know if you nicked his mobile. Walid told him you've been sittin' 'ere the whole time." Saunders flashed a hint of doubt when he said this, but he did not question Court.

A couple other men at the table backed up the assertion. It was apparent to Court that no one at the table had seen him leave the room, with the possible exception of Saunders, so there was no more suspicion on him than anyone else.

Walid and Saunders continued talking to the angry soldier, and Walid himself was getting pissed off about the exchange. The younger Syrian said something Court didn't understand, and then Saunders turned back to Court. "Bloody hell. All these guys are Qiwat al Nimr. Tiger Forces." Court knew that the man whose phone he'd taken had been a special forces soldier, but he hadn't known that the other nine or ten guys with him were part of the same group. Saunders had explained earlier in the day that the Tiger Forces unit of the Syrian Arab Army were bitter rivals of the Desert Hawks Brigade.

For an instant Court was worried about this turn of events, but he wanted to slip away from the bar for a few minutes to call Paris, so it very quickly occurred to him that nothing would serve his purposes right now like a good old-fashioned bar fight.

That said, he had no illusions that if a brawl did kick off, it would be anything like a normal bar fight. There was one inebriated Desert Hawks major and five foreign mercenaries against ten or fifteen Tigers paramilitary men. He saw that at least one guy in the mix had a pistol. He doubted any of the mercs here with him were armed, and if Walid *did* have a piece, in his inebriated state he was probably more of a danger to himself than anyone else.

It was clear to Court that a fistfight in a bar in a nation as wrecked as Syria wouldn't be the same as one in most other places. If it did come to blows around here, it probably would end with somebody getting killed.

And if a fight did start, it would help Court's cover if it happened organically. If he just picked up a chair and threw it at the Syrians now to instigate action, everyone in the room would point him out after the fact, he would be the least likely in the room to slip away, and the suspicions that would arise from this would threaten his entire cover and his operation here.

So he hoped a confrontation would start without him being the one identified with starting it.

And to that end, things looked like they were going his way. The Russians were up and heading over towards the commotion, with a couple of the Tigers in tow.

A big Russian stepped up to Court, and he spoke in English. "You take this guy's mobile phone?" It appeared one of the Tigers was a Russian speaker, and he wanted a translator he thought would be on the side of his friend missing the device.

Court stood from his chair, not aggressively but certainly not passively. A group of a dozen Russians and Syrian special forces men stood around the KWA table now, so all the other KWA men at the table stood up, ready to defend themselves if necessary.

Court lifted his shirt and turned around, exposing his bare stomach and back. In English he said, "This guy is full of shit. I don't have his phone."

The Russian spoke in Russian to the Syrian special forces man, Walid butted in with a comment of his own, and several Arab men began shouting at Walid.

Court stepped forward a half step, and the big Russian saw it as a provocation. He put a hand out and shoved Court in the chest. It was an aggressive move, but it didn't constitute the opening to a brawl. Court realized if he started slinging punches it would be obvious he was the one who started the fight, and if that happened, it would further single him out among the other patrons in the bar.

Walid and the Tiger soldier whose phone was now in a garbage can in the back alley began yelling at each other again, and the KWA men had more or less squared off against the Russians. Brunetti—the Argentine—put his finger in the face of another Syrian and began threatening him in Spanish that was understood by no one else in the room save for Court.

The semispontaneous fight Court had been hoping for was gathering steam. But none of the confrontations going on in the room had crossed the line to the jumping-off point where all the testosterone present would lead to the massive melee he was looking for.

An idea came to Court that he hoped might just make the fight break out without him being the one to throw the first punch. The big Russian—still looming over him—looked like he was about to turn around and go back to his seat, so Court addressed him in Russian.

"My friend here with the Desert Hawks thinks you Russian Air Force guys are pussies because you are afraid to fight on the ground like men."

The man looked at Court cockeyed. Court's mastery of Russian wasn't complete, but he'd clearly gotten his idea across. The Russian turned to Walid and pointed angrily but he spoke to Court in Russian. "Take this militia loser out of here before we beat his ass." Court put his hands up, as if to say *Okay*, and he smiled, and the Russian Air Force soldier glared a moment more before looking back to his friends. The Tiger Forces men seemed to think the drama was over, so they, too, seemed to relax their guard a little.

But Court turned back to Walid, and as he did he dropped his smile and adopted an expression of astonishment.

Walid saw the look on the Westerner, and he'd heard Court speak to the Russian in his own language.

In Arabic, Walid asked, "What did he say?" He looked to Saunders for the answer, but Court understood the question, and he replied in Arabic.

"Something in Russian. Just talk. Forget it."

But all Court's facial cues were controlled to give the impression the man had said something horrible while pointing to Walid. Not satisfied with Court's answer, the Syrian major shouted now. "What did he say?"

The Syrian men turned back towards the table with the mercs and the Desert Hawks officer.

Court took a brief moment to weigh his options. He had been in the

Middle East many times with the Goon Squad years ago, and back then he and the guys had a running tally of all the creative ways people swear in Arabic. Court's personal favorite was *Khalil aire wa kloo*, which meant "Pickle my dick and eat it." But for purposes of sending Walid over the edge right now, he decided to take a bigger tool out of his toolbox. "He said, '*Yelan el kees hali khalakak*.'"

Court knew there *might* have been a ruder phrase to an Arabic man than "Curse the pussy that made you," but if there was, he sure couldn't imagine it.

Walid's eyes narrowed, and then they flashed over to the Russian. The big Russian saw the anger, and he froze to evaluate the Arab's look. The special forces soldier missing his phone turned to the Russian in surprise, not having heard what the Russian had said but hearing Court's translation over the music.

Other Arabic speakers near Court's table gasped.

It was as if all the air in the room had been sucked away in a breath.

And then, in the center of nearly twenty angry men, Walid was the first to move.

With a jolting and frantic motion, he reached behind his back, under his shirt, and he pulled out a gun.

CHAPTER 36

Court hadn't known that Walid was in possession of a firearm, which meant the major had done a good job concealing it, both from Court and from the bouncer downstairs. Apparently the other contractors also were clueless, because they all reacted with shock and surprise.

Broz was closest to Walid, and he saw the pistol as the militiaman swung it up towards the Russian. The Croatian's reflexes were damn good, but consistent with the principle that action beats reaction, all he could do was stick a hand out for the gun as the Syrian leveled it at the Russian.

Walid got a shot off but managed to miss a room full of people and hit the ceiling. Broz disarmed Walid with a shoulder shove and a pull of the weapon, but not before the Tiger Forces man who had been looking for his phone pulled his own pistol.

Anders, the Dutch KWA man, kicked a chair across the floor and it slammed into the Tiger's legs, knocking him forward. His weapon went off before he had it leveled, and the round struck the table between Saunders and Brunetti, and by now all the women in the bar and half the men had either hit the deck or begun running for the exit. The other half of the patrons, including all the Russians and the Syrian Tigers, had enough training to know better than to turn away from a gun when it was in range of their backs, so some of the men attacked in the direction of Broz to get the pistol he'd yanked from Walid, and the others began swinging at what they perceived to be the greatest threat within reach.

The bar fight that Court wanted so badly had begun, but he was already regretting it.

The big Russian was only four feet away from Court, and he turned to grab a vodka bottle off a table behind him. On Court's right Saunders, Brunetti, and Anders began mixing it up with a group of Syrians. Court counted three Russians grabbing bar stools and coming his way, while Broz swung the pistol he'd pulled from Major Walid up towards the Tiger Forces man who, while now flat on the ground, still had his gun raised.

But the gun in the hands of the man on the floor was accidentally kicked away by a Syrian who tripped and fell on his back, and at the same time, Broz was tackled hard from the right.

The weapon the KWA contractor held skidded away from him and across the floor.

Court ducked a flying bar stool, deflected the swing of the vodka bottle by the big Russian who'd accosted him, and fired a hard forearm into the man's trachea, temporarily collapsing the man's windpipe and dropping him to the ground. To his right Saunders had been tackled by a Syrian, and together he and his attacker rolled over the table where Court and the KWA men had been sitting.

Brunetti threw a beer bottle that hit a Syrian holding a chair over his head, and Anders blocked a hook from a Russian and countered it with a punch to the stomach and an elbow uppercut to the jaw.

As Court moved towards one of the pistols on the ground, he couldn't help but notice that this bar fight had devolved into an every-man-for-himself situation on the part of the KWA contractors; the mercs weren't engaged in helping one another but instead were either fighting for the pleasure of it or fighting to beat back the men attacking them.

The camaraderie Court had known while working on a paramilitary team in the CIA or around other civilian security contractors over the years was nowhere in sight with these mercs.

The armed bouncer from downstairs came through the stairwell with a gun in his hand and was immediately set upon by a pair of Russian soldiers, who both decked him and hit him with a beer bottle, sending him crawling out of the room and back down the stairs.

Court blocked a spinning bar stool with a chair, and then he slung the chair fifteen feet across the center of the room, where it slammed into the back and head of a man kneeling to pick up one of the two loose firearms on the floor. The man went down hard after taking the hit, but the attacker with the bar stool got a second swing in, and Court could only fire an arm up to absorb it.

The blow caused Court to stumble ten feet to his left, all the way over to the windows that looked out to the street in front of the club. The Russian who hit Court charged again, but this time the American ducked the swinging bar stool, causing the man to spin with the momentum. Court used the opportunity to grab him from behind, and he slammed him into the wall between the windows.

The man crashed face-first against the bricks, and the bar stool left his grasp and slammed hard against the window, sending fissures across the one-meter-by-two-meter pane.

The Russian was dazed but not out of it. Court grabbed him by the head and tried to drive him again into the wall, but the man spun and caught Court in a bear hug and lifted his feet off the ground for an instant, nearly toppling him. An elbow into the eye of the Russian short-circuited his offensive move, and while he recovered from the stunning blow, Court separated himself enough to deliver a heel kick to the crotch. He spun back around and sent a knee hard to the falling man's nose.

The knee sent the man's head snapping back as he fell backwards, and it slammed into the cracked windowpane, shattering it outright.

As soon as the sounds of breaking glass dissipated, Court could hear sirens outside in the street. It sounded like several emergency vehicles were just pulling up out front. This would mean guns and truncheons and handcuffs and express rides to jail, and Court didn't want to hang around for any of that.

As the Russian dropped onto his face and out of the fight, Court turned around to see Saunders pounding a Syrian on the floor behind the table, and Anders and Broz kick-stomping the Tiger Forces soldier whose phone Court had stolen. Brunetti was bleeding from the head and face, standing in the middle of the room looking for another challenger, and Walid had miraculously staggered closer to the stairwell without taking a beating from anyone involved in the fight.

Court saw him there, legs unsteady, with the half-empty bottle of Jack Daniel's in his hand. He wasn't wielding the bottle as a weapon; he was holding it up to his mouth to take another swig.

Court had missed a Syrian on the floor on the far side of the table till the man pulled himself back to his feet just three feet from where Court stood. The soldier lunged at Court, but the American's reflexes were good enough to wristlock the man's hand, spin behind him, and yank him pitilessly back down to the floor onto his back, where he kicked the man in the head, knocking him unconscious.

Quickly Court scanned around the room for the loose pistols; he saw one on the floor and the other in the hands of a bartender, who picked the weapon up and took it behind the bar, as if to protect his bar against any attempts to steal the booze.

Court started again for the one gun he could spot on the floor, but a young bearded Syrian got to it first. He lifted it into the air and fired a single round over his head, bringing the fighting around the room to an immediate halt.

From the direction of the stairwell Court heard the whistles, the fresh shouting, the sounds of voices that could have only come from police or soldiers here to break up the fight and break the heads of anyone who resisted.

The armed man dropped the pistol, but a Russian standing near the stairwell threw a punch at the first uniformed officer through the door.

Court knew there would be a lot more cops behind that one, so he decided to make a break for it. He still planned on using the fight as a means to slip out to make a call, so he hustled to the shattered window and climbed out, careful to avoid lacerating himself in the process. He put his feet on the window's ledge and looked down, but just as he did so he heard the police in the room behind him. A large commercial window unit air conditioner was in the next window, and he decided that if it was braced from the bottom, it *should* support his weight. He climbed over and up onto it quickly, shielding himself from being seen from inside the second floor.

He saw no fast way down to the ground floor other than a straight drop of twelve feet. It was just sidewalk below, so he decided against this approach. Instead he lay down on his stomach on the window unit, and it creaked and squeaked against the strain. Feeling down below it he was happy to find braces that led at 45-degree angles to anchor into the wall of the building, and he held on to one of these, lowered himself off the unit, and swung down below it.

With his feet just three feet off the ground now, he dropped the rest of the way onto the sidewalk. Here dozens of men and women—patrons of the bar, mostly—stood around. Parked in the street not far away, Court saw two Toyota Hilux pickup trucks bearing the symbol of the NDF, the National Forces, the pro-government militia that had been co-opted as a secondary law enforcement entity here in the police state of Damascus. The vehicles seemed to be unmanned, and Court thought about stealing one to get away, but since there were people watching him right now, and since the phone he'd gone through so much to get was still sitting in the garbage behind the disco, he decided to go for that instead.

Court entered the front door of Bar 80 now, heading to the back exit. There were a surprising number of patrons still inside, idiots all, Court told himself, and the police and NDF were all over the place. With Court's dark hair, beard, and civilian clothing, he didn't stick out in the crowd, so he just moved through, heading to the back exit so he could get to the alley.

As he passed the stairwell, a group of police and NDF descended, with Saunders at their center. He was handcuffed, his upper lip was fat, the buttons of his shirt had been ripped off, and sweat mixed with a little smeared blood on his bald head. The Brit, who had been cursing out the cops in Arabic, saw the man he knew as Wade and switched into English.

"You lucky prick, how did they miss you?"

Court kept walking, but gave the man a wink.

"Find Walid and get back to base. Don't go alone. You'll get popped at a checkpoint if you try. We'll be out in a few hours, but Brunetti's got 'imself a busted nose."

Court nodded but kept walking towards the back; he didn't want the cops to pay any attention to him.

At the back door he turned around and looked towards the stairs. Brunetti, Anders, and Broz all were being led out in restraints by NDF and police, along with Russians and even Syrian Tiger Forces soldiers.

Court was alone.

He exited the back door, stepped into the alley, and walked over to the garbage can. The phone was still there, lying on a pile of beer bottles. He plucked it out, wiped it on the leg of his cargo pants, and then began running off, back in the direction of Walid's car.

He realized the opportunity he had now. This was no longer about finding five minutes to make a phone call before deploying to another part of the nation tomorrow.

Instead, Court knew he had to go for the baby. *Right* now.

No . . . this wasn't a perfect situation . . . Far from it. But he would have to make it work.

CHAPTER 37

Court was astonished to find Walid in the parking lot by his car, still holding the bottle of Jack Daniel's in his hand. The Desert Hawks officer had apparently staggered out of the club with the booze, and while he was obviously shitfaced drunk, Court determined he was not drunk enough to suit Court's purposes.

Together both men took a swig out of the bottle, and they spent a few seconds talking about the fight that had just taken place. Court's sudden rudimentary Arabic surprised the major. Walid took a second swig of the booze, and then Court directed him to the front passenger seat of the car.

Court climbed behind the wheel, took the keys from a compliant Walid, and then began driving west through Old Town Damascus.

After less than a minute on the road, however, Walid looked out the windshield, then told Court in slurred Arabic that he was going the wrong way. In response Court encouraged him to drink some more whiskey. Walid did so, and as soon as he lowered the bottle, Court removed his own seat belt, then carefully shifted in his seat. He turned his body to the side so he could face Walid and drive at the same time with his left hand. Walid noticed the odd positioning, and he looked at Court with dopey, tired, and just slightly puzzled eyes.

"What are you doing?"

Court answered by firing a blazing right jab out, connecting with

Walid's left eye socket and knocking him flat against the passenger window. The big man went unconscious, then slumped forward, hanging there by his seat belt.

. . .

A minute later, Court pulled into a dark parking lot at the edge of the Old Town. Here he climbed out, then looked under the dashboard of the car, using the light of the mobile phone to help him. He began identifying fuses that led to different lights in the vehicle. He pulled out the fuses for the rear lights and the brake lights until the lights went out when he tried to deploy them, but he left the fuses barely in place so he could unplug them easily. Righting himself in the driver's seat, he leaned down and indexed the correct fuses so he could both disconnect and reconnect them without looking.

He spilled a little of the Jack Daniel's on the major's tunic and put the bottle in the unconscious man's right hand. He pulled Walid's head back to where he didn't look completely out of it, and when the drunk man's head drooped forward again, Court lowered the angle of his seatback a few degrees so that his head would stay up.

Court looked at the man through the window with the door closed. He hoped if he got stopped at a checkpoint he could talk his way through with a story about how the major had passed out and Court was taking him home.

This was *not* a good plan, Court knew, but he didn't know what else he could do.

He got back on the road, and while he drove, he opened the secure communications app on the cell phone and dialed a long number. It took a full minute for the call to go through, but when it did, Vincent Voland answered quickly.

Court said, "It's me. I'm here."

"In Damascus? Already?"

"Yep."

"Incredible. Any problems?"

"Nothing *but* problems. Problems all over the fucking place, as a matter of fact. But I made it, I'm operational, and I need to talk to Bianca, now."

"Of course. I'm heading downstairs to her room to put her on the phone."

Court drove the Hyundai one-handed, holding the phone to his ear with the other. While he waited he asked, "Any sign of Drexler?"

"No sign at all, but that means nothing. He's coming. I feel it in my bones."

"Have you beefed up security there at the house?"

"*Oui*. We are ready should he bring associates."

Court could only hope Voland had the situation in hand up there, because Court had more than his share of problems of his own down here.

Seconds later Bianca came on the line. She had a hopeful sound to her voice, which buoyed Court to hear. "Is it you?"

"It's me. I'm in Damascus."

"I did not think I would ever hear from you again."

"No time to talk. I need your address, and I need you to tell me the best way to get to your place."

"Of course. Where are you, exactly?"

"I'm leaving Old Town, heading west, towards Mezzeh. I'm going for Jamal right now."

"*Now*? You . . . you *can't* be on the road at this time of night! They'll spot you."

"Unfortunately, this is something I can't take care of on my lunch hour tomorrow."

Court saw a line of brake lights on the road ahead, and he worried it might indicate a checkpoint. He scanned around quickly for some way to turn off, and he looked down at the map on the phone for help, as well.

He slowed and took a left turn down a darkened side street. This led him to the south, and on the phone he saw he could pick up an east/west street that would put him back on course.

Bianca spoke through the speakerphone. "Hello? Are you there?"

"I'm here."

"Please listen to me." He could hear the worry in her voice. "I drive at night from Old Town and must pass through several roadblocks. My security detail gets me through, but who's going to get *you* through without them catching you?"

Court turned and looked at the passed-out militia major slumped against the passenger door next to him. "Let me worry about that," he said, but the truth was he was *very* worried about that.

"What street are you on?"

The street signs were in Arabic and English, and Court rolled past an intersection with his eyes on the signs. "I'm on Fawaz al Laham."

"There is a checkpoint on Fawaz al Laham where it turns into Omar bin Abdulaziz!"

Court made another turn to the south that took him down a quiet street with tall apartment buildings on both sides. He gave her the name and she said, "No checkpoints, but that won't get you to my house. I live in Mezzeh district in the Western Villas neighborhood. You'll have to turn around."

"Shit. Okay, I'm going to keep picking my way west, and I'll tell you what I see. Get Voland to pull up a map on a computer or a phone, and you can talk me to your neighborhood."

In under a minute Voland relayed that he had his computer open to an interactive map. "All right," Bianca said, "I am ready. The good news is I know where the checkpoints are, but the bad news is that to get into my neighborhood, you have to pass a guard shack and gates. I live on Zaid bin al-Khattab, number thirty-six."

Bianca was adamant that he should not drive all the way into her neighborhood. She claimed there would be a large checkpoint and security officers patrolling in a truck within a few blocks of where she lived, so she convinced him to go to a less active neighborhood a kilometer away and use the night to his advantage to close on the property.

She spent several minutes giving relative details of her home, and while she talked Court listened, but he also focused on avoiding any roadblocks, busy intersections where he might be spotted, or major thoroughfares.

It was slow going, but he kept heading to the west.

Minutes later he found a place to park up a hill from her home. Over the sound of a snoring Walid, Court asked Bianca more questions about the walls, windows, guards, neighbors, vehicles on the street, and police and military presence in the area. He committed it all to memory and tried to think of any possible information he might need in the next couple hours.

When Court had exhausted all his questions about the property, the personnel, and the area around it, he changed focus. "Tell me about your situation there."

"I'm still in the room in the basement, but Rima is coming down and talking to me two times a day."

Court imagined there was some indoctrination or deprogramming going on during those talks, but he didn't bring it up.

"How many guards does Voland have around you?"

"I have no idea. I saw some European men today, two or three of them, but there might be more. They had guns."

He wished he knew more about just what Voland and the Halabys were doing to protect Bianca, but he had no time to dig into the matter further.

Court said, "Tell me something that only you and Yasmin know so I can establish to her that you sent me."

Bianca thought of something, told Court, then said, "If she refuses to go with you, call me and I'll talk to her."

Court had no illusions that he would be able to make phone calls while in the house confronting Yasmin; he had to just hope like hell he could convince her to comply. If not he figured he'd tie and gag her, throw her in a closet, and leave her for the security men to sort out the next morning.

Bianca said, "Good luck. Please hug and kiss Jamal for me when you see him and tell him his mommy misses him."

"This ain't the movies."

"I'm sorry?"

"Let me talk to Voland."

Court expected Voland to come back on the line, but instead Rima Halaby's voice crackled over the connection. "Sir, I know you don't want to use any of my connections, but I *must* give you the name of someone there in the city who can be a great help to you if you have any difficulties."

"You don't know that this person is not compromised."

"He's been living in the capital for years while helping us move aid to the rebels from abroad. If his actions were known to the authorities, there is no chance he wouldn't have been thrown in Saydnaya Prison long ago.

"He is a surgeon at a regime hospital. He spends his days saving the lives and limbs of young soldiers, but he knows what's going on in other parts of the nation, and he refuses to turn his back on any Syrian in need. He's helped relief agencies get supplies into the war zones in the north, and he's saved thousands of lives by his actions. He is a good man . . . and if you tell him we sent you, he will help you in any way he can." She then gave him the address and phone number of the doctor. Court had to commit both to memory.

"Are you in contact with him?" Court asked.

Rima replied, "I haven't spoken to him directly in two years. But I am able to get messages to him."

"Do not reach out to him about me. If I get desperate, I'll know where to find him."

Court spoke with Voland a moment more, and then he hung up.

. . .

In the dark parking garage he went through Walid's car quickly. He found the backpack the major had put his uniform in when he changed into civilian clothes outside Bar 80, and while Walid was a much thicker man than Court, Court knew the uniform would give him at least a momentary advantage when walking through Bianca Medina's neighborhood. He quickly dressed in the Hawks Brigade uniform and put his own boots back on, leaving Walid's boots in the trunk of the Hyundai.

In the trunk he also found Walid's emergency bag, set up for if the major was caught off base during a terror attack or civil strife. It was filled with food, water, and medical supplies, as well as other items.

From the bag Court took a pair of binoculars, a flashlight, and a long but cheaply built fixed-blade knife in a sheath.

Then he went around to the passenger side and pulled Walid himself out of the car. He tied the unconscious man's hands behind his back with rope pulled from the emergency bag, then hogtied his hands to his ankles and gagged him. Court then dragged and hefted the big man from the passenger seat and rolled him into the trunk of the car.

He closed the trunk lid on the major, put the extra items into the uniform backpack, and threw it onto his shoulder.

At one a.m. he began walking off through the neighborhood.

CHAPTER 38

Captain Henri Sauvage wanted to smoke, but the Syrian communications team working around him forbade it. The tension was high here on the dark wet country road in the center of the woods, so Sauvage didn't know how he was going to survive without a cigarette. But he didn't press the issue; the Syrians were dangerous-looking men with intense, angry demeanors, their hands never far away from the submachine guns under their leather jackets or the small hooked knives in the sheaths near their belt buckles.

The two men here with Sauvage were tasked with using the big heavy jamming equipment in the car to kill the cell phone and Internet traffic in the area. Another man was on a telephone pole on the northern side of the property, waiting for the cue from Malik to cut the hard lines into the house.

In front of Sauvage six more men, all dressed in dark clothing, moved off through the thick trees, separating as they walked through the rainy night. Drexler was at the center of the group, picking through the foliage next to Malik, and both men were easy to distinguish because, unlike the others, they wielded pistols.

When they fully disappeared from view through the dark and the woods, Sauvage leaned back against the white sedan. As the two Syrians worked on laptops on the hood, the Frenchman's only job was to sit here and wait.

Sauvage told himself this would all be over soon, but he didn't really believe it.

This event was going to be big and loud, he was certain. An outcome that involved him staying both alive and out of prison was getting harder and harder to imagine.

. . .

One hundred meters to the east, Sebastian Drexler adjusted the night vision optics over his eyes and moved along with the rest of the Syrian commando force.

He'd been on special forces raids in a half dozen African and Middle Eastern countries over his career, usually without night vision, but always with a weapon and surrounded by paramilitary forces that rushed through the desert, jungle, urban center, or grassy plains towards some objective. From this expertise he'd determined that these Syrians were unquestionably well trained. Even with the fuzzy, two-dimensional image afforded by the night vision, they were able to negotiate their way adroitly through the thick flora, they kept their separation from one another, and they advanced on the target location in near-complete silence.

Five more Syrians would be making their way through the woods around the southern end of the property, with the objective of hitting the farmhouse on the front side. The communications team, along with Sauvage, was also ready to move vehicles around to the front of the house or even to provide a follow-on attacking force if the situation called for it.

Drexler struggled to keep up with the Syrian commandos, but he knew he needed to exert his authority over all aspects of this operation. Malik was the epitome of an alpha male, and if Drexler backed off at all, Malik would walk all over him. If that happened, he'd lose his chance at achieving his true objective here.

He did not want or need a large battle this evening. Too much noise would bring a lot of law enforcement, and that would make flying out of Paris tomorrow difficult if not impossible. If he could get out of here with the woman without this turning into a loud and flashy massacre, then he could more easily get out of France and get to Serbia, where he'd eventually be free of the Syrian GIS men and have the time, space, and opportunity he needed to take care of Bianca Medina.

. . .

After moving through the trees for ten minutes, Malik called a halt over his radio, and the line of men stopped as one. Malik and Drexler picked their way forward carefully until they came to the edge of the woods.

Sebastian Drexler saw the back of the French country estate now. It was completely enshrouded in darkness, with the windows blacked out and all the external lighting extinguished. But even though it was sprinkling and overcast, the house could not hide from the night vision goggles, which pulled the tiny amount of ambient light from the stars above and enhanced it. The home appeared as a large, barely distinguishable green haze, but soon movement caught the attention of Malik and Drexler both. A pair of men stood on a patio; they held short-barreled weapons and shifted from one foot to another, bored and unaware of the danger in the woods one hundred meters from their position.

As Drexler looked on, a white-haired man stepped outside and spoke with the two guards for a moment.

Drexler reached over to Malik. "Hand me your five-power night vision binoculars."

Malik did so, and Drexler swiveled his unenhanced goggles up on his forehead so he could bring the binos to his eyes.

He looked at the white-haired man for some time through the night vision binoculars. Slowly, a smile widened on Drexler's face. "Vincent Voland is here."

"Yes. We know." Malik looked at Drexler. "You two know each other?"

"We've never met, but I know who he is. An ex–French intelligence man, both foreign and domestic. He's been after me for years. Tonight he'll get his wish to see me up close. Doubtful the event will go as he had dreamed it might."

Malik took the binos back and looked through them himself. "He won't see you up close. We're not here for you to participate in some old feud. We're here to rescue the girl, and then we leave."

"Believe me, I know exactly why we are here," Drexler replied.

Malik took his eyes out of his binoculars and looked at Drexler, but he made no reply. He looked again through the night vision. After a few seconds, the silver-haired man by the pool turned and stepped back into the house.

Malik radioed his communications team and ordered them to begin jamming operations in the area. He then brought two members of his team forward and whispered to Drexler, "I'm sending a pair of men closer to eliminate the rear sentries silently. They'll use knives. We need to be ready to advance quickly when this is done."

"How are your men going to get across one hundred meters of open ground? It's dark, but it's not *that* dark."

"They'll low-crawl. It will take a half hour, and I'll have sharpshooters ready to drop the guards if my men are spotted. That will not happen quietly, so in that case, we need to be prepared to attack the house from right here."

Drexler didn't want to attack the Syrian expat safe house from here; it would be noisy and exponentially more dangerous to do so. And he knew a gunfight would bring authorities into the area, and that could waylay his plan to reach Bianca Medina.

But the fact that Vincent Voland was at the property now gave him a new idea.

He said, "No. Tell your men to wait."

"Wait for *what*?"

"For me to negotiate the terms of Voland's surrender."

Drexler removed the holstered Beretta from inside his jacket and put it down on the ground. He removed the revolver from his ankle and the extra magazines and a folding knife from his jacket. He took off his night vision goggles and stacked them with the other items. He then pulled out a tiny tactical flashlight from his pocket. Turning it on, he stood and began walking across the back lawn alone.

Malik called out to him in a whisper. "What the *fuck* are you doing?"

Drexler ignored him.

277

CHAPTER 39

Court had wanted high ground that would give him a good view of the movements inside Bianca Medina's walled property, and he found it by heading up a hill to the east of her neighborhood, entering the open parking lot of a pool and fountain supply store, and climbing the wall of the building by using hand- and footholds afforded by a stone planter, a PVC pipe protecting electrical wiring, and a wooden sign.

Court was a nimble climber, and in seconds he was kneeling on the roof, Walid's binos in his hands, looking some four hundred yards down the hill. Past a mosque, past an upscale pizza parlor, and past several other private homes, he could see right into the gated rear grounds of Bianca's walled property. From his vantage point there were areas within her property he could not see, but the entire back half of the compound—including a tiled swimming pool, the garden around it, and the back windows of the large, two-story home—was in view.

The villa had Mediterranean architecture and was built in a U-court shape, with wings extending back perpendicularly to the main house on both sides, a courtyard in the center, and a high wall in back that closed off the courtyard.

There was no question that it was a nice residence, but considering that the man paying the bills for the place was the most powerful and wealthy man in the nation, it wasn't all that ostentatious. All around in the neighborhood were dozens of properties of similar size and luxury.

Court knew that Ahmed crafted everything towards Shakira not finding out about Bianca and the baby, so even though Bianca had been living in plain sight here, Ahmed wasn't going to have her living in a home so grandiose it invited special scrutiny from the neighbors.

Through his glass Court saw a single guard on the flat roof of the villa sitting on a chair on the eastern side and facing the street in front of the property and the short circular driveway to it. The large court area in back seemed to be unguarded, but Court suspected there would be cameras and motion detectors.

After a minute of searching he saw a patrolling guard with a flashlight and a short-barreled weapon with a folded wire stock walking slowly around the grounds.

Nope, Court said to himself. *No motion detectors to worry about.*

He'd asked Bianca about the security force, and she'd said nothing about a patrolling sentry. Court hoped this was the only way Azzam had beefed up the security of the residence in the past few days.

It would be tough to get in, but it didn't look like it would be much tougher than the hundred other buildings Court had infiltrated in his career.

Court continued scanning the scene over and over, back and forth with the binos. Softly to himself on the rooftop he said, "What am I missing?"

There *had* to be another level to the security. Ahmed Azzam knew Bianca was missing up in France, and he also knew this was where her son, Ahmed's son, was being kept. Because of matters out of his full control, Ahmed could not risk moving Jamal, but even if Ahmed trusted Bianca implicitly, Court couldn't believe for an instant the one stationary guard, who looked as relaxed as he could be, plus another bored guy roving the grounds would be the full measure of the external security set up here.

"Where *are* you?"

Through the binoculars he scanned the property once more, then widened his search to the streets nearby.

And now he had his answer.

Bianca had warned there would be security at the front gate of the neighborhood, but scanning around inside, Court saw vehicles of the NDF, the National Defence Forces.

Three parked NDF trucks in all. It could easily mean fifteen armed militiamen. All within two hundred yards of the front door of Bianca's house. This was why the regular security force had relaxed its guard despite the heightened threat to the location.

The neighborhood was protected, the actual block Medina lived on was protected, the front gate of her property was protected, and the grounds were protected, albeit by only a couple of goons who realized they were the fourth ring in from danger, and therefore probably assumed they would be well aware of any threats long before the grounds were breached.

And Court figured it would be safe to assume there would be security men inside the home, as well.

He focused on the closest National Defence Forces unit, parked in a military SUV ahead and on Court's right, equidistant between himself and Bianca's home. Through his binos he saw three men standing by the vehicle, all with rifles slung on their shoulders. He figured these guys had no idea they were here protecting one particular home; they'd just been sent to an intersection, likely night after night after night, and although he was certain their leadership read them the riot act about remaining vigilant, it was human nature to let one's guard down as the hours and days began adding up.

He figured if he could get over the fence into the gated neighborhood, he could probably get close enough to take these bozos out without making too much noise.

But maybe he didn't have to. He looked down to the uniform he wore, and compared it to the uniform worn by the NDF men. Other than some extra patches on the shoulders of the Desert Hawks Brigade tunic and a slightly more involved camo pattern, the tunic and pants looked virtually the same. The NDF men had black berets, and Major Walid had left the base with only an olive green baseball cap in the back pocket of his trousers, but Court figured his own dark hair, and his short beard that looked just like the short beards worn by a third of the men in their twenties and thirties around here, along with his "I know what I'm doing" attitude, would get him close to the compound, especially if he moved outside the glow of the electric lights of the streets in the neighborhood.

Court took another minute to plot his approach through the streets, alleys, commercial spaces, and residential property between himself and Bianca's home near the bottom of the hill, then climbed down from the pool and fountain shop.

He muttered to himself as he descended. "Okay, Gentry. Time to steal a baby."

CHAPTER 40

Former French Foreign Legionnaires Boyer and Novak stood on the rear steps of the farmhouse outside Paris with their Heckler & Koch MP5 subguns held on their shoulders at the ready, their barrels aiming to a figure approaching from the woodline. In the distance the single flashlight bobbed and jittered as it closed, a man clearly walking behind it.

Boyer said, "Call it in to the others."

As Novak radioed Campbell and Laghari at the front of the house, warning them to be ready, the door to the hearth room off the farmhouse opened behind them. Boyer chanced a look back, and he saw Tarek Halaby standing there in corduroy pants and a dark cardigan, his eyes on the light closing on the house from the back lawn.

His voice revealed his concern. "Who is that?"

In French, Boyer answered, "We don't know. But if he tries anything, he dies."

When the light was just forty yards away, Boyer called out in English, "Stop where you are."

The light stopped moving, and then it clicked off. A voice in French replied, "I am unarmed. I will comply with all your orders, monsieurs."

The two men illuminated the figure with their weapon lights. The man covered his face and eyes with his hands to block it from his eyes.

"This could be a trick," Tarek said, and this annoyed Boyer, who hadn't spent the vast majority of his fifty-five years in third-world hell-holes just so he could be told how to do his job by a surgeon with an address on the Left Bank of Paris. Still, Halaby was the client, so Boyer just said, "Go back inside, Doctor. We'll search him and bring him to you for questioning."

Halaby did as instructed, shutting the door behind him.

Novak called out to the man in the light now. "Turn around and step backwards with your hands raised."

The figure obeyed, but as he stepped up a gentle slope in the grass and through a waist-high hedge, he looked back in the direction of the two men holding guns on him.

"Turn back around!" ordered Boyer.

But the man only halfway turned, and he stopped moving. After a moment, he called out. "Paul? Paul Boyer? Is that you?"

Boyer looked to Novak, who looked back to Boyer. The Frenchman said, "Who the fuck is asking?"

The man with his hands raised laughed loud enough to be heard across the patio. "What are the chances, my friend? It's me. Sebastian. We worked together in Malawi. Again in Entebbe. Not so many years ago."

Boyer lowered his weapon. "Drexler?"

"In the flesh. As I said, I'm unarmed, so if you would do me the courtesy of not shooting me, I would greatly appreciate it."

Boyer looked to Novak now but kept his gun up and on Drexler. "Go check him out. And be careful . . . he's a sly fox."

Drexler heard this, and he chuckled in the dark. "How's that exquisite wife of yours, Paul?"

"She left me. Married a Kenyan government minister."

"Never could stand that bitch, if you don't mind my saying."

"Not in the least. How've you been, Drex?"

. . .

Tarek Halaby stood in the hearth room at the back of the house, his hands on his hips, as Sebastian Drexler was brought inside by the two ex-Legionnaires. Novak returned to the rear grounds, but Boyer remained behind Drexler, his weapon low, but ready to raise it in a hurry if necessary.

Tarek spoke to the prisoner. "Do you speak French?"

"I do, Doctor. In fact, you and I have spoken before. On the phone the other day."

Tarek's eyes widened. "Eric?"

"Correct."

"Why are you here?"

Drexler said, "With apologies and with respect, I will speak with Monsieur Vincent Voland alone, or I will not speak at all. I *should*, however, let you know that I have colleagues close by and, unlike me, they have not come this evening to talk. I only ask that you allow me to speak with Vincent with an aim to preventing a *very* unfortunate event from taking place tonight."

Tarek asked, "What makes you think I know this Vincent Voland you speak of?"

Drexler smiled. "Because five minutes ago I saw him enter this door right here. Please, Doctor, there is not much time. Let's not play games."

CHAPTER 41

Like a knife through butter, Court passed the first and second rings of defense with ease. He'd entered the grounds of a mosque, then climbed the wall into Bianca's gated Western Villas neighborhood via a Turkish pine, and dropped down into the paved and walled rear courtyard of a patisserie. He moved in the dark through the café tables of the closed eatery, then climbed a smaller stone lattice wall and found himself two streets over from Bianca's home.

Just as Bianca had suggested, it was clear now to Court that security here had indeed been heightened in light of what had happened in Paris. But also as she'd guessed, it was also clear that Jamal was still here. Court could imagine no other reason for all the guns and guys.

A Toyota Hilux pickup bearing the colors and insignia of the NDF drove by with two men in the cab and two more sitting in the bed. Once they were past, Court crossed the two-laned street and entered the property of a small apartment complex, passing a lighted guard shack and the man inside it by no more than twenty-five feet.

At the rear of this property he looked down a gentle hill, through a gardened property, and to a road beyond. Halfway down the road, an NDF vehicle was parked, and at the far end sat the target location.

Medina's Mediterranean-style home.

Court descended the hill in the dark and walked through the property, and a motion light turned on. A door opened on a second-floor balcony and a man looked out into the light.

Court gave the man a bored wave and kept walking.

The man waved back—seeing the uniform, no doubt—and closed the door behind him.

Court marched along the street for a moment, still in the dark, and was seen by a pair of teenagers holding each other while leaning against the wall of a parking garage adjacent to an apartment building. They paid him little attention and quickly returned to their intimate moment.

It occurred to Court that in many of the Middle Eastern nations he'd visited, this unmarried girl alone with this boy would find themselves in a great deal of trouble. Here in Syria, however, the nation's liberal views protected them, even if its leadership threatened to condemn them all to death in a never-ending civil war.

He skirted the NDF men in the street by moving through another apartment building property, but this meant he found himself walking through lighted areas next to men and women still out past one a.m. on this Sunday morning. A small market was open, an outdoor café cooked sizzling meat on a grill, and he passed a tea shop with tables spilling out into the common areas of the apartment building where men and women smoked hookahs.

Court marched straight through it all, even past a pair of Syrian police officers who acknowledged him with little head bobs, but he maintained his visage of authority, his air of entitlement to be exactly where he was, doing exactly what he was doing.

No one gave him a second glance, and no one thought of him after he passed.

A minute later he moved back into the dark, through the private gardens next door to Medina's walled home. His eyes scanned for lights, guards, motion detectors, homeowners, and dogs, and when a Syrian police car rolled to a stop next to the NDF vehicle, Court just held his position against the wall in the forecourt of the residence until he satisfied himself that the arrival of the cops did not mean he'd been sighted. He moved out again and soon reached the wall that adjoined Bianca's rear courtyard.

He pulled himself up onto the eight-foot-high masonry partition. Once he was settled, he peeked over the edge of the wall in an attempt to spot the roving guard. It was too dark to make out the man, but he could see a flashlight moving around the northern wing of the home towards the front of the grounds. He hoisted himself quickly over and then hung down, dropped silently onto the tiles along the wall, and began moving up towards the house. He avoided pathway lighting by stepping into garden beds, and soon he passed the tiled pool and arrived at a cluster of patio furniture protected just under the second-floor balcony that ran the length of the base of the U-shaped house. Court moved between a sofa and a large chair and knelt down, placing his back to a wall that ran perpendicular to three sets of doors to the home.

A large set of glass double doors was in the middle, covered on the inside with curtains, and next to the doors on the outside wall was a keypad for the alarm system. Twenty feet to the left of the double doors was a single sliding glass door. Court imagined it would lead to a downstairs bedroom. And on the far right, fifty feet from where Court knelt, was a single wooden door. This might have led to the kitchen or perhaps to a garden room.

He saw no movement through any of the windows, but he was sure there were armed men inside. Bianca had explained to him that the guards he'd find on the property were a Ba'ath Party security unit made up of only Alawis. Ahmed pulled from this unit to staff his presidential protection detail, so it was no surprise he used other members as his clandestine security force to look over the woman he saw as the future first lady. And since they were Alawi, they would not hold any sectorial or familial allegiance to Shakira Azzam, a Sunni Muslim.

Whoever was in the house right now, Court knew they would have more skill than the NDF men he'd waltzed past to get there. And since he could see the red light on the alarm keypad by the door, he also knew the three exterior doors at the rear of the home would all be alarmed and, most likely, locked.

Getting inside the house itself was always going to be one of the trickier parts of his operation. Coming here tonight, without the benefit of the tools he'd hoped to acquire for a successful break-in, meant he had to be flexible about his points of entry, and he'd have to be as patient as he could be, while still keeping in account the fact that he wanted to be at the Jordanian border before the sun came up in six hours.

He had the alarm code that Bianca had given him, but he had no way of knowing if it had been changed since she'd been kidnapped, and the last thing he wanted to do was key in a string of numbers that would set alarms squealing all over the grounds.

He knew he could grab one of the outside guards and get the number from him, but he was hoping to avoid any chance of detection as long as possible. He moved to the sliding glass door, careful to keep from being seen through the glass by anyone in the room. As he got to the wall next to it, he peered around the side and saw it was, indeed, a bedroom, but there was no one inside.

He didn't try the door; even if it had been unlocked, the home alarm system was engaged, so opening it was the last thing he wanted to do. Instead he looked inside at the track the door would travel along to open, checking it for any secondary bracing or locking system. He saw nothing and decided this door would be his entry point when the time was right.

For now he retreated a few feet on the patio, tucked himself into the darkest corner of the grounds near the door, and waited, his eyes on the alarm keypad by the double doors, twenty-five feet away. He was hoping a roving guard might switch positions with a static man inside, a man inside might step out to check on his mates, or a person in the house would decide they needed some fresh air. In any of these cases someone would have to turn off the alarm, and Court told himself he'd be ready.

Court couldn't wait all night for good luck, but he told himself he'd give it an hour before tackling the guy with a flashlight and beating the alarm code out of him.

Brute force often wasn't the best option, but sometimes it was the only option.

CHAPTER 42

Vincent Voland had dressed for bed and lain down on the sofa in the library of the farmhouse, on the far side of the property from the activity at the back, but after taking a minute to change back into his suit and arm himself, he was brought into the kitchen by one of the Syrian guards. Here Tarek Halaby told him the man he'd been warning everyone about was sitting on a bench in the hearth room, he was unarmed, and he said he had come to prevent a tragedy.

Voland smiled at this. Drexler probably had a car full of half-drunk French cops up the road whom he'd use as a bargaining chip to get Medina handed to him without a fight. It wouldn't work; Voland would simply take Drexler into custody and pass him over to French authorities, and if the dirty cops came up the drive, the houseful of armed Syrians and the four veteran security men would make short work of them.

Voland took an extra moment to compose himself, to steel his mind to finally meet Drexler face-to-face, and to control his hands from shaking with the excitement of finally catching this elusive quarry. To Tarek he asked, "Are all six of your men inside the house?"

"Yes. The Legionnaires are outside, but my men are inside. I have three resting and three watching the property from second-story windows."

"Tell them all to be ready." He stormed past Tarek without another word and disappeared into the hearth room.

Seconds after Voland left the kitchen, Rima stepped up from the wine cellar where she had been watching over Bianca. She saw the worried look on her husband's face. "What is it?"

"They're here," Tarek replied.

"What do we do?"

"I have no idea." And with this, he pulled her close and hugged her.

. . .

Sebastian Drexler sat on an old bench in the hearth room, eyeing Voland as he entered from the kitchen. The older Frenchman's wavy silver hair was a little askew, telling Drexler the man had been lying down, and he saw that Voland had a pistol jammed into his waistband under his jacket.

Drexler said, "A gun in the pants? Really? I didn't take you for a man of action."

Voland put his hand on the grip of the Walther self-consciously. "Yes . . . well, when killers are bearing down on one's location, one must take precautions." He sat in a wooden chair across from the Swiss agent, looking him up and down as he did so. "I've seen photos of you, of course, but you're younger-looking than I expected for a man who's caused so much trouble for so long."

Drexler gave a half shrug. "I got an early start on my career in mayhem, I guess."

"I was thinking it was the plastic surgery."

Drexler smiled. Unoffended.

"You know I have been looking for you for a long time."

"Of course I know. You could have had me in Tripoli, in fact. You hesitated, and I got away. Indecision is a recurring theme in your career that I've noted over the years."

Voland nodded. "Well, you can trust that I won't hesitate tonight."

"We shall see," Drexler replied.

Voland regarded the comment, then asked, "Why did you come here like this?"

"As I told Dr. Halaby, I am here to prevent further catastrophe. Simply put, you are *seriously* outgunned, Vincent. A few Syrian expats and some over-the-hill mercenaries aren't going to slow down what's waiting out there in the trees."

Voland chuckled. "If I thought we were in any danger I would simply contact the local police. There is a station in La Brosse; they could be here in minutes."

Drexler shook his head. "I doubt that. You are working off book tonight, and if the police come you'll go to prison for kidnapping Medina and causing death and chaos in the streets of Paris. No . . . you are affiliated with like-minded intelligence officials inside the French government, but you have no sanction for any of this. You are *not* going to reach out to the police."

Voland didn't seem fazed by being called out like this. "Actually, you are correct. But while I might not call the gendarmerie myself, someone else here certainly will, especially if they are in fear for their lives. I am a consultant . . . I am not in charge."

Drexler smiled. "The landline is cut. The mobiles are jammed."

Voland had not expected this, Drexler saw. He reached into his pocket for his phone and checked it. After confirming Drexler's assertion, he looked up. "I'm impressed. But you've underestimated us. We have a satellite phone."

"Which is nothing more than a radio that connects to a satellite network. They are jammable, too, Vincent, over a limited area." He waved a hand in the air. "Like if you know the exact house the sat phone is located in, for example." With a frown he added, "Technology is hard to keep up with, true, but maybe you should have tried a little harder before bringing these poor people out into the country where they could be so easily surrounded."

Voland cleared his throat. Now the insecurity was clear, both on his face and in his voice. "What is it you are offering?"

"I want the girl. That's all. Give her to me and you will walk out of here."

"So you can kill her to satisfy Shakira al-Azzam?"

"It's more complicated than that, I'm afraid. And it's more complicated for you, too. Your original plan, I assume, was to get intel on Azzam by using his mistress. But that scheme is sunk, man, and you *have* to know that. Now you are just holding her for no good reason."

Voland laughed. "Don't be ridiculous. You might have us surrounded, but now *we* have *you*. Your men out there won't dare attack us now for fear of you getting killed in the process. I could shoot you myself, in fact."

"Of course you could, but it won't help you. Just like you, I'm not running the show."

Voland's white eyebrows furrowed. "What does that mean?"

Drexler did not answer immediately.

Voland's chin jutted out a bit. Drexler wondered if it was real confidence or fictitious bluster. "And you don't know what assets we have assembled here on the estate to protect her."

Drexler replied, "I'm sure you're hinting about your American. I hear he was quite good. But I do *not* believe he is here."

Voland smiled now. "Attack the house, and find out."

Drexler stared Voland down, trying to determine if he was telling the truth. "Who is he?"

Voland maintained his grin. "He is the Gray Man."

Drexler leaned back against the wall, confident and relaxed. "I was almost ready to believe you, but then you ventured off into fantasyland."

"Believe what you want, Drexler."

"Matters not. We've been watching the house; we know who's here. None of my people have reported any mythical uber assassin sightings."

Voland said, "He is still part of our team. If something happens to any one of us, he'll come for you."

"I seriously doubt that. You aren't as important as you think you are. Why would the world-famous Gray Man take on such a futile assignment for the Halabys?"

Voland did not answer the question. Drexler determined with certainty that the Frenchman had been lying.

Now Voland asked, "Since we're having such a frank conversation, why don't you tell me who is out in the trees?"

Drexler did not hesitate. "Fourteen Quds Force–trained commandos of the Syrian GIS. Their leader has worked for me in the past all over Europe. Perhaps he is not the Gray Man . . . but I can assure you, he *does* exist, and he *is* here."

"Do you take me for an idiot? Azzam himself controls GIS paramilitary forces. You are working *against* Azzam, for his wife."

"What must be going on in that head of yours right now. You calculated that Shakira would send me up here to kill Bianca, because that had been my original mission. Yes, I've figured out that you have somehow intercepted my communications with the ISIS cell in Belgium. You know who I am working for, so that is why you are confused as to what GIS is doing here. They work for Ahmed, after all, the unfaithful husband, not Shakira, the jilted wife. Well . . . as I said, it is more complicated. I've changed alliances midoperation. I only want to bring Bianca home to her child."

This was a lie, of course, but Drexler had determined there would be a greater chance he could get Voland and the entire house to surrender if they felt Medina would not be harmed.

Voland swallowed, and Drexler could see the true fear of a man unaccustomed to being outsmarted. "The leader you spoke of. Is he the one they call Malik?"

"One and the same."

"He killed four counterterror police in Bruges last year."

"Not my operation, and this is certainly no official-channel corroboration, but I can confirm he was the gunman. Multiply him by fourteen, and that's what you're facing, right now, if you do not agree to my terms." When Voland did not reply, Drexler said, "All you need to do to prevent a bloodbath is to allow Bianca to leave with me. She will return to Syria unharmed, and you will survive."

Voland looked at the tile floor for a long time. Drexler felt bad for the old man. So many miscalculations.

"If what you say is true . . . if you could take this building over at will . . . why would you let me live?"

"I'm glad you asked that, Vincent. I won't be working for Syrian interests much longer. I will turn that page and take on something new. I have beaten you tonight, but I have need of men like you. I use people in the field, yes, but they are paid well for their work. As I mentioned, I've studied your career, and you are a good intelligence officer. Not great. You haven't been willing to stick your neck out when operational duties required it, but you've done your best. I will offer you survival tonight, and in exchange I would hope you might consider my requests for contract work in the future."

Voland seemed stunned by it all, the employment offer included. "I've made the last several years of my life about putting you in a French prison. Now you want me to serve as your hired hand?"

Drexler shrugged. "You needn't die for a lost cause. I would much rather put you to work."

It was silent in the room for most of a minute. Then the Frenchman stood on unsteady legs. As he turned away he spoke softly, almost to himself. "I must talk to the Halabys to discuss your terms."

"By all means."

CHAPTER 43

Tucked between the sofa and the chair in the complete darkness on the back patio of Bianca Medina's Damascus home, Court tuned his ears to the scene around him, listening for any movement either inside the home or out on the grounds of the house. He knew from Bianca that the baby's room was in the southern wing on the second floor and Yasmin slept right there in the room with him, so he considered climbing the outside of the house and trying to gain access via the balcony.

But again, the alarm code would be impossible to defeat without tools, so he was hoping to be able to wait for someone to turn it off.

He checked his watch and saw it was one thirty. He told himself he'd give it another twenty minutes before taking down the patrolling guard for the access code. He felt like he had to get to the Jordanian border well before first light, so he couldn't wait much longer.

And then, right before his eyes, the light on the keypad turned from red to green. Someone was on his or her way into or out of one of the doors, though he saw no movement at any of the three ground-floor doors in front of him.

A sound came from the balcony above. Soft footsteps, right over Court's head. Apparently a single individual had exited there, and now he or she stood at the railing, looking out over the rear courtyard.

Court wondered if it was Yasmin, but then it occurred to him that he'd been lucky enough to see the alarm deactivated in the first place. There was no way in hell he would be so lucky as to have the woman he needed to grab make it that easy for him.

Just as he decided now was the time to head for the door, he could hear the footsteps turning away, heading back to the house.

Court realized the person above might reset the alarm as soon as he or she was inside. He looked around quickly, stood up, and darted towards the sliding door to the bedroom, since he'd identified this as the one of the three doors easiest to breach.

First he tested it, making certain it was locked. When it did not slide open, he knelt and leaned against the glass, put his right hand under the handle, and shoved it up while coming up higher on his legs. The door lifted a fraction of an inch in the track, but the latch held. He did this a second and a third time, worrying he was making too much noise but aware this was still the quietest way to get into the house.

On the fourth try the latch popped up audibly, and Court lowered the glass door back down into the track and slid it open. He stepped inside, then turned to close the door.

The alarm keypad on the bedroom wall beeped softly, and the light remained green. The man upstairs had indeed tried to set it, but he'd received a warning that this downstairs bedroom door had been open.

Court had been too slow.

Quickly Court closed and locked the door, and he turned to find a place to hide, but before he could move, he heard a different soft beep from the keypad. The alarm turned from green to red. The man upstairs had tried again to arm the alarm, and this time it had worked.

Court knew if the man was any good at his job, he would either call someone and have them check on this bedroom door, or else he'd come do it himself. Court wanted to be out of the middle of the downstairs bedroom before that happened.

He hurried over to the en suite bathroom and stepped inside, tucking himself behind a half-open door while pulling Walid's fixed-blade knife.

The wait was interminable, but eventually footsteps in the hall indicated someone *had* come to check the door.

• • •

Sayed Alawi flipped on the light to the spare bedroom and looked around. He held a walkie-talkie in his left hand, and he brought his right hand down to the pistol on his belt there.

The room was empty. He glanced into the dark bathroom as he headed around the bed to check on the door, but he didn't go in. Instead he looked outside on the patio first, then pulled on the door, making sure it was, indeed, properly locked. He was already glad he hadn't broadcast over the radio the fact that he'd received the alarm exception message, because clearly, there was nothing to worry about.

Still . . . Alawi found this curious. He'd been working here since just before the birth of the child, and the alarm had never once erroneously signaled an open door when the door was locked. Also, none of the other security men on the premises should have been in this wing of the home.

He wondered if the new guy outside had come in to take a leak, or if one of the other men in the house had gone outside for a stroll. No one was supposed to move from his post, either static or mobile, without first making a request to the agent in charge.

Alawi wasn't the agent in charge, but he would have heard that transmission in his earpiece, and he'd heard nothing over the radio in the past hour.

He decided he needed to find out if there was either a problem with the alarm system or a problem with one of the new guys following orders. He reached for the transmit button on the radio on his belt, and as he did so he turned away from the glass door and back towards the well-lit bedroom.

And then he stopped.

A uniformed soldier stood in front of him, feet away, near the threshold to the bathroom.

Alawi was confused. "Who are you?"

• • •

Court launched at the guard, desperate to get to him before he made a noise. The American knocked the radio away with a backhand, then punched the man in the jaw, staggering him on his knees.

297

He began to fall backwards into the glass door, but Court leapt closer, caught him by the collar, and spun him around, back into the room.

Court punched him hard in the face again, knocking him unconscious onto the bed. Court then moved over to the door to the room and shut and locked it softly, then flipped the lights off again.

Court stood there in the darkness of what was obviously a guest bedroom, and he shook the pain out of his right hand. His jab had hit more cheekbone than he'd intended, and his fourth and fifth fingers throbbed from the impact.

Back at the unconscious man, Court rolled him face-first off the bed and onto the floor of the bedroom, knelt on the man's back, and grabbed his head.

With a single swift movement Court pulled and turned, snapping the guard's neck and killing him. He stripped the man of his shoes, his suit, his shirt, his tie, and all the while he listened to the walkie-talkie on the floor for any hint that the guards on the premises were alerted to the noise or the absence of this man.

Court stripped his uniform off and dressed in the guard's clothing; it fit a lot better than Walid's too-loose tunic and too-short pants.

Then Court put the Desert Hawks Brigade uniform on the dead body.

This was surprisingly arduous work that took him nearly five minutes, but when he was through, after he'd holstered the guard's big SIG Pro pistol and clipped the radio onto his own belt, he knew he would be able to move through the darkened house more easily now.

He put the earpiece in his ear and began rifling through the man's identification, hoping to learn his name, but the writing was in Arabic, so Court just pocketed the wallet and dragged the body into the bathroom. Here he placed it in the bathtub, closed the curtain, and headed back for the door that would lead him to the rest of the home.

CHAPTER 44

Vincent Voland sat with Rima and Tarek in the library of the French estate, while Drexler was kept under guard in the hearth room by Boyer.

Voland told the Syrian couple about the offer made by Drexler, and he added, "I don't know why the Syrian GIS men are here, but this changes the equation totally. None of us stand a chance against—"

"You want to surrender!" Rima screamed it as the realization came to her.

Voland held up his hands. "Face the facts! They will kill every last one of us in here, and we will lose Medina anyway. If we withdraw, then perhaps we—"

Tarek snapped now. "By 'withdraw,' you mean run away."

"We will have our chance, I feel certain. Just at a later date."

Tarek shook his head. "There *is* no later date. My nation is dying! You have spent three days telling us no one could take Medina from this house. A lone, unarmed man walks up and you want to surrender without firing a shot?"

"I know Drexler, and I know the Syrian out there leading the attack against us, and I know the capabilities of the force he has with him. They promise Medina won't be harmed if we—"

"She won't be *harmed*?" Rima shrieked. "Drexler sent ISIS to kill her just days ago."

Tarek added, "He's lying! There is no one here but him."

"He's *not* lying. He's a cold, calculating individual, but he has survived this long in his work by always acting from positions of strength. He wouldn't walk in unarmed unless he really did have the unbeatable hand. And he says his mission now is to bring her back alive to Damascus."

Rima said, "This is insane! We sent the American to rescue the child in Damascus, and he is doing so as we speak. And now you want to give the mother back to Azzam?"

Voland put his hands up. "We know the American is going alone into a fortified building in the middle of Syria. We certainly don't know he's getting out of there, and we certainly don't know he's going to make it out of Damascus and all the way to Jordan."

Tarek said, "You are saying that even though the American has more going against him than we do, you still want *us* to give up?"

"It's not what I *want*. It's what I see as the only rational choice."

The Halabys went into another room to speak in privacy, but quickly they returned to Voland. Tarek said, "Speaking for myself and my wife, we owe it to our nation, and to the American who is risking everything to help us. We will not surrender."

Voland looked down at the floor a moment. "You are making a mistake that will likely get us all killed. Nevertheless . . . I will respect your wishes. I will go tell Drexler he will remain our prisoner and we will fight to defend the Spaniard."

CHAPTER 45

Court took the stairs in Bianca Medina's villa slowly because he could hear talking in the living room, just out of view behind him. Two men in idle conversation; Court picked up something about someone named Sayed, but that was all he understood.

On his way to the stairs he'd passed a guard sleeping soundly in a tiled alcove and moved within five feet of him in the dark hallway. At the top of the stairs he found an empty hallway that went to the left and right and then turned to form the arms of the U of the home. He went to the right first, because Bianca had said the baby's room was there, right next to her own. Peeking around the corner, he could see a man sitting in a chair at the end of the hall near a door. It was so dark in the hallway Court could not be sure if the man was awake or asleep at thirty feet away, but he could see that the man was wearing a similar dark suit to the one Court had taken off the man he'd killed downstairs.

He went to the other side of the second floor and looked up the hall there, but there were no guarded doors, so he decided the baby was probably being held behind the first door. He returned to the corner and thought about what he needed to do.

There was no getting around that guard; this he knew. He only hoped he could kill him quietly.

Court touched the knife under his jacket, checking its placement, took a calming breath, and stepped around the corner. He began walking purposefully up the hall. He just had to hope his clothing and the dim light would disguise him until it was too late for the sentry in the chair to stop him.

He continued on, his hands idly at his sides, closing on the guard by the door. He was still twenty feet away when the man shifted and said, "*Salam.*" Hi.

"*Salam,*" Court replied, trying to use the same low voice he'd heard from the man who owned the suit he now wore.

At fifteen feet the man sat up in the chair and said something else. He spoke in a whisper, which was good news for Court because it meant the other guards in the house would not hear anything, and it also meant someone was likely sleeping on the other side of the door behind him.

When Court did not respond, the man said, "Sayed?" and then he sat up even straighter, suddenly on alert.

"*Nem,*" Yes, Court replied, slowing the man's decision making a fraction of a second. But then the man began to stand, and he reached into his jacket.

Court closed the remaining eight feet in two quick steps and shoved his left hand over the man's mouth, and with his right hand he sank the long fixed-blade knife he'd taken from Walid's trunk hilt-deep into the Alawi guard's solar plexus.

The Syrian's legs gave out in two seconds, and his struggling stopped after a few seconds more.

Court slid him down the wall, back into his chair. He pulled the knife out and leaned the man's head back against the wall.

Other than a brief and muffled gasp and some scuffling of leather shoes on a tiled hallway floor, the killing had barely made a sound.

• • •

There had always been a chance that even if Azzam did not move his baby from Bianca's home in the Western Villas section of Damascus's Mezzeh district, he would, at least, move the room the baby was being kept in. It would have been a simple security measure designed to slow anyone who came after the child, at least long enough for them to be spotted by security in the house.

But when Court finally got to the room at the end of the hall where Bianca said he would find the baby's room, he opened the door and found a baby lying in a crib, and a mattress on the floor next to it with a girl sleeping soundly on it.

Court closed the door behind him and moved slowly across the bedroom. The rugs on the tile floor made it easy to keep his footfalls silent. All his senses were tuned to high, still focusing on any noises from other parts of the villa.

In seconds he was on his knees next to the mattress, inches away from the sleeping au pair.

Court could think of absolutely no way to do this without scaring the living shit out of this poor girl, which served no purpose here. Intimidation was an effective means of gaining compliance, he well knew, but in this situation he needed more than compliance; he needed Yasmin to become his partner in crime, and for this he wanted to earn her trust.

And that was going to be hard considering the fact that her first impressions of him were going to be as some sort of monster leering over her in her bed at night.

He placed a hand over her mouth, knelt over her face, and pressed down.

Her eyes opened slowly, then popped wide when she saw the strange man in the low light above her. He placed a finger over his own lips.

"Écoute, s'il vous plaît, mademoiselle." Please listen, miss. He continued in French. "I have been sent by Bianca. I am not going to hurt you, but we must not make any noise. Do you understand me?"

A tear formed in and rolled from each eye. She blinked. And then she nodded.

Court kept the hand in place. "Bianca is safe in France, but she will not be returning. Shakira Azzam has tried to kill her, and she will try again if Bianca returns to Syria. We have come to retrieve Jamal so he can be with his mother." There was just Court, there was no "we," but when he'd worked out what he'd say to the nanny, he'd decided there was a greater chance she would buy into this entire improbable escapade if she thought there were more people involved with the getaway.

Court took a moment to listen for sounds in the house, and then he continued in French, speaking softly and quickly. "I am taking Jamal now. Bianca wants you to come with him for your own safety, no other reason. But no one will make you do this. You can stay right here if you want to, but she is worried Ahmed will become angry when he finds the baby gone, so Bianca thinks it would be best for you if you came with us."

The girl just stared at Court with wide, frightened eyes.

"Do you understand me?"

She nodded.

Court decided he needed to be more explicit. "I have a gun. As I said, I won't hurt you, and I won't hurt Jamal, but I will kill anyone else who gets in my way."

Yasmin began nodding emphatically under Court's hand.

"You want to leave tonight?"

Another nod.

"Good. I am going to take my hand off your mouth. Please don't make any noise, because if you do, you will be in danger from those who will come."

As soon as he took his hand away, Yasmin did speak. She kept her voice in a whisper. "Please speak slower, monsieur. Your French . . . it is not so good. How do I know Bianca really sent you?"

Court ignored the slight because he knew she was right. He slowed down a little. "She told me to remind you of the day Jamal was born when it was just the three of you in the room at the hospital, and you sang to him. Bianca told you that you have a beautiful voice, and she asked you to sing to him every day. You promised you would. She wants to know if you've been keeping your promise while she's been away."

Yasmin nodded slowly.

"As soon as we're out of here you can talk to her; she's waiting for me to call and tell her I have you and the boy."

Yasmin closed her eyes and nodded, still lying there in the bed. She was terrified, Court knew, but she would also know by now there was no way she could stop him from taking the child, and there was also no way she was going to remain behind if he did so.

"You need to get dressed. You will only take your clothes, and things you need for the baby on the trip."

"How long is the trip?"

Good question, thought Court. He gave her the optimal version. "We will travel tonight to the Jordanian border and slip over before dawn." And then he added, "But I don't know what happens immediately on the other side of the border, so bring enough food, diapers, and clothing for him in case we are delayed."

"Okay."

Now Court said, "I have a car, but it is several blocks away. Do you have a vehicle?"

She shook her head no. "Bianca has a Range Rover. It's out front. The keys are in the kitchen."

Court nodded.

"But," she asked, confusion on her face, "why don't the others just pick us up?"

"What others?"

"The other people helping you."

Oh, yeah. All those guys, Court thought. "They're out there, but we have to do this part alone." He meant they were *way* out there, as in France, but he didn't get specific.

She nodded again. "So you can really kill ten men?"

Court cocked his head. "What do you mean?"

"There are ten men in the house."

"You mean . . . *right now*?"

"*Oui.* Since Ahmed came the day before yesterday. He doubled the guard."

Bianca had told him five. He'd killed two already, a third man walked the grounds, and a fourth sat on the roof. He'd seen a fifth in the alcove near the stairs, and he'd heard two men talking in the living room.

That was seven. Court wondered if there could really be three more armed men in the house he didn't know about.

"Where do the guards congregate at this time of the night?" he asked the girl.

"Usually a group of them sit in the living room and watch TV or look at their phones. I have to get the keys and Jamal's formula out of the kitchen; it's right next to the living room."

"Formula?"

Yasmin blinked in surprise at this. "Food."

305

Court just stared at her.

"It's what a baby eats," she said.

Court nodded his head. "Right. There's no formula here?"

She went over to a small refrigerator in the room and looked inside. She pulled out one bottle. "It's not very much. Two feedings at most."

Court cocked his head. "Two feedings . . . what's that, about a day?"

Yasmin looked at the stranger with confusion. "A *day*? No . . . three or four hours, *maybe*."

"Shit," Court said, looking at the tiny human lying asleep in the crib. "Can you get his formula at night without the guards being suspicious?"

Again she gave him a funny look. "I do it all night, every night. Do you know *anything* about infants?"

"Look . . . until we get to Paris, the baby is your department. I'll take care of everything else."

"*Oui*. I think that would be best for Jamal."

CHAPTER 46

Vincent Voland opened the door to the hearth room and was surprised by what he saw. Sebastian Drexler stood in the middle of the room talking to Boyer, and the former Legionnaire wore his submachine gun hanging down over his back, not pointed at the prisoner.

Voland said, "What is going on here?"

Boyer said, "Look, Vincent . . . This isn't our cause. When you hired us, you said an agent not aligned with the Syrian embassy might come with some bent French police officers to try to take the woman back. You definitely didn't say *anything* about tier-one Syrian government paramilitaries being involved. We're surrounded, and it's suicide to hold our ground. I've made a deal with Drexler, and I've ordered my men to lower our weapons."

Voland nodded solemnly. "I understand, Paul. You may consider yourself and your men released from duty."

Tarek Halaby had entered from the kitchen, and he'd heard this. He looked at Voland like he'd lost his mind. "*What?* What are you saying? We agreed we would not surrender!"

Voland turned to the Syrian doctor. "And that was the wrong decision even when we *did* have four top-level security men on our side. Now . . . there is absolutely no chance."

Tarek Halaby pulled the radio off his belt, triggered the mic, and spoke into it in Arabic. "The Legionnaires have surrendered! For Syria, we will never give in to—"

Vincent Voland pulled the Walther pistol out from under his jacket and held it to Tarek Halaby's right temple. "I'm so sorry, Doctor, this is not what I want. I am doing this for your own good. For your wife, as well. Put the radio down."

Tarek lowered the radio to his side, but at the same time he turned his head slowly to the Frenchman. "Bastard!"

Voland said, "I am saving your life with this gun, Tarek." He turned to Boyer now. "Let them in."

Boyer stepped to the door of the hearth room and opened it. On the other side, Malik and three of his men stood there, dressed in black, their short-barreled rifles at the ready. Novak was with them, too, but he had already been disarmed.

Clearly Drexler had convinced Novak and Boyer to allow the Syrians to advance up to the building while Voland was talking to the Halabys.

The men in black flooded into the room, but as they did so, Tarek Halaby swept his walkie-talkie up and into Vincent Voland's pistol, knocking it away from his temple.

He reached down with his other hand and grabbed his own gun out of his belt, and he began raising it towards the Syrians.

Malik shot Tarek Halaby twice through the heart at a range of ten feet.

The fifty-five-year-old Syrian doctor stumbled backwards, then fell onto the cold tile floor as Syrian government commandos flooded through the room, racing for the door to the kitchen. Boyer was disarmed, as well as Voland, and Sebastian Drexler was handed Voland's pistol.

Boyer immediately radioed his two men at the front driveway and told them to leave the property.

While this was going on, Drexler took Vincent Voland by the arm. "Where is Medina?"

Voland did not reply. He just stared down at Tarek Halaby's dead body, tears forming in his eyes.

"Tell me and you walk out right now! Don't tell me and I shoot you dead!"

Voland replied with, "Promise me you won't hurt Rima Halaby!"

"If she's as foolish as her husband, I will make no promises." He repeated, "Where is Bianca Medina?"

"Off the kitchen there is a stairwell that leads down to a wine cellar. In the back of it are two doors. One leads to storage, the other to a servant's quarters. She's in the servant's quarters, the door on the right. She's locked in. You will not hurt a hair on her head!"

Malik and his men had already moved as a team to the door that led to the kitchen. Drexler gave Voland a menacing look and waved the pistol in his hand. "Why would I hurt Mademoiselle Medina? I only want to return her to her home."

Voland understood that there was a dynamic here between Malik and Drexler. The Syrian did not know that the Swiss intelligence officer had been, initially at least, planning on killing Medina. Voland only had to tell Malik about Drexler's work for Shakira with the ISIS cell, and there was a chance the Syrian would shoot Drexler here on the spot. But there was also a chance he would not and, Voland knew, Drexler would shoot him immediately for incriminating him.

So Voland said nothing.

Malik called from the door to the kitchen. "How many Free Syria Exile personnel are on the property?"

"Other than Rima and Tarek, six more."

Drexler said, "*Bon.* You and the Legionnaires may leave now, just walk away. After tonight you no longer work for FSEU. If you work at all . . . you work for me."

Voland did not reply; he just looked down at the floor.

Drexler took the barrel of his pistol, put it under the older man's chin, and pushed up, lifting Voland's face up to meet his own. The men made eye contact.

"Say it," Drexler said. "Who do you work for?"

"I . . . I work for you, Monsieur Drexler."

The Swiss agent pulled the pistol away and holstered it. "Go."

Vincent Voland looked back down, and he did not lift his eyes from the floor as he followed Boyer and Novak towards the back door.

Voland had only made it a few steps when the man at the front of the first commando at the door to the kitchen opened the latch and pulled the door open, his gun high.

Instantly the first man in the stack was shot through the head. He fell back into the hearth room, while his teammates returned fire. In seconds all the Syrian GIS men began pouring forward through the doorway, guns blazing, as they assaulted the house.

CHAPTER 47

The baby remained sound asleep as Yasmin followed behind Court through the hallway, past the dead guard in the chair. The American had told the young Syrian woman to keep her face tight into his back and to hold on to his suit coat so he could know where she was at all times, but he had no idea if she was complying with his wishes.

Court was only using the guard's suit for camo in the dark now; there was no pretense of him actually looking like a member of the security unit here in the house since over his shoulder he wore a blue backpack full of diapers, the bottle, and other baby-related odds and ends, and Yasmin carried the child in her arms and remained tight against Court's back.

At the bottom of the stairs he stopped and listened carefully. He could hear the sounds of slow and steady breathing from the living room. After fifteen seconds he turned to Yasmin, gave her a nod, and put his hands out to hold the baby. She refused to hand over the child at first, but Court took her by the arm and glared at her. He figured there was less chance Yasmin would alert the guards if she was worried about the kid, so he decided to use Jamal as insurance.

Finally she handed the sleeping baby to Court, who took him awkwardly, then brought him into his chest, hoping like hell he didn't wake up.

Yasmin walked into the living room silently, then into the kitchen, out of Court's view. He worried for a few seconds about what she might really be doing, but soon he relaxed when he heard the sound of a refrigerator opening, and then the soft rattle of bottles.

One of the men in the living room spoke, and Court took the baby in his left arm so he could wrap his grip around the pistol at his waist.

Yasmin replied to the man, but it was a quick, relaxed exchange that did not worry Court at all from its tone, although he could not understand the words.

He looked down at Jamal now and put his right hand on the top of the baby's wispy black curls. *So, you're the little troublemaker,* he thought.

Yasmin returned to the stairs an instant later, put four full bottles in the backpack over Court's shoulder, handed him the car keys, and took the baby back in her arms. She clutched the tail of Court's suit coat again, and the three of them began walking down the hall.

They passed the man in the alcove; Court had the long knife in his hand clutched close to his chest where Yasmin couldn't see it, ready to launch himself on the guard if he showed any alarm at all, but the sentry remained soundly asleep.

He did not kill the man, but he knew the man had not exactly been spared. Court figured all the guards in this building would be executed as soon as Azzam found out about the kidnapping.

They entered the spare bedroom where Court had killed the first guard, and he headed over to the keypad in the dark. Yasmin stayed on his heels, just as he'd ordered, but now Court could hear the baby stirring. It was just soft noises, so he was not too concerned yet. He remained concentrated on his exfiltration.

Court leaned close to Yasmin. "I hope you know the alarm code."

"Of course. They changed it when Bianca disappeared." She told it to Court. He recognized that disarming the system would, no doubt, alert anyone in the house near a keypad, but there was no other way out.

He reached up to deactivate the alarm, but then he stopped and turned to the bathroom.

He had an idea.

First he gave Yasmin the backpack, and she struggled to put it on and handle the baby at the same time. Jamal lifted his head and looked around a little, and he gave off a soft cry. Court left the two of them at the glass door and went into the bathroom, where he scooped the dead man in the

Desert Hawks uniform out of the bathtub and hefted him into a fireman's carry.

When he returned to the bedroom Yasmin gasped audibly, and Court shushed her. She looked in shock at the man slumped on the stranger's shoulder.

Court had decided that if he could get out of here with the body undetected it might look, for a short time, anyhow, like this guard had been involved in the kidnapping of Jamal. Anything that would buy him some time as he left the city would increase his chances of success in getting to the Jordanian border.

Court went back to the keypad, struggling to carry the man, but he did stop to whisper at Yasmin. "It's okay. He's just asleep."

It was a lie, but she was stressed, and now the baby was almost fully awake in her hands. He'd do anything he could to keep his two new cohorts from freaking out.

He looked out onto the back patio of the home and searched for the patrolling guard's flashlight. He didn't see it, which meant the guard carrying it would be in the front of the property now, or else making his way on one of the walkways on either side, out of Court's vision. This was good as far as getting out of the building, but since he needed to get the girl, the baby, and the body in the car in the front drive, he hoped like hell the guard would be strolling around back to the west just as they moved around the house to the east.

But he didn't think for a second he'd get that lucky.

He took a step back from the door and drew his SIG pistol from its holster on his hip. He gave Yasmin the car keys and told her to deactivate the home alarm, and then to be ready to move fast on his heels. When they got to the Range Rover she was to use the keyless entry so Court could dump the body . . . he corrected himself, the sleeping guard, in the back. Then Yasmin was to get in the backseat with the baby, crawl down to the floorboard, and cover herself and the child with the backpack.

He made her repeat everything, and then the baby started to cry.

"What the hell is wrong with it?" Court asked in an angry whisper.

"*It?* He's hungry."

"For God's sake, not now. We've got to go."

She turned and deactivated the alarm, then opened the sliding glass

313

door, and Court shot out, moving as fast as he possibly could while holding a 170-pound dead man on his back.

Past the patio furniture, a right turn into a small arched passage that led to the northern side of the property, then another right turn towards the front and the driveway there. Court swept his pistol left and right, looking for any threats ahead as they walked along a lighted footpath.

He had no idea where the guard with the flashlight was, but he knew he needed to be certain he saw the man's light before the man's light saw him.

They turned around the northeastern corner, and the silver SUV was right there in the drive, just ten yards away. The baby began to squeal just as Yasmin popped the tailgate on the vehicle, and as Court moved around the back to dump the body inside, he saw the flashlight's beam across the front driveway sweeping towards the noise there.

Court heaved the body off his shoulder and down into the back of the Range Rover, spun towards the light to his left, and fired off four rounds.

The flashlight spun in the air and fell onto a narrow strip of grass between the walkway to the front door and the driveway. Behind it a body lay still on the path.

Court swung his pistol towards the roof now, aimed at the area where the man had been sitting, and saw he did not have a line of sight from this angle. Just as he was about to head for the driver's-side door of the silver Range Rover, a man stood up with a rifle, almost directly in the sights of Court's pistol. Court fired a single round, hitting the man high on the top of his head above his left eye and knocking him back and out of view.

Court climbed behind the wheel, fired up the engine, and slammed the SUV in reverse. He spun around to make sure Yasmin was in the back, and she was, but with the shooting and her panic she'd neglected to close the door behind her.

He smashed through the gate at the end of the drive and reversed into the street.

Men began pouring out through the front door of Bianca's villa now, running towards the Range Rover and shouting, but Court ignored them, hoping like hell these guys knew better than to start slinging lead at a car carrying the son of their president.

The crack of a pistol told him he'd neglected to consider that these guys

314

just *might* be unaware the kid had been kidnapped at all. All they were sure of at the moment was that someone was trying to steal Bianca's car.

Shit.

More pistols snapped off and glass shattered behind Court; he threw the transmission into drive and floored the accelerator.

"Stay down!"

CHAPTER 48

The gun battle inside the farmhouse southwest of Paris turned against the Syrian expat rebels and in favor of the Syrian government commandos the moment Malik and his remaining men linked up with the squad that had assaulted from the front of the building. Malik had left one of his team in the kitchen to cover the stairs to the wine cellar for the purpose of trapping Bianca Medina down in a hole, while he and his unified team fought their way through the ground floor and then up the stairs, where three of the six remaining Syrian guard force members had set up a hasty block. After being bogged down there for a couple of minutes, one of Malik's commandos threw a pair of grenades over the blockage, killing the surviving Syrians, and then the team raced up the stairs on their hunt to find and kill all the remaining FSEU gunmen, one by one.

And as the commandos working for Ahmed Azzam cleared the big farmhouse, Sebastian Drexler waited in the kitchen with Voland's pistol in his hand, just feet away from the lone paramilitary left guarding the stairwell. Drexler listened to the broadcasts over the radio announcing the positions of Malik and the rest of the team, and he fantasized about shooting this one GIS man in the back of the head, strolling down the stairs, and dispatching Medina, but he saw no way to do this without running the risk of Malik finding out about it. Further, he didn't know what he would encounter once he got downstairs, and he assumed Medina would be protected. He needed Malik's men just to get to the girl, and there was no way he could do it without them.

No . . . Medina was safe from Drexler, at least for now.

After five minutes, Malik announced a cease-fire over the radio, proclaiming the two main levels of the property clear. He'd lost three of the ten commandos who had raided the home, and three more were walking wounded, but these men he positioned in upstairs windows to keep an eye out for police.

Then all his attention turned to his preparations to assault the wine cellar. As Drexler watched, Malik stacked his team up by the door in the kitchen that led down to the lower level. The breach man opened the door, then peered around the corner, shining the light on his P90 submachine gun down the darkened stairs.

Drexler called softly over to Malik. "Have you encountered a middle-aged woman with red hair?"

Malik shook his head but kept his eyes on the stairwell as the first man prepared to descend.

Drexler moved up close behind the stack of men and shouted out, startling the gunmen. "Rima Halaby! If you are down there, you need to come up now! You have no chance!"

Malik looked back angrily at Drexler, but then a voice called out. "I'm coming up! I am unarmed!"

Drexler spoke to Malik now. "You are not to harm her if she complies with your orders."

Malik reluctantly relayed this order to his men, and they stepped back into the kitchen but kept their weapons high on the doorway.

When Halaby did not appear at the top of the stairs after thirty seconds, Drexler called to her again. A few seconds later she did appear, however, and she shut the door behind her. She was grabbed by a Syrian, spun around, and pushed roughly up to a wall. She was frisked by a second man, while the rest of the unit re-formed at the door, ready to descend.

Malik spoke to her in Arabic. "Anyone else down there other than Medina?"

Rima spoke with her face against the wall. "I wish to make a statement."

All eyes turned to her. Drexler said, "You can say whatever you want once we have Bianca. Is she still locked in the back room on the right?"

Rima shrugged off the hands on her and turned to face all the men in the room. With a brave gaze she looked to Drexler. "You are Eric."

"I am."

"And Monsieur Voland told you where Bianca was being held?"

"Yes."

"My husband. Is he dead?"

"I am sorry. He resisted." He added, "He was brave, but foolish. Don't be the same."

She looked on the kitchen floor now. There, lying near a heavy wooden table, was the body of Firas, her nephew. He had been the man who opened fire on the commandos as they breached the door from the hearth room, and he'd killed one of them before he himself was shot to death.

Malik said, "No time for this. Let's go."

The veins in Rima's throat pulsated, and her face reddened, but she kept her shoulders back and her head high. "We have failed . . . but so have you."

"What do you mean by that?" asked Drexler.

Rima said, "You won't be returning to Syria with Bianca Medina. I killed her."

"You *what*?" He turned and looked at Malik, then gave him a nod, urging him to go down the stairs with his team.

Malik instantly gave the order in Arabic to his team. The door was opened, and one by one they headed down the stairs in a tactical train, their weapons' lights probing the darkness below. Malik himself joined the rear of the stack.

He'd advanced just a few steps down before he smelled smoke.

The breacher—the first man in the line—was already at the bottom of the stairs in the wine cellar. His voice crackled over the radio.

"I've got smoke pouring out of both doors at the back of the—"

Malik shouted down the stairs, ignoring the radio. "Get in there and get her out!"

By the time the Syrian commandos arrived at the door on the right, the smoke in the wine cellar was choking them. The breacher put his hand on the iron door latch. Even through his gloves he felt the searing heat. He fought the pain, urged on again by his leader shouting from behind, and opened the door.

Flames launched out into the fresh air of the wine cellar, nearly enveloping the men there. The inside of the bedroom was completely ablaze.

Malik shouted over the radio, "Put the fire out! Find the woman! That's an order!"

But the door to the storeroom on the left burst open now, and flames roared out and traced along the wooden ceiling of the wine cellar, above the heads of all the men standing there. Fire spread in seconds to the wall tapestries and area rugs and licked across the wooden wine racks along the walls. None of the commandos had anything with which to put out a fire so large, and no one dared penetrate deeper into the room to enter the servant's quarters where Medina was supposedly being held. Clearly large amounts of flammables had been ignited in both rooms, and the men knew if they did not evacuate instantly they could all be consumed by smoke and fire.

Despite the direct orders to recover the woman, the commandos began pulling back to the stairwell. Malik himself tried to push past them and into the room, but in seconds, he, too, turned around and ran for the stairs.

. . .

Sebastian Drexler stood at the top of the stairwell, saw the flames and the smoke, and listened to the frantic transmissions over his radio.

While the men downstairs fought the outright terror that came with the realization that they'd failed their mission to recover the Spanish woman, Drexler fought the urge to grin from ear to ear because he could not believe his good fortune. Turning around into the kitchen, he met the stare of Rima Halaby.

In French she said, "You wanted her dead, didn't you?" she asked.

Drexler had no idea if the Syrian holding Rima up against the wall spoke French, so he maintained his cover by saying, "Of course not!"

"Voland told me you did."

"Voland has misjudged everything, and it has led to your husband's death. But I will see that you are not harmed, as long as you do as I say."

Rima smiled. In Arabic she said, "What will Ahmed Azzam do to all of you now when he finds out you failed?"

Malik was the last man up the stairs, smoke pouring from his clothing

319

and gear. One of the commandos slammed the door shut, cutting off flames that had already swept to the top of the stairwell.

Malik dropped to his knees, coughing and hacking for several seconds, but once he recovered, he stood and staggered over to Rima Halaby. He wrapped his hand around her throat. "What did you do?"

Drexler turned to him. "Malik!"

Rima looked into the eyes of the dark-haired commando leader. She laughed wildly. "I slit her throat in bed, poured turpentine on her body, and set it alight."

Malik shook his head. "Liar! You don't have the stomach for—"

"I've been a heart surgeon for almost thirty years! You think cutting living flesh is beyond my abilities? Are you a fool? I did her a favor. She's better off dead than having to return to that monster you work for!"

The man at the door to the wine cellar called out across the kitchen. "Sir! There is a lot of wood in this farmhouse. That fire is going to spread. We have to get out of here!"

Malik put his hands in his curly hair now, on the verge of panic. Drexler could see that the man knew Medina's death meant his own death, as well. He paced the room for a moment, in full view of his men.

Then he looked at Rima again.

Drexler sensed the thinking of the Syrian. He said, "We need Dr. Halaby. We take her back to Damascus. She is the one person who can corroborate the story of what happened to Medina."

As Drexler watched, Malik brushed his slung submachine gun behind his back, drew his pistol, and stormed over to Rima. He jammed the barrel of the weapon between her breasts.

"Think, Malik!" Drexler shouted. "Don't do it!"

Rima whispered, "I die a proud daughter of Syria."

Malik fired once into Dr. Rima Halaby's chest, knocking her back against the wall. She slid slowly down to the floor.

Drexler shook his head in frustration. He didn't care anything about the woman, but the Swiss operative wanted her to confirm to Shakira that Bianca was dead.

Just then, smoke began pouring out through fissures in the wooden door.

Malik stood over the dead woman on the wooden floor as he said, "I want two men with hoses spraying water on the fire to slow it. The rest of you, check upstairs for anything of intelligence value. You have fifteen minutes until exfiltration." His men began following his orders, although it was clear they would all rather get the hell out of the burning building.

Drexler stood nearby and was still nearly euphoric about his good fortune, but he did his best to feign the same worry that Malik felt. He said, "You really think it will help to get intelligence on the FSEU?"

Malik shook his head. Softly to Drexler he said, "Not really. I think Azzam will have us all shot because Medina is dead. But I don't want my men to know this, so I'll give them some hope."

He turned away from Drexler and began following his men out of the kitchen.

Drexler smiled after the man had turned away. He knew he sure as hell wouldn't be shot by Azzam, because he wouldn't be returning to Syria.

As for the rest of them? *Of course* they would die.

CHAPTER 49

The entire time Court had been sneaking his way into Bianca Medina's gated neighborhood, he'd also been planning his route to get out. Exfiltration would be harder than infiltration, he'd known full well, because he wasn't hauling a baby and a nanny *into* Bianca's house. And it wasn't hard for him to determine that getting out of Western Villas would not be something he could pull off with stealth. No, he was a realist, so he knew escaping with the girl and the kid was going to require revving engines, squealing tires, gunfire, and car crashes.

The gunfire had begun almost immediately, but now as he barreled along up Zaid bin al-Khattab Avenue, directly towards a green Toyota Hilux with NDF markings, he knew it was time to ratchet up the noise and drama. The truck full of regime-aligned militia started to move, turning perpendicular so as to block the Range Rover's escape. Men in the back raised their weapons, and men in the cab leapt out and leveled their rifles over the hood.

Court knew that four AKs dumping rounds into the Range Rover's engine block would knock the vehicle out of commission in seconds, so he decided his best defense would be a good offense—he'd give the gunmen up ahead something more important to do than shoot at him.

With the pedal to the floor he raced directly at the pickup. A short burst of AK fire came from a man shooting over the hood, tearing into the windshield of Bianca's SUV just to the right of Court's head, but then the shooting stopped, and Court saw four men sprinting away from the pickup in multiple directions. Two dived onto the sidewalk to the east of the road, and the other two flung themselves over the hood of a car parked along the sidewalk on the west side. Court turned the grill of the SUV away from the Hilux and towards the sidewalk, sideswiped one of the men as he climbed back to his feet, and knocked him back into the road like a rag doll.

The three other men at the roadblock had only a brief chance to grab their weapons and fire again before Court smashed through the gate at the end of the street, and their rounds went high and wide.

Court jacked the SUV to the east as two men came out of the guard shack with pistols, firing off rounds, but Court weaved back and forth across the four-lane road and then took a hard right just a hundred meters on.

The window in the tailgate shattered just before he weaved out of the line of sight of the men at the guard shack, but he knew he wasn't out of the woods, because the sounds of sirens, screeching tires, and revving vehicle engines echoed through the streets from all directions.

He shouted to the girl on the floorboard behind him. *"Ça va?" Are you okay?*

"Oui, ça va," Yasmin replied, but Jamal was wailing now.

"What's wrong with the baby?"

"He's a baby! He's upset, of course!"

"Right. Look, we're going to switch cars and we have to do it very quickly. Be ready to move, okay?"

"What about Mr. Alawi?"

"Who the hell is . . . ? You mean the guy in the back?"

"Yes."

"He's coming with us."

This was problematic, of course, because Court already had Walid bound, gagged, and drunk in the trunk of the Hyundai, but he figured there was room enough for both, even if it would be a tight fit.

As he drove to the parking garage close to the pool and fountain store to pick up Walid's car, he rolled down his window and listened to the sound of sirens on several streets around him. While there was certainly a large law enforcement presence hunting for him, it didn't seem like anyone

323

was right on his heels at the moment, though he knew that could change any second.

He'd given some thought to the likely response there would be to this crime here in the city. He felt sure the guards would call in an immediate police report about some sort of attack in Western Villas, and they might even say that a woman and child had been kidnapped out of a house, but Court knew the guards at the house would not broadcast to the local police that the child who had been taken was the illegitimate son of Ahmed al-Azzam.

Crimes of various kinds in other parts of Damascus were commonplace with the war going on and the insurgency active in the city, so even though this was undeniably a big event and different from a regular terrorist attack, it wasn't going to cause one fifth the uproar it would have caused if word got out about what had *really* taken place.

. . .

Just six minutes after stealing the Land Rover, he parked it close to the Hyundai in the garage and leapt out. He pulled the dead guard from the back of the Land Rover, opened the trunk to the Hyundai Elantra and dropped the body in the back right on top of Walid. He shut the trunk lid again without even checking on the Desert Hawks Brigade officer.

From the lack of any noise, it seemed as if Major Walid was still passed out drunk, and if he wasn't, Court wondered if he'd be able to tell that the dead man sharing the tight space with him happened to be wearing his uniform.

Court then helped Yasmin with the backpack and had her climb into the backseat of the car and get down low, as before. Quickly he changed out of the dark suit and back into the gray pants and black T-shirt he'd worn since changing at the KWA base hours before.

Yasmin was more focused on the baby and his cries than on the foreigner taking his clothes off outside the Hyundai.

The entire vehicle transfer took just over three minutes, and soon they were back on the road and heading to the south, in the direction of Jordan.

Court knew he needed to get in touch with Voland, but he decided for now he wanted to concentrate on avoiding checkpoints.

For five more minutes they drove along in very light traffic; only once did Court need to leave his route and find another road to avoid a checkpoint. All the while he questioned Yasmin about which way he should go, where the roadblocks could be found, and which suburbs would have less military and militia activity.

But in this endeavor, Yasmin Samara had proved utterly useless.

Finally Court asked, "How is it you don't seem to know anything about the police and military situation around here?"

"Because I haven't been outside Western Villas since Jamal came home from the hospital, and I haven't been out of Mezzeh since last fall."

"I thought you used to live in Paris."

"Yes, but I moved home last year, and as the granddaughter of a minister I was told it wasn't safe to leave the regime strongholds of the city."

Court thought he could quiz a random twenty-something-year-old girl in Wichita about the situation in Syria right now and she might know more details than this woman did.

He began to worry about Yasmin's potential for allegiance to the regime. She worked for Ahmed Azzam, obviously, but if her grandfather was one of his ministers, he thought it likely she would be fully indoctrinated into the belief system of the regime. "Tell me about your grandfather."

Her response surprised him.

"He's dead. Ahmed Azzam had him hanged."

"What? When?"

"Over a year ago. I am not supposed to know. I was told Grandpa had a heart attack. But I heard Azzam's men talking about it late one night in the living room. My grandfather had business dealings with Azzam's brother. There was an argument over money, and Ahmed sided with his brother."

"I'm sorry," Court said, although he felt this news lessened the chance Yasmin would hit Court over the back of the head with a baby bottle and bolt out of the Hyundai at the next intersection.

Next Yasmin said, "But my uncle is a minister, too. He will be killed if I flee the country."

Court fought an eye roll. *Jesus*, he thought. *I don't have time to save every motherfucker in this country from imminent peril.* But instead, he feigned concern. "Who is your uncle?"

"A member of the National Council."

Then to hell with him, Court thought, but again, he did not say it.

"He's your only family remaining?"

"My brother was killed in the second year of the war. I have cousins . . . all in the Army or Air Force."

Good fucking riddance to them, too, Court thought. He said, "You are doing your part to end the war."

He looked in the rearview mirror and saw her making a face like what he said made no sense, and it was an expression Court had found himself adopting from time to time on this operation, but he dropped the conversation. Yes, she was probably right. Her loved ones would be put to death for what he was, in effect, forcing her to do. But that wasn't going to stop him from doing it.

Court said, "Bianca said Azzam was going out of town."

Yasmin said, "He leaves tomorrow. He told me he would return Tuesday afternoon."

This matched with what Bianca told Court the other day about Azzam's trip to review troops at forward bases with the Russians and Iranians.

"Did he tell you where he was going?"

She shook her head. "The president does not tell me things like that. But one of the guards from his detail said something about flying back to Damascus via military helicopter on after a meeting with the Russians."

"Tuesday morning," Court said, mostly to himself.

Yasmin changed gears. "When do we see the other people helping us?"

"What? You're not happy with my performance?"

After a pause, Yasmin sat up fully in the backseat, the baby in her arms. "You are alone, aren't you?"

"Just until Jordan."

"So . . . the entire time you are getting us out of the country, you are working alone. But once we are safe . . . others will help?"

"Doesn't sound so great when you say it like that."

They began driving along through the Damascus suburb of Daryya, and here they found fewer cars on the highway than in the city. This unnerved Court because he'd felt some safety in numbers, plus the road-blocks had been easier to spot when there were long lines of red taillights ahead to tip him off.

There was a turn ahead in the highway and Court worried that there might be a roadblock ahead he could not see; it had been a long time since he'd skirted the last checkpoint, after all. So he decided to take the off-ramp before the turn, then pick his way through the suburb before rejoining with the highway to the south.

Court said, "I might need your help reading signs if they aren't in English."

"You speak English?" she asked.

In Arabic he said, "I speak many languages."

"Poorly," she replied.

Court smiled a little; he'd expected Yasmin to be a mousy and scared little nanny with a conservative Muslim countenance, but instead he found she was handling all this pretty well.

He made a left to follow the road under the overpass, and then, as soon as his headlights centered on the street in front of him, he slammed on his brakes.

Right in front of him, blocking the oncoming lane, was a stationary Syrian Arab Army T-72 tank surrounded by a low wall of sandbags. Uniformed men stood there in the dark. When they saw the Hyundai they flipped on spotlights and motioned for Court to pull over to the side of the road.

There was an urgent intensity to their actions. Court didn't know if this meant they were somehow looking for Walid's vehicle, or if they were surprised to see *any* vehicles here at two in the morning.

Court began rolling forward to where they were leading him, but then he cranked the wheel and floored it, streaking by the tank and the men, racing under the overpass, and then pulling across the road and into a narrow alley that went up a hill.

Lights flashed on, gunfire roared behind him, and the strikes of heavy-caliber bullets sparked the street to his left and in front of him on the broken alley. He completed his turn, then quickly reached down to the fuses he'd readied under the dashboard. He extinguished all the lights in the vehicle, but this did nothing for him at present, because within seconds the heavy beams of light from multiple pursuing vehicles glared in his mirrors.

"Shit! Get down on the floorboard!" he shouted. There were no streetlights in this area, which seemed odd to him at first, but when he made a quick turn, away from the lights behind him, he looked out the driver's-side window and, at first, thought he was looking at a steep hill just off the road.

A second glance showed him that it was the rubble of a huge apartment building. The lights from behind reappeared, and as he raced down the street, he looked ahead. More mountains of rubble in all directions. It appeared this entire town had been razed.

The buildings on the hill were nothing but wreckage; this neighborhood had been bombed to broken bits by the regime years ago to uproot a rebel stronghold. The devastation seemed to go on for miles, but it was clear some of the rubble was, in fact, occupied. As he shot along in the darkness, Court saw lights in deep recesses of the buildings or dark human figures standing by the side of the road watching the sedan flee the pursuing military.

Court floored the Hyundai. He drove faster than he felt comfortable with, especially with the absence of streetlights or headlights. He took turns that led him towards higher elevation, but just before each turn, the lights of the military trucks flared in his rearview.

After five tense minutes of this he thought he was in the clear. He pulled up onto a raised overpass, now looking for a way back to the highway to the south. He made it just a hundred yards, then saw four green UAZ-469 light utility vehicles parked at the National Defence Forces militia checkpoint on the overpass. They were Russian in manufacture, but they looked like slightly larger and more robust WWII-era U.S. Army Jeeps.

Court slammed on the brakes, reversed, and executed a J-turn that had both Yasmin and the baby crying out in back. One of the UAZ-469s was in hot pursuit as he shot along an empty four-lane road running through the bombed-out buildings.

Court looked into his mirror and saw the UAZ-469 bearing down on him. The NDF truck got closer and closer, its driver unencumbered by low-light conditions.

Gunfire erupted behind them, Yasmin screamed and the baby wailed, and more glass in both the rear window and the windshield shattered. The rearview mirror spun off the arm holding it, and Court felt a sharp sting on the right side of his head, just above his ear.

He felt blood running behind his ear, down the back of his neck. He didn't know if he'd been shot or cut, but he could still see, still drive, so he kept going.

And he could still think. The UAZ-469 closed to within fifty feet of the Hyundai, and Court pulled the steering wheel to the right. He stomped on his brakes again, even yanking the parking brake up, and put the sedan in park. The utility vehicle overshot him on the hilly road, and then it, too, slammed on its brakes, but before the driver could put his Jeep into reverse, Court had jumped out of the Hyundai, leveling his pistol in the passenger window.

The passenger swung his AK up to the threat, but Court shot him through the forehead, knocking him sideways and out of the way of the driver.

The young National Defence Forces soldier just had time to switch his focus from Court to the barrel of the gun in his hand before Court shot him in the face, killing him instantly.

Court opened the passenger-side door and dragged both bodies out of the UAZ. He helped a now nearly unresponsive Yasmin and the baby in her arms out of the Hyundai, then reached to pop the trunk to drag Walid out.

Before he put his hand on the trunk, however, he saw a line of at least a dozen large-caliber holes in the rear of the Hyundai. Blood ran freely out the back, and this told him Walid had been hit by the shooting at the checkpoint.

He shined a flashlight in and saw two dead men, both riddled with bullets.

Court moved back to the driver's-side door, reached in, and put the sedan in neutral. It began rolling forward down the hill instantly, picking up speed as it went.

It veered to the left somewhat, but rolled over broken concrete and rebar on the sidewalk and then angled back, plunging once again down the middle of the four-lane street.

Court didn't wait to watch it roll away. Instead he turned off the lights of the UAZ and helped Yasmin and Jamal inside. He climbed behind the wheel, ignored the smeared blood on the driver's-side window, and looked down the hill, just as a pair of Syrian Arab Army trucks pulled into the intersection two hundred yards on.

The Hyundai rolled towards them, picking up speed.

Men bailed out of the trucks and began shooting at the vehicle. They had no idea they were shooting at an unoccupied car.

"Hit 'em." Court urged the sedan on as he turned the UAV to the right and bumped up onto the low concrete rubble there.

The Hyundai missed the Syrian trucks off to his left, but the soldiers there kept firing into it as it continued along the road lower down the hill. A round struck the gas tank and the vehicle exploded in a fireball but kept rolling downhill while the Syrians climbed back into their trucks to pursue it.

Court turned away again, focused in the terrible light, doing his best to pick the safest line through the wreckage of an apartment building.

It took him nearly a minute, but he made it through the destroyed building, then out into an alleyway on the other side. Without his headlights he scraped obstacles every few seconds, but he made it to the end, turned right, picked up speed, then ran over obstruction after obstruction.

The bumps flung Yasmin and Jamal into the air in the backseat. The baby cried, but Court knew he had to put distance between himself and the last place the Hyundai was seen as fast as possible.

Out of the wreckage of the bombed-out neighborhood, Court pulled out into light southbound traffic on a two-laned north-south road. He turned on his headlights. A caravan of military trucks raced towards him, but they passed by, and three NDF militiamen standing by their vehicles at an intersection a mile to the south barely looked up as he passed.

Somehow he'd done it, but he'd only managed to get out of the district where the kidnapping had occurred.

He still had to get himself, a terrified young girl, and a crying infant out of Syria before the sun came up.

Yasmin sat in the back of the truck, feeding Jamal from a bottle.

Court turned back to her as he drove. "I need to make a phone call."

She looked up at him. "To tell your friends that we've survived so they can throw you a party when we get to safety?"

Court smiled, and turned back to the road. "Yeah, but I'm sure it will be a great party."

He could feel Yasmin looking at him for a long time. "You okay?" he asked.

"Monsieur," she replied, "your head is bleeding badly."

"Yep," he replied, but he didn't know what he could do about it at the moment.

CHAPTER 50

Vincent Voland stood alone in the soft rain, his tweed suit soaked through. Boyer and his three associates had left the property; Voland assumed they would go to the road and hitch a ride, but he could not be certain. None of the five men who'd been allowed to leave the farmhouse had made eye contact with any of the others, and aside from a few mumbles here and there between the mercenaries, there had been no words.

But Voland did not leave. He *could* not leave.

He stood still now in a grove of winter pear trees south of the farmhouse, along the driveway that snaked to the east to the road a quarter mile away.

As soon as he'd left the house he tried making a call on his mobile phone, but just as before, there was a jammer in the area that prevented him from getting a signal. So he stood there, watching, waiting to see what would happen, positioning himself as close to the driveway as possible while remaining out of sight.

He heard the gunfire in the house peter out after five minutes, and then for another five it was utterly still, until one final crack of a gunshot rang out. And then, the smell reached him, and he realized somehow a fire had started in the building. In the darkness and misty rain he didn't see anything for the next few minutes, but eventually smoke began pouring from the attic vents and the chimney and out ground-floor windows. He began praying for Rima and Bianca to find some way out, either on their own—which he knew was likely too much to wish for—or at least in the custody of the Syrians and Drexler.

But they never came out.

Thirty minutes after Voland exited the farmhouse a sedan raced up the driveway, past his position, then skidded to a stop on the wet stones alongside the side door. Black-clad commandos began rushing out of the building and piling into the car. A second vehicle arrived soon after.

Sebastian Drexler himself appeared, running out of the house, rubbing his eyes and falling to the ground, coughing and choking.

Behind him, more men, Syrians all.

But no women. No Rima. No Bianca.

Voland watched Drexler get control of his coughing fit, and then he stood and began shouting at one of the commandos. This man was tall with curly black hair; he was the one who shot Tarek. Voland took him as the leader, but this was just a guess, because there were no known photographs of the Syrian operative called Malik.

The sixty-five-year-old Frenchman standing in the mud, in the rain, told himself that if he only had a rifle or a rocket launcher, he'd extract payback on Drexler and Malik right now. They were only fifty meters away.

It would be so easy.

But even he did not believe this. No . . . he had surrendered tonight—rightly or wrongly, this was a simple fact. And the untrained husband-and-wife heart surgeons, who didn't belong in the world of espionage and rebellion, had both died fighting for what they believed.

Voland wanted to be sick.

He was close enough to see everyone on the driveway climb into the sedans and then race away from the house. The roof of the building was fully engulfed in flames now, and it was clear the entire place would burn to the ground before the fire department came.

And it was Drexler and the Syrians who had escaped. Not Rima. Not Tarek. Not Bianca.

No one else would be leaving that building with their lives.

He assumed Drexler himself must have killed Bianca, somehow doing it right under the noses of the other men.

As soon as the last of the three vehicles raced back down the driveway,

Voland stepped out of the pear trees and up to the driveway. He told himself he should be running into the burning building, screaming the names of the women, pulling them out on his back.

But again, just as his thoughts of shooting the madmen who'd caused this all drifted away, so did his fantasies of coming to the rescue.

A portion of the burning roof overhang collapsed down on the parking circle, right on top of Voland's car.

He turned away from the farmhouse and towards the road, hundreds of meters distant through the trees. He shuffled as he walked . . . because he had nowhere to go.

His mobile phone rang in his pocket, and this startled him. Whoever had been jamming the signal must have shut down their equipment. Quickly he snatched it up to his ear, hoping against hope it was Rima telling him she'd made it out somehow.

"Yes?"

But it was the voice of the Gray Man. "I've got them. We're ten klicks south of Mezzeh, clear for now, but I have over one hundred klicks to go to the border and less than four hours before daylight. Tell me where to—"

Voland had stepped off the driveway and begun walking through wet grass towards the winter pear again, because of approaching lights and fire truck sirens on the driveway ahead. As he did this he interrupted the American. "There has been an . . . an event."

"What kind of event?"

Voland sniffed, cleared his throat. "She's dead. Bianca is dead. They are *all* dead."

A pause. "Tarek? Rima?"

"As I said. They are dead."

"*Dammit!* How?"

"I tried to help them. Rima and Tarek. But they wouldn't listen."

"Was it Drexler?"

"*Bien sûr* it was *fucking* Drexler, along with Malik, a Syrian government assassin, and his team. Guns, night vision, communications jammers. They burned the house down to embers. They slaughtered everyone!"

Another pause on the line, but not for long. The American said, "Well . . . they didn't slaughter *everyone*, did they, Voland?" Vincent Voland had expected to hear just exactly what he heard next. "I cannot *fucking wait* to hear the explanation of why *you* didn't die in that fire with the rest of them."

"I . . . I *swear* to you. I tried. I fought with them to understand we were outnumbered. I told them it was futile to—"

"Stop right there. You ran out on them, didn't you?"

"Did you hear what I said? Azzam's men were here! GIS. Mukhabarat paramilitaries. We didn't know GIS would be involved."

Slowly, the Gray Man said, "Did you, or did . . . you . . . not . . . surrender to Drexler and the Syrians?"

"I did!" Voland shouted defiantly, his voice echoing off the trees around him. A fire truck raced past on his left. "It was exactly the right move! The move Rima and Tarek *should* have taken for themselves."

For the next twenty seconds, all Voland could hear was breathing over the phone. Then the American said, "You and I will talk about this again when I get to Jordan."

To this Vincent Voland made no reply. Fire trucks continued rolling past, and he walked deeper into the cover of the trees.

"*Hello?* The pickup at the border? Remember? I need you to focus and give me my coordinates for—"

"*Monsieur* . . . I realize how this will sound, and I'm truly sorry. If it were just me I would get you and the child out of there . . . but, with the mother gone . . . it's not me making the decisions, you understand."

Court's voice lowered an octave. "Be very careful about what you say next."

"What *can* I say? The child was a bargaining chip, nothing more! The extraction of the baby was only to earn the compliance of Bianca Medina. But Medina is dead, so there is no way to exploit everything she knew about Azzam."

"He's leverage."

"*How?* He's an infant! Azzam will disavow that baby the moment he knows Bianca is dead. He won't bring a bastard child into his palace without a mother, and Shakira surely won't accept him. Maybe Azzam will find another mistress, make another heir, but Jamal Medina is worthless to him now. That means he is worthless to those trying to stop Azzam."

The next response from the American was delivered in a matter-of-fact tone that made it all the more frightening to the Frenchman. "I'm going to kill you, Vincent. You know that, right?"

"Listen to me carefully. If you give me time, I *will* find a way to get you out. I owe you that for your heroism over the past week. But the Syrian resistance group based in Jordan won't help now, so it won't happen tonight. And even when I *do* find an exfiltration route for you, it will just be for you. The girl and the baby. That operation is played out. They can't come."

"We had a deal, you son of a bitch! I was to bring the child to—"

"What *deal* did you have with me? If you will remember, I was firmly *against* you traveling to Syria! I wanted you up here, where you could protect the Halabys from Drexler."

"You promised me you had that end of the operation covered. I was wrong to believe in you."

It was silent for several seconds, until Voland said, "I will find a way to get you out."

"Yasmin and the baby, too. If I come out, they come out."

"Then you have put yourself in a hopeless condition, haven't you?"

The American did not reply.

· · ·

Court sat on a pile of rubble in the half-destroyed underground parking garage of a completely destroyed office building. He held the phone to his left ear, and with his other hand he picked out what he hoped was the last shard of protective windshield glass from where several pieces had been lodged under a flap of skin right above his ear. The wound bled freely still, but it was superficial, and hardly his biggest concern of the moment.

The NDF vehicle he had stolen sat parked twenty feet away in the deepest shadows of the large empty space. He looked over at Yasmin and Jamal, whom he could just barely see through a shaft of moonlight that came through a crack in the concrete roof. She held the baby in her arms and sat with her back against the wall of the garage looking up at Court. She didn't speak a word of English, this was obvious, because she showed no reaction to the fact that her fate was being discussed in front of her, and things weren't looking good for her right now.

But she could clearly see there was a problem. She watched Court intently, certainly wondering why he was yelling at the people that he'd promised were waiting right over the Jordanian border with open arms.

Court turned away from the young girl and blew out a long sigh. "What would it take for you to agree to extract the child and the girl?"

The Frenchman on the other end of the line said, "What do you mean, 'what would it *take*'? This is not a negotiation. I have to find people in Jordan or Syria or Lebanon or Turkey who will risk their lives to get you out. I can find someone, probably, but only to get out an able-bodied man of incredible skill. No one would be foolish enough to take on the added danger of an untrained civilian and an infant. There is *nothing* that would—"

Court said, "What if I helped you eliminate Ahmed Azzam . . . would *that* do it?"

"Eliminate?"

"Assassinate. I won't do it myself, that's impossible. But it might be possible for me to acquire intel that helps the FSA or the SDF or *someone* out there to kill him. Intel better than anything you could have gotten from Bianca Medina."

Voland sniffed out a surprised laugh. "Ha! Well, yes, of course, in that case I could find someone who would help me bring out an entire nursery school." The Frenchman clearly thought Court was joking.

But Court just sat there with the phone to his ear.

Voland slowly realized the American was serious. "What are you talking about?"

Court said, "I know where Azzam is going. *Exactly* where he is going. And I can get there myself. Close, anyway."

"How do you know this?"

"Bianca told me he was going to make an appearance at a Russian military base outside Damascus."

"There are a half dozen that I know of, and I assume there are others I don't know about. You can't—"

Court cut him off. "And then, tonight, a regime-backing militia officer told me the SAA was creating an unprecedented security cordon around a new Russian special forces base outside Palmyra, possibly for a high-profile visitor."

"That's it?"

"No, that's not it. Yasmin tells me Ahmed told her he'll return to

Damascus on Tuesday. I think he'll be at a Russian base in or near Palmyra on Tuesday morning."

"That's not enough intelligence to get the FSA to attack a Russian base."

"Of course it's not." He said, "But here's my offer. You talk to your people in the French government. You know, the ones you *aren't* working with right now."

"Go on."

"Find a way to get the kid and the girl out of here, and I'll stay in Syria. I'll go north, I'll try to get more intel on Azzam's exact location and the time of his visit. I'll push any intel I get to you, and you push it to the FSA. If they have any assets in the area at all, I'll give them a target."

"How on earth can you possibly get close enough to provide intelligence?"

"That's my problem, not yours. Do we have a deal?"

Voland took a long time before replying. "What is wrong with you?"

"Meaning?"

"Those are not your people. That is not your war. What is your personal motivation? Why are you doing this?"

"We had a shitty plan from the start. That plan got a lot of people killed, and so far, it's achieved nothing. But I am not going to let Jamal and Yasmin swing in the wind because of our mistakes and miscalculations. I won't abandon them!"

"But . . . it wasn't *your* plan."

"No, it was *yours*. You should feel the responsibility for these two that I feel, but apparently you don't."

"I am a realist."

"You are a piece of shit!" Court's rage threatened to overtake him. At this moment he wanted to kill Voland almost as much as he wanted to kill Azzam. But he got control of his emotions, enough to reply. "This is my offer. I will serve as your agent in place here in Syria, but if I do this for you, then it will leave you with two choices. *Only* two. You can get the boy and the nanny out of here through your contacts, or you can do the other thing."

"What . . . what is the other thing?"

"The other thing is run and hide, because if you *don't* come through on this and I *do* survive Syria, I'll come hunting you. And since you now see what I will do *without* any personal motivation, just imagine what I'm capable of when I'm on a mission of revenge."

Voland sounded utterly terrified now. "No threats are necessary, I assure you. I agree to your request, and I *swear* I will not let you down."

"Your promises are less than worthless. Show me action."

"Of course. Rima gave you the name of someone there in the city you could call on in an emergency."

"She did."

"Take Yasmin and the boy to him. I know how to reach him, so when all is arranged, I will contact him about the extraction."

Court looked at his watch. "Okay." And then, "You're all I've got, Voland, and I don't trust you. But I *do* believe that I scare the living shit out of you, so I think you'll do your best to come through."

"You have my personal motivation figured out. And you're all I have down there with the ability to change the outcome of this horrible war. With you working as my man in Syria, there is some hope for that wretched place."

Court hung up the phone. He didn't find himself filled with the same level of optimism as Voland, and he chalked that up to the fact that Voland wasn't relying on a man who'd double-crossed him and then turned his back on his clients.

He looked to Yasmin and switched to French. "Back in the car. We're going back to Damascus."

Yasmin did not hide the confusion and displeasure from her face.

"Yeah . . . tell me about it," Court said as he pulled himself off the rubble.

CHAPTER 51

While Vincent Voland continued marching purposefully along the driveway towards the road, two full kilometers west of him a woman stumbled through a large field waist high with barley. She caught her tennis shoe on a plow track and tumbled to the ground, then struggled slowly back to her feet. She was exhausted; her hands, arms, and face were covered in cuts and bruises, and she was soaking wet, both from the rain and from the creek she'd fallen into in the woods behind her.

Bianca Medina whipped her long black hair out of her eyes with a shake of her head as she pushed on.

Thirty-five minutes earlier Rima had unlocked the door to Bianca's room and told her that she and Tarek wanted her to run. Ahmed's men had arrived with a man working for Shakira, Rima had explained, and while this meant they didn't know what would happen to her if she was caught, as far as the Halabys were concerned, she needed to get out of the house and into the woods. Rima told her to hide there till either she or her husband came for her later, and to reveal herself only if she heard Rima's or Tarek's voice.

The Frenchman, Monsieur Voland, was no longer to be trusted, Rima had hurriedly told her without providing any explanation.

Rima remained in the wine cellar as Bianca ran with Firas up to the kitchen, and then he, too, stayed behind, holding his gun on the door to the hearth room, as Bianca raced upstairs following Rima's instructions. She saw several FSEU guards at the top of the stairs, all checking their weapons and making a hasty blockade there from pieces of furniture, but she ran past them, heading over to a bedroom on the northern side of the house. She opened a window and climbed out, then hung down in the darkness, covered from the back by the long side of the farmhouse and partially covered to the front by the long greenhouse that blocked anyone in the drive from seeing her. She dropped down into the wet grass and entered the long, narrow greenhouse so she wouldn't be seen by anyone at the front of the property.

On the far side of the greenhouse she stayed low, ran along the lawn there with long fast strides, then entered the woods on the northern side of the property, running as fast as her long, athletic legs would take her.

She estimated she made it three hundred meters or so, where she found a place to both hide and get out of the rain in the form of the wide trunk of a toppled oak. She sat there for ten minutes; for much of the time she listened to the pops of gunfire, and then all was still. Around the time she'd expected to hear Rima's voice calling to her, she saw a faint glow through the trees in the distance. Minutes after that came the sirens of fire trucks and police cars.

Even before Bianca left the wine cellar she'd seen Rima pulling plastic bottles of turpentine out of the storage room. She hadn't known what she was up to at the time, but as the roof of the farmhouse caught fire and the glow through the trees increased, casting terrifying shadows all around her, she realized what had happened.

Rima had been trying to cover Bianca's tracks, to make it look like she'd been killed in the fire. Bianca also realized, although she did not know how she knew, that Rima and Tarek were now dead.

She waited another ten minutes, and then she decided she needed to run again. No one was coming to help her, she could feel it.

So she moved out through the dark woods, fell into the creek, and cut herself so many times she'd stopped reacting to each new individual pain. She broke out into the barley field and then saw a road in the distance, and she pushed on.

Bianca had a plan as to what she would do now. She would get to the road, find a phone, call her friends with the fashion designer that invited her to France, and they would come and pick her up. Of course she knew she would need a story for where she had been since the ISIS attack three nights earlier, but for now all she wanted to do was get away from there.

As soon as she came to the road, a car's headlights appeared from the southwest and she waved at it frantically, standing by the side of the little road and shivering.

The white car slowed and pulled over.

Utterly exhausted, Bianca all but collapsed on the passenger-side door as she leaned into the window.

In the front passenger seat was a Caucasian man in his forties, a cigarette in his hand. After a moment he rolled down his window. In French she said, "Thank God, monsieur. Please, I need help!"

The man just gaped at her, a dumbfounded look on his face. He said nothing, made no movement, just sat there holding his cigarette and staring.

But the driver's-side door opened, and a young dark-haired man launched out of it. He ran around to her, helped her into the backseat, and then knelt down in the open door, looking her over.

It was then she realized the man held a walkie-talkie in his hand. He brought it to his mouth, and he spoke in Arabic. "This is Number Twelve; I'm on the D91, west of the property. I have the subject! I repeat, I *have* the subject! She appears to be unharmed."

Bianca blinked hard, then harder still.

Over the radio a voice in Arabic said, "*What?* You're sure?"

"Yes, sir. She came running out of the field right in front of my car, Allah be praised. I'm taking her to the warehouse now."

The man lowered the walkie-talkie and smiled at her. "Madam, I am with the Syrian embassy. We have rescued you, sister! We will get you out of here and, *inshallah*, back to Damascus where you will be safe from all harm. I promise I will protect you with my life."

Bianca collapsed to her side in the backseat of the car and began sobbing uncontrollably.

• • •

The Syrian commando ordered Henri Sauvage to drive, and he remained in back with the woman, ready to cover her with his own body if there was any danger. The young man was almost euphoric, and Bianca, it appeared to Sauvage by looking in the rearview, seemed utterly despondent.

But Sauvage was thinking about himself, and he realized he had just helped the Syrians grab a missing Spanish national out here in the French countryside, and he, a captain in the Judicial Police, was the guy driving the getaway vehicle. He'd go to prison for life for this, which meant he'd want a bonus from Eric, for *damn* sure.

And he'd want to get the fuck away from France, probably for the rest of his life, as soon as this was over.

The Syrians had what they'd come for now, so he saw the light at the end of the tunnel for the first time in days, and he told himself he just might survive this, after all.

CHAPTER 52

Thirty-four-year-old Dr. Shawkat Saddiqi parked his Nissan Sentra in the reserved space in front of his apartment building and turned off the engine. He sat there a moment with his eyes closed.

It was three a.m.

He'd worked a twelve-hour shift in the ER of Al-Fayhaa Hospital that had turned into a fifteen-hour shift when the nine wounded occupants of a bus bombing were brought in shortly before he was due to get off work at midnight. He'd performed surgery on three of them himself, and saved two lives.

But he wasn't happy, he wasn't proud of his work. No . . . now at three a.m., he was just *fucking* spent.

He climbed out of his vehicle and walked along the sidewalk towards the back entrance of his building. He was surprised to hear footsteps behind him at this time of the night, but not worried. This was an upper-middle-class neighborhood in Al Midan, in the center of Damascus. This part of the city had been spared much of the war, at least the physical scars of it, anyway.

The emotional scars? No one in this city was immune from those, just as almost no one in this city was blameless from responsibility for the carnage.

Saddiqi arrived at the door and reached forward with his key, but a voice behind him called out softly.

"Shawkat Saddiqi?" The doctor turned around.

In front of him on the pathway stood a man with a beard wearing a wrinkled dark suit. Standing behind him was a small young girl wearing a chador and a long-sleeve cotton shirt with black warm-up pants and a blue backpack. He didn't notice at first, but quickly he realized she held an infant in her arms.

Saddiqi might have been nervous to be accosted in a dark parking lot at this time of the morning, but there was nothing threatening about the group in front of him at all.

"*As salaam aleikum,*" *Peace be unto you,* Saddiqi said, touching his hand to his heart. It was a polite greeting, but he fought a little disappointment inwardly. He was not unaccustomed to people showing up at his apartment in the middle of the night. It usually meant he wouldn't be feeling the coolness of his pillow any time soon, and he desperately needed rest.

"*Wa aleikum salaam,*" *And peace be upon you,* replied both the man and the woman simultaneously.

Saddiqi looked them over for any obvious injuries. He saw some blood on the collar of the man's shirt. "How can I—"

The man said, "Do you speak English?"

Saddiqi's guard went up, but he wasn't sure why. In Arabic he replied, "Who are you?"

The man continued, still in English. "Doctor . . . I've been sent by Rima Halaby. It is a dire emergency."

Saddiqi turned away.

He put the key in the door lock and opened it. In heavily accented English he replied, "Please. Come inside."

. . .

Ten minutes later Yasmin sat on a vinyl sofa in a small but tidy apartment on the fifth floor of the building. Jamal was in her lap, and he ate greedily from the bottle she fed him.

Court and Shawkat Saddiqi sat at a small bar area in the apartment's kitchen, just feet away from Yasmin. The doctor had already made tea for his guests, and he'd put out a plate of cookies and sweets that Yasmin politely declined. Court, on the other hand, dug shamelessly into a stack of cookies made of dates and flour because he hadn't eaten all day.

Saddiqi took out a first-aid kit he kept in a back room and began cleaning the wound on Court's head. As he did this he asked, "So, how is Rima?"

Court put down his cookie. "I'm very sorry to have to tell you this. But she's dead."

Saddiqi looked up from the bloody wound. "When?"

"Rima gave me your name two hours ago. One hour ago she was killed."

"My God. What about Tarek?"

"Tarek is dead, as well."

Saddiqi sighed and poured more antiseptic on a fresh cotton swab, and he went back to work. Court thought the man showed little emotion, and he tried to gauge Saddiqi's relationship with the Halabys from his lack of reaction to hearing about their deaths, but he stopped himself. This guy was a trauma doc in Damascus. He must have seen death every hour of every day of his working life, so his internal meter of heartbreak and sadness must have been so off-kilter Court knew he couldn't judge the man by how he acted.

Saddiqi closed the torn flap of skin, holding it until the bleeding stopped. "The Halabys' two children died last year. I assume you were aware."

"Yes. How did you know them?"

"I was a couple years older than the kids, but their parents and my parents had been friends when we were children. We lost touch after they emigrated when the war began.

"I had been helping the rebellion here in secret, treating wounded insurgents who showed up at my door. Someone who got out of the country told the Halabys that even though Dr. Saddiqi was working at a regime hospital in the capital, he could be trusted. Tarek reached out to me via encrypted chat, and we've shared information to help save lives."

Saddiqi added, "This is back when they were just involved with nonviolent aid."

Court said, "And then, somehow they became leaders of the insurgency."

Saddiqi used glue to seal the skin closed above Court's ear. "Leaders? No. After their kids died, the only way they could sleep at night was to dream about killing Ahmed Azzam and his supporters. Two people in their fifties who'd spent thirty years saving lives learned to dream of *taking* lives. But now they are dead. All for nothing."

"No," Court countered. "For something. But only if you can help us."

"The Halabys sent you to me. Why?"

"This girl . . . and the baby. They need a place to stay. It might be a few days."

Saddiqi seemed surprised by the request. He'd obviously expected much more. "Of course. They are welcome in my home."

"There is something else. It might be that Yasmin doesn't really want to be here."

Saddiqi stood up and looked over Court to the girl feeding the baby on the sofa behind him. "She seems okay."

"What she's been through tonight has been a shock. People react in different ways. Trust me, I've seen it. She might be totally compliant now, and then wake up in the morning and try to throw herself out the window to get away."

Saddiqi had cleaned the blood from Court's neck, and now he took off his gloves and threw them into the trash. As he did this, he looked again at Court. "You are asking me to hold a mother and her baby prisoner?"

Court did not want to tell Dr. Saddiqi everything, but he realized he had no choice. "Sit down, Doctor."

Saddiqi did so. "In my profession, we tell people to sit down when we are about to give them very bad news."

"It's the same in my profession. That baby? His name is Jamal."

"So?"

"Lots of people name their boys Jamal around here, right?"

"Of course. It is the given name of the man who ran the country for thirty years before his son took over."

"Right," Court said. "But that boy? His father named him Jamal because *his* father's name was Jamal."

"Who is the boy's father?"

Court shrugged. "Ahmed Azzam."

Saddiqi shook his head emphatically. "Ridiculous. Ahmed Azzam's son

347

is dead. It's a secret, but Shakira took him to my hospital many times, and we all know—"

Court shook his head now. "This isn't Shakira's boy, and Yasmin isn't the mother, either."

It took a moment for the doctor to understand, but when he did he covered his face with his hands and muttered something in Arabic that sounded like a prayer. Finally he switched back to English. "Who is the mother?"

"A Spanish woman who has a house here. She's currently out of the country."

"And you brought Ahmed Azzam's child here, to *my* flat. I assume people are looking for him."

"I'd say that's a very safe assumption. I can promise you that no one tailed me to your place. The main danger is the girl. She is complying because she's worried she'll be blamed for this even if she somehow manages to get away. But who knows? Like I said, tomorrow she might have second thoughts."

"Again, sir. Do you think I just happen to be running a jail in the back of my flat?"

"I didn't have any other place to take her. I have to leave town . . . just for a few days." Court looked off into the distance. "I think. I *hope*." He looked up at the doctor. "If I don't come back by Friday . . . then I'm dead, and you're on your own."

"You aren't making a good case for me helping."

"I hear you've been helping for seven years. You'll help now, because that kid back there might just lead to the end of this war."

"How will the child end the war?"

"Better if you don't ask any questions."

Saddiqi rubbed his tired face again. After a long time he nodded, as if to himself, and said, "I have a neighbor. He is involved in the local resistance. He's not a leader, but he is a good man, and I suppose he can watch over a girl and a baby for a couple of days in my apartment. If he can't manage that, then I guess that means the resistance is useless."

"That's good. How soon can he be here?"

"I patched him up after he was shot two years ago. Since then he's brought me other wounded fighters. If I need him, at any time, he will be here. I'll call now."

Court told Dr. Saddiqi about his contact in France who was looking for a way to bring the girl and the baby out of the country. He gave Saddiqi Vincent Voland's phone number.

Saddiqi asked, "This Frenchman. Is he reliable?"

"If he screws you or me over, then I will tear off his nuts and shove them down his throat. He knows this. I think he has all the motivation he needs to come through for us."

The doctor looked at Court a long time. Court broke the staring contest by glancing at his watch and standing up quickly. "I have to get to Babbila."

"What's in Babbila?"

"The Desert Hawks militia base. I'm sort of working for them at the moment."

Saddiqi seemed as stunned at this as Court had expected.

"Long story," Court explained. "It was my cover, and I wasn't planning on using it again, but I'm going to need to find a way to get back in there like none of this happened."

"You shouldn't be out on the streets. But I can go anywhere. I'll drive you where you need to go as soon as my neighbor comes to watch the girl."

CHAPTER 53

At the warehouse just off the grounds of Toussus-le-Noble general aviation airport, the Syrian commandos tended to their wounded, bagged their dead, and cleaned and reloaded their weapons.

Bianca barely spoke a word as she was shown to her quarters, an area in the corner of the warehouse floor partitioned off with sheets hanging from ropes. Inside was a cot, a change of clothes, and a new pair of tennis shoes in her size. For the third time in the past week, people had given her clothes to change into, although it occurred to her that only the Lebanese fashion designer she'd come to Paris to model for had given her anything she much felt like wearing.

As soon as she arrived Malik told her that President Azzam wanted to speak with her via sat phone, but she surprised everyone by saying she was just too tired and emotional to talk. She asked Malik to relay the message that, thanks be to God, she had been rescued and was unhurt, and she would speak with him in the morning. It was obvious to Bianca that Malik did not want to disappoint Azzam, but also clear he did not want to offend the woman who obviously held a special relationship with the president, so he reluctantly let it go and offered her canned food, which she declined, and bottled water that she took with her to her makeshift quarters.

Rima had warned her that someone with this group had been working with Shakira and had been involved in the ISIS assassination attempt. But even though Rima didn't specify the attractive blond-haired Westerner standing on the far side of the warehouse floor, Bianca Medina had decided all the Syrians were working for Malik, and Malik was definitely in the Syrian intelligence services. That left two possibilities as to the identity of the man working for Shakira Azzam.

There was the gruff man who'd said not a word to her during the drive from the field to the warehouse, and the blond man . . . she thought he might be Swiss because of his accent and word choices. He had shaken her hand and told her he had been sent here to Paris by Ahmed himself to help with her recovery.

He seemed genuine, and sincere, but she had met many men who could charm and deceive simultaneously.

She didn't dare say anything to anyone about what Rima had told her. Any hint that the Halabys had allowed her to escape or had communicated information to her would tip off Ahmed's people that she had been complicit in her own disappearance. If not at first, then at least after the fact.

She just lay down on her little cot and stared up at the rafters ten meters above her. She thought about the American down in Damascus, about Jamal, and about the things Rima had told her and shown her about the crimes of Ahmed Azzam, and she wondered what the hell she was supposed to do now.

. . .

Sebastian Drexler gazed across twenty meters of dusty warehouse floor to the beautiful young woman lying on the cot, just barely visible through an opening in the bedsheets hanging around her. He looked her long, slender physique up and down, then fantasized about pulling his pistol from his coat right now, firing a round into that exquisite body of hers, and then spinning around and dispatching Malik's men with perfectly placed bullets to their heads. He could then burn this building to the ground and catch the next train to Bern or Zurich or Gstaad or Lauterbrunnen.

It was fantasy, of course. There were still eleven GIS operators here, nine of whom were fit enough to fight effectively.

No . . . Drexler would have to wait, but he didn't think he'd have to wait too long.

An opportunity would arise to kill Bianca as they traveled to the east; he just had to be ready to take advantage of it.

As he thought about the hours and days ahead, he looked down at his phone and saw that he had four missed calls and a text on his encrypted commo app. He opened the text.

Answer your fucking phone.

It was the first lady. He sighed, long and hard, because he'd have to call and give her the news that Bianca was still alive and, for now, at least, she was surrounded by men who would give their lives to protect her.

He walked over to a darkened distant corner of the warehouse and dialed the number to her satellite phone.

Shakira answered on the first ring. "Dammit, Sebastian!"

Missed you, too, he thought. "The woman has been recovered."

"Dead or alive?"

"At present she is alive. I have a plan to—"

"There was a shoot-out in Mezzeh tonight. In Western Villas. A man escaped. It's on the news, and I'm having my staff bring me updates from GIS."

Drexler was utterly confused and had no idea how this related to him. "Wait. *What* man? What are you talking about?"

"They are saying this man kidnapped a baby after fighting security forces! He killed several Ba'ath security officers, and more NDF forces that chased him until he disappeared."

"Who was the baby?" Drexler asked, but he knew the answer.

"On television they aren't saying anything about the identity of the victims, but they wouldn't, would they?"

Drexler's eyes closed and squinted shut, and he gripped the phone just as hard. He understood now, understood even better than Shakira what was going on. "A highly skilled killer who can slip into Syria and kidnap the child of the president. There is only one person who fits that description on this Earth."

"Who is he?"

"They call him the Gray Man. He is American."

"What's he doing in Syria?"

"Apparently, he was working for the Halabys."

Shakira gasped. "The man who rescued Bianca in Paris?"

"One and the same. And then he went to Damascus to rescue her son."

Shakira said, "Once Bianca is dead, this won't matter. He can put the kid on CNN for all I care. Ahmed won't admit to being his father."

Drexler did not reply.

"When will you do it? When will you kill her?"

"I am told we will fly to Serbia in the morning. There we will wait for documents to be sent to us so we can continue on to Russia. From there we'll come home. I'll take care of everything before we leave for Russia."

"You had better," Shakira said.

Drexler passed on a few more promises to the first lady that it would all be over soon, and they would be together again. Then he hung up the phone and looked up to see Henri Sauvage standing over him.

Drexler wasn't in the mood. "What?"

"Why am I still here? I have done every last thing you asked."

Drexler knew Malik was the only one who could release Sauvage at this point, and Drexler figured the only reason Malik had not released Sauvage already was that Malik was going to shoot the French cop in the head at some point and dump his body in a muddy field, simply to tie off one of the many compromises of the past week.

Drexler said none of this. Instead an idea came to him. "Henri . . . you might not know it, but you are crucial to this operation, and you are in a position of power right now."

"What the hell are you talking about?"

"The next phase, you might have gathered, involves getting Medina back to Syria. To do that we have to travel across Europe. I do not have credentials that can pass scrutiny, and neither does Malik. Unlike me, he is here in Europe legally, but as soon as Rima and Tarek are found dead in that house, men with Syrian diplomatic credentials traveling across Europe are going to be looked at with the highest suspicion."

"What does this have to do with me?"

"You are a French citizen and a law enforcement officer. If you came with us, you could facilitate any dealings we had at airports, with chance encounters with police or others. You could go out and purchase supplies, rent cars, things of that nature. Logistically you would be a tremendous help."

"And in the process I would incriminate myself even more into this crime?"

353

"My dear captain, at this stage of the game I imagine you are already in as deep as you could possibly be. Why not make, say, another one hundred thousand euros in the process? That money could help you as you transition your life to someplace safer for you."

Sauvage just stared Drexler down. Finally he said, "Two hundred fifty thousand euros."

Drexler didn't imagine Henri Sauvage would see fifty cents of this money they were discussing, so this was purely a hypothetical conversation. But to the Frenchman he said, "Two hundred. This will be two days of work. Three at most. Then you can have the rest of your life."

Sauvage did not look happy, but Drexler doubted this man ever looked happy. He nodded slowly. "Fine. But three days at the most and then I return."

"Agreed." Drexler didn't really need the Frenchman along on the journey; he could tend to any logistical arrangements himself, using his powers of persuasion and charm, but he saw how Sauvage could prove useful.

A plane would land at the airport in a few hours and it would only accommodate four people apart from the pilot. That was Drexler himself, Malik, Medina, and one other person. The Swiss operative would find himself in the air with fewer threats around him, and more opportunity to deal with Bianca Medina.

If Drexler managed to kill the passengers and crash the plane, and if Sauvage's charred remains were found in the wreckage of a smoldering aircraft crashed on a mountain or somewhere along the way between here and there, and if in said remains Drexler's watch, glasses, and other personal effects were found, then Shakira would think Drexler died along with Medina.

This would satisfy Stefan Meier at the bank, it would satisfy Shakira Azzam, and it would more than satisfy Drexler himself.

Just as Drexler had used the dead body of the Finnish photographer to get into Europe, he would use the dead body of the French police detective to finally free himself of Shakira Azzam.

Now the only real concern he had was to figure out where the hell he could find a parachute between now and when he boarded the plane in the morning.

CHAPTER 54

Court had Saddiqi drop him off three hundred yards from the hole in the gate of the Desert Hawks' base, and he went the rest of the way on foot.

He made it through the hole after five minutes of prizing open the metal links, then belly-crawled through the dirt behind the shack next to the motor pool. He brushed himself off and then, when he felt sure the coast was clear, he ran across the street. He then made his way in the shadows through row after row of metal buildings until he arrived back at the KWA barracks.

Infiltrating the facility turned out to be as easy as exfiltrating, if not more so, because there was so little going on in the area at four a.m.

He saw that the lights were off in the team room, and he slipped inside, heading to the back for the barracks.

The lights were off in here, too; a dozen men lay in their bunks, and some snored.

As Court moved to his own bunk he was surprised to see that both Saunders and Broz had already made it back to base after getting picked up by the cops and National Defence Forces militia. He did not see Brunetti or Anders anywhere in the room, but he wondered if Brunetti's broken nose might have had something to do with their absence.

He sat down on his bunk and pulled off his shirt, shoving it in his backpack. Just as he leaned over to untie his boots, he heard a banging on the back door of the barracks. KWA men all around him leapt up out of their bunks, grabbing rifles and pistols as they did so.

Saunders was first to the door and he looked out, then unlocked and opened it.

Four Desert Hawks officers moved into the room aggressively, and behind them, several armed militiamen. The mercenaries in their underwear leveled their guns at the new arrivals in the confusion, and shouts were exchanged.

Court saw from the action of his teammates that, whatever the hell was going on, this was definitely *not* a nightly occurrence.

The overhead lights came on, and Court was in the center of the action, standing there shirtless; his lean upper torso had several scrapes and bruises he'd picked up in the past few hours.

Van Wyk, the South African KWA team leader, addressed the Desert Hawks colonel angrily. "What the hell is this all about?"

The Syrian officer spoke reasonably good English. "There has been an attack in the Western Villas neighborhood in Mezzeh district tonight. A boy and his caretaker were kidnapped, and several security forces were murdered. We have been ordered to do a bed check to make sure all KWA contractors are present."

Van Wyk looked around the room. "We've got a guy in the hospital and another there with him. Everyone else is present and accounted for, so we're obviously not out kidnapping children." He stuck a finger in the colonel's face, treating the militia officer with no deference at all for his rank. "I want to know why you are lookin' at us for a crime across town."

The colonel replied coolly. "There was a fight tonight at a bar in Old Town Damascus between Western security contractors, Russian Air Force personnel, and SAA Tiger Forces soldiers. Four KWA men were arrested but not charged. This tells us at least four of you were off base, within a few kilometers of the attack.

"In addition to this, the security forces in Mezzeh told the police that the kidnapper had top-flight abilities. It wasn't an insurgent group that pulled this off. It was one man. He killed or wounded multiple highly trained men in commission of his crime."

Court saw Saunders flash a quick look his way. Court did not meet his gaze.

Van Wyk said, "Look, a few of the boys went out for drinks. No harm, but some Tigers were lookin' to start a row. They got picked up by the police, but the cops let them go."

As he'd feared, one of the young militiamen pointed at Court. "Sir . . . the others are in their underwear. But this one has his boots and trousers on."

All eyes in the room turned Court's way.

The colonel asked, "Where did you get those marks on your body? That cut on your head?"

Court said, "I was in action yesterday afternoon on the road from Latakia. You must have heard about that."

The colonel nodded. "I did hear about that. But those look fresher." He walked over to Court, looking him up and down.

"Yeah . . . I was in the bar fight tonight, too."

The colonel seemed to accept this explanation, and Court thought the danger was behind him, but the Croatian contractor Broz spoke up. "Wait a minute. You were the one guy who didn't get arrested. And when we got back here an hour ago, you weren't in your bunk. Where you been for the past four hours, Wade?"

What an asshole, Court thought. There was no other team he could have run with in any other part of the world where one teammate would sell out another so quickly.

These mercenaries were hard men who didn't give a shit about camaraderie.

Court looked around him. He couldn't fight all these guys, and he didn't see a way to talk himself out of this.

But just then Saunders said, "He's not your man, gents."

Now the attention in the room turned to the British mercenary standing there in his underwear.

Saunders said, "Tell 'em, Wade."

Court said nothing.

"It's all right. Go on, now. Tell 'em where you were."

"I . . . uh . . ." Court thought Saunders was trying to help, but it wasn't working. "I was . . ."

Saunders took over. "After the NDF brought me and Broz back to base, Broz came back here and I went to the loo. Not the one off the team room,

357

but the one off the loadout room, the next building over. Wanted some peace and quiet to take a shit without all the other smelly asses. I walked into the loo, took one look, and turned back around.

"That bastard right there was pukin' his guts out in the sink, but it was all over the floor, as well. Tell me you cleaned that shit up, Wade."

"Uh . . . yeah. I did. Not a hint anything even happened," Court replied.

The Desert Hawks colonel turned to Court. To make sure he understood the English slang, he said, "You were sick? Vomiting?"

Saunders answered for him, "Aye. Somethin's got a hold of him. It's either the killin', the booze, or the food."

After a moment Court shrugged. "It's not the killin'."

Broz looked incredulously at Saunders. "You told us this man can really fight. He shows up tonight, disappears, and later the Syrians come in and tell us someone with special skills snatched a kid. You're *certain* you saw him after we got back from the police station? Because I sure as shit didn't."

"On me mother's grave," Saunders said.

The colonel addressed Court again. "If you were not arrested with the others, how did you get back to base?"

Court didn't bat an eyelash. "Met a girl on the street in front of the bar who spoke English. I told her what happened. Figured she could help me get a taxi back, but she offered to drive me herself. Tried to pay her, but she wouldn't take it."

"The girl, what's her name?" the colonel asked.

"I didn't ask. I just needed a ride."

Broz and Saunders both looked at Court now. They'd known that Walid had been their driver, and he hadn't gotten himself arrested, so they figured Court would have returned to base with him. But even though his story was confusing to them, they weren't going to say anything about Walid in front of the colonel that might get him in trouble.

It wasn't that they were being kind. No, he was their ticket off base, and they'd do nothing to screw with that setup.

The Desert Hawks colonel left the room with his men a moment later, satisfied he could report to his higher-ups that his highly trained contractors had nothing to do with any crimes in the city that evening beyond cracking a few bottles over heads in a disco.

Court wondered how long it would take for the Desert Hawks forces to find out Walid wasn't anywhere to be found, and what danger that might bring to his operation.

Broz and Van Wyk both asked about Walid as soon as the militiamen were out of the room. Court just shrugged and said he went looking for him after the fight but had no idea what had happened to him.

. . .

Thirty minutes later Court lay on his bunk, his eyes open, staring into the darkness above him. He had a million worries on his mind, but he wasn't able to process them all, because he knew this long night was not quite over yet.

When Saunders appeared standing over his bunk, Court told himself he'd finally be able to deal with the last hanging thread of his interminably long first day in Syria.

Court sat up without a word, stood, and followed Saunders out into the team room. They continued through the front door, and walked through the dark for a full minute before arriving at a secluded area near an empty storage shed within sight of the main gate.

Here Saunders turned around and faced him. "You might think about sayin' thank you."

"Thank you."

"Yeah? Well . . . I knew since you got here you weren't who you said you were. I read Graham Wade's CV, and you, mate, *ain't* him. That shit on the road yesterday? You aren't some old, washed-up, Canadian ex–infantry officer. You shoot, move, and communicate better than any other contractor I've ever worked with in me life."

"You're no slouch yourself. Look, what do you say tomorrow morning we tell each other how awesome we are? I really need to hit the rack."

Saunders ignored him. "I *knew* you were up to something. All that wonderin' about who we were fightin' as if it fuckin' matters around here. I sussed out you had another objective in Syria beyond comin' down and fightin' for the Hawks to earn a paycheck. I knew, but I didn't know if whatever you were here for was good, bad, or indifferent."

"I'm a good guy," Court quipped.

"Right. Kidnapping kids? That'll earn ya a sainthood for sure."

"I had nothing to do with—"

"Sell me another. I told myself after the contact with Jabhat al Nusra that I was gonna watch you close. So I did. At the disco, I saw you leave with the Tiger Forces bastard's phone, then walk right back in and deny it. I watched you trying to get the fight goin' in the bar. Couldn't figure out what your game was, but when we got back here and you still weren't around, I went lookin' for Walid. He's not back, either."

Saunders continued, "He was too bloody pissed to help out with a kidnapping, so I figure you just needed his wheels and his uniform. Is that it?"

"*You're* the drunk one, Saunders."

"Not too drunk to notice that gash on the side of your head. You didn't have that in the bar."

"Yeah . . . I did."

"You aren't the only man here with a brain, Wade. I know you've been moonlightin' tonight. So . . . tell me. Who's the little shit bird you nicked, eh? He belong to somebody important? A general, a Ba'ath Party official? Where do you have him stashed?"

"Why the hell would I come here to snatch somebody's baby?"

"Dunno. Money, I reckon. We were at the police station when the call came in. Once word got out about the kid, the cops couldn't get rid of us fast enough. They had a real crime to deal with. Whoever's kid was taken was so important the whole city's police force was trippin' over each other to look for him. Must be a nice payday for you."

Court did not reply.

"C'mon, man. I can walk outta 'ere and go tell the colonel that on second thought it wasn't you pukin' in the loo, after all."

Court realized he might have to kill Saunders to keep him quiet. The man had done him a favor, but he was expendable if he tried to do anything to impede Court from assisting in providing intelligence on the Syrian president.

But then Saunders said something that changed everything.

"Fine . . . don't tell me. But here's how it's gonna be. I want a quarter of the take, not just for getting the guns off you thirty minutes ago, but I'll help out with your exfil. You managed to slip away tonight, but you can't do that whenever you want, especially considering the Desert Hawks are going to have their eyes on you now."

Court was hopeful about this turn of events, but he continued to feign ignorance about the kidnapping. "Again . . . we have to muster at six a.m. Can I just go back to the bunkhouse and—"

A look of realization flashed in Saunders's eyes. "Wait . . . you didn't have time to go far after you snatched that baby. Where do you have him stashed?"

Court realized arguing with this guy was going to be futile.

Saunders smiled. "I'm your problem solver. Where is the kid going?"

Court sighed. He gave up the ruse. "The West."

The Brit's eyes went wild. "Fuck me, mate! You have to exfil him from the *country*? Are you bloody mad? That's a tall order."

"I don't have to do it. I just had to get him out of where he was, and deliver him somewhere else in the city. I did it."

"Good. Is he somewhere safe for now?"

"It's Syria, Saunders. Nowhere is safe."

"True enough."

"But, yeah. I think so. My job is done, but I won't get paid till he gets out."

Saunders started to reply, but Court cut him off. "And that means *you* don't get paid till he gets out. We'll go up north tomorrow, get out of here, do our jobs, and when we get back to Damascus I should have the money in an account I can access."

"No tricks, Wade."

This whole operation was nothing but a big bag of tricks, Court thought, but he simply nodded at the Englishman, then looked at his watch. "If I'm lucky, I can get myself about twenty minutes' sleep tonight before I have to get up and get my gear together."

"Sweet dreams then," Saunders said. "But remember . . . I'm expecting a cut for what happened tonight."

"You made that clear," Court said.

Saunders led the way back to the bunkhouse with a spring in his step, because he thought he was going to make some money.

Court walked behind him, and it occurred to him that the three con-federates in his scheme now consisted of a Syrian doctor with no espionage or military experience, a Frenchman who had either double-crossed or turned his back on everyone he had worked with over the past week, and now a cutthroat mercenary who seemed tickled *fucking* pink at the chance to take part in a kidnapping of a baby so he could earn some quick cash.

He told himself, and not for the first time on this operation, that the only one he could rely on was himself.

CHAPTER 55

There was no sleep for the Gray Man. After he lay in bed awake for just minutes, the lights came back on, the men began climbing out of their bunks, burping and farting and cussing, and within moments they were gearing up for the trip to the front lines to the northeast. As had been the norm since he got here, the team was a surly group, with little conversation between them, even after Brunetti and Anders returned from the hospital to join the others for the mission.

To Court it was as if these guys were already prepping themselves for the action ahead. Not the danger; that had a tendency to draw men together and increase comradeship. No, these guys, from the perspective of Court's trained eye, were getting their heads ready to kill people, whether or not the killing had anything to do with the war going on.

Van Wyk took Court into the loadout room in the next building and told him to grab whatever he wanted from the well-stocked crates, racks, and shelves full of KWA gear. From the weapon racks he pulled a pristine-looking Kalashnikov with a short barrel and folding wire stock, and a desert-sand-colored Glock 9-millimeter pistol in a drop leg holster.

He chose a set of ceramic plate body armor in a plate carrier, which he then hung over his shoulder and cinched to his body by means of a Velcro cummerbund. He grabbed ammunition, a combat knife, a pair of fragmentation grenades, flashlights and batteries, and emergency medical supplies, and all this went onto a load-bearing vest he donned over the plate carrier.

He put on kneepads and elbow pads and selected a pair of tactical gloves, cutting off the trigger fingers on both hands with a tactical knife.

He filled a backpack full of bottled water, vacuum-packed rations, and a camouflage jacket.

Lastly he found a Kevlar helmet that fit him, retrieved a pair of ballistic-rated sunglasses from a case, and headed outside.

Completely geared up he looked like all the other KWA men, which meant he didn't look too much different from the Desert Hawks Brigade soldiers themselves, except for the white hawk badge on the left shoulder of their uniforms versus the unadorned shoulders of the KWA men.

At six a.m. on the dot Court stood in front of the barracks as a long procession of trucks, infantry fighting vehicles, armored personnel carriers, T-72 tanks, and utility vehicles passed by on the way to the front gate.

Van Wyk addressed the group with a short briefing, basically telling the men they were to assist with pacifying a couple of villages an hour to the east of Palmyra, and they'd learn more details during the four-to-six-hour transport to the area. He pointed to the new man, the one he knew as Wade, and gave him the call sign Kilo Nine.

For years while working in SAD's Ground Branch, Court's call sign had been Sierra Six. It was so ingrained in his consciousness, even after all this time, that he figured he would probably still answer to it if someone addressed him as such, but he was hoping he wouldn't be stuck in this unit long enough to remember Kilo Nine the same way.

As the massive procession of Hawks Brigade armor passed, two BMP-3 infantry fighting vehicles pulled over to the mercenaries and stopped, and the rear hatches on both opened. Court, Saunders, Broz, Brunetti, Van Wyk, and Anders climbed into one of the vehicles, while the other six KWA men climbed into the other.

The six men in Court's infantry fighting vehicle sat on two benches facing one another, and the three-man crew already on board waited for the signal to move out. The heavy, tracked machines folded back into the procession leaving the base, and soon Court could feel the driver make the hard left turn that indicated they'd departed through the main gate.

It was low, cramped, dark, and hot inside the vehicle. It bounced up and down roughly on its chassis as soon as it encountered the first bumps outside the wire of the base, and it smelled like the interior had been sprayed down with engine lube and body odor.

This was Court's first time inside a BMP-3, and to say he wasn't impressed would have been an understatement. He had been hoping to get some rest on the several-hours-long journey to the north, but now he couldn't imagine any way to pull that off.

Court had never served in the U.S. military, and he'd only sat in Strykers and Bradleys, the U.S. frontline infantry fighting vehicles, a handful of times. All those occasions were during training evolutions at military bases around the United States or a few times when in Iraq and Afghanistan working operations with the CIA's Special Activities Division.

Normally his Ground Branch task force helicoptered into a location to grab or eliminate their target, and they'd leave the same way. When they did travel over roads, they normally did so in low-profile vehicles: local cars and trucks.

The Special Activities Division left the driving around in big, bouncy armored vehicles to the military guys.

Court did not want to be here, working with mercenaries who were, themselves, working for a militia that was working for the evil Azzam regime, but he knew of no other way to get up near Palmyra, the place where Azzam was allegedly visiting Tuesday. He had to continue on this mission, to remain in cover as a mercenary deploying to support combat troops, and then, when he got as close as he could to his real destination, he would find a way to pick up the intel that would pinpoint Azzam's location.

For this he would need a phone, and he knew Van Wyk didn't have one, but there would be a Desert Hawks command post wherever they were deploying, and there would be all the commo gear there he needed.

In his fantasies, Court imagined his intel would send a squadron of French Mirage fighter-bombers over Palmyra to take out Azzam from the air, but in reality he was under no illusions the French would do anything so brazen. No, if this was to work, it would involve indigenous forces.

In the meantime, however, the KWA men around him seemed very certain they were heading into some sort of a fight, although whether it was going to be a two-sided affair, with people fighting back, was as yet unknown. Court would be going in with them, doing what he had to do to keep his cover, but the first chance he got to acquire some actionable intel about the reasons behind this security option, grab some means of communication, and get the fuck out of there, he told himself he would take it.

Court took off his helmet and rubbed the sweat already soaking his hair. Putting it back on, he met Saunders's gaze, and the British man leaned forward and spoke into his ear. "When we get where we're goin', you're gonna have to do your job."

"You doubt my abilities?"

"If we make contact with armed fighters? No, I know you can do it, although if it's not ISIS or Al Nusra you'll probably whine about it before, during, and after. But the Hawks like to use us for suppression ops, and that means dirty work. If they send us into the city to round up town leaders or anti-regime suspects, I'll warn you, it won't make for stories you'll want to tell your grandkids by the fire."

Court just shrugged at Saunders, still trying to figure out the psychology of a man like him. He said, "This is KWA, Lars Klossner's company. I knew what I was getting into on the way in."

Saunders nodded at this, and then said, "How much you getting paid for the kid?"

Court pulled a number out of his ass. "One hundred thousand."

"Dollars?"

"Pesos."

Saunders's face showed genuine confusion.

Court rolled his eyes. "Yes, dollars."

The Englishman stared him down for several seconds. "Bollocks. Wouldn't be worth it to a man like you. You've got a lifetime of training. You're not Canadian, you're a Yank, so I figure you for SEAL Team Six, or one of those Delta boys. Maybe even CIA para ops."

"You've got one hell of an imagination."

Saunders shook his head and repeated himself. "Bollocks. I bet you're making two hundred, minimum, which means I want fifty."

"Not gonna happen."

Saunders turned to the team leader, at the far end of his bench. "Oy! Van Wyk?"

The older South African turned to Saunders.

"Thirty-five," Court said.

"Fifty."

A sigh. "Fine."

Still with his eyes on the American, Saunders said, "Never mind, boss."

Van Wyk went back to his thoughts, and Saunders smiled at Court.

The Englishman said, "I want to know more about you. I get that the money's nice in this line of work, but it's only worth it if you don't have other options. Me? I'm what they refer to as unemployable in the security and private military contractor industry. And since I don't have any other skills other than fightin', I took the job for KWA five years ago knowing what I would have to do. Told myself I'd follow orders for whoever I was working for, full stop. They want me to fight insurgents, jolly good. If they want me to blast my way into a mosque and shoot a village elder, then I'll do that, as well."

Court looked away.

"But you? I don't have you sorted out yet. It's mad, really. Why the risk? Why not stay wrapped up in your bed at home when you're not fightin' the good fight for your country and not out here in the shite with the Ali Babas?"

Court had been thinking the same thing about Saunders, but he didn't reveal it. Instead he said, "Look, man, if you're trying to be my guidance counselor, you're about twenty years too late."

Saunders kept a skeptical eye on Court, who found the look unnerving. Finally the Brit said, "Something got switched off in you, and you ended up here, filching children. What was it?"

Finally Court said, "Here's where you and me stand, Saunders. I owe you some money, but I don't owe you any explanations. For anything." Court leaned forward, menacing. "Now . . . get the fuck out of my face and let me get some rest."

Saunders raised an eyebrow, and then he leaned back and away.

Court closed his eyes and hoped the bouncing and knocking of the armored infantry carrier would somehow rock him to sleep.

CHAPTER 56

The Frenchman tossed back the dregs of his fifth coffee of the day, and it wasn't even ten a.m.

He'd spent the morning in his office in the 5th Arrondissement, working his satellite phone while the one suit he had with him dried in the window.

He'd come here directly after hitchhiking away from the farmhouse, because he was too tired and overwhelmed to conduct a surveillance detection route in order to make sure he hadn't been followed from the property. He didn't want to go home without being assured he hadn't been followed, but there was reasonably good security in the office building where he worked, so he'd decided that would be sufficient protection. He'd slept for five hours on his leather sofa, but by eight a.m. he had a pot of coffee on the burner, his laptops opened, and his phone wedged between his neck and his ear, and since then he'd been talking almost nonstop to various intelligence operatives in Jordan. These were exactly the men he knew would not agree to extract the son of Ahmed Azzam when they learned about the death of Bianca Medina. But they were men who would do damn near *anything* to bring about the end of the Azzam regime, so if rescuing the baby and the nanny from Syria was the purchase price for the death of the dictator to their north, the Jordanians would find a way to come through.

Originally they had been asked to do nothing more than pick up the kid and the asset at their northern border, but now Voland was asking for something several orders of magnitude more complicated. He told the Jordanians he thought he could persuade a man to drive to the border to deliver a woman and the child, but this man wouldn't be trained in cross-border movements, personnel recovery, or any sort of intelligence tradecraft at all.

In short, the man who would be delivering the two subjects to the Syrian/Jordanian border wouldn't have a single skill necessary to facilitate this difficult and dangerous act—other than the ability to drive a car—so the Jordanians would have to somehow pick up all the slack on their end.

The Jordanians would come through, Voland felt confident, but they'd need a couple of days to plan and put the assets in place.

He did not want to reach out to Dr. Saddiqi until he knew exactly when and exactly how he was going to get the girl and the baby out of Syria. But he knew he needed to have a plan by the time the Gray Man contacted him, because he'd let the American down so many times already that nothing short of imminent action was going to convince him to keep up his end of the bargain and provide intelligence about Azzam's movements.

Voland also had contacts in the SDF, the coalition of predominantly Kurdish anti-regime groups fighting in the northern part of Syria, as well as in the Sunni-dominated Free Syrian Army. These connections came via the Halabys, but Voland knew if he did get the actionable intelligence from the Gray Man that he'd promised, the groups fighting Azzam would do anything in their power to attempt to exploit it.

Once he felt he'd done all he could for now on the Jamal Medina front, his thoughts turned to a new topic: a topic he told himself he would do well to put out of his mind, but a topic he could not, in spite of himself, force himself to ignore.

Sebastian Drexler.

Vincent Voland had spent years looking for information that would lead to the capture of Drexler. It was a job he'd begun while working in foreign intelligence; there were domestic warrants aplenty for Drexler in France, and the domestic intelligence service turned to foreign intelligence for help in locating and planning the man's capture, since it was clear Drexler was outside Europe. But when Voland left active service with DGSE, he continued his hunt for Drexler as something of a passionate hobby. The word was that Drexler had been living in Syria for two years, and he was doing the bidding of the regime, specifically focused on the private wealth of the Azzams. The rumors had come out of Switzerland, but they were just rumors and no specific bank had been positively pegged as the location of the Azzams' money.

When Voland had received word of the contacts between Drexler and ISIS in Brussels, he knew Drexler was indeed in Syria, indeed working for Shakira, and he came up with a plan to draw him out.

That plan had worked as far as phase one, but phase two, the capture of Drexler, and phase three, the exploitation of Bianca Medina as an intelligence source for rebels fighting against the regime in Syria, had both failed as badly as any intelligence operation could possibly fail.

And Vincent Voland put all blame for this on himself.

That was why his thoughts were now locked on Drexler: where he was now, what his next play was. With Medina dead, Voland assumed Drexler would head back to Syria.

Malik, on the other hand, was a European theater operative for the Syrian government, and he would likely stay somewhere on the continent in a safe house. He'd melt back into Europe's massive Arab population and disappear. The Syrian assassin had probably been here on the continent for years, so finding him with the scant clues Voland had would be difficult if not impossible.

But Drexler had come here to Europe within a specific date range; he would most likely be leaving the continent soon, and *this*, Voland felt sure, presented him with an opportunity.

He made a series of calls to acquaintances in French domestic intelligence and pulled some strings to have them download images from French immigration control. He specified time parameters that made safe assumptions about when Drexler arrived from Syria. Voland felt sure Drexler was not in Paris until after the ISIS attack on Thursday, and he must have arrived, at the latest, Saturday afternoon, to be involved with the attack on the farmhouse late Saturday night.

He requested images and passport information of all white males between ages thirty-five and fifty-five, knowing Drexler was in his forties but might have tried to disguise himself in person, on his passport, or both.

He requested the pulls from Charles de Gaulle, Orly, Marseille, and

Lyon, the most suitable airports for someone coming from abroad, although Voland didn't even know for certain Drexler would have flown into France. He could have traveled through Brussels, Frankfurt, Amsterdam, or even farther away and taken a high-speed train.

But Voland knew he had to start somewhere, and he also knew from his study of the man over the years that Drexler was an exceedingly assured, almost cocky intelligence asset. He'd formulate and execute a plan straight up the middle of an intelligence operation. He wasn't a risk taker, per se, but instead a man with absolute confidence in his skills, borne out by years of success.

Voland figured Drexler wouldn't have snuck into the country on a fishing trawler in the dead of night. No, he'd fly first class with papers to back him up all the way.

At eleven a.m. he received a file with all 4,974 immigration arrival photos he'd requested. At eight minutes till noon he scrolled to the 1,303rd image. He continued to the 1,304th, but then he scrolled back.

He shouted in his office, *"Voilà!"*

Voland had spoken at length to Drexler the evening before, so there was no mistaking the face. Sebastian Drexler had arrived at Charles de Gaulle on Saturday afternoon under a Finnish passport carrying the name of Veeti Takala.

The scanned passport photo was in a thumbprint size below the image taken when Drexler passed through immigration, and Voland enlarged it. The picture showed a bearded man with sandy brown hair, several shades darker than Drexler's, but noticeably so, because while Drexler's hair was short, the Takala passport showed a man with much longer hair and a full beard.

Still, Voland could see that the passport photo was not Sebastian Drexler.

The sixty-five-year-old Frenchman picked up the phone and dialed the number of a friend in the DGSE, intending to have him run the name for any details on the passport or identity of Veeti Takala. While the phone rang, Voland spent his wait Googling the name, on the offhand chance he'd find a social media account that matched the passport photo.

And then he put down the phone.

The name Voland entered into Google appeared in a Reuters article that had posted the previous day. Veeti Takala was a photographer for ITN who had disappeared in Damascus two days earlier. The photo of the man clearly matched the passport photo that Drexler used.

It occurred to Vincent Voland that if he were a betting man, he'd bet against Veeti Takala ever making it back home to Helsinki.

Curious as to how Drexler could have entered Europe using a false passport, he scanned through all the immigration data in the file sent by his intelligence agency contacts and saw that the fingertip reader recorded a match for the fingerprints on record for the Finn. Voland did not understand this at all, but he did realize it didn't matter.

Drexler wouldn't be leaving the continent going through immigration control or using the passport of Veeti Takala. No, he'd used that means once, and he'd surely burned the passport as soon as he got into the country.

For Voland, this wasn't about finding out what name he was traveling under. This entire exercise was simply to acquire the one thing Voland needed above all else to find Sebastian Drexler before he left Europe.

A close-in, high-resolution, color photo of his face. The photograph taken by immigration at Charles de Gaulle was perfect, and it was of Drexler, not Takala. Drexler would have no time to change his appearance much or at all before he left the continent again.

Voland had two missions now, and he was fully engaged in both. He told himself he would not rest until he got the kid and the nanny out of Syria, and he would not rest until he found Sebastian Drexler and made him pay for what he'd done.

CHAPTER 57

From a dead sleep the sounds and the movement of the infantry fighting vehicle came to him in a rush, and then Court's eyes opened as he woke with the taste of grease and fuel in his mouth.

He wiped his sweat-drenched face with a towel he had jammed in his load-bearing vest, swigged warm water from a plastic bottle in his pack, and splashed more onto his face and down the back of his neck. He looked down at his rubber watch and synchronized the bouncing of his head with the swinging of his arm so he could focus on the numbers on the display. It was noon; he figured he'd slept on and off for close to four hours, which meant he'd really needed it, and it also meant the Desert Hawks Brigade convoy should be getting close to their destination.

The BMP drove along a poorly maintained road; this Court could tell from the jarring bumps, but he couldn't see anything from his position. He looked over closer to the rear hatches and saw that Van Wyk was on the headset that allowed him to communicate with the vehicle's three-man crew, and he was struggling to write something down on a notepad propped on his knee.

Saunders was awake next to him, and he caught Court's eye. The two men looked at each other but neither spoke.

Just then Court heard a boom outside the vehicle, and he looked around to see that the other men in the back of the infantry fighting

373

vehicle were all reacting to the same sound. It was either a large weapon firing or a shell detonating, and though it wasn't much louder than the noise of the machine surrounding him, he figured it had to have been pretty loud for them to hear it at all.

Another boom, then another.

Van Wyk shouted to the men around him. "That's outgoing! One hundred millimeter."

The main weapon of the Russian-built BMP-3 was the 2A70 launcher, a 100-millimeter gun that could fire high-explosive or antitank missiles. Court found himself hoping Ali Company of the Desert Hawks, the company he and his team were embedded with, had not come into contact with tanks, because the Gray Man had no magic ninja fighting solution to avoid getting blown up the same as everyone else.

If the BMP Court was riding in was hit with an antitank round, Court's body would just turn into canned beef stew along with the other eight guys in the vehicle.

Seconds later Court heard the unmistakable sound of heavy machine guns firing, and his feeling of helplessness and claustrophobia only increased.

"Outgoing," Broz confirmed.

The 30-millimeter gun on Court's BMP joined the fray, and the sound was deafening.

The team leader put his hand on his headset to press it closer to his ear, and he spoke to the driver of the vehicle for several more seconds. He looked up and said, "Look alive! We're heading into an oil refinery, one kilometer square. Two dozen buildings in all, all either partially damaged or completely destroyed. Opposition presence is unknown, but Ali Company is taking some small-arms fire from some of the structures. Our target is the central control building in the middle of the complex. It has been used as an SAA command post in the past. Daesh took over the refinery last month, and SAA intel is guessing Daesh will be using the same building as their HQ. We're being sent in to clear it so the Hawks can use it as their battalion CP for the clearing operation."

Saunders said, "Why don't the Hawks do this shit themselves?"

"They are sending Bashar and Chadli Companies one klick north to hit an enemy encampment in the hills. Ali Company is with us, but they will secure the other refinery structures while we clear the central control building."

Broz said, "This is grunt work, boss!"

"And you're getting paid fifty times what any of those grunts are getting paid, so put on your helmet and deal with it! Ali Company only has one platoon of special forces, and they are hitting the three pumping stations."

Court could see on the faces of the others that none of the KWA men seemed interested in this fight, but they all tightened straps, took last swigs of water, and hefted their weapons.

Van Wyk said, "Our crews will deploy smoke ahead. Both of our BMPs will get us up to the building. We will go out the rear hatches and continue straight on for twenty-five meters to the door of the target building. From there we will clear the building bottom up."

It was a suffocating feeling for Court to have someone relay second-hand info about the area right outside the armor from where he sat. An area he was about to attack into. He couldn't see a thing now, and he didn't imagine he would see the location he was hitting at all until he crawled out through the rear hatch.

Anders shouted to be heard over the thirty-cal firing above his head. "Are the BMPs taking fire from the control building?"

Van Wyk spoke into his mic, then addressed the team again. "Unknown, but the gunner reports possible movement on the third floor of the building."

Fun, Court thought. After rolling for hours with his knees to his chest, he was about to bound out through a smoke screen and race into a building that might be full of ISIS fighters.

But the movement reported could also have been noncombatants. Court eyed the men around him and told himself he wouldn't put it past any one of them to commit an atrocity or two before nightfall today.

Court heard the outgoing pops of smoke being deployed via the grenade launchers on the turret of the BMPs, and then the vehicle stopped so violently that at first Court thought it had taken a hit from an RPG. The BMP then turned 180 degrees on one of its tracks, lurched backwards a few feet, then stopped roughly again.

The main gunner began firing the PKT vehicle-mounted machine gun. At what, Court had no idea.

375

"Go!" Van Wyk shouted. Anders opened the left rear hatch and Broz opened the right. Court was the third man out on the left. His boots crashed down into broken bits of concrete big enough to break an ankle if he didn't watch what he was doing, but he ran on through it, into thick gray smoke spewing from the grenades fired from his BMP. It was hard to tell with all the machine-gun fire from his vehicle, but Court didn't detect any incoming rounds as he made his way through the smoke. Soon all he could see was Saunders's back and helmet ahead of him, and in seconds he slammed with Saunders and the others against the wall of the building, flattening their backs out so they couldn't be seen by a shooter inside any of the shattered windows.

They were next to the door, or at least next to where the door used to be. Instead there was a massive hole where it looked to Court like a main gun round from a tank had blown the door and a good portion of wall away.

But Court hadn't heard any of the Desert Hawks' T-72s firing, and he didn't see any tanks around now. So if this had been from a tank, it had been in a battle fought earlier.

This was Syria, so for all Court knew, the destruction could have been seven years old.

Court stacked up at the back of the six-man team, and seconds later the half dozen KWA mercs from the other BMP appeared through the smoke and arrived at the other side of the big hole. Together the team breached the building—Van Wyk's six went right and the other KWA unit went to the left.

The first few rooms downstairs were empty other than tons of trash and broken bits of concrete and glass, but Court saw sleeping mats, tea-kettles, clothes, and other evidence that someone had been living here in the rubble. He didn't see any weaponry or ammunition, or even anything in the clothing that gave him the impression there was some sort of military unit encamped here.

Anders took point as the team moved up a set of cement stairs. Court was still in back, but at the top of the staircase, Van Wyk sent Saunders, Broz, and Anders on to continue straight down the hall towards an open room ahead, while he directed Court and Brunetti to follow him down the hall to the right.

Court liked Van Wyk's thinking from a tactical aspect. There were few people on Earth with more close-quarters battle experience than Court Gentry, and he knew that when room-clearing a building, if you don't have the manpower to leave an operator in each room you clear, you must consider the room enemy territory as soon as you leave it behind. With only six men clearing this wing of the building, it made sense to clear close-proximity open spaces simultaneously to reduce the risk of the enemy backfilling the rooms they'd already been through.

The hall to the right led to an office with a broken door that wasn't completely detached, so Brunetti shouldered it down while Court and Van Wyk flooded in to the left and right respectively. Court found the left side of the office to be nothing but a wrecked collection of filing cabinets and broken desks, but before he could call "clear," he heard gunfire right behind him.

He spun around, dropping to his left kneepad as he did so, and he saw a man with a sniper rifle at the wrecked window of the office. He'd been shot multiple times already by Van Wyk, but somehow he was still on his feet.

Gentry, Van Wyk, and Brunetti all fired into the man, throwing him back into the corner of the room. He spun against the wall and fell forward onto his face.

Court had no idea if he'd just killed a Free Syrian Army soldier or a member of ISIS. Just like the day before on the highway, his survival instincts superseded everything else.

They cleared the rest of the room, a hall that ran off the back to the bathroom, and then the bathroom itself. On the way back through the office, Court stepped over to the body and rolled the man over. He was bearded, with long hair and a black T-shirt. An old brown sling full of rifle magazines hung around his neck. Court said, "Looks like ISIS."

Brunetti re-formed tight behind Van Wyk to continue clearing the rest of the building. At the doorway he said, "*Everybody* looks like ISIS around here to me."

Court re-formed at the back of the group and the three moved along the western end of the second floor of the control center building and prepared to go up a metal staircase to rejoin the other three men, but just as they started to climb, a burst of automatic gunfire erupted at the top of the stairs.

Quickly Van Wyk, Brunetti, and Court moved up in a tight three-man stack. They found a hallway with a pair of doorways at the end. Van Wyk called out, "Coming in!"

Saunders replied instantly. "All clear! We're on the right."

Court followed the other two into a large room. At the far corner, Saunders stood over a group of bodies lying by the window.

"What you got?" Van Wyk asked.

"Three dead."

"Combatants?"

Saunders spit on the floor. "Enemy sympathizers."

Court lowered his weapon a little and walked across the room to the bodies. Two women wearing hijabs, both in their twenties, were perforated from their collarbones to their pelvises. A third body was a boy of no more than fourteen. He had taken a round through the stomach.

Blood splattered the wall low behind them, giving Court the impression they had all been sitting on the floor when they were shot.

The three had been living in this wrecked storage room; that was clear from the blankets and boxes of crackers and trash and the two half-empty plastic jugs of water nearby. None of the three had any weapons Court could see.

"You motherfuckers!" Court couldn't help it. He said it out loud.

He knelt to check for a pulse on the boy.

"What are you doing?" Broz asked from across the room.

Court did not reply. The boy was dead, and the ladies appeared dead, as well, but he began checking them both for a pulse.

Van Wyk said, "Kilo Nine is new here. You boys popped your cherries once. He'll get used to it." After a moment Van Wyk called out to Court. "That's enough, Nine. Come on, a lot of rooms to check."

Reluctantly Court climbed back up to his feet and rejoined the mercs, his jaw flexing as he thought about flipping his weapon to fully automatic fire and gunning down all five of these men from behind.

But he didn't flip his selector switch, and he didn't fire. Instead he spoke to himself. "Stay in cover, Gentry. Stay in cover and end this fucking war."

CHAPTER 58

President of the Syrian Arab Republic Ahmed al-Azzam smiled, looked into the eyes of his beautiful wife Shakira, and kissed her sweetly. They hugged tenderly, and then they both looked up, to a point across the room.

Ahmed wore a blue pinstripe suit, warm in the hot lights around him, and a thin sheen of perspiration glistened on his forehead, despite the makeup he wore. He spoke in his native tongue. "Shakira and I have been blessed with a beautiful family, wonderful friends, and work that we both find fulfilling. While ours is a happy life, many of our fellow countrymen are less fortunate. You know I am engaged tirelessly keeping Syrians prosperous and safe from terrorists and foreign invaders, but you should also know that my lovely wife works day and night on the social programs that help the impoverished among us live healthy and gratifying lives."

Shakira took her husband's hand and squeezed it tightly. "Thank you, darling. We hope you will all join us in making a contribution to the First Lady's Children First antipoverty campaign by calling the number on your screen now. Operators are standing by, ready to receive your donations."

Ahmed put his arm around his wife and looked into the same camera. Together they said, *"Shukran, jazelaan."* *Thank you very much.*

The lights flipped off, the director called "cut," and the Azzams unfolded from their embrace without another glance towards each other. Shakira stood from the sofa in the main reception room of the palace to

379

speak with her assistant, while Ahmed launched from the sofa himself, stepped over to his bodyguards, and left the room without a glance or a word to anyone, least of all his wife.

In the long corridor that would take him back to his office he felt his phone vibrate in his coat pocket. He answered it.

"Yes?"

"Ahmed? Ahmed, it's me."

His eyes narrowed as he heard Bianca's voice. The facial expression belied a look of mistrust, but his own voice carried a light and thankful tone. "How wonderful to hear you. How are you feeling, my darling?"

"Thanks to God I am safe. Your men rescued me last night. I'm sorry I was too exhausted to talk when they freed me. My emotions had been so strained over the last days."

Ahmed stepped over to a huge window that looked out over the gargantuan thirty-acre front court of the palace grounds. As he did so he waved his guards and attendants away. He spoke softer now. "Were you hurt in any way?"

"No, Ahmed. I was locked in a basement, but I was fed, attended to. I managed to escape just as your men attacked. The terrorists holding me tried to burn me to death, so I'm glad I was able to get out in time."

"Yes, I heard. Very fortunate for you."

It was silent for a few seconds. Then Bianca said, "When will I see you, my love?"

"The men who are with you now are competent. They will bring you home to me soon, *inshallah*."

"Good. I can't wait to return to you and Jamal."

Ahmed analyzed every word Bianca said, each inflection, each breath he could hear. "Bianca . . . what did you tell your captives?"

"*Tell* them? I told them nothing."

"Nothing? Did you mention anything about Jamal, perhaps? It is all right if you did, I just must know so I can keep him protected."

"I . . . I said nothing. Not a word. Why . . . ? Is something wrong?"

Azzam did not know if something was wrong. He couldn't detect a lie over a satellite phone. No . . . he needed to see his lover face-to-face to find out if she had told the terrorists about the existence of her son and where she lived.

"Nothing is wrong. Everything is just right, now that you have been rescued."

"Good," she said. "When I get off the phone with you, I will call Yasmin."

Ahmed's narrow expression of mistrust returned. He said, "I have ordered Yasmin and Jamal moved, for their safety, and there is no phone where they are. You will see them as soon as you return."

"I . . . Yes, all right."

"Come home to me. We have much to discuss."

"Yes, love. *Inshallah.*"

Ahmed hung up the phone and adopted an impassive expression for the benefit of the men across the corridor. But in truth his body steamed with rage. His child had been taken from his city, and it would be days before he knew if his mistress was involved in the crime.

But for now he had to hurry to the airport. His flight north to Homs to appear at an Iranian base would be tomorrow, and then, the next morning, he would go to Palmyra to a Russian facility on the edge of the desert.

He didn't want to go to these places. His son, the heir to his reign here in Syria, was missing, and even though he had thousands of police and internal intelligence officers looking for him, while this was going on it was hard for Ahmed to focus on other matters.

And doubly so because of Bianca. When she came home he was going to have her visited by his best intelligence interrogators under the guise of asking about her captors. But the real objective of his people would be to find out if she had any culpability, either in her disappearance or in Jamal's disappearance. His people had been extracting the truth from terrorists, rebels, dissidents, turncoats, and political rivals for a long time. They would find the truth from beautiful Bianca, and if the truth was what he feared, he would have her tortured and then executed for her disloyalty.

As he walked back to his office, he decided he might even take part in the torture himself.

• • •

Bianca Medina did her best to keep from crying. She handed the satellite phone back to Malik, who stood there with Drexler and the French police officer, who clearly did not understand a word of Arabic.

After sleeping through the morning, Bianca had asked to call Yasmin, but Malik reminded her that the president himself was waiting to hear from her. She did her best to sound innocent, to reveal nothing about the Halabys, the American killer, the French spy. But she did not think Ahmed believed her.

She did not believe him for a moment that Yasmin and Jamal had been moved to somewhere secure. No . . . the American had taken them, and that was why Ahmed was suspicious of her. Ahmed had determined the truth: that she had told her captors everything.

If she returned to Syria, she would be killed; this she knew without a shadow of a doubt. But she saw no opportunity to get away from the men who held her now.

She did not believe she would ever see her son again, and she did not believe she was safe in Europe, or safe at home.

She returned to her cot amid the hanging bed sheets, and she sat down, and there she could hold it no longer.

She started to cry.

. . .

Malik and Drexler watched the woman cry alone for a moment, and then they turned away and stepped into an office in the warehouse building to talk. Drexler knew all about the kidnapping of Bianca's son, from Shakira, but Malik knew nothing about the child, even of his existence. All he knew were his orders—to get Drexler and Bianca back to Syria—and he knew that this plan had hit a stumbling block.

Drexler said, "You told me we'd go to the airport at noon. It's five till."

Malik said, "I had one of my men go to Toussus-le-Noble. He says French military troops have arrived and are searching it top to bottom. They are setting up tents off the tarmac, preparing for a longer stay. We won't be flying out of there."

Drexler rubbed his face in frustration.

Malik said, "You shouldn't have left Voland alive. This is his doing."

Drexler shook his head. "No, it's not. I wanted a peaceful resolution so we could exfiltrate France quietly. Voland did his best to give that to us. But the massacre and the fire that could be seen from a jumbo jet . . . *that* is what brought the authorities out en masse."

Malik turned away. "I have my men acquiring some vans. We will drive east. Not to Serbia; I don't feel confident in the private flight to Russia any longer."

"Why not?"

Malik shrugged. "Again, you left Voland alive. I think he will be involved in the search for us. He could have distributed photos of Bianca everywhere, even to a small airport in Serbia."

"So . . . where are we going?"

"We will go to Athens, and then—"

"Athens, Greece? That's a twenty-four-hour drive!" Drexler shouted.

Malik kept his voice calm. "We will drive for twenty-four hours. When we arrive in Athens, we will wait for a ship to pick us up. You, Bianca, and I will travel to the Syrian coast."

"What is this ship?"

"It's been used in smuggling operations for years, but right now it is off the coast of Lebanon. A dozen of my Mukhabarat colleagues working in Beirut will board today, and it will make the two-day crossing to Athens, where it will meet us."

Drexler thought this over. He wasn't getting on board that ship, obviously, but he saw how this change of plans might work to his advantage.

"When do we go?" Drexler asked.

"We will leave here within the hour." Malik looked over at Sauvage, sitting and smoking at the front loading dock of the warehouse. "What about the cop?"

"He will come with us, he might be useful," Drexler said. "I'll see that he earns all the money that I have promised him, even if he never lives to see a cent of it."

CHAPTER 59

At the refinery in central Syria, Van Wyk finally announced the "all clear" to his KWA mercenaries, after twenty minutes searching the control building. In all that time, the two KWA teams found a grand total of three armed enemy: the one Van Wyk sighted in the first room, and a sniper-spotter team on the roof that was killed by the men from the other BMP.

While this was going on, there had been a lot of shooting taking place all over the refinery as an entire company of Desert Hawks Brigade militia, some two hundred men, took outbuildings, pumping stations, storage facilities, and other structures, but Court couldn't tell much from the cadence of fire. It could have been that the Desert Hawks were involved in multiple skirmishes with the enemy in different parts of the massive property, or it could have been that they were simply executing civilians they found hiding in the ruins.

As soon as the control building was clear, the battalion command of the Desert Hawks Brigade began pulling up in trucks, armored personnel carriers, and other vehicles. As the building had been used as an HQ by the Syrian Arab Army when they owned the refinery, there was already space for them to move their equipment into. Three large command center rooms on the second floor were used to bring in communications equipment, maps, headquarters staff, and senior officers, while a platoon of security was positioned on the roof and in the large building's windows.

The twelve-man KWA strike force climbed back in their BMPs to catch up with the main element of Desert Hawks Brigade, but when they didn't move out after twenty minutes, Van Wyk got on the radio with company command and found out that Ali Company had been ordered to halt here at the refinery to await further instructions. The mercenaries filed out of the vehicles again, went back into the command building, and found a shattered, ruined office with blasted-out windows on the top floor in which to wait.

The body of a man well into his fifties, perhaps even his sixties, lay in the center of the room. Blood splatter on the floor told the story. He'd been engaged from the doorway; the blood was fresh, so Court knew it was someone on the KWA team that shot him. The body wore a simple white button-down and brown slacks, he wasn't geared up in any way as a fighter, and there was no weapon nearby.

Court couldn't say for certain this man had been a noncombatant, and for all he knew the dead man had charged right at the men who came through the door, but Court seriously doubted it. From what he'd seen and heard of KWA, he assumed this man had just been squatting here in the building and was shot dead while unarmed by the mercenaries who encountered him.

When the team moved into the office, Saunders and Broz picked up the body in the middle of the room, dragged it over to the blasted-out window, and swung it out, letting it drop down onto the concrete below.

Court just looked away.

Van Wyk had been with the Desert Hawks leadership in the command post to find out the reasons for the delay, and now he leaned his head into the room. "Bashar and Chadli Companies are heavily engaged to the northeast. They think it's FSA, company strength at most, but well dug into the hills. Nothing for us to do; it's long-range engagement, snipers and mortars and RPGs. Definitely *not* the CQB stuff they use us for. The militia is calling the Syrian air force for assets to disrupt the enemy in the hills, but so far nothing's available.

"We're to wait here at battalion HQ for orders, but I don't expect it will be long before the Hawks need us. I'll be downstairs in the CP."

The rest of the twelve-man team found places to sit or lie down around this ruined office. Court took off his rifle and his backpack and leaned against the wall. He was still fuming about the murder of the noncombatants, but he knew the sooner he focused his attention on his real mission here, the sooner he'd be done with these KWA assholes.

And he was well aware that being positioned here near the Hawks Brigade command post had presented him with an opportunity. Court knew he needed to find a way downstairs into the CP. There would be maps, plans, men discussing the tactical needs of this security operation, and, somewhere in all that intelligence, Court was hopeful he'd find some information about Ahmed Azzam's rumored trip to Palmyra.

Sure, Court was embedded with one militia unit that, from what he had been told, had been positioned at the outer edge of the security ring around Palmyra. It was too much to hope for that that tactical operations center for the Desert Hawks Brigade was going to have all the plans for the entire operation laid out for him to see, but he didn't necessarily need to know everything.

He was looking for a definite time and an exact place, and he would love to know as much as he could about the security setup for the president during his visit.

He had no illusions that he'd learn everything he needed to know. Still, he'd take whatever he could get and he'd make the most of it, but first he needed a way to get into the TOC.

Court had been thinking this over for several minutes, lost in his thoughts, when he looked up and saw Broz leaning back on his backpack, sitting on the floor by the wall and staring at him from across the room.

Court looked away, but the Croatian mercenary said, "What's your problem, Kilo Nine?"

"Go fuck yourself," Court answered.

Saunders was sitting nearer to the window. He said, "Don't worry about him, Broz. The new bloke will come through when the fight is on."

"Yeah? Sounds like he wants to do an interview with every son of a bitch in every firefight before deciding whether they get a bullet. Is this asshole going to have my back when he sees some lady pull out a pistol on my six? I don't trust him."

Court turned back to the Croatian. "So you don't trust the guy who *doesn't* shoot innocent kids? Are *all* you guys that twisted?"

Saunders gave Court an "eat shit" look, while some of the others mumbled curses Court's way. But Broz was the one who stood up from his position. He left his M4 rifle on the floor where he'd been sitting, but he walked over to Court.

Court stood up and faced him.

Broz said, "You're a little better than the rest of us, aren't you, Wade?"

"I didn't come here thinking that, but you guys aren't impressing me much with your actions."

Broz stuck a finger in Court's face. "Bastards who look just like those three we shot downstairs wear S-vests all the time!"

"Which three? You mean the boy and the two ladies? I didn't see any S-vests on them."

"I've lost men to women and kids before. You might not have to worry about that in Toronto or wherever the fuck you come from, but you're in the real world out here in the desert."

"So . . . what? You just shoot everybody you see to be sure?"

Broz said, "That would suit me. God'll sort 'em out. Seriously . . . why are you here?"

Court said, "Maybe God sent me to sort *you* out."

Court and Broz went for each other simultaneously, locking up and falling to the floor. Court rolled on top of the bigger man, pinning him by his chest, but as Court brought his fist back to deliver a punch to the man's face, the Croatian shifted his weight onto his right hip, shoved his right elbow inside Court's knee, and bridged his body up, thrusting hard to the right.

Court knew judo, he knew the move Broz was trying to execute, and he knew how to counter it. He made to slide his left leg away from his body to stabilize himself so he couldn't get thrown, but as he moved his foot he realized Broz had brought his own left leg over his own body, then hooked it down around Court's foot, trapping his leg tight.

Court's weight was on his knees, not back at his feet where he could fight Broz's new leverage, so the Croatian easily flipped Court off to the side, and Court slammed down onto his back.

Broz didn't hesitate to exploit his advantage; he rolled onto Court, pinning his shoulders to the dusty concrete floor. He head-butted Court, using his helmet in an attempt to break the pinned man's nose, but Court's helmet blocked the brunt of the strike, so the Croatian changed tactics, sitting up to get enough distance to rain punches down on Court's face with his hard-knuckled combat gloves. But as Broz postured up, Court realized the danger he was in, so he moved with the man above him, shot his arms around Broz's body armor, and grabbed his own wrists behind the man's back. He pulled Broz back down close to him. Here Court used his right leg to trap Broz's left, used his right arm to overhook Broz's left shoulder, and clamped in tight, so when he pushed off the man wouldn't be able to catch himself with his left hand on the floor. Court exploded hard up with his left foot and let go of his grip behind Broz's back, sending the two-hundred-pound man and all his gear rolling to his left, where he slammed onto his back.

Court rolled on top of Broz's torso, pancaking his shoulders to the floor.

He felt Broz reach for something with his left hand down at his waist, so Court himself used his left hand to reach for his own boot.

Broz brought a fixed-blade knife from its scabbard and pressed its tip under Court's body armor at his right hip. Simultaneously, Court thumbed the button on his switchblade, springing the four-inch blade like a bullet.

Just as the Croatian began putting pressure on the knife at Court's hip, Court brought the razor-sharp edge of his switchblade up and against Broz's carotid artery.

Both men froze in this position.

"I'll gut you!" Broz said.

"And then you'll bleed out right where you lay!"

Court turned his head to the sound of movement and saw Saunders leaping up to his feet from where he had been sitting and watching the fight. He charged over, reaching for his pistol on his leg as he moved. Court kept his left hand, and his knife's blade, right where it was against Broz's neck, but he untucked his right arm from its clutch around Broz's head and fired it down to his right hip, over the knife jabbing into his lower back. In less time than Saunders could make two bounding steps towards the fight, Court drew his SIG pistol, whipped it around and over his body, and pointed it at Saunders at a range of ten feet.

The Englishman stopped, raised his hands, and froze in place.

And then Van Wyk stepped back into the room. "What the *holy fuck* is going on in here?"

Both Broz and Gentry breathed heavily, but neither man moved their edged weapons from their lethal positions. Van Wyk shouted, "Knock it off! Wade! Broz!"

Still neither man moved. Court thought Broz was a psychopathic murderer; he wasn't about to relax his guard as long as the man had a knife pressing against him.

Van Wyk realized this was a tense situation that had to be untangled the right way. The team leader said, "All right. First . . . Saunders, turn away and walk back over to your kit. Do it slowly, and Wade won't shoot you. That's right, isn't it, Kilo Nine?"

"That's right," Court said through labored breath, his pistol still aimed at the Brit's face.

Saunders lowered his hands, turned slowly away, and returned to where he was sitting.

"Right. Pistol down, Wade. Slide it over to me."

Court did as instructed but kept the switchblade tight against Broz's neck.

Van Wyk next said, "Brunetti?"

The Argentine sat on his backpack near the window. "Yeah, boss?"

"You got a dog in this fight?"

"No, boss."

"Good. Raise your weapon. Shoot the first man who doesn't do as I tell them."

The man with the broken nose reached for his AK leaning against the wall. He leveled it at the two men lying together on the floor across the room, then flipped off the safety lever. "Okay."

Van Wyk said, "On three you will both lower your weapons, unravel, and go back to your kit. One . . . two . . . Brunetti, you good?"

"Yes, boss."

"And three."

Court retracted his switchblade with a snap, and Broz dropped his knife to the floor next to him with an audible clang. Both men climbed to their knees without looking at each other, and then stood.

Seconds later their knives were restowed, Van Wyk kicked Court's pistol back to him, and the men sat down on opposite sides of the room.

The South African team leader said, "That doesn't happen again or I start killing men for the good of the mission. Now, I came up here to give you a sit rep. Companies Bashar and Chadli are moving into the northern hills; they've broken up the opposition lines there. Battalion command can't get any SAA air online to attack the FSA while they're on the move, so they are trying to reach out to the Russians.

"Either way, we'll be heading due east in fifteen mikes, bypassing the hills and staying on the highway. There is a town we have to take by dusk to get us into position for tonight."

Saunders asked, "What's tonight?"

Court noticed that Van Wyk glanced his way before saying, "Looks like a raid is in the works. That's all I know."

The team leader left the room, but Court climbed to his feet, grabbed his rifle, and followed along into the hall to the stairs there.

"Sir?"

The South African turned around at the top of the stairs. "Don't call me sir. It's boss, Van Wyk, or 'hey, mate.'"

"Right, boss. Look, sorry about that back there."

Van Wyk put a gloved finger in Court's face. "I've got enough to deal with. Don't let it happen again."

"I won't."

"Klossner told me you were good but didn't have a lot of experience on the dark side. You'll learn . . . not to love it, but you'll learn to do it."

This guy was as lost as the rest of these cutthroat killers, Court could see. He changed the subject. "You said they were trying to get Russian air to the hills?"

"That's right."

"I speak Russian, if they need someone in the operations center."

Van Wyk seemed surprised by this but said, "SAA has Russians embedded with them, but the Hawks don't. If the Hawks want Russian air, they've had to go through the army."

"Maybe I can raise them on the radio directly."

"Come with me," Van Wyk ordered.

Court went back to collect his gear, then followed Van Wyk without a look or a word to the other men.

CHAPTER 60

After traveling from Damascus up to the interior of the nation, Court finally found himself about twenty-five feet away from where he really wanted to be. This was progress, yes, but he also found it frustrating as hell.

He'd been led into the Desert Hawks battalion command post on the second floor of the refinery control building, but he'd been moved along a wall and taken to a communications station at a long table in the corner. He stood there with Van Wyk and a few Desert Hawks captains and majors, but twenty-five feet off his right shoulder was an open and damaged doorway to another part of the command center, and right inside this room was a detailed map lying flat on a large table. The map appeared to Court to be the size of a twin bed, and militia officers moved around it, talking to one another and on handheld radios.

He was certain the map held the secrets for whatever this security operation was all about, and if, in fact, an Azzam visit to Palmyra was the reason behind the operation, then Court knew he needed to find his way into that room.

Court stole glances over to the table every chance he got, but from his position he couldn't make out a single feature of the map.

He had been standing here waiting for the radioman seated in front of him to dial in the Russian Air Force frequency that would put him directly in touch with Russian forces. It was weird, he had to admit. He was about to request that the Russians send air support to attack retreating Free Syrian Army forces. The thought made him feel nauseous, but he was in cover, and he'd seen no other way to finagle an invitation down into this room, where he knew he might be able to find the answers he was looking for.

Court was in this mission all the way now. He'd do what he had to do to get the intel for the FSA that could target Azzam personally.

Finally Van Wyk gave Court a long list of instructions relayed from the Syrian officers standing around the radio table, who themselves were in radio contact with the two companies pursuing the enemy forces to the north. When Court had everything written down, he took the radio and actuated the microphone. "Calling Russian air assets on this frequency. This is Desert Hawks Brigade battalion tactical operations center." Court gave the code name of the Hawks unit commander, as instructed by the Syrian officers standing around.

"Send your traffic, Hawks Brigade," came the terse reply in Russian.

Court was working off a map in front of him, although it wasn't the map he wanted to see. On the table where the radio was set up was a laminated map with grease pencil notations, showing this command position in the refinery, the highway to the north, and the hills farther north where the FSA were running from the two regime militia companies. Court glanced at the map and said, "We have enemy in the open, fleeing to the northeast. Request any air assets in the area to prosecute. How copy?"

There was a long wait before any reply, and when it came, it was a different Russian voice.

"Who is broadcasting on this network?" the Russian asked.

Court replied, "I'm a contracted PMC officer for the Desert Hawks Brigade." Court repeated the code words for the unit commander.

There was a pause. "You're not an Arab."

"That is correct. I am Canadian, Klossner Welt Ausbildungs security."

Another pause from the Russian. "We have a Russian officer who speaks some Arabic. Put a Syrian on the radio."

Court translated this for Van Wyk, and added, "These Russians have something against Canadians, apparently."

Van Wyk translated for the Desert Hawks officers, and one of them got on the radio to speak with the Russian air assets.

To Court it looked like he'd just outlived his usefulness. There was a good chance he was going to be sent back to the KWA room upstairs because he wasn't needed here.

He realized the only way he'd learn anything here in the command center was by walking into the other room and right up to the map, so he decided he needed to risk doing just exactly that.

Van Wyk was engaged with the majors, and none of the other men in the commo room noticed him slip away.

Court walked into the room with the map table like he had every right in the world to be there, and he judged the movement of the group of men around the table to position himself where he could see the most. The men were engaged in their conversation; Court wasn't picking up the words but it seemed to be something of an argument.

He walked the length of the room and through an open door on the far side. Here was a small empty room with a window, but no way out. It would be awkward to just turn around and retrace his steps, but he was the Gray Man; he knew he could pull it off.

Court turned around and walked right back past the map, again as if he belonged, and headed back to the radio room. He'd spent fewer than ten seconds close to the map, and had only looked at it for two or three.

But he saw what he needed to see. The map clearly displayed the city of Palmyra, and a series of concentric circles. Different unit markings were evident around the maps, although Court didn't recognize all the units.

To the far east it was easy to decipher, because this part of the map was a much more detailed version of the smaller laminated map Court saw on the radioman's table. Court couldn't read the Arabic script, but he had seen the location of the Hawks' position in the refinery and also north in the hills.

Court could also see that there were two more small towns to the east of the refinery along the highway.

To the west were markings for other units, and from what Court had heard in the bar the night before, the SAA was providing the inner line of defense around the Palmyra area.

Inside of the SAA protective ring, the nucleus of the entire map had not been drawn around the city of Palmyra itself, but instead, it looked like it was about a mile or a mile and a half outside the city. And the nucleus was not a circle . . . it looked like the outline of a dumbbell lying at a 45-degree angle. At the center of the entire map, the nucleus around which the dumbbell emanated, was a spot on the M20 highway just a mile or so east from the eastern edge of the city of Palmyra.

Court had no idea what was at the center of this security cordon, but whatever it was, it involved two locations close to each other, and a protected zone between them. Clearly the focus of the entire security operation lay both north and south of the highway to the east of Palmyra.

This was key. He couldn't just call Voland and have him tell the FSA that Azzam would be in Palmyra at a certain time. The FSA couldn't flatten the entire city. But if there was some sort of a Russian base a mile or so to the east of Palmyra, and Azzam was planning on visiting it Tuesday, then that might represent actionable intelligence. The FSA might be able to send rocket crews close enough to attack the base, or set up shoulder-fired surface-to-air crews to target Azzam's helicopter.

Yes, Court now knew the "where." As for the "when," it was sometime between tomorrow, which was Monday and when the security cordon was supposed to be in effect, and Tuesday afternoon, which was when Azzam had told both Bianca and Yasmin that he would return to Damascus.

The "what" was not hardened intel. This was all still speculation that this security operation involved Ahmed Azzam at all, but Court had executed many operations in his career on less solid intel than what he'd managed to acquire that corroborated his theory, so he was confident that the president would be coming to this area.

Court stood back by the radios, behind Van Wyk, and concentrated on committing all the information he had just seen to memory. In the middle of thinking over what it all meant, he looked up and was surprised to see Van Wyk looking directly at him.

"Kilo Nine! Pay attention."

"Yeah, boss?"

"You're up."

"What?"

"The Russian's Arabic sucks, apparently, so you're back on the mic."

Court took the radio and began speaking again with the Russians. He looked up to Van Wyk. "They say they can send a pair of Mi-24s for a couple of runs with rockets, but they are low on gas. After about two passes they will have to leave to refuel, and it will take them an hour to return."

While Van Wyk discussed this with the Syrians, Court thought about this bit of information. Quickly he realized *this* was intel he needed. He figured the turnaround time to fuel an Mi-24 would be up to a half hour, and certainly not less than fifteen minutes. If the Russian attack helicopters had to fly both ways from the hills north of the refinery to their refueling bladder, and they could make the entire trip, including refueling, in an hour, Court thought there was a significant chance this meant there was a Russian refueling operation set up around Palmyra, and possibly in the "dumbbell" on the map in the other room.

There was nothing scientific about any of this, but all circumstantial evidence continued to point to a Russian base just off the highway east of Palmyra, and less than twenty-five kilometers from Court's present location.

A Syrian major handed Court a sheet with the latest coordinates for the concentration of enemy forces trying to escape out of the hills. He wanted these exact coordinates relayed to the Russian helicopters.

Court decided to slightly alter the coordinates when he read them out over the radio, with the effect being to send the Russians to a location about two klicks west of the actual position of the Free Syrian Army forces. He wasn't sure if it would save the guys on the ground or not, but he knew he couldn't send the helos too far off course, or it would come back that they'd been fed completely incorrect coordinates.

. . .

Minutes later Court and Van Wyk left the command center, and minutes after that the entire KWA strike force was outside the control building, hustling back to their BMPs to leave the relative safety of the refinery and head out with Ali Company towards the east. As Court surveyed the scene around him, he saw bodies in the distance, slumped forms near some storage tanks. He was too far away to know if the people killed had been combatants or not, but he was well aware of the Hawks' reputation for barbarism against civilians.

He climbed into his infantry fighting vehicle with the others, then looked up to see that Broz was sitting right in front of him. The Croatian still stared Court down.

Court said, "Dude, any time you want another shot."

Broz clearly did want to start something, but Van Wyk sealed the hatch and looked in at the team. He saw the posturing between the two men. "Broz! Wade! You start fighting in this tin can with me in here with you, and I swear to God I'm going to shoot you both."

Court and the Croatian both calmed down, but when the vehicle began bouncing on the road, it became obvious that any fight in these conditions would have likely resulted in more comedy than tragedy.

CHAPTER 61

In his office in central Paris, Vincent Voland hung up his phone and rubbed his tired eyes.

While he had spent his morning coordinating with the Jordanians a means to rescue the baby and the nanny in Syria, and the noon hour spent pushing Drexler's photo out to all the airports and train stations in Europe along with warnings that he was behind the attacks in France and might be trying to leave the continent, he spent the afternoon hours on deeper research into every shred of intelligence of known Syrian Mukhabarat activities in Europe.

He focused on the physical logistics of the GIS, Syria's General Intelligence Service, because he assumed Drexler would use Syrian government resources to get back to Syria. He researched airports first, looking for any examples in the past five years of known Syrian intelligence forces using international airlines, charter outfits, or privately owned aircraft. He even examined examples of Syrians sending freight via air, thinking it possible they might simply use the same means to ship a Swiss spook working for the Azzam regime as they would a shipment of jet avionics equipment or high-tech radar parts.

When he knew everything there was to be known about how Syrian government spies had moved men and matériel via air, he targeted every company, route, and middleman, and he communicated with contacts he maintained in the intelligence agencies in the different locations involved. He sent the new, high-quality photo of Sebastian Drexler and asked them to use their existing facial recognition assets to plug the image into the computers that analyzed security cameras around all the properties used by Syrian intel.

When the air routes back to Syria were as well covered as he knew how to make them, he began looking into ship traffic: specifically any instances of the GIS in using oceangoing vessels to move themselves, other people, or items. A couple of private yachts in the Med had been flagged as belonging to shell companies owned by Syrian interests, and Voland had the yachts located and the facial recognition software scanning video in the areas around the marinas where the yachts were in port.

Also through his work he'd found out that in the past year, two cargo ships from Europe had been stopped in the Mediterranean and found with illegal goods bound for Syria. Voland had been in this game long enough to know that for every shipment stopped on the water, certainly a dozen if not more made it through. Reading over the maritime investigations done by the EU into those responsible for the shipments, he learned that one of the two confiscated cargos had originated in Split, Croatia, and the other had departed from Athens, Greece.

Digging into the cases deeper, he found the actual ports where both cargo ships took on their illicit cargo.

Here both trails went cold. In both Split and Athens, investigators had uncovered no paperwork showing a freight company, a trucking company, or any other details of where the goods came from or how they were loaded on board. Instead in both cases it had been random spot checks on the water that determined the ship had been carrying contraband, and the contraband had been sent using forged manifests that could not be traced back to a person or company.

Still, Voland realized a ship from Europe to Syria would be a high-probability means of transportation for Drexler to return to Syria, especially since he must have known that by now he was being hunted at all the airports.

The Frenchman sent Drexler's photo directly to the harbormasters of both ports where illegal Syrian cargo shipments had departed from the year before. Within an hour he was told that facial recognition suites were up and running at every camera at both ports, including the marinas, the traffic cams, police cameras, even restaurant and retail stores in the two locations.

Voland didn't celebrate this positive step in his hunt because he knew Drexler could be driving to Russia, or taking a ship to South America, or simply hiding out in Europe for a month before returning to his patron nation.

These were just small steps, a few of many he would need to take today. Still, this was intelligence work. It required time, patience, and, more than anything else, dogged determination.

And in Voland's case there was one more ingredient in the recipe. Voland was filled with and fueled by an intense passion to make Sebastian Drexler pay.

CHAPTER 62

Court and his group of mercenaries spent the afternoon climbing into and out of their BMP-3 as the KWA team worked to clear buildings behind Desert Hawks Brigade Ali Company's spearhead to the east.

None of the mercs had been read in on the entire operation, of course, but it was becoming clear to Court that the objective for this day was simply to move through some villages along the M20 highway for the purpose of looking for a fight. Recon by fire, it was called. The Hawks rolled down the road, shot off a few rockets and rounds, and looked to see if there was any sort of fighting force in the area interested in mixing it up.

In the few cases during the afternoon where the militia did receive fire, Ali Company devastated the building or street where the gunfire came from, and then rolled on in their vehicles.

If any structure in the target area was left standing, the KWA men were sent in for room clearing.

Court hadn't fired his weapon in the past three hours of action, simply because he'd seen no targets in the buildings he'd entered. He had seen dead and wounded; some were fighting-aged males, and others were clearly civilians. They'd all been killed or maimed by Desert Hawks weapons before KWA arrived.

It was scene after scene of sickening atrocity, and all the while Court wondered how the hell he was going to get away from this so he could report what he'd learned earlier in the day in the oil refinery.

• • •

About five in the afternoon Court's BMP threw a tread, so he and the other five men from his team rode on the other KWA armored vehicle down a broken street, their weapons up in their arms. They'd been ordered to push on to the eastern edge of the little town and to find some hard cover high enough to get overwatch on the last village down the highway at the far edge of the security zone.

The KWA men were alone in the village with their one vehicle. The main section of Ali Company had been called out of the town and sent up to the north. Court heard from Van Wyk that somehow the Russian helos that they'd requested to pulverize the retreating FSA force had not located them, so nearly the entire battalion had been ordered to go out into the desert east of the hills to make sure the FSA was out of the perimeter the Desert Hawks had been ordered to secure.

The reason a dozen foreign mercs and a few vehicles had been the only ones left in the town had become clear to all minutes after arriving.

There was nothing here left to kill.

Court had seen the first decayed body the moment he climbed onto the other BMP and sat down next to the turret. Just off the broken road, inside a shelled storefront, a cadaver lay with most of its clothing still intact. He saw more bodies, some lying out in the open, over the next few minutes.

He found himself confused by the placement and disposition of the corpses. They weren't blown to bits; they were just lying around, either in rubble or out on the sidewalks and streets.

Saunders was seated at Court's shoulder and answered the question before Court posed it by leaning into his ear to speak over the big engine and grinding tracks below them. "Chlorine."

"What's that?"

"Gas attack. From the look of the bodies it happened a couple weeks ago. The Syrian Air Force dropped barrel bombs on the town. Looks like they used conventional bombs first, and a lot of them, and then just said 'stuff it' and dropped some chlorine. Killed anyone left who was out in the open. Bet it sank down into the bunkers and tore up some lungs and throats in there, too. Some of these poor buggers probably came running out of their holes to try to find air, but there was no air to be had." Saunders sniffed. "Yeah. The gas is gone, but the stink of dead flesh is bloody obvious."

"Right," Court said. And then, "This doesn't bother you at all, does it?"

"Said the bloke who nicked somebody's baby."

Court turned away. "You guys are pure evil."

"You'll catch up, mate. The day isn't done yet, and tonight's gonna be a horror show."

■ ■ ■

Two hours before sunset the unit had made it to the southeastern side of the village and found an overwatch on the top floor of a five-story apartment complex. Court sat in a corner bedroom filled with trash strewn around amid the broken masonry. Through a window to the east he could see the next town, and through a window to the south he could see desert, with low rolling hills.

Anders sat nearby in the same room, and he scanned the south with his binos. "Wonder who's hiding up there."

Court had been thinking the exact same thing. While all day long he'd been hearing reports of fighting in the hills to the north, the hills to the south loomed much closer and more ominous to this little town.

Van Wyk assembled the men in the living room of the apartment a few minutes later. He held his radio in his hand, and he was in comms with a Desert Hawks major back at the command post. The two men spoke in Arabic for a minute more before the team leader addressed the eleven men. "Right. Here's the plan. The Hawks have finished their work in the northern hills and they're on their way back here. Ali is linking with them ten klicks out of town in the open desert, and at sunset they're surrounding the next town on the highway.

"I am told they believe there might be some FSA elements in there from the force they encountered in the hills. They are going to start shelling after sunset, and you can expect the Hawks to pound that town with rockets, tanks, and mortars for a few hours. This is the outer edge of the security perimeter they've been asked to establish, and they don't want any enemy forces remaining."

403

"What about us?" asked Anders.

Van Wyk said, "We'll go into the town behind the main element."

"More room clearing?" Broz asked, a grumble in his voice telegraphing his feeling about it all.

Van Wyk said, "There is a mosque in that town that has supported anti-regime forces in the past. The Desert Hawks don't feel great about flattening the mosque, so we're going in to clear it."

Saunders mumbled, "Pussies."

Court said, "ROEs?" He was asking about the rules of engagement, and there was a snicker from one of the mercs in the back of the apartment's living room.

Van Wyk said, "If they are in that mosque, they are considered hostile. No quarter given."

Court wanted to hear Van Wyk point-blank say he was ordering his people to kill unarmed civilians, but he decided he wouldn't press it. The insinuation was clear, and anything else Court did to reveal that he was uneased by what was happening around him would just detract from his cover.

Anders said, "Boss, can you ask the TOC about those hills to the south? We're sitting ducks from any indirect fire positions up there."

Van Wyk looked out the window at the hills, and then he spoke into the radio. The major replied and the South African translated. "He said those hills are outside the security perimeter, but SAA intelligence says it's a heavy opposition presence, so use caution. Still, he's not worried about an attack from the south."

Anders said, "Of course he's not, because he's back at the *fucking* command post in the refinery."

Court asked, "Is it FSA or ISIS?"

Van Wyk looked at Court. "The major said it was terrorists, which is the word they use for any opposition."

Saunders chimed in. "Wade, the only thing you need to know is that it's a bunch of hatey, beardy blokes who will pull the trigger as soon as they can get your melon in their gun sights."

Court let it go.

Anders pushed the issue of their isolation here. "There's a dozen of us total in this little town. If somebody attacks across that strip of desert from those hills, they could be on us in minutes."

Van Wyk said, "All right, Anders, I hear you. Just stay out of the windows on the south. Do not reveal your positions to anyone with long glass in that direction."

. . .

The meeting broke up, and a few minutes later Court was back at his post by the windows to the east. He could still see out to the south, as well, but he was staying far back in the room so he couldn't be sighted from that direction.

He was frustrated about the intel he had about Azzam and his inability to pass it on to those who could exploit it. He needed to get the hell out of here, and now. He'd done what he could to search the apartment for a cell phone while the team was settling in to their defensive positions, but he'd not found anything other than a dead wall phone that had been ripped from the wall when bomb shrapnel had destroyed most of the unit. But even though this one apartment was a dry hole, he figured if he had enough time to search the ghost town around him he would be able to find a phone, and with it he could contact Voland.

But he wouldn't have the time because he was going to be posted right here till it was time to climb back aboard the BMP and hit the next town.

And getting back on mission wasn't the only reason he wanted to get the hell out of here.

His stomach churned thinking about the attack to come.

The late-afternoon sun was low now in the west; looking to the east through binoculars, Court could see flickers of reflections from the few bits of glass still in the windows of buildings of the next town on the highway. He wondered if he'd find that this area had been hit with chlorine bombs like the one he was in now, and he also wondered if the Desert Hawks were going to utterly level it tonight when the sun went down.

He was all but certain they would, and then he and his colleagues would go in and eradicate any survivors hiding in the rubble.

With an entire battalion of militia raiding in the dead of night, along with a small team of shock troop mercenaries used to raid the mosque and kill anything that moved within, this was going to be a massacre; that much was clear.

Court lowered his binos, then crawled back over to the window to the south. Anders was in the room with him, but the Dutchman ignored him as he dug into a bag of rice and ate it with his fingers.

Court looked out to the southwest, into the low sun again, and then he looked out to the hills to the south.

And he got an idea, but it was not an idea that made him feel particularly buoyant. No, the sickening dread that he'd felt about taking part in this evening's slaughter was replaced by a sickening dread about what he'd just decided to do.

CHAPTER 63

From his position on the floor in the corner of the apartment, Court looked around the bedroom a minute, searching for an item necessary to implement his plan. He couldn't find what he was looking for here, so he told Anders to cover his position for a moment, then went out into the living room. A few men sat around at the windows looking east, and none paid much attention to him.

When he'd surreptitiously hunted for a phone earlier, he'd noticed a completely shattered boom box on the floor of the apartment, next to the overturned shelf where it had obviously stood. On the floor around the shelf were a dozen CDs, some in their cases, some lying loose.

Court checked the men around him, and when no one was looking his way, he knelt and snatched up three of the CDs, then dropped them into a cargo pocket in his pants and returned to the room in the southeast corner of the building.

Anders finished his meal, then looked over at Court. "Hey, you got any WAG bags?"

Court knew what a WAG bag was from his time in Ground Branch. WAG stood for "waste alleviation and gelling" and it was, effectively, a toilet in a bag that an operator could use to dispose of his solid waste. It wasn't pretty, it didn't make the highlight reels of snipers or Navy SEALs in action, but soldiers, sailors, and operators in the field had been defecating into plastic bags for a long time.

Court sighed a little to himself, because this meant his battle buddy was about to take a dump right next to him in this four-meter-square room. "No, Anders, I don't. How 'bout you try to hold it?"

The Dutchman was already undoing his utility belt and heading to the corner. "Nope."

Court resigned himself to the fact that the next few minutes were about to get even more unpleasant than the last few, but then he turned to Anders as he realized this was the opportunity he needed. "Look, you Neanderthal. There is a shitter somewhere in this apartment. Why don't you go find it, and I'll do the same when my time comes?"

"You think the plumbing works in this apartment's bathroom?"

"Of course not, but it's a little room with a porcelain bowl, and that's a lot better than you taking a big crap in the corner here. Have some respect for the homeowners, at least."

"Why? They're dead."

He was probably right, Court realized, but he needed him out of the room. He said, "Dude, I'll watch your sector."

Anders refastened his belt with a shrug. "You're like a damn woman." And with that he left to go find the bathroom.

As soon as he was gone, Court crawled across the floor over to the window that faced to the south. He sat with his back to the concrete eastern wall and looked back into the open room. He took one of the CDs from his pocket and held the shiny "down" side out the southern window, half pointing it towards the setting sun to the west. Turning around and looking through the hole in the middle as a sight now, he angled the disc towards the mountains to the south and moved it back and forth.

He was careful to keep his head and body behind the wall next to the window, and also careful to keep his ears tuned to sounds around the apartment. If he was signaling the enemy with his head out in the open, a sniper hiding on the desert floor would have a prime shot at him. And if he was caught signaling the enemy by the KWA men, Van Wyk would shoot him dead right here without question.

For a full minute and a half he flashed the hills, broadcasting his location to any possible enemy there, making it look like the lens of a pair of binoculars or a sniper scope had gotten caught in the setting sun.

He heard footsteps right outside the room, so he dropped the CD and brought his hand back inside the window. The shiny disc fell to the street below.

Court's elbow was still on the window ledge when Anders reentered.

He looked at Court there in the corner. "You moved."

"I can see both sectors from here."

"Yeah, well you are going to get your arm shot off if you keep it there."

Court brought his arm in, then crawled back over to his side and began looking once again to the east.

His idea had been for enemy fighters to begin harassing the building, with either snipers or mortars, just enough for the decision to be made for the KWA men to withdraw from the area before dark.

He didn't think his simple action was going to prevent the Desert Hawks Brigade attack of the town to the east outright, but he hoped it would at least get the Hawks to actually engage with soldiers on the other side of the fight, be they FSA or Daesh or al Jabhat or SDF, instead of simply eradicating civilians of the neighboring town.

And he also hoped some sort of an attack might give him the opportunity to slip away, at least long enough to find a working cell phone. It occurred to him this was like yesterday's bar fight, with stakes raised by a factor of one thousand.

He felt like going AWOL would be the only way he could transmit his intel. He had two days' rations in his pack, and he could go to ground, make his way west back towards Palmyra, and provide even more intel if the FSA did try to engage Azzam while he was at the Russian base.

Just then Van Wyk leaned into the room. "Just got word from battalion. Shelling of the next town begins in thirty mikes."

"Roger that," Court said, and Anders echoed this.

Van Wyk looked at his watch. "Thirty minutes after that and we load up in the BMPs. Keep eyes on that village, get me any intel you can."

Court and Anders sat in silence for twenty minutes, and by now Court had figured his plan to use the CD as a signal mirror to invite an attack had failed. He had a couple more CDs in a cargo pocket, but the sun was very low now, and he didn't see any way he could get another chance to—

Saunders shouted from the living room. "Hey! I heard some pops! Keep eyes out for IDF."

IDF was indirect fire, and Court realized his grand scheme to get himself shot at was going to work out after all.

Seconds later Van Wyk started to call "incoming," but before the second syllable was out, three explosions ripped the desert floor in quick succession, just eighty yards south of the apartment building where Court sat. A few tiny bits of debris pinged off the building, not far from where Court sat near the southeastern corner.

He knew these first shots would be ranging rounds. A spotter would determine how to adjust the mortars so that the next rounds would hit closer.

Saunders stormed into the bedroom where Court sat. The two men locked eyes, and Court looked away. "What did you do?"

"What?"

"Did you signal somebody?"

"The fuck are you talking about?"

"There's no way we were seen from that distance. Impossible. You signaled them."

Anders looked at Saunders like he was crazy. "Why would he signal them?"

"You weren't going into the next town. I saw it in your eyes when boss gave the order. Figured you were gonna throw yourself down some stairs to get out of—"

"Incoming!" Van Wyk shouted now from the next room.

Three more rounds came in; this time they were much closer. The first two hit in the street just to the south of the apartment building, but the third impacted against a lower floor. The resulting shaking knocked Saunders to the floor and sent loose debris and dust flying in all directions.

Anders shouted now. "Why would he signal for an attack?"

Saunders pointed at Court, and he stood up in the cloud of dust, his face red with fury. "This fucker isn't here to work with us. He came here to—"

"Mortars!" Van Wyk screamed. "And we've got multiple technicals inbound from the south. One klick out! All call signs, withdraw to the BMPs!"

Court hadn't expected them to attack that hard and that accurately.

The three men in the corner room ignored the order from the team leader. Saunders answered Anders's question. "Wade came to Syria just to snatch that kid in Damascus, and he's using KWA for cover. He's stuck with us but he's trying to find a way out of the country."

Three more mortar rounds slammed into and around the building, sending everyone flying, and filling the apartment again with dust and smoke.

Anders looked at Court. "You kidnapped that baby they were talking about this morning?"

Court climbed to his feet. "Boss said exfil!"

But Saunders blocked Court's exit from the room.

Court said, "Not now, Saunders!"

Anders climbed to his feet and made a run for the door. Saunders let him pass, but he pointed a finger at Court.

"You're fucking mad! Calling in the enemy? You're gonna get us killed!"

"Not if we get out of here before we get—"

Court stopped talking when he saw Saunders move his hand to the long knife he wore on his vest.

A mortar shell crashed squarely on the roof, directly above the room. The ceiling collapsed in different portions of the apartment, and a dust cloud filled the room so thick that Court could no longer see Saunders.

He slung his rifle over his shoulder, threw his backpack on his back, and charged forward like a linebacker.

Saunders had drawn the long knife from the chest of his load-bearing vest, but he hadn't expected the man hitting him so hard with his head low. Both men tumbled onto the ground in the debris, and Court threw knees into Saunders's body and punches to his face.

The knife came up in an arc that Court couldn't see, but he felt the arm swinging freely and he fell back and away quickly. The blade cut deeply into the magazine rack on Court's vest. Realizing he was now in a life-and-death struggle with the British mercenary, Court continued rolling backwards, kicking his feet over his head and flipping over onto his knees.

He reached down to the SIG pistol in his drop leg holster and pulled it free as heavy machine-gun fire began raking the building. The entire scene

411

was still clouded over with dust and building materials. Court fell onto his back, worrying that the man with the knife could be inches away, and then he kicked himself backwards along the floor, gear and pack and all, until he hit the far wall.

He couldn't see Saunders, but he knew where he'd been, and he aimed and fired eight rounds as fast as he could press the trigger.

His ears rang, and another mortar hit just outside the building, sending shrapnel into the room over Court's head. He stared forward in the thick dust and raised his weapon again to fire more rounds, but then Saunders appeared just two feet away and coming fast.

Court fired once into Saunders's chest plate before the British mercenary fell onto Court, knocking him onto his back.

The man was already dead, a bullet wound in his left temple and another in his throat.

Court pushed the gear-laden body off him, fought his way up to his feet, and ran out the door to the bedroom.

One flight down in the stairwell he turned to go down to the first floor, and then he stopped abruptly. Anders lay facedown on the landing, blood pooling under him. There was a ragged hole in the wall where a high-explosive mortar round had entered the stairwell, sending shrapnel out in all directions that eviscerated the Dutch KWA employee.

Court continued his descent.

He got to the front door of the building, and in the low light of dusk he saw the two BMPs in the street, their engines running, their lights on. The rear hatches of both vehicles were closed, but a top hatch on the second BMP was open, obviously waiting for the three contractors still in the building.

Court considered making a run for the vehicle and climbing in, but he saw this as an opportunity. If he could lay low in the apartment building while the KWA men egressed, they would assume he'd been killed in the mortar attack.

KWA wasn't a "no man left behind" type of outfit.

Of course, Court realized staying behind would still leave the nonsignificant issue of dealing with whoever was heading this way on the technicals Van Wyk had reported, but he figured he could try to find a basement and wait out the attack, then search for a phone to report his intel to Vincent Voland.

It was a good plan, but the plan ended when Van Wyk rose up out of the hatch and saw Court standing there in the front door of the building. "Move your ass!" he shouted, and he brought his Galil assault rifle up through the hatch and aimed it down the road, as if to cover Court.

Court stood there, decided he would be better off exfilling with the contractors and then searching for another opportunity, and then he started running towards the armored vehicles.

He made it fewer than five steps before he heard the unmistakable whiz of an incoming rocket-propelled grenade round. He ran on another two steps, and then his body was tossed into the air. The sound and fire came simultaneously, and after the incredible assault to his senses, he was blind and deaf. He did feel his body slam back into the street, pounding his right shoulder and right leg.

He lifted his head and shook it a moment until he could just barely see a foggy distorted image. It was the darkened road by the apartment building, and on it the two infantry fighting vehicles raced off to the west.

Court dropped his head back down into the street, and his helmet clanged. He felt a trickle of wet on his lips, and he licked it, tasted blood and concrete and dirt. He brought a hand to his face, rubbed his eyes a moment, and then focused more clearly.

Three pickup trucks raced past him in the street, coming from the southeast, and then they slammed on their brakes, skidding in the rubble all around.

Armed men with beards and dark clothing leapt from the beds of the trucks, not twenty-five meters from where he lay.

Court raised one hand to the men in surrender, but only for a moment, because his hand dropped back down as he lost consciousness.

• • •

Court woke with a bag on his head and his hands tied behind his back. He was lying on his left side, bouncing up and down against the hard surface, and this told him he was likely in the bed of one of the technicals he saw just before passing out. He didn't know how long he'd been out, but he felt

413

cool night air blowing on his arms that he'd not felt before, so he imagined some time had passed.

His body armor had been removed, as had his boots, utility belt, and drop leg holster. His watch was gone, as was his helmet. He realized he must have been stripped down to the dirty white T-shirt and the green, black, and brown camo battle dress uniform trousers he'd gotten from the KWA loadout room down in Babbila, and the two pairs of boot socks he'd put on that morning.

Men spoke Arabic above him. From the positioning of the voices he suspected they sat on the sides of the bed and back at the tailgate, and he lay between them at their feet, but his ears rang still and his head hurt too bad to even try to concentrate on what the men said. It didn't matter really, he figured, because he knew all he needed to know about what was going on.

He'd seen the dark clothing and the beards, both common with ISIS fighters, and he knew he was fucked.

They'd only taken him alive so they could execute him more dramatically than a bullet to the head as he lay unconscious in the street. Whatever they did to him would be for show now, and he'd seen all the various manners by which they put someone to death on video. The beheadings, the burnings in cages, the drownings, tying men to landmines and IEDs. He'd seen children ordered to kill prisoners with guns and knives, and he'd seen mass executions where dozens of men would be taken, one by one, and put to death, as a crowd looked on.

The only thing ISIS had generated in its five years of existence, as far as Court could tell, was a lot of inventive ways to instill terror via torture and death.

And now he could do nothing but await his own miserable fate.

. . .

The drive lasted a long time, but Court had no ability to determine how long. He figured it must have been eight or nine p.m. when the vehicle began ascending into hills, and for another hour or more it climbed and descended, turned on hairpin curves, and even stopped a couple of times.

He'd nodded off but came to when the tailgate slammed down behind him, then hands grabbed his ankles and pulled him roughly out of the pickup. He braced as his torso was dragged on the tailgate, hoping who-ever was pulling him had the decency to help him to the ground so he didn't fall four feet, although he knew there was no reason to expect such decency.

As he feared, he fell straight down and crashed hard onto his back on dirt and rock.

Multiple arms pulled him up to his feet now, then half walked, half dragged him down a gravel path and into an enclosed space—some sort of a building. He was shoved against a wall and then pushed down on his butt; even through the bag he could tell it was pitch-black in the room, and then the hands guiding him let him go.

The door slammed shut.

He thought about his predicament, and he held out no hope. His bind-ings were well tied, and he'd heard the trucks of a dozen vehicles at one time or another during his ascent into the hills, so whoever owned this territory seemed to own it outright.

The door to the room opened and Court felt other men being shoved against him, pushed down onto the floor. These would be more prisoners, and this made him think that ISIS was storing prisoners so they could execute them en masse as soon as the sun came up tomorrow.

CHAPTER 64

At some point Court fell asleep, and he dreamed of his own death. He was with dozens of other men, all wearing the orange suits that ISIS loved to dress its prisoners up in as a way to dehumanize them. They were each taken, one by one, on a short walk, then pushed to their knees and shot in the back of the head.

The dream was horrific, but more so as Court had watched his fellow prisoners receive the shot that blew their brains out. When Court's time came, in contrast, he found himself oddly at peace.

He thought about Jamal Medina and Yasmin Samara, and Dr. Saddiqi, and he lamented that he could not fulfill his promises to help them, and he thought about Tarek and Rima Halaby and their two children, and about Bianca Medina, who, while certainly not innocent, was nonetheless still a mother who loved her child, and wholly undeserving of all that had happened to her.

It was sad he wouldn't fulfill his mission here in Syria, but there was nothing he could do about it, so as he walked to his death in the dream, he told himself it was finally time to let go, as if he knew a long-awaited and much-earned rest was coming for him.

He welcomed the rest as he bowed his head and waited for the gunshot.

· · ·

Court woke suddenly to the sound of a man calling out in shock and fear next to him. He recognized the man's voice. It was Broz, the Croatian mercenary. He'd obviously kept his own mouth shut all night long to hide the fact that he was a European, a non-Muslim, and thereby would suffer more at the hands of these monsters.

There was a small amount of light coming through his bag, and he thought it must be morning now.

Court could hear Broz being dragged away, out of the room, and as soon as he was pulled away, Court felt hands grabbing him. He was yanked roughly to his feet, frogmarched out of the room, and shuffled ahead.

He heard a wooden door open and he was turned, walked along a moment, then pushed down on a chair. Seconds later the door he'd entered through slammed shut. His bag had been left on his head, but even through it he felt the presence of someone standing in front of him.

This would be an interrogation, of this Court was sure. He wasn't going to reveal to anyone here that he was an American. If these assholes were going to execute him, they weren't going to do it with the special fanfare reserved for high-profile Islamic State prisoners. No, he'd rather get his head chopped off for a small crowd and his body dumped in a sandy ditch and be forgotten than show up on YouTube in some insane music video–style execution.

A man spoke to him now. It was in Arabic, of course, but Court understood the words. "What is your unit?"

Court did not reply. If he said anything in Arabic, that would be just the same as indicating he was a foreigner, because he couldn't fake the accent, dialect, or language skills of a native Arabic speaker.

He felt a blow on the side of his head. "Hey! What is your unit?"

Still Court didn't reply. The man stepped away, then muttered something to someone in the room, but this Court couldn't make out.

Again the interrogator tried. "You were with the Desert Hawks, but you don't wear their uniform. Where do you come from? Are you Syrian?"

It occurred to Court that if this asshole just pulled the bag off Court's head he'd probably be able to figure out for himself that he wasn't a local.

He received another smack to the side of his head, and although he had fantasies about launching himself up and head-butting his interrogator into a coma, he did not react to the hit.

From the far corner of the room Court heard the sound of a wooden chair being pulled across the concrete floor slowly. He tracked the sound all the way up to him; whoever was dragging it along was making a dramatic show of coming closer, slowly and ominously. The chair stopped just a couple of feet in front of where Court sat, and then it was swung around; again Court could hear its placement by the scraping sound.

The wood creaked as an obviously large man sat down on it.

It was already dark inside the bag, but it suddenly got even darker, as the man seated in the chair in front of him leaned right into his face.

Nothing was said for several seconds. Whoever this guy was, he was patient, intense, and he knew how to intimidate a prisoner.

Finally he spoke.

"English?"

Court did not reply.

A few seconds later, the man repeated himself. "English?"

Despite his decision to show no reaction to his interrogator, Court cocked his head a little. Something was off about this guy's accent.

The man spoke a third time, and this time as soon as the words left his mouth, Court felt the hair stand up on the back of his neck, because the accent was unmistakable now. "Hey, dickhead. I asked if you spoke English."

This asshole was from the United States.

Court hesitated just a moment, and then he replied, "Dude, you take this bag off my head, I'll quote Shakespeare."

The bag came off slowly. Court blinked away the brightness of the room, even though the only light came from a large opening in the plywood ceiling of the stone block room that looked like it had been created by a direct hit from a mortar round. He then focused his eyes on the man sitting three feet in front of him. He was American, clearly, in his late twenties or early thirties. He wore a gray T-shirt under tan body armor. There were tats on both forearms, and he had sandy brown hair and a thick beard that looked like it had been growing for months.

His green eyes looked at Court with absolute suspicion, but Court was almost overcome with relief. The man wore no insignia on his gear or clothes, but he was clearly a member of the U.S. military.

The man said, "Well, well. Aren't *you* an interesting son of a bitch? What's your name, Slick?"

"Why don't you just call me Slick?" Court found he could barely talk, his throat was so dry.

"All right then, Slick. What's your story?"

He swallowed roughly, then said, "No story. Just passin' through."

"Sweet. Thanks for dropping in on our little corner of paradise."

"Pleasure's mine. Got any water?"

"Yeah, loads. But we don't hand it out to terrorists."

"I'm not a terrorist."

"Oh, cool. Then I guess you can go."

Court looked past the American and saw a half dozen smaller Arab men back by the door of the dim room looking on. Some had AKs and some were unarmed, but to a man they all wore black tracksuits with no uniformity, and some wore headbands. They looked like a sloppy soccer team.

A couple had short beards or mustaches, but most were clean-shaven.

Court could tell in an instant this wasn't a jihadi group, like he'd first thought when he saw them from a distance in the low light the evening before.

No . . . these guys were likely FSA, the Free Syrian Army. And this was the best news he'd had in a *very* long time.

Court tried to determine exactly who the American was now. Most likely he was U.S. Army Special Forces, a Green Beret, though he could have been from one of the "White Side" SEAL units, or possibly even the Army's special-mission unit, commonly referred to as Delta Force.

The bearded man just looked Court over, saying nothing, so Court added, "Let me help you out. This is the part where you ask me who I'm working for."

The man smiled. "Is it? Okie-doke. Thanks for the tip. Who are you working for?"

"I can't tell you."

"Is that because you're workin' for ISIS, workin' for Jabhat al Nusra, or working for the SAA?"

"None of the above."

The big American stood up fully, reached into his belt, and pulled out a pair of thick contractor gloves. As he began putting them on, he said, "Let me tell ya 'bout a little unwritten rule we have around here when it comes to prisoners."

"Can't wait."

"Talk shit . . . get hit."

"I wonder why you haven't written that one down."

The soldier laughed, genuinely enjoying the repartee. "Bunch of tight-asses at the State Department and Pentagon send us memos tellin' us we can get in trouble for coldcocking a prisoner without cause, but somethin' tells me I can get away with it as long as the prisoner is another gringo. I think I might have to bust your smartass mouth just to find out."

Court smiled. He liked this guy. "You're SF. Fifth Group? Third? No . . . you're Tenth Group."

The American blinked when Court said the third number, so faintly the man didn't realize it himself.

Court said, "Yeah, Fort Carson, but doubt you're seeing much of Colorado these days."

"Who the hell *are* you?" the man asked. He sat back down in the chair, forgetting about his gloves and his plan to punch his prisoner in the face.

"Can't tell you that, but I bet you twenty bucks I can guess your name." Court squinted in the sunlight beaming through the hole in the ceiling, looking over the man's face. "Bobby? Billy? Randy . . . Ronnie? You look like a Ronnie."

The bearded man now made a slight but obvious reaction.

Court took this to mean he'd nailed it. "Okay, Ronnie. How about you have one of your little guys back there bring me some water? It will help me talk."

The American in the body armor called out to the men behind him without taking his wide eyes off his prisoner. *"Meyah lal shereb!"* Water!

A young man with a wispy beard and a shiny black Adidas jacket with white stripes pulled a bottle of water out of a pack on the floor and brought it over. He spoke English to the soldier as he handed it to him. "Who is this guy?"

"Dunno yet."

Court was not untied, but the American soldier squirted several ounces of water into his mouth. Court drank it down, closing his eyes a moment as he let the water bring him back to life. Then he said, "Ronnie, you've got a tough job. But I'm going to make it a little bit easier today."

"Are you?"

"I'm going to give you a phone number that will connect you to an office building in McLean, Virginia. Call it yourself, or kick it up to your command and have them call it. This will get straightened out and I'll get out of your hair."

"McLean, huh?"

"That's right."

"You're saying you're CI—"

Court shushed him before he could finish it.

The SF man scratched his beard. It was clear to Court that the man wasn't sure what to do.

Another bearded American with body armor and forearm tats entered the room and spoke before he looked up and saw his colleague in the middle of an interrogation. "Hey, Robby, second platoon snipers spotted SAA helos about ten klicks north of—"

He stopped dead in his tracks.

Court nodded to him. "Hey, man. Any chance you could run and grab the sat phone for Robby? He's got a *really* important call to make."

The new Green Beret stared at the prisoner for several seconds before turning to the big man sitting with Court. "What the fuck?"

"He says he's an American."

Court chuckled. "Either that, or I'm a Bedouin camel herder who just watched a shit-ton of *Sesame Street* growing up."

Robby said, "And he's tellin' me he's OGA." OGA meant "other governmental agency," and it was the "down low" way of saying CIA when out in the field.

Court shook his head. "Didn't say that, Rob. Said they'd vouch for me. Look, you're obviously in charge here, so that makes you, what, a captain?"

"None of your business, Slick."

Court said, "Lieutenant, then. Got it."

The other man in the room laughed despite himself. Court was clearly the last thing they'd expected to run into in the hills of the Syrian Desert. He said, "You want me to get the phone?"

Robby said, "Negative. Take the FSA guys and give me a few minutes alone with my new friend here."

When the room was empty other than Robby and Court, the American Green Beret said, "You gotta help me out, man. You're saying you are, or are *not*, CIA?"

Court shrugged. "I'm *something*, Robby, that's really all I can tell you. Just put me on the phone with them. That's not me playing tricks, that's me doing you a favor. The person on the other end of the line is going to be *really* pissed off that I'm right here, right now, in your custody, and there is no sense in them taking out their anger on you."

Robby just stared at Court another minute, still in silence.

Court said, "All right. I'll cut you in just a little, but I'm code word, so your TS/SCI clearance doesn't get you into the party. You can't even know I exist, understood?"

Robby nodded, a dazed look on his face now.

"I'm on the job. I was in cover as a contractor for a regime-backed militia, but one of your little buddies RPG'd me and I ended up right here. Now I've got to get back on my time-critical mission, and the only way I can see to do that is to have you talk to Langley so they can tell you to let me go."

Robby said, "The other guy the FSA picked up?"

"He goes by Broz; he's a Croatian mercenary, working for KWA."

"*Those* bastards."

"Yep. They shot civilians yesterday at the refinery along the M20 highway. Don't know what you can do about it."

Robby shrugged. "Me, either, in the grand scheme of things. But I sure as hell can make him miserable while I've got him."

Court said, "Talk shit, get hit?"

The man smiled. "I bet a merc who just committed war crimes is gonna talk some serious shit."

"Before you tune him up, you mind making that call?"

Robby nodded slowly. "Okay, Slick. I'm curious enough to play along."

He was on board now, at least partially. He squirted some more water in Court's mouth, radioed for the sat phone to be brought to him, and then went out into the hall, leaving Court tied up alone in the room.

Robby was curious—he wasn't stupid.

. . .

A half hour later Robby and three other Americans walked purposefully back into the room. Robby pulled a knife off his chest rig and cut Court free.

As Court stood, the soldier extended a hand. "Captain Robert Anderson, Tenth SF. Pleasure to meet you, sir."

Court shook his hand. "I was pretty happy to run into you myself."

"I apologize about the treatment. We hear some tall tales in this job, and I've run into a couple of Brits running with ISIS and Al Nusra, so even your American accent didn't prove you were on the level."

"You'd have been a fool if you acted any other way."

"I checked with my command, and they okayed me calling the number you gave me after they checked it out to make sure it went to Langley. I spoke with a woman there, she wouldn't give her name, but she confirmed you were one of hers. She didn't seem too happy to hear from me."

"Her name is Suzanne, and I'm only telling you that because it would piss her off if she knew that I did."

"Yeah, well, she wants you to call her ASAP. Here's the phone."

Court took the phone. "I'll call her boss. He'll be just as pissed about this, but he'll also be a little more helpful."

"I don't really have much of an office, but you can use my hooch for some privacy."

. . .

Captain Anderson led Court out of the little mud, stone, and plywood building and through a warren of similar structures, all built deep in the hills. This Special Forces forward operating base was well hidden here, protecting it from possible Russian or Syrian aircraft above, and the FSA unit they were embedded with held a solid-looking defensive perimeter. Robby told Court there was one ODA here, or Operational Detachment, Alpha—meaning a dozen Green Berets working with some seventy-five

423

FSA fighters. The Americans were here fighting against ISIS, not the Syrian regime, but the FSA fought against both groups.

Anderson led Court into a small room on the ground floor of a bombed-out building and told him no one would disturb him during his call.

Court sat on the cot, looked at the phone in his hand, then took a deep breath.

He dialed a number from memory, but he wasn't really sure what he would say when the call went through.

CHAPTER 65

As the director of the National Clandestine Service of the CIA, Matthew Hanley often worked late into the evening. Today had been no different. He'd arrived at his office in McLean, Virginia, just before eight a.m., and it was just after nine p.m. when he crossed the Potomac River on his way home to D.C.

His driver got him back to his Woodley Park neighborhood by nine fifteen, but just a few blocks from home, Hanley changed his mind and decided to go out to dinner instead.

Hanley was a bachelor in his midfifties, a former Green Beret, and he didn't splurge on much in life apart from good food and wine. Tonight he made the last-minute decision to indulge at the Bourbon Steak restaurant in the Four Seasons hotel, not because he had anything special to celebrate, but rather because the pressures of his job had him certain it would kill him one of these days, so why shouldn't he enjoy a good meal while his heart was still beating?

He and his four-man security detail entered without a reservation, but a table for one was found in the center of the room, and Hanley ate while his detail maintained a discreet 360-degree watch over the dining room and the street out front.

Apart from an urgent call from the office, he enjoyed the first half of his meal in silence at his table while he listened to the soft murmur of conversation from others seated around him. Well-heeled couples talked about their kids and marriages, businesspeople discussed their work, and foreign travelers to D.C. spoke in foreign languages, most of which Hanley understood, and the big man in the middle listened in on it all while he dined alone.

At ten thirty he poured the last of his first full bottle of cabernet into his glass, and was just about to cut off another slice of his twenty-two-ounce bone-in rib eye, when his cell phone rang. The sound of the ring told him it was on his encrypted app, so he decided he should answer it.

This was his second encrypted call of the past forty-five minutes, and he was certain it would have some relation to the first.

"Hanley."

"Hey, Matt. It's me." It was Violator. Courtland Gentry. Hanley's wayward lone-wolf asset.

Hanley put his fork on his plate and leaned back from the table. "Yeah, I know. Brewer called. She's about to have an aneurysm."

"Fingers crossed."

Matt smiled but didn't let Court hear him chuckle. He took a sip of his cabernet with his free hand. "So . . . last I heard you were in Frankfurt, about to go on vacation. Did you get off at the wrong bus stop on the way to the beach?"

"Yeah, the one in the Syrian Desert."

"Right. Some indigenous forces working with an A-team captured you in the middle of a firefight, thought you were ISIS or Al-Nus. I trust you've charmed the hell out of them and smoothed things over."

"Yes, sir. We're all gonna get matching tats when this is over."

"And you want my help in getting the hell out of there."

There was a pause on the line.

"Court?"

"I don't want to leave, but I do need some help."

"You are on the job?" Hanley said it as a question. "Aren't you getting support from your employer?"

"Negative. The guy running me is untrustworthy. I might just go it alone from here on out."

Now Hanley put his glass down. "If you were going it alone, we wouldn't be talking. What do you need?"

"Not sure how much I should tell you, actually."

"The line is clean, but you know that. You don't know how much you should tell me so that I maintain plausible deniability over what you are about to do. Is that it?"

"In a nutshell."

"Well . . . maybe keep it vague. Theoretical. Hypothetical."

Court breathed into the phone a moment. Then, "Let's say an opportunity arose where someone could eliminate a very bad actor at the center of a very bad situation."

Hanley looked around for the waiter, and when the two men met eyes, the big man lifted his empty wine bottle. He had a feeling he was going to need some more alcohol in the next few minutes. Court was talking about assassinating Ahmed Azzam; there was no question in Hanley's mind. He controlled his own breathing and said, "Go on."

"The elimination of this bad actor might well help things . . . but it might not have any real effect. Who knows . . . things could conceivably get worse."

"The future's hard to predict."

"That's right. I guess I'm trying to decide, should this person in a position to do this thing to this bad actor act . . . or should he wait for someone with more knowledge of the situation to decide if the elimination of the bad actor is the right thing to do?"

Hanley said, "You want a vague answer?"

"I want an ironclad thumbs-up or thumbs-down, but I'll take what I can get."

"You are after my blessing, then."

"Something like that . . . I guess."

"Well, kid, I can't just give you carte blanche to delete anyone in the world you want to delete. Officially or unofficially."

"I understand."

"Having said that," Hanley continued, "I've learned over the years that you have pretty fair judgment."

Court did not reply to this.

"And . . . if the question is, 'do we take a bad actor off the game table, even if we don't know what will come next,' I kinda have a philosophy about that."

"I'd be very interested in your philosophy, Matt."

Hanley kept his voice low as his eyes flitted about the room. "If a bad guy gets dead, well, it might make the next bad guy think a little bit. It might not, there's no silver bullet to fix every problem, but at the end of the day, a little street justice, an eye for an eye . . . well, that might be the most sure thing there is out there to hold back the monsters."

There was a long pause. "I've been thinking pretty much the same thing."

"I know you have. And you've got to do what you've got to do. Officially speaking, though, I haven't said shit, and you have not been tasked. You got that?"

"Got it."

The connection crackled for several seconds.

"Court, old buddy, I've got a rib eye staring me down here."

"I'll let you get back to your steak. Sorry to bother you."

"You kidding? Between you and me, this little phone call has made my week."

"Guess that means you had a shitty week."

"I'd say you have no idea, but you probably do." Hanley sipped water now. "Your mom misses you."

"Suzanne Brewer's definitely not my mom, and I doubt she misses me. She probably was hoping I hadn't checked in because I got hit by a bus."

"Brewer knows she's not that lucky." Hanley laughed aloud, then adopted an authoritative tone. "I want to hear back from you again, soon. You copy? We still have an arrangement, if you remember."

"Copy. Let me figure out my current predicament, then I'll reach out."

"Put a couple weeks in between," Hanley said. "For the sake of plausible deniability."

"Will do."

Hanley added, "I guess I'll keep one eye on the news for a few days to see what the hell you're up to. Be careful, kid. Come through whole, okay?"

"I'll do my best."

Hanley disconnected the call and immediately put a call in to a number he had stored on his phone. It went directly to a desk at the Pentagon, and a watch officer answered on the first ring and sent Hanley's call on from there.

While he waited for the transfer, he picked up his fork and took a bite of his sherry-glazed mushrooms. As he looked around the room, it occurred to him that no one else sitting in the restaurant could have possibly guessed that the thickly built man dining alone had just given tacit approval to the assassination of the president of Syria.

CHAPTER 66

Court Gentry sat alone in Captain Anderson's hooch for twenty minutes, drinking water, eating rations, and waiting. A Green Beret medic came in and cleaned and stitched the vicious cut he'd received over his right ear from the exploding windshield glass in Damascus, then wrapped Court's head with a dressing.

Finally the captain came through the door, followed by two other members of his A-team. He introduced them as Danny, a master sergeant, and Cliff, a first sergeant. Court did not introduce himself but shook their hands.

Once this was done, Robby said, "All right, mystery man. I've been told to hand you over whatever you want, equipment-wise, food- and water-wise, et cetera, and follow your instructions. I am then ordered to forget I ever saw you. Not sure if that means you have friends back at Langley, or enemies."

"Yeah, our relationship status is complicated."

Robby said, "We are staying here for the next several weeks, so unless you want to join our op, you'll need to get extracted somehow. If your friends in high places can scare up transport for you, I'll certainly get you safely to your LZ."

Court shook his head. "Thanks, but I don't need babysitters."

"Sir, you're smack-dab in what's left of ISIS country."

"Well, *that* blows. My travel agent said this was a clothing-optional resort."

All three men laughed, but to Court it still appeared they were regarding him as if he were a unicorn. Robby said, "Seriously, you aren't going anywhere without a lot of help." Cliff unrolled a large satellite photo of the area and put it on a table in his hooch. He showed Court where they were in the hills, a few hours' drive south of the highway where he'd been captured. "The FSA has technicals, but you'll need a helicopter. The Iraqi border is one hundred twenty-five klicks east. The Turkish border is three times that to the north."

Court just looked at the Army men. "I'll be heading northwest, actually. To Palmyra."

All three looked up from the sat photo. Robby said, "Now why would a smart fella like you go and do a thing like that?"

Court shrugged. "Work."

Cliff said, "We've had our drone up north. Not to Palmyra, but east, over the M20. We've been seeing all the activity. A couple days ago the Iranians moved out of the area, then the SAA moved in, and yesterday the militia pushed east along the highway. We even spotted some Russian attack helos. You know anything about what's going on?"

Court nodded. As far as he was concerned, an American A-team right here a few hours' drive from enemy lines should know as much as possible about what was going on. "Ahmed Azzam is going to be visiting a small Russian Spetsnaz base located about two klicks east of Palmyra tomorrow, probably in the morning."

"*What* Russian base?" the men asked simultaneously, and this surprised Court.

"You don't know of a Russian base along the M20?"

Court looked down to the photo and put his finger on the place where he'd seen the nucleus of the security operation. "I saw it on an enemy map right here. Just north of the M20 highway. Also, there is something they want protected down here."

Court remembered the "dumbbell" on the map and traced his finger down. There, displayed on the photo, were a few bombed-out buildings and the unmistakable shape of a single runway. "What's this?"

"It *was* the Palmyra airport. It's been shuttered for years. Since ISIS came in. The SAA hasn't reopened it."

"How old is this image?" he asked.

Danny checked the back. "Almost a month. That's so far out of our sector we haven't updated it. Mostly we use our UAVs for real intelligence, not sat images."

Court's eyes were on the airfield. "Holy shit!" he said aloud, as it came to him. "Not only is that airport back open, but I think the Russians are running it."

Robby was incredulous. "Where are you getting this intel?"

Court said, "Can't say. But I can say I'm pretty sure I'm right."

Robby looked at him. "And you want to go there?"

"I wouldn't say 'want to.' More like 'have to.'"

Danny said, "Shit, sir, I wanna be you when I grow up."

Court shook his head. "You *really* do not, Sergeant."

Cliff looked to his senior officer. "Hey, Rob. What about hooking him up with the Terp? He's from Palmyra."

Robby nodded. "An FSA soldier . . . he's our interpreter. You met him this morning, sort of. He's one hundred percent reliable, the bravest and hardest-working kid I've ever met. Seriously, I'm going to adopt the Terp when I get out of here, and he's only a couple of years younger than me."

"If he knows Palmyra, then I'd really like to talk to this guy."

. . .

The Special Forces team's FSA translator was called in over the radio, and he entered the captain's hooch with a very worried look on his face. Court saw that he was the young man who wore the black Adidas jacket with the white piping that he'd seen earlier in the day. He was in his midtwenties, with a scraggly beard.

Robby said, "Meet Slick. He's American. That's all you need to know."

The young man nodded and shook Court's hand. "Sorry I hit you on the head when you had the bag on. I thought you were Desert Hawks Brigade."

"No hard feelings," Court said. "Why is your English so good?"

"My father grew up in the UK, then moved back to Palmyra. When I

432

turned seventeen I studied languages at the University of Homs. French and English. But only for two years. Then the war came."

Robby said, "Slick needs to go somewhere in Palmyra, high up enough in a building to where he can see this area here." He pointed on the photo to where he'd been told by the stranger that a Russian base had been erected. "You know a way to get there?"

The Terp furrowed his eyebrows. "It is very dangerous. Maybe if you sneak across the desert you can get there, but the SAA is all over Palmyra since they took it back from Daesh."

Court said, "Sometime tomorrow Ahmed Azzam himself will be two klicks east of Palmyra. I want to be close enough to see him."

An astonished look crossed the Syrian's face. Thinking a moment, he said, "Maybe we can get into the hills to the north. You will be able to look down onto that land. It's very flat."

Court shook his head. "They will be ready for that. This base will have berms and structures built up to protect against that high ground to the north. There's no way we can set up there and expect to get a look at Azzam." He spun the map around and put his finger on a point to the west. "But if we can somehow get *into* the city of Palmyra . . . they won't be expecting eyes on them from that direction."

The Terp said, "Of course they won't. Why would they? It's full of SAA and pro-regime militia units. I have friends who live in Palmyra; I lived there for three years fighting for it myself, before we lost it to ISIS. Then SAA came and took it from ISIS. Trust me, nobody knows the place like I do. But the FSA can't go into Palmyra."

"Maybe not the FSA. But what about a couple of idiots with a long rifle?"

The Terp looked at the Green Berets as if he did not understand.

Cliff said, "I think he's talking about you and him."

The young Syrian looked back to Court like he couldn't believe the American was serious.

Court looked down at the area on the photo, checked the scale, and then touched a building on the far eastern side of the city. It was the only building of any size in the area; the next group of large structures was three blocks west.

"This building here looks like it's about a mile and a half from the center of the camp, assuming it's where I think it is. Farther to the run-way." He looked up at the others in the room. "I want to go to this building."

The Terp puffed his chest out a little. "I am a proud fighter of Usud al-Sharqiya."

Court looked at Robby. "What's that?"

Robby said, "Lions of the East Army. It's the name of his militia."

"I thought he was FSA."

"Slick, there are thirty different groups that make up FSA that I know of."

Court addressed the young man again. "Okay, you are Lions of the East. What's your point?"

"My point is that I have no fear. I will go with you, Mr. Slick."

Court nodded at the young man. "I appreciate it."

Cliff spoke to Court now. "I can gear you up, unless you were looking for a cold beer or a bottle of scotch."

Court shook his head. "You got an M107?" He was speaking of the Barrett M107 anti-matériel sniper rifle.

Cliff shook his head. "Negative. But we have a TAC-50. The FSA has one, as well." The McMillan TAC-50 was another fifty-cal sniper rifle.

"How pissed will the FSA sniper be to give his up?"

Robby said, "My command says to get you whatever you want, but no U.S. forces are to accompany you when you leave my base. I'll get you that rifle, and I'll straighten it out with the FSA."

"Good. Other than the sniper rifle, I need an AK with a folding stock, a pistol, a technical, and some water. Fuel to get me fifty klicks."

The Terp shook his head. "Others will want to come."

"We have to keep this small-scale. If we're detected, either we'll be killed before Azzam comes, or they'll cancel his visit."

"If we are bringing a truck anyway, it doesn't matter if we are two men or six men."

"You have anyone in mind who might tag along?"

The Terp looked to Robby. "Yusuf and Khadir. Plus a driver and a man to protect the driver."

Robby said, "Yusuf and Khadir are the Carl Gustaf team."

Court knew a little about the Carl Gustaf recoil-less rifle, but not much.

He did know that it was an 84-millimeter weapon that fired an array of standard and rocket-boosted munitions. "Trained by you guys?"

"Yep. U.S. Army ordnance, given to the FSA along with training. Those two guys are as accurate as you'll get in all the FSA. They've been together for years as an RPG team. We outfitted them with the Carl and now they are rock stars around here. If you need a piece of armor hit at up to four hundred yards, Yusuf and Khadir are the ones to do it for you."

"Sure," Court said. "That might just come in handy."

CHAPTER 67

Two Mercedes Viano vans, each carrying a driver and six passengers, arrived in Athens, Greece, in midafternoon. They parked in a lot near the Port of Piraeus, and then Malik, Drexler, Sauvage, Medina, and three of Malik's men walked along Kastoros Street, while the rest of the GIS men did their best to melt into the neighborhood without being noticed.

Soon Drexler and his entourage turned into the doorway of an office building by the water, and they climbed three sets of stairs to a large office space overlooking the yachts in the marina.

The sign on the door read "Hellenic Carriers of Ocean Freight, Inc."

It appeared to be a working office, but a key had been left under a mat for Malik, and when they all entered through the door, the lights were off and no one was inside.

Malik turned to Bianca after flipping on the lights. "Mademoiselle Medina, there are a few cubicles in the corners with some privacy, and there is a large corner office that is at your disposal if you would like to rest. I am sorry this is not more comfortable for you, but this office is owned by my department, and it is the closest and safest place near the marina. We will stay here until the boat from Syria arrives, early tomorrow morning."

"It is fine, of course. *Shukran*," she said.

Bianca sat down in an office chair and idly looked over some brochures, reading about the services of the freight forwarding company written in French. Malik saw her interest and said, "This is a front of ours. We use this place to help get weapons and supplies into Syria past the embargos. I don't think the war would be going nearly so well for us without this office, and others like it in Italy and Croatia."

Drexler had been standing by the window looking down on the neighborhood below. Soon he asked Malik to join him there.

The Swiss operative said, "You can't keep all your men here. They will stick out like sore thumbs."

"It is my job to protect Medina until she gets on that boat tomorrow."

"And you will have failed if someone calls the local police to tell them ten Arab men wearing jackets are standing on the hot streets at a port in southern Greece. *Think*, Malik. Medina can only be hidden here for the next twelve hours if we remain low profile."

"What are you suggesting?"

"I'm suggesting you send all your men home. Between you, me, and Sauvage we can watch her. When the skiff from the ship lands tomorrow there will be more GIS men to protect her all the way to Syria."

Malik looked down at the port, then shook his head. "Not all of them. I'll send some home, but I'll keep my top three men here with me."

Drexler nodded. "Thank you."

Malik turned to him. "The policeman. You haven't armed him, have you?"

"*Armed* him? If I armed him, the first person he'd shoot would be me." Drexler smiled now. "Don't worry about him. He's my problem, and I'll take care of him."

And this was true. Drexler was not worried about Sauvage. Now he was only worried about the four men between himself and Medina. Malik and his three men. He'd managed to thin the herd by talking the Syrian operative into releasing most of his force here, but the four who were staying, Malik included, would be the best of the best.

He knew he could kill four men in most circumstances, but these were no ordinary men. Certainly he would be killed if he tried. He told himself he was just missing one piece to the puzzle, and then he would make his play.

Drexler and Malik left the office to go down to the marina to make arrangements for the boat to dock the following morning, so Sauvage,

437

Medina, and the three Syrian GIS men remained in the large office space. Bianca and Sauvage sat across from each other at different desks, both with a view out the window to the port, and then beyond to the Aegean Sea.

The three security men took up watches in different parts of the sprawling office, leaving Sauvage and Medina effectively alone together.

Bianca recognized this as an opportunity, and after several minutes to ensure no one was close enough to listen in, she looked over to the French police officer. "I've been sitting with you in a van for over a day, and you've barely said a word."

Sauvage seemed surprised that the woman spoke to him at all. He shifted in his chair uncomfortably. "I don't have much to say."

"How do you fit into all this?"

Again Sauvage shuffled in discomfort. "I'm just happy you have been rescued, madame."

"That doesn't answer my question."

"No? Well then . . . if you must know the truth, just as you were a captive in Paris, I am a captive now. Drexler has involved me in all this, and I came along unknowingly, until it reached a point when I could no longer walk away."

Bianca said, "I am sorry."

Sauvage looked at the woman a long time. Bianca smiled at him a little, and he looked away. "You shouldn't be sorry. This isn't your fault. It's mine."

Bianca checked the Mukhabarat officers on the other side of the room to ensure they couldn't hear her. Then she said, "This European. Monsieur Drexler. He wants me dead, doesn't he?"

Sauvage looked down at the floor. "Why would you think that?"

She didn't answer him. "And since you just admitted he was the one who got you involved in this, I guess that means *you* want me dead, as well."

Now Sauvage looked up to her. "No. Of course not. I haven't wanted anything that's happened in all this. I just wanted . . . I wanted money for a vacation house in Nice, for my kids' university days." He shrugged and sighed. "And a little more. A lot more, I guess. I was a fool, but I am not a murderer."

"What is your first name?" she asked.

He looked at her again, nervously now. "Why does it matter?"

"Because I would like to know."

"It's Henri."

"Perhaps, Henri, you and I can help each other."

Sauvage looked away once more, out the window and towards the harbor. He stood up, ready to move farther away in the office. *"Je suis désolé."* *I'm sorry.*

"Attendre!" *Wait!* "Listen to me. I see good in you, Henri. You are not like the others. I know you don't want to have anything to do with this."

Henri shifted on his feet now, kept looking out the window, but he did not walk away.

Bianca said, "You must ask yourself why you are here."

"I am helping them get you to safety in Syria. Since I am a police officer, I have credentials they need in case—"

"Don't be ridiculous. You must know they have you along for another reason, and when they are done with you, Drexler will kill you. Think about everything you know about what's going on here. Why would men like Drexler and Malik allow a man with that knowledge to return home? Ever."

Sauvage sat back down slowly. Soon he put his face in his hands.

Bianca said, *"Non!* You *must* remain strong. We must help each other if either of us is to survive."

"How are we to survive?"

"That depends."

"Depends on what?" Sauvage asked.

The Spanish woman looked him over a long time. "On whether you are brave enough to fight for your life."

CHAPTER 68

Court Gentry wore a threadbare gray T-shirt with a black track jacket zipped over it, brown cotton pants, and tennis shoes. He'd gotten the clothes from FSA fighters here at the outpost in the hills, and with these clothes he looked just like most anyone else here, even though word had spread around the camp about the new visitor.

He donned a chest rig that carried his AK magazines, but no body armor. Few of the guys in the FSA had plates, so he'd opted to go without himself in case he was spotted by someone close enough to notice he wasn't outfitted like the others.

He'd taken the dressing off his head; the fourteen stitches over his ear were holding, and the wound wasn't visible through his hair without really looking for it.

He went through his gear one last time before departing. He had a large backpack full of equipment, food, and water on the ground next to him, a worn Beretta M9 pistol in good working condition, and an AK-47 with iron sights and a folding wire stock. He wore the pistol on his belt, and the AK lay on the ground next to his pack.

All this he considered extra equipment, because his main weapon for this mission lay cradled on a cushioned case in front of him. It was a McMillan TAC-50, a fifty-seven-inch rifle that fired the .50 caliber Browning machine-gun round.

Court didn't know the TAC-50 at all, but he'd hit living targets in the field at over one mile distance with fifty-cal sniper rifles, and he'd spent the last half hour with the Terp and the FSA sniper who operated the gun to ask specific questions about the weapon and the scope attached to it so he'd know how to best employ it when the time came. He'd been given a laser range finder and notes on the ammunition, the air density in the region, and other relevant data that would make it possible for him to hit a one- to one-and-a-half-mile shot.

He zipped up the camel case, slid three ten-round box magazines into pouches on the outside of it, and slung it over his back on the right side, slinging his other pack over his left shoulder.

The AK he carried in his hand, and then he struggled forward to the pickup truck waiting for him at the edge of the camp.

Captain Robby Anderson met the American a few yards from the waiting vehicle, already loaded with the five Syrians. The vehicle would take the sniper, the Terp, and the two-man recoil-less rifle team to a spot in the desert a few miles from Palmyra, and then the Terp and the American would go on alone to the northwest, and the Carl Gustaf team would head due north. The technical driver and the machine gunner in the cab would return to base, while the four men on foot would spend the nighttime hours doing their best to remain undetected as they infiltrated the security cordon to get as close as possible to where their target was due to arrive the next day.

Court shook Anderson's hand, and the younger man said, "Good luck, Slick. If this works, you're gonna be famous."

"If I become famous, a black helicopter is going to land right here and pick you up for a conversation."

Robby nodded at this. "My lips are sealed. Same as the other guys. I just mean . . . if you actually do it, you will be making a hell of a difference around here."

Court looked out over the hills and down to the desert in the distance. "Who knows?" He gave a nod to the other Green Berets standing near buildings higher on the hill, then turned to leave.

"Any chance you'll tell me your name? I'd look you up back in the States. Maybe we could grab a beer."

Court smiled. "Let's keep this a one-night stand. Trust me, you won't respect me in the morning, anyway."

Court slapped the younger man on the shoulder good-naturedly, then began lumbering down the hill towards the pickups.

. . .

The stranger Robby called "Slick" had climbed into the technical, and the vehicle had just begun to roll out behind the others, when Danny walked up to Robby. Both men watched the FSA truck disappear around a bend in the hills.

Danny said, "I hate to state the obvious. But that dude is a dead man."

Robby shrugged. "Yeah, probably. But can you think of a better way to go?"

"Got me there, Captain. You think he understands this is a suicide mission?"

"I think that man understands the odds, and understands what's at stake. He figures his life is a worthy trade for a shot at taking down a monster."

The two men turned and began walking along a switchback that climbed up the hill. They'd have to heighten their defenses for the next couple of days, because if the FSA technical was caught in the open and any survivors were taken, it was a good bet someone would come looking for their tiny outpost in the desert hills.

. . .

Court sat in the bed of the Toyota Hilux pickup with the Terp next to him. Both men had handheld radios with earpieces, and these had also been given to the Carl Gustaf crew and the driver of the vehicle. All four men spoke through the back window to the driver about their route as they picked their way across the rough ground. The Terp had a good map of Palmyra, so he and Court could make even more detailed plans about the ingress phase of their operation.

The Terp knew of a tunnel Daesh fighters had used when they owned this territory a year earlier. According to the young interpreter, the tunnel attached to the sewer system in Palmyra, and it extended outside the city to the south, connecting with an irrigation canal there that had brought water to farms ringing this ancient city out in the middle of the desert.

The Terp asked the other men in the technical while they traveled, but

442

none of them knew if the sewer system or the pipes that ran into the fields had been damaged, destroyed, or filled in. Still, Court decided heading to the farmland south of the city seemed like it might be the best way to get a couple of men close to and then inside the city itself without being seen.

. . .

After three hours driving across open desert, Court and the Terp's technical stopped in a deep channel created in a wide alluvial fan. All four men on the operation climbed off the truck, grabbed their gear, and took a reading with both the GPS on Court's watch and a compass. By their calculations, Court and the Terp had three hours' walking ahead of them to reach the farmland, and from there it would take another one to two hours to get into the city of Palmyra itself.

Court said, "Five hours carrying gear and hoofing it, kid. Can you do it?"

"Of course. Can you?"

Yusuf and Khadir had just as much equipment, but their walk would be shorter, because they would find a hide sight on the eastern side of the supposed Russian base.

Court and the Terp said good-bye and good luck to the others, then headed off to the northwest across the alluvial fan, towards a point in the distance they could not yet make out. Khadir and Yusuf heaved their heavy equipment on their backs and went north, planning on finding a layup position as close to the area as possible without compromising themselves.

CHAPTER 69

The dishes were piled one upon the other. There was the breakfast egg soufflé dish, then the lunch croque monsieur dish, and now Vincent Voland placed the green salad and onion soup dishes on top of the rest.

Voland had purchased all three of the day's meals at the café downstairs from his office, and he had devoured all three of the day's meals at his desk. Now that it was seven p.m., the thought occurred to him that he should clean up his mess lest the rats he often heard in the attic above him find the courage to risk coming down into his office in search of the source of the scents.

Just as he rubbed his eyes, breaking the staring contest with his monitors so he could get up to go wash his dishes and return them downstairs, an automatic e-mail popped up on his screen. It was a potential facial recognition hit on Drexler's image.

He'd received a half dozen of these so far this afternoon, and none had played out, but he still felt the tingles of anticipation as he blew up the file and the picture loaded on his screen.

He looked at the picture carefully to orient himself, and then he rubbed his eyes again, possibly for the hundredth time of the day.

A group of people walked along a sidewalk in front of the window of some sort of shop. The camera that took the image was apparently positioned across the street, but it was a small road, and the light was perfect for photography.

Voland zoomed in on the people, and the software cleaned up the resolution.

"Mon dieu," he said. The man in the tan sport coat with blond hair was Drexler, no question in Voland's mind. Next to him was Malik, and next to him was an unknown man of Western appearance. Behind them were three dark-complected and dark-haired men, close enough to where Voland could tell they were all together.

And there, right in the middle of the entire entourage of men, was a tall and thin woman with long black hair.

He zoomed on her. Bianca Medina looked even more tired and fraught than she had the last time he saw her, but she was *very much* alive. He had no idea how he could have missed her leaving with the Syrians the other night on the driveway, but he was elated that she had not been killed.

Voland's hands shook as he clicked the file to read the details. The image came from a camera at a travel agency on Kastoros Street near the Port of Piraeus, the location where the cargo ship caught smuggling into Syria had picked up its contraband nearly a year earlier.

He went online; his hands still trembled with excitement, and he found a nonstop Aegean Air flight from Charles de Gaulle leaving in an hour and a half. Flight time to Athens was three hours, fifteen minutes, and before Voland had even checked what time the flight was due to touch down in Greece, he was out the door of his office, with phone, briefcase, and passport in hand.

He had contacts in Athens he could call, and he could get them to canvass that area around the port. If Drexler and Malik had not left with Bianca for Syria already, then he would damn well know about it when they did try to leave.

CHAPTER 70

Court and the Syrian known as the Terp thought it would take three hours to make it across the strip of desert and into the farmland just south of the city, but five hours after setting off on foot, they still hadn't arrived.

They had a lot of good excuses for their slow advance: rolling Syrian Arab Army patrols to the southeast of the city; small temporary outposts; BMPs and trucks, and even a T-72 tank sandbagged out in the desert with an entire platoon of infantry encamped around it.

Upon seeing the T-72 the Terp admitted he'd never run into that sort of defensive setup before, and this just gave Court more reason to believe Azzam would show up near the airfield the next day.

The mobile patrols were sporadic, but even these, the Syrian said, were more prevalent than he'd seen in the area, especially this far away from population centers. The two men had to go to ground several times while vehicles passed, but with the wide expanse of desert around them, it was difficult for anyone with a light on their vehicle to sneak up on two men on foot, so Court and the Terp managed to remain undetected.

After dealing with the tank and the patrols, they spent a half hour lying flat in a low wash as a pair of Mi-24 attack helicopters circled high overhead. The FSA soldier couldn't tell if the helos were Syrian or

Russian—both nations used the Russian-made Mi-24—but Court worried the Russians might have thermal equipment on board that would make them easier to see if they were up and moving around, so they remained small, flat, and still.

After the helos moved back to the north, the men climbed back to their feet, reorganized all the gear on their bodies that had been displaced when they hit the deck, and began walking again.

It was past midnight when they entered the trees and farmland just south of the city. It was like an oasis to Court; the air smelled better, the cool of the night felt better with the moisture off the plant life.

But more than anything, the chickpea and lentil fields, and the rows of trees that grew alongside them, made it easier to move without too much worry of long-range spotters in the city seeing them approach.

They arrived at the irrigation canal and found the tunnel supposedly dug by ISIS when they were under siege by the SAA.

Court shined a tactical flashlight into the hole, and even though the beam stretched out for a hundred yards, it still ended in blackness. "How far till the tunnel attaches to the sewer?"

The Terp admitted he had no idea.

"I thought you said you knew this town."

"Even when we were fighting here, we didn't live in the sewer. Once we get into the city, I'll show you what I know about the area, but this part right here . . . I don't know. It looks tight. Maybe we should just stay above ground."

Court shook his head. "We'll just take it slow, turn around if it gets too tight."

Court went first and began crawling through the tunnel with his small tactical flashlight in his mouth.

. . .

The two men spent a miserable, arduous, backbreaking hour below ground, but when Court and the Terp finally did find a place to climb back to the surface, it was easier than he'd expected. Court had envisioned a heavy manhole cover that would have to be pushed away, or rusty metal bars of a storm drain that would have to be prized apart, but instead the men simply climbed up on a pile of rebar and concrete rubble where an aerial bomb had impacted the street above the sewer line, and they emerged into a darkened neighborhood of seemingly abandoned buildings.

There was no light or movement on this street, and at first the Terp did not know where he was, but when he climbed totally out of the sewer and struggled with his cramped muscles and heavy equipment to move down to a nearby intersection to look for street signs, Court could barely make out that the young man was waving him forward.

When Court showed up a minute later, encumbered by his own various weapons and packs, the young man took him over to the stoop of a ruined building to sit down.

The Syrian man said, "Okay, I know where we are. Not far from the eastern edge of town."

"Good."

"There will be SAA patrols, but no one else will be outside. Better we use rat holes to move, so no one sees us on the street."

"Rat holes?"

"I'll show you."

The Terp stood and entered the building next to them, and Court followed along, still slowed by his gear. They climbed two flights of stairs, passed a silent family of seven living among the ruins, and then continued on through the building. Court expected they'd have to find a way back downstairs, but to his surprise, the Terp took him down a long corridor, which ended at a wall with a man-sized hole in it.

The Syrian said, "This is a rat hole. When the Syrian Army was in the street, we broke holes in the walls between the buildings so we could travel through the city without going outside. You can cover an entire city block without having to expose yourself."

"Great," Court said. "How many blocks do we have to cross to get where we're going?"

The Terp pulled out his small map of the city, oriented himself, then looked up to Court. "Twelve."

Court sighed. "Christ. Are you kidding?"

"I'm sorry. The damaged sewer means we're farther away than where I thought we'd be."

Court was pissed, but at the situation, not at the kid. He said, "Let's move out."

The Terp looked the older American up and down. "You look pretty tired. You want to rest for a few minutes first?"

Court was exhausted, but he figured he'd have time to rest once he got where he was going. "I want to be in position before daylight. We have to push on."

CHAPTER 71

In the top-floor offices of the Athens freight forwarding company, Malik sat outside on the balcony, speaking on the satellite phone to the men on board the ship on its way into the Aegean Sea from Syria. Inside, his three remaining men rotated watches and rest. Bianca slept on a small sofa in one of the corner offices, and Henri Sauvage sat at a desk by an open window and smoked morosely.

Sauvage hadn't seen Drexler in the past hour, so he was surprised when the blond-haired man appeared in the dim light of the room and sat down in a swivel chair in front of him. He then rolled the chair around the desk, positioning himself at whispering distance from Sauvage.

"I don't have long to explain, but you and I are in a difficult situation."

"Of course I know that. You put me here."

"Perhaps I did. But I can assure you one thing. Right now I am your best chance for survival."

"What do you mean?"

"When we get down to the dock in the morning, the Arabs plan on killing us."

"The *Arabs* do?" Sauvage asked. Bianca had all but convinced him that this was Drexler's plan.

But Drexler said, "Yes. I found out through a source inside the Syrian Mukhabarat."

This sounded like utter bullshit to the French cop, but he played along. "Why?"

Drexler shrugged. "Loose ends, you and me. But there is something we can do to save ourselves."

"I'm listening."

Drexler looked around to make certain no one was around, then reached down to his right ankle and pulled out a stainless steel revolver with a black grip. Sauvage blinked hard when Drexler turned the small weapon around in his hand and handed it over.

"What . . . what is this?" Sauvage asked.

"Tell me you've seen a gun before."

"Of course I have. I mean, why are you giving it to me?"

"If we went after the four men right now, we'd be slaughtered. They are separated around the entire office, they are all armed with submachine guns, and as soon as we got one man, the others would be on guard. But tomorrow morning we will all walk together to the marina. You and I can walk apart from each other; try to lag back behind the Arabs a few meters. Then, when I pull my gun to shoot Malik, you kill the two men closest to you. You must *not* hesitate. One bullet into each man's back. I'll take Malik and then whoever is left."

Sauvage was deeply mistrustful. "I don't . . . I don't know."

"Once we get on the ship we are dead men. We have to do this to survive."

"What about Bianca?"

"What about her? We let her go. I won't be returning to Syria knowing they have targeted me for termination. She can do whatever the hell she wants. She can get on that boat, or she can stay in Europe."

There was much here Sauvage did not take at face value, but the fact that Drexler had just handed him a loaded gun caused him to doubt his earlier thoughts that Drexler was planning on killing him. If so, how would Drexler know Sauvage wouldn't just shoot him last? The little snub-nosed revolver carried five rounds, after all.

He gave Drexler a nod, the Swiss man went over the timing and the

451

order of the action again, and then he drifted off into the darkness of the office.

Sauvage looked down to the pistol in his hands.

None of this made sense to him at all.

. . .

Bianca Medina had finally fallen asleep on the sofa in the corner office, and she'd dreamed of her son. She'd planned on taking him to the ocean for the first time in his life this summer, and in her dream she was there with him, and it was warm and wonderful.

He'd turned to her and he'd called her "mama" and she'd smiled when he spoke, and then she started to speak back to him, but she could not say a word.

She tried again but her mouth would not move, and Jamal looked at her with suddenly frightened eyes. She tried to scream now, but still she could not open her mouth.

. . .

Bianca opened her eyes to darkness, but she felt the presence of the man over her, his hand pressing hard against her mouth. It was Drexler, she just knew, and he'd come to slit her throat in her sleep.

She reached up to swing at him, but a hand caught her hand. Her eyes focused on a face that came down close to hers, and she realized it was the face of the Frenchman, Henri.

Bianca went limp as her heart pounded.

"Ecouter." Listen, he said. "You really want to fight them?"

She swallowed hard, blinking away the tears of panic. "Yes."

"Then I'm with you."

He took his hand off her mouth, and she recovered quickly. "You are? Good."

She sat up in the darkness, and he sat next to her on the sofa and waved something in front of her. It was a small revolver.

Bianca gasped in surprise.

"Drexler gave me this. He told me the Syrians are going to try to kill me and him both just as soon as we get on board the ship. He wants me to shoot two of them as we walk to the marina. He will kill Malik and the other."

452

"But . . . I don't understand. He just *handed* you a gun?"

Sauvage nodded. "He did." Then he opened the cylinder and dumped out the five bullets. He fished around in them for a moment. "These two? They were the ones in the cylinder next to fire when he handed it to me. These are live rounds. Three fifty-seven. Very dangerous." He held up the other three bullets now. "But these three cartridges have been opened, and the gunpowder has been removed. The primer is intact, the bullet is back in the casing, but the weight was just slightly off, so I checked them. Drexler doesn't know it, but I worked in the ballistics lab at La Crim for four years. I can tell if a bullet is real or a dummy round." Sauvage smiled now. "He wanted me to shoot both men in the back, one round each. Then he would kill Malik and the final Syrian and then, when they were all dead, he could turn his seventeen-shot Beretta on me, and on you, and there would be nothing we could do about it."

Sauvage reloaded the pistol, taking care to put the two live rounds back in the cylinder so they would fire with the first two trigger pulls. He then slipped the weapon under his shirt at the small of his back.

"What do we do? Will you shoot him?"

"Not with the revolver. We need his help killing the others, so we go with his plan. But you walk close to him. When I kill my two men, I will try to get one of their weapons. But to do that I will need time. A few seconds. You must grab Drexler, stop him from killing me before I kill him."

Bianca nodded at this. "I can do it."

Sauvage said, "For both of our sakes, I hope you can."

CHAPTER 72

Court Gentry lay on his belly perfectly still, looking through the wreckage of a destroyed and empty pet shop on the ground floor of a large apartment building and out into the street. The view ahead of him was not what he wanted to see. The scene was entirely too vivid. Now that dawn had broken, the light of the morning would make crossing the next street next to impossible.

The young man Court called the Terp was a few feet ahead. He'd taken off his equipment so he could move with more dexterity, and was all the way up at the doorway in the front of the shop, chancing a look out at the street whenever possible. Rolling patrols of Syrian Arab Army vehicles passed by at regular intervals.

The Terp turned back to Court, thirty feet away, and made some sort of motion, but even though the dawn had broken outside, here in the pet shop that had no pets, it was still too dark to see.

When the Terp's gestures became more emphatic, Court took off much of his gear and moved forward. As soon as he crawled up next to his partner, both men had to move out of the doorway as a single BTR-50 armored personnel carrier rumbled by.

When the rumbling ceased and the vehicle disappeared from view, Court looked to the Terp. "What's up?"

"The building you wanted to use. It's not there."

Court looked ahead. They were near the far eastern edge of Palmyra, but the going had been painfully slow over the past few hours, and they'd only now made it to within three blocks of their intended desti- nation. But when Court looked across the street, over the low buildings there, he saw nothing to the east other than the top of a distant pile of rubble that had once been the seven-story structure he'd wanted to use as his overwatch position. It was less than half the height it had been before.

"Shit," Court said. He was so fucking tired and sore and scratched and bruised from his hours of crawling and climbing through the rat holes, abandoned buildings, and rubble of Palmyra.

The Terp said, "We can move two blocks to the south of where we are. There might be some taller buildings to the southeast."

Court shook his head. "Too much light to keep going. Even if that building were still intact, we'd never make it across open ground to get there."

He took the map from the Terp and looked at it with a penlight. "This building we're in now. It looks pretty big. How tall is it?"

The Terp had no idea. The two men went back for their gear. Then they crawled back to the rear entrance of the pet shop, made their way down the hallway that made up the ground-floor spine of the building, and began climbing the stairs.

Slowly. Very slowly, because both men were exhausted.

• • •

Fifteen minutes later shafts of morning sun shone through holes in the wall as Court and the Syrian interpreter climbed the last of the broken staircase to the sixth floor of a seven-story apartment building that had been half destroyed by shelling and bombs. Court walked down a hallway that sloped where the floor had suffered a partial cave-in, and then he crawled on his hands and knees the last few feet to make his way into a room on the eastern side of the building. Here he saw that the entire east- ern wall of the apartment was missing, so he was able to look out onto a wide vista with the sun rising over it. He saw that they were three blocks from the far eastern edge of the city, and all the buildings in front of him were significantly lower.

He peered out beyond the edges of the city, but it was too far away to make anything out.

If the base *was* out there, the shot he took at Azzam now was probably going to be three or four hundred meters farther than he'd planned.

But there was no way he could get any closer.

He turned to the Terp, who was just crawling off the slanted hallway and down into the room. "You did great, kid. This is a good hide, but we are a *lot* farther from the base than I want to be."

He found a dark corner in a back hall near a bathroom, and he sat against the wall, facing the opening ahead. He put down his AK, his backpack, and his rifle bag, and he leaned back against the wall, finally allowing his body to rest a moment.

Instantly his body began cramping. "Water and salt, kid. As soon as we're set up, we both need to hydrate."

The Terp peered out into the morning light. "Are we supposed to see a Russian base from here?"

Court lay on his stomach now, pulled his Zeiss binoculars out of his pack, and stabilized them on his backpack. Through the twenty-power magnification, he began scanning the desert floor to the east.

It took him just seconds to see a Russian Mi-8 helicopter hovering over a large cluster of low buildings, all surrounded by concrete fortifications, wire, and other bunkering material.

"Got it." He pulled out his laser range finder. "Two thousand, seven hundred fifty-two meters to the center of the base." At 1.71 miles, this was a full quarter mile farther than any shot Court had ever attempted, but he knew it was within the capabilities of his weapon, his ammunition, and his scope.

Scanning around the distant base some more, he saw Russian military vehicles, mortar and rocket positions, men going about their day, and a second helo resting on a dusty pad.

The young Syrian's binoculars weren't as good as Court's, but through them he scanned to the southeast. "You were right about the airport. Take a look."

Court did so, and he saw a second baselike development just off the runway, far from the shattered airport terminal. This base was much smaller, but it was fortified with several armored vehicles, and four Russian military helicopters were parked on the sandy tarmac.

A pair of Kamaz Typhoon MRAPs, or mine-resistant ambush-protected vehicles, also sat in the center of the base. Court knew these big transport vehicles were used in Syria by Russian Spetsnaz special forces units.

Only by carefully scanning the desert floor and the highway that bisected it here could Court see more infantry, more armored BTR wheeled troop carriers, and an assortment of big trucks and smaller military utility vehicles. It appeared to Court that at least two companies of regular Russian infantry were here, which was interesting, because he thought this was supposed to be a Spetsnaz or special forces base.

Clearly the area had been augmented with additional forces, and this meant to Court that something special was going on.

Next both men worked on their hide. Court pulled out the TAC-50 and set it up on its bipod, and he put his AK-47 within reach on the floor next to him. Now that he had his thirty-five-power scope on his rifle to use to sight on the base, he gave the Terp his twenty-power binoculars, along with a security sector to keep an eye on, and then he went back to work on ranging in his rifle for the approximate distance he'd be firing from later.

The young man asked, "Should we check in with Khadir and Yusuf to make sure they are in place?"

"Not yet." The Motorola military-grade handheld radios the men carried were encrypted, and their range was over thirty miles. Still, Court had ordered the other team to stay off them until he transmitted, except in extreme cases. He was less worried about the transmissions themselves being picked up, but he knew it was always possible the transmissions could create an electronic signal that could be identified as an unknown force in the area on UHF, and the Russians could thereby determine they weren't alone.

He looked at his watch. "It's almost seven a.m. No idea what time Azzam is coming, but you can be damn sure we will see him when he comes."

Court didn't say it, but he was worried that seeing the Syrian president was all he would be able to do. He was just too damn far to feel confident in his ability to hit a man-sized target.

Court opened up an MRE packet of red beans and rice, which was full of the sodium he needed since he'd been sweating away salt for the past twelve hours. While he ate he drank an entire bottle of water, and he made sure the young Syrian did the same next to him.

While the Terp ate rations, he looked at Court a long time. Finally Court said, "I'd rather you didn't stare at me."

"Sorry. You don't look like the other soldiers I've seen."

"No?"

"No. What is your unit?"

Court spooned some rice into his mouth. "I'm with a unit that doesn't feel the need to tell everyone about what unit we are."

The Syrian seemed to think this over. "I don't think I've ever met anyone from that unit."

Court smiled a worn-out smile at this. "Tell me about you, kid. How did you end up here?"

"I'm the idiot who agreed to come with you."

Court smiled again. "You've been hanging around smartass Americans too long."

The Terp chugged water, then said, "As I told you, I was in the university in Homs. I started going to the protests when they were peaceful, just singing songs and stuff. But the protests got rougher, people started throwing rocks at the police, and the police started shooting back. Some of the students managed to get guns. I was against that, but what could I do? Soon enough the protests turned to battles, but I refused to fight. The Mukhabarat picked up my brother, said he was a ringleader, but I don't believe it.

"He never came home."

The young man looked off into the distance as he recalled those days.

"I had done a year in the army when I was eighteen, but by then I was twenty-one, and I'd driven a tractor when I was in SAA, so I didn't know much about fighting. Still . . . when Mohammed didn't return and my mother's and sister's hearts were broken, I decided to join the resistance. I wasn't special, just another rebel fighting in Homs and Palmyra, but when the Americans came, they needed someone to translate."

"What will you do when the war is over?"

The young man gave Court a strange look. "When the war is over I will be dead."

Court glanced at him a moment, then crawled back to his rifle's scope to scan the Russian base. "You don't think you'll live through this?"

"No. I will die Shahid. You call it . . . a martyr."

Court just sighed, and the Terp heard the noise.

"You don't want to be Shahid?"

"I'll let some dumb son of a bitch on the other side be a Shahid."

"I don't understand."

"Patton," Court said. "General Patton. That was his line. Well . . . sort of."

This did nothing to rectify the young Syrian's confusion. "Who is that?"

"I'm just saying . . . that if you go into a war ready to die, then you're probably going to die. And if you die, then the other side wins."

"Of course, but I know that Allah can take me at any time."

Court took his eye out of the scope and looked at the Syrian. "You think you could ask him to wait till I'm done with you?"

The young man smiled. "It . . . it does not work that way."

"You guys talk five times a day and you don't get to ask him for stuff?"

The Terp laughed. "You are a Kuffar. A nonbeliever."

Court shrugged. "A nonbeliever thinks they have all the answers. That's not me. I don't know what's out there beyond my ability to see. All I know is that I don't know, and I *do* know that a hell of a lot of people in this world are dead set on killing each other over stuff they seem so damn sure of."

"Yes, my country has been crying blood for a long time. My friend, we share the same destiny. You and I are going to die like everyone else."

Court scanned to the south again, at the airport. There were no fixed-wing aircraft in sight, which he found interesting. He said, "I don't plan on dying till I kill at least one more asshole."

"Azzam?"

"Can you think of a bigger asshole around here?"

"No . . . He is definitely the biggest asshole around here."

As he finished saying this, Court took his eye out of his scope and looked out at the blue sky in front of him. Off his right shoulder an airplane came into view, flying low, its gear down. Court recognized it as a Russian Yakovlev Yak-40, an old but trusty transport jet.

The Terp said, "The airport is open!"

In the sky above it both men saw a pair of MiG-29 fighter planes circling. These were not preparing to land, but they were clearly protecting the transport.

Court said, "And a VIP has arrived."

"Do you think it's Azzam?"

"We've come a long way, so I'm shooting whoever gets off."

The Terp said, "I like this plan."

Court reached into his backpack and took out three liters of water. It was all he had left. "Kid, I need you to pour this all around the floor and on the walls, three meters in every direction."

"But . . . why?"

"When I shoot this gun, it's going to kick up a lot of dust. If we don't wet the area, I'll have to wait for follow-on shots." Court added, "We won't have time for that."

The young man opened the first bottle and began pouring it on the floor, sprinkling it on the walls around him.

CHAPTER 73

Just before seven a.m. Bianca stood with the three Syrian GIS men, their leader Malik, Drexler, and Henri Sauvage inside the door to the office building. The ship from Syria was just offshore, and a skiff would be arriving in the marina shortly to pick everyone up. Malik was on his phone, talking to a man on the skiff, and she could hear him coordinate the exact location for the pickup.

Malik slipped the phone back into his pocket and turned to the group. "We want to arrive at the dock at exactly the same time the launch does. It's still dark. We do this right and no one sees us."

Drexler looked out the window, then back to Malik. "Let's go. What are we waiting for?"

The Syrian Mukhabarat operative shook his head. "We have a minute to wait so it is timed properly."

"What the hell does it matter if we get to the water a few seconds before they do?"

Malik just shook his head. "My operation, Drexler. My rules."

Drexler wiped sweat off his brow.

. . .

Vincent Voland parked his rented Toyota Yaris four-door compact on a hill just a block away from the camera that had recorded the sighting of

Bianca Medina, Drexler, and the Syrians the day before. It was not yet seven a.m.; he'd come straight from the hotel after his late-night flight and his early-morning check-in, and he'd just spoken with the two watchers he'd hired to keep an eye on the port and told them they could go home for a few hours' rest.

His men had seen nothing, so Voland worried the Syrians were no longer in the area.

Voland needed more rest himself, but he was too wired to sleep. He figured there was little chance he'd see Drexler and company walking around the dock, and that he'd probably already boarded a ship, but as soon as offices at the marina opened up he'd start pumping the workers there for information.

In the meantime, however, he wanted to walk the area to get a feel for the location.

He walked along Akti Kondili, where the images had been taken, and then he went down to the water. An occasional car drove by behind him, but this was near the closed private marina, so there wasn't much going on this early in the morning.

He turned to go into the city a few blocks, to try to get a feel for where Drexler and his entourage had been coming from on their way to the port, because he felt certain he knew where they'd been going. They'd gone to the marina to board a boat, and that boat was gone.

On the corner of Egaleo and Kastoros he heard a noise off to his right. It was a door closing, and this surprised him, because the only buildings he saw were commercial, and none of the offices would open for hours.

In the dim light a block away, he saw a group of people walking south, towards the water.

There were six men and one woman. The woman was tall and beautiful; the Frenchman could tell this even from a block away.

Vincent Voland turned and began running down Egaleo, parallel to the group but out of sight behind a row of buildings. He didn't have a gun, and he didn't even know the number for the police here in Athens. He was a sixty-five-year-old man with no hand-to-hand fighting skills, and after half a block he was already feeling the pounding of exertion in his heart.

He had no plan other than to try to see if this group was, in fact, Bianca and her captors.

If these were the people he'd come from France to find . . . he hadn't a clue what he would do about it.

. . .

Drexler had pushed and pushed for Malik to begin the movement towards the docks, for the simple reason that he knew his plan to kill the three Syrians, then Sauvage and Medina, would only work if there wasn't an additional skiffload of Syrian operatives on the shore to stop him.

Malik had pushed back, of course, because he wanted the skiff to arrive at the water's edge at the same time as those boarding it to reduce the chance that any passing police or harbor official would see the illegal transfer.

But Drexler had won the fight. Although he would have liked to have left the office minutes ago, so there was no chance the men in the boat would be near enough to the marina to see what happened, he decided instead to rely on the darkness of the alleyways leading to the docks and a quick getaway.

Malik put his earpiece in so he could stay in constant communication with the men on the skiff, and then the entourage walked down Etoliku, a two-lane street with cars parked on both sides, making for a narrow advance. The street ended perpendicular to the docks, and already in the distance Drexler could see a dark skiff approaching, with several men dressed in black on board. He had positioned himself behind Malik and one of the GIS men. Bianca was walking along silently at his right shoulder, and Sauvage was on his left a few feet away, behind one of the GIS officers.

The last GIS man brought up the rear.

Drexler looked right at Sauvage as he walked, willing him to look his way. When he finally did, Drexler saw the terror in the man's eyes.

The Swiss operative only needed the French cop to fire his gun twice, shoot or slow down two of the four operatives, and then, when he invariably tried to shoot Drexler himself, Drexler would simply kill Sauvage and then Medina.

463

All his problems behind him, right here in this alley, and all he needed for this to happen was for Sauvage to reach for his gun.

Just then, Sauvage glanced to Bianca, nodded to her, and then his right hand went into his jacket.

Drexler sensed something was wrong, and he went for his own weapon.

. . .

Henri Sauvage's legs would barely function, but he forced them forward, and though he had similar trouble reaching for his weapon, the moment Drexler reached into his own coat he knew he had to act.

As he felt the grip of the revolver under his coat, Malik put his hand to his ear and said, "Wait." He stopped, and Drexler stopped in midreach for his pistol. Sauvage took his hand away from the gun in the small of his back lest the man behind him see him telegraph his draw.

Without turning around to face Drexler, Malik said, "The skiff reports an old man running down the street a block to the west. I don't know who—"

Sauvage saw Drexler begin moving again, executing his draw stroke. With speed and skill he raised his weapon to the back of Malik's head. The GIS man walking just behind Drexler saw the movement and began to call out to his boss, but Sauvage reached back for his gun, spun around on the balls of his feet, and fell to his knees.

The GIS man in back shouted, "Malik!"

Malik tried to spin away, but Drexler's gun cracked in the narrow street, and the GIS leader stumbled forward into the street.

Sauvage's pistol fired into the chest of the man just behind him a fraction of a second later.

Drexler swiveled to shoot one of the two standing operators, and Sauvage spun back around 180 degrees towards the man who had been walking in front of him but was now turned towards Drexler and drawing a submachine gun from under his jacket.

Drexler and Sauvage both fired at the same time, both their targets fell, and the man closest to Sauvage dropped onto his back with his submachine gun out in front of him.

Sauvage dove for it.

Sebastian Drexler swiveled his Beretta towards Henri Sauvage now, just as the French cop leapt for the little Uzi, but as Drexler was about to press the trigger, he felt an impact on his right side.

Bianca Medina slammed into him, grabbed his gun arm with all her might, and threw her 110 pounds of weight into his torso, knocking him off balance.

But Drexler did not go down. He fought to free his arm, then stumbled back as he pushed her away and down to the asphalt, and as she landed on her back below him next to a parked car, he leveled his gun at her face.

The sound of automatic gunfire chattered in the alley now, and Sebastian Drexler arched forward, his weapon spun away, and his face slammed hard into the hood of the parked Citroën.

He slid off the hood and fell onto his back between the Citroën and the car parked in front of it.

Henri Sauvage fought his way back to his feet, took a step forward, and leveled the gun at Drexler, prepared to shoot him again.

Bianca screamed, "Henri!" She pointed to Malik. He sat up in the street on Sauvage's left, his pistol out in front of him, the right side of his face red with blood.

Sauvage turned to the man, but another crack and flash of gunfire in the alley sent Henri Sauvage tumbling backwards, shot through the chest.

Bianca rolled onto her hands and knees and crawled between two parked cars. She continued around to the dark and narrow sidewalk, but soon she heard the grunt of a man blowing out his last breath, then the thud of Malik as he fell onto the cement on his back. She then heard the clanking sound of his pistol falling away.

"Bianca?"

Bianca stood up from behind the cars, looked down the street in the direction of the port, and saw a man running through the low light towards her. Behind him, some 150 meters away, she could see the black skiff full of men landing at a dock there. Men leapt from it and began running in her direction.

• • •

"Bianca!" Vincent Voland ran up to her and helped her away from the scene of blood and bodies, and then together they scrambled up the street and back towards Voland's car. They climbed into it a minute later and raced off through the night, with shadowy figures just appearing in their rearview as the Frenchman floored it around a corner.

Bianca hyperventilated for over a minute while Voland drove.

"It's all right, my dear. You are safe. I promise you, you are safe. It's over."

But when she could finally speak, Voland realized it wasn't her own safety she was concerned with. "The American. He . . . he took Jamal?"

"*Oui, mademoiselle.* He took him and delivered him somewhere safe."

"Where? He is in Jordan? In Paris?"

Voland hesitated.

"Where is he?" she demanded.

"He is still in Damascus, but tonight we will get him out. It's all arranged."

Bianca went catatonic. She sat quietly in the passenger seat for over a minute more. When she finally spoke she said the last thing Voland expected her to say. "I want to return to Syria."

"*What?*"

"I want to die with my child."

Voland shook his head. "No one is dying, I promise you." He turned to her as he drove. "No one *else* will die. I will get Jamal out. Please, believe me. Just give me until tonight."

. . .

Back in the alleyway, the bodies of six men lay motionless. The dawn's light increased, seemingly by the second, as did the sound of approaching sirens.

But the men did not move.

A new sound entered the alley: the noise of racing footsteps, coming back from the north, the opposite direction from the port. Five men in black, pistols in their hands, skidded to a stop when they reached the figures, and they began checking each body for a pulse.

They almost missed the sixth man, but one of the Syrian operatives from the ship noticed a pair of feet sticking out from between two parked cars. He shined a light on the feet, tracked it up the body, and saw a blond-haired man, lying on his back. His eyes were open and blinking.

"I've got one alive!" he shouted.

The leader of the group turned and looked at him. "That's Drexler. Get him to the boat."

. . .

Sebastian Drexler offered the men no help at all in extracting him from Greece. He'd been wearing a Kevlar vest, but when Sauvage shot him multiple times in the back, it knocked him into the car. He'd banged his head and lost consciousness. When he'd come to, the GIS men were already on top of him, and he had no choice but to go with them back to the skiff.

But still, he wasn't going to make it easier. He lay limp, and they carried him, one man on each appendage, and as soon as they were back on the landing craft and racing towards the ship, they checked his wounds and found them to be nothing more than bruises, and then they began interrogating him about what had happened.

Drexler couldn't answer at first; all he could do was stare ahead, at the ship out in the distance. That ship meant Syria, and Syria meant Shakira, Ahmed, and certain death.

And the ship kept nearing. Despite him willing it to get smaller, it got larger with every second the skiff churned the water towards it.

One of the Syrians leaned over him, asking him again about who showed up to shoot Malik and the others and to steal Medina, the precious cargo. As the man spoke, his pistol in his shoulder holster hung tantalizingly close to Drexler's reach.

In a moment of panic the Swiss operative went for it and tried to draw it free, but the Mukhabarat officer subdued him. Others came and pinned him to the hull of the boat, and then they shined a light in his eyes.

Drexler spoke perfect Arabic, so he understood what they said.

"Fucker tried to take my weapon!"

Another said, "Bastard's in shock. He thinks he's still fighting back there. Just watch him, and we'll get him some help when we get him on board."

Drexler went limp now, because there was nothing left to fight for. No matter what he did now, he knew.

He was a dead man.

CHAPTER 74

Ahmed al-Azzam had been waiting to hear reports on the pickup of Bianca from Athens before deplaning, but no word had come, and he knew the Russian military reception was waiting just outside the main cabin door. He stood from his seat, moved forward within his cluster of guards, and climbed down the air stairs pushed up to the door of the Yak-40.

When he stepped onto the tarmac of the Palmyra airport, feeling the cool morning desert air, he realized he hadn't set foot in this part of his nation since well before the beginning of the civil war. Even though his armies and militias had taken back the territory over a year earlier, much fighting had remained close by, so it had been too dangerous for the president to make such a journey.

But now he was surrounded by over three hundred Russian soldiers, a half dozen Russian attack helicopters, and even more Syrian army and air force personnel and equipment. Beyond this cordon of protection, he'd been told, his militias had fanned out and pacified the towns and villages for twenty kilometers in all directions, solely for his ninety-minute visit.

This area was as safe as it could possibly be made, and, for the first time in a long time, Azzam finally felt comfortable in a location outside the capital other than the regime-held bastion of Latakia on the western coast.

Still, Azzam wore black body armor over his light blue button-down shirt, and his eight-man protection detail kept tight with him as he deplaned.

He wasn't crazy. There was still a war going on, and this was still on the edge of contested territory.

But, Azzam thought, perhaps on his next trip out of Damascus he wouldn't need the body armor. Russia had all but won this war for him, with help from the Iranians. A year from now the last pockets of resistance to his rule would be confined to somewhere out in the desert or up in the mountains, and the civil war would be over. His patrons in Russia and Iran would trade with him while other nations fretted over sanctions, and although his nation would not be as prosperous as it was before the war, Azzam himself would be even more prosperous from the under-the-table deals he fashioned with every Russian commercial opportunity that crossed his desk.

This Russian base would be the last nod to Russia's power over him, because Azzam had worked out a secret agreement with the Iranians. In a few months, when the end of the war came, he would agree to allow the Iranians to create permanent bases in his country, just as he had done with the Russians. Moscow would be furious; they had forced him to agree to their patronage in a moment of weakness, but now that he had grown strong again—albeit in large part due to Russia's help—he would dampen Russia's hold over his nation by taking more support from the Shia regime in Tehran.

Azzam stepped down from the stairs, up to the welcoming committee of military men, and shook the hands of a Russian general and several colonels, who themselves had been ferried into this remote location for today's photo op.

Within moments Azzam ducked his head and stepped into the back of a Kamaz Typhoon, a massive Russian armored transport vehicle, for the five-minute drive northeast to the Russian special forces base on the other side of the highway. This vehicle was followed by a second Typhoon, in case the first became disabled.

. . .

Almost two and a half miles away, two men lay on the cheap linoleum flooring of a bombed-out sixth-story apartment and looked through high-powered optics at the vehicle as it began rolling north.

The man on the right spoke English with both excitement and confusion in his voice. "That had to be him. That *had* to be Azzam."

"It was him." Court had confirmed through the higher-power optics of his rifle. He couldn't make out the man's face from this distance, even through the impressive scope, but the bearing of the figure, the treatment of the figure by those around him, and the fact that he was the one person who deplaned who earned the attention from the mass of Russian military officers arrayed at the bottom of the stairs told him he had acquired his target.

The Terp asked, "But . . . why didn't you shoot?"

"Dude, it's two and a half miles to the airfield. When he gets to the base, assuming he is somewhere around the main buildings, it will still be a one-point-seven-mile shot. A cold-bore shot from one point seven miles is not impossible, for the best snipers in the world, but long-range shooting is a perishable skill and . . . I'm a little out of practice."

"You are telling me this now?"

"I can hit him, I just need him within one point five miles and a clean look at his entire head first. Don't worry, kid. I'm patient."

"But . . . shouldn't we find out where Khadir and Yusuf are? What if they attack the base before you fire?"

"Why the fuck would they do that?"

The Syrian shrugged. "Maybe they think they can hit him."

Court thought about this. "Break radio silence. Send a brief transmission telling them to stand fast. I will initiate any attack."

· · ·

Ahmed Azzam spent an hour touring the Russian camp, meeting with the Spetsnaz soldiers, getting photos and video of him asking questions, posing on weapons, and listening to stories of the men telling him about killing terrorists and rooting out resistance. They talked of Daesh, the SDF, and the FSA as if they were all the same unit, a group of foreign-led terrorists out to destroy the peaceful and prosperous way of life of the Syrian people.

Throughout the base he was shadowed by his eight-man security detail, his SAA translator, and a throng of officers from the Russian army and the SAA—more than two dozen men in all.

Azzam found himself enjoying his time out here with these men, but he'd already signaled to his entourage that he would be cutting his trip short. He wanted to get back on board the aircraft and back to the palace, where he could monitor the rescue of his mistress in Greece and the search for his son here in the capital.

Originally he'd planned to helicopter to a couple of Syrian bases to the west and then back to Damascus, but he'd already changed his mind. The aircraft would get him back to the capital faster, so he'd bypass the bases and return to the palace.

As soon as he shook hands with a dozen Russian soldiers at three 120-millimeter mortar emplacements, the general taking him on the tour spoke through his interpreter.

"Mr. President, we have prepared a meal in your honor. If you will follow me to the mess tent, I would like—"

Azzam smiled and held up a hand. "Thank you, General. I only wish I had time. But my duties force me to return to Damascus immediately." He looked at the video crew following him on his trip. "Can we set up for my announcement here?"

The producer of the unit said, "Of course, Mr. President, but it would be good if we could get some more Russian equipment in the shot. Perhaps we could have them bring the armored transport carrier over here and park it behind you."

The Russians obliged, and both big Typhoons lumbered across the small base and parked behind the mortar position. Azzam and the Russian general stood in front of the staged vehicles, and several Russian and SAA colonels were brought in close.

When the cameras were ready, Azzam's bodyguards backed away a few feet.

. . .

In the wrecked sixth-floor apartment, 1.81 miles away from the mortar position, Court said, "I can see his head plainly now. But he's still too damn far. Everywhere I've had a shot for the last hour has been on the far side of the compound, and every time he was on the near side, he was too wrapped up by the men around him."

The Terp said, "But the armored vehicles are there. When he gets inside, you can't hit him, and if he goes back to the airport, you can't hit him. You might not get another chance."

Court adjusted the scope for the distance, using a ballistic calculator and the range finder, and taking a wild-ass guess about the wind from the movement of the flags at the front gate of the base. But when he put his sights on the target, he saw that the point where the crosshairs met in his scope was wider in his field of view than Azzam's head. He could approximate where he needed to position the rifle to fire, but it would take a miracle for the round to hit a head-sized target at such a distance.

Court closed his eyes and cussed. "I don't have a shot," he said.

• • •

When the camera was rolling, Azzam did not look at it. Instead he leaned an arm on the sand-colored Typhoon APC next to him and addressed the Russian and Syrian military forces standing around the armored vehicle. "I am very proud to reveal to my nation that this will not only be a small special forces base for our friends the Russians, but we are also constructing, with both Russian and Syrian input and assistance, a new, permanent airfield here in central Syria. In addition to our joint Syrian-Russian air base at Hmeymim, now Russia will have complete and total air superiority in the skies over the Syrian Arab Republic, bringing a new dawn of security and prosperity to all here in our nation."

Ahmed Azzam shook the hand of the Russian general, and then the two men held their hands in the air as those around clapped and cheered.

• • •

Court blinked away sweat and peered through the thirty-five-power scope. "What the hell are they doing?"

On his right, the young Syrian resistance fighter looked through his binoculars. "I don't know. I also don't know why you are not shooting." The young man was obviously frustrated. "You told me back at our base that if you could see him, then you could shoot him."

Court did not move from his prone position behind the Tac-50. "I lied. He's still effectively out of range. We'll only get one chance at this. I don't want to—"

"Sir . . . this *is* your chance. What if he gets back inside one of those vehicles and leaves for the airport as soon as he finishes talking?"

Court shook his head and took his eye out of the scope. "I need you to contact the Carl Gustaf unit. Tell Khadir and Yusuf that wherever they are, they *have* to find a way to the airfield. Tell them to keep low, keep out of sight, but try to move to within six hundred meters."

The Terp made the call, then listened to the reply. "They are nine hundred meters east, southeast of the airport, but an Mi-14 is almost directly overhead their position, so they are moving very slowly. They think they will be spotted in moments."

Court scanned over with his scope. He saw the Russian helo hovering a thousand feet over the desert, and the gullies and low rises below it that were apparently hiding the FSA rocket crew.

"Shit," Court said. "They *can't* let themselves get compromised. They are going to have to try to take out the Typhoon when it returns to the plane. We can spot for them from here to see which vehicle he gets into. Tell them they *have* to get closer, but to hold their fire until we tell them, no matter what else happens."

The Terp did this, then turned to Court. "You aren't going to shoot at all?"

Azzam was still 1.81 miles away. Court recognized that he wasn't going to get the shot he wanted today.

"No. Sorry. I can't reach him."

The Terp made the transmission, then turned to Court. "It will take them an hour to cover the open desert, and they will probably be spotted. You are still the best chance to kill Azzam. You *must* try."

Court looked at the kid once more, then lowered back to his scope.

Court's mentor at CIA, a man he only knew by his code name of Maurice, was the first of many instructors who turned Court into a world-class long-distance marksman. He taught the young CIA recruit the math and the craft; he gave Court the confidence he needed to use his scoped rifle in the field to hit targets out over a mile.

Court could remember months of lying prone in fields in West Virginia, East Tennessee, and North Carolina, wearing ghillie suits, with a man-sized target so far away it couldn't be seen with the naked eye.

473

Maurice would spot for him, sitting at his side just like the young Syrian interpreter did now.

Maurice was a Vietnam vet, and he always said the same thing on the final shot of the day, which was always the most difficult. As Court concentrated on his breath, his heartbeat, while he labored to exert as much control over his involuntary muscles in order to line his sights up on a mile-plus long shot, Maurice would lean into Court's ear and say a phrase that never left him.

"Send it and end it, kid."

Court would fire, sending a boat-tail round across fields and lakes, over cabins and farms, and, more often than not, much more often than not, he'd hit his target, thereby ending the "threat."

He'd send it, and he'd end it.

He thought back to those days, the fundamentals of the craft, and he fought again to remain calm. He forced himself not to feel any emotion at all. Any increase in heart rate, fluctuation in breathing, new sweating on his skin that could cause reflex muscle contractions. Anything different with his body at the moment he fired would affect his shot. It could send the round out of the barrel one hundredth of an inch from where he wanted the muzzle positioned for firing, but translated out across 1.81 miles, the round would end up several feet off target.

He blinked hard.

No . . . this was insane. He couldn't even put his crosshairs on the target's head at this distance, much less hold them there.

But as he peered through the optics, an idea came to him, and again, it came to him in Maurice's calm but intense voice.

"Got a problem you can't solve? Change the question, son. Branch out."

Maurice had taught Court all about "branching," or the ability to change tactics and plans as the need arose. It kept him from panicking, kept him flexible and on track.

He couldn't hit Azzam's head, and he knew the man was likely wearing plated body armor. The only chance in hell he had of hitting him at all would be if everyone around him simply moved out of the way.

Court spoke aloud in the darkened apartment hallway now. "Sending."

He moved the scope off the men in front of Azzam, and he instead shifted his aim fractionally to the left. The crosshairs met on a flat steel plate of the big Typhoon armored personnel carrier positioned directly behind the group.

Court cleared his mind of thoughts, blew out half his air, paused briefly, and pressed the trigger.

Boom.

He knew the flight path of the round would take seven and a half seconds, so Court racked the bolt quickly, resighted through the scope, and aimed again, this time back to the right. He fired again. He'd rushed his second shot somewhat, but he'd taken just enough time to put the crosshairs back in the group of Russians, approximating where Azzam was standing among them.

Both bullets were in the air at the same time, and Court had time to rack the bolt and line back up to prepare for a third shot before anyone on the Russian special forces base had any idea that death was screaming their way at 2,700 feet a second.

CHAPTER 75

Ahmed Azzam shook hands again with the general for the camera, then turned slightly to reach for the hand of a tall Russian colonel. Both men smiled and made eye contact, and then both men's brains registered a sudden, jolting, whip crack of noise between them. Before either man could perceive any danger, there was an impossibly loud clang of metal on metal, a spray of sparks on Azzam's right and on the colonel's left, and then Azzam shut his eyes as an involuntary response.

An instant later he spun away from the flash and sound, and he crumpled down into a ball.

. . .

Court just had time to get his eye focused back in the glass as the first round struck the steel wall of the APC, inches from where Court had been aiming. As expected, the sound, sparks, and flying bits of metal caused an immediate reaction in the group.

The idea was that the Russian soldiers would be well trained at hitting the ground when under fire, whereas the Syrian president, who was no combat vet, would take longer to react.

Unlike his sniper craft, this was no science. This was just a guess about how individuals would respond in a heartbeat.

. . .

But the second round Court fired at the crowd didn't come anywhere near the Syrian president, who was already dropping to the ground. It instead struck the Syrian Army captain serving as a translator on the outside of his left upper arm, traveled through his body lengthwise, and tumbled out and into the side armor of a Russian major. If the bullet had still been traveling ballistic it would have likely made it through this man's Kevlar, but since it struck the armor sideways, it merely pitched the officer over the Syrian president, and he fell onto the ground alongside the armored personnel carrier.

Every one of Azzam's eight bodyguards had reacted to the sound of incoming sniper fire the way all humans react to such sounds; they recoiled automatically. But before anyone else on the scene had the presence of mind to act, the men recovered, turned for their protectee, and moved to cover him.

The eight men looked in the tight group for their president and panicked when they did not see him at first, but as the close-detail members realized he was on the ground, they worried even more.

Burly Syrians pushed their way through the Russians, some dead or injured; there was blood everywhere. Many of Azzam's guards fell down in the process of getting to their president, but within six and a half seconds of the first shot hitting the Typhoon's armor, two bodyguards had enveloped Azzam, and others began pushing Russians out of the way to get him clear of danger.

"He's bleeding!" the lead protection agent shouted as soon as he saw the blood on Azzam's collar. The president lay facedown in the dirt at first, but just as his two men shielded him, and others fought their way through the mass of Russians, both dead and alive, to get to their protectee, Azzam pushed himself up onto his knees. All the security men knew the bullets had come from the direction of Palmyra to the west, so they lifted him by the arms and began moving him around to the far side of the APC.

And it was in the execution of this move to safety that his lead bodyguard saw that Ahmed Azzam's chin and right cheek were deeply cut, pouring dark rich blood.

It hadn't been Court's intended second shot that wounded Azzam, but rather the first shot. The big 647-grain bullet fired from the McMillan sniper rifle had exploded upon striking the steel APC, sending lead and brass fragments in all directions. Three men in the group were wounded with the shot, but none as much as Azzam. A hot, sharp, twisted fingernail of brass had ripped into his right cheek next to his lip at a speed of nearly six hundred feet per second, and it tore its way into his mouth, where it chipped two teeth and then exited out below his lip just above his chin.

The president pressed hard against the pain with his hand, and blood dripped through his fingers.

· · ·

In the destroyed apartment building Court fired a third round, and on his right the young Syrian FSA soldier watched the scene through the binos.

He made out the distant image of a Russian officer spinning and tumbling, men on their hands and knees crawling, and the ones in the dark suits who came off the plane, clearly Azzam's bodyguards, rushing to a point low on the ground next to the Typhoon MRAP.

Court fired again and again, draining the five rounds in his weapon, and then he ejected the magazine, knocked it away, and banged in another five-rounder. This took him less than three seconds, but when he got his eye back in the scope and looked at the area where Azzam had been speaking, he saw only a few still or writhing forms prone in the dust.

"Shit," he said.

"What?" the Terp asked.

"I don't think I got him."

The Syrian scanned with his own glass. "I don't see him. He must be behind the vehicles."

A transmission came over the radio from the Carl Gustaf team. The Terp listened, then turned to Court. "Good news! Yusuf says the helicopter is leaving his area. They have not been spotted and are moving towards the airport."

Court said, "Yeah. Great news. What do you want to bet that helo is inbound for us?"

Behind the rear Typhoon, one of Azzam's bodyguards took off his black jacket and pressed it against the president's face to stop the blood.

"He's shot in the face!" he shouted, and his colleagues converged on him.

Russian Spetsnaz officers raced over, as well. Bodyguards tried to fight them back until they saw one with a medical kit, and this man was allowed to follow Azzam as he was ushered into the back of the Kamaz Typhoon.

The Syrian president was conscious and alert but had a look of utter disbelief over what had just occurred, as if he were still unaware he'd been struck by a fragment of a sniper's bullet.

Two of Azzam's bodyguards laid him down on the side-sitting seats in back of the armored vehicle, and then the Russian medic began treating the president's wounds, while Azzam's lead protection agent knelt at his shoulder, ready to assist.

The bodyguard called out to his teammates, most of whom were still outside the vehicle. "He's not critical! Repeat, *not* critical! But we need to get back to Damascus. Contact the aircraft and tell them to be ready to roll as soon as we get on board, then call Dr. Qureshi at Tishreen. He can tend to him better than anyone else in the country."

Azzam tried to talk but blood filled his mouth.

His guard patted him on the shoulder. "Mr. President. You will be fine. It's just a small ricochet that hit your face. This medic is Spetsnaz, the best. He will take care of you. We will expedite you back to Damascus and get you to Tishreen Military Hospital, where they can make you good as new." The guard looked up. "Get this vehicle moving to the airport, now!"

• • •

While the president was being tended to at the mortar position, the base's leadership shouted orders into their radios. "The sniper rounds came from the city! Get helicopters to the west. Check the high buildings in Palmyra out to four kilometers."

The Russian Spetsnaz colonel in charge of the base said, "This contact is limited. It's one sniper. Everyone calm down. We will deal with the attack."

· · ·

By the time the Typhoon bounced over the highway and continued down the new asphalt road to the airport, the lower part of Azzam's face and right cheek were completely bandaged, and he was sitting back up.

He was having problems being understood by his men, which was understandable considering the location of the wounds, but he had regained control of the moment. There was no real pain in his torn face— that would come later—but for now he was more concerned with making sure whoever fired at him was destroyed.

"You have helicopters looking for the shooter?" he asked the Spetsnaz medic, who didn't speak Arabic and would have no idea, anyway. The translator from the SAA was dead, still lying back at the mortar position, so communication in the Typhoon was done with nods, finger pointing, and a lot of shouting.

The medic just tied off the president's dressing behind his head and radioed to his platoon commander that he'd like to fly with the president all the way to Damascus to monitor the bleeding.

The bodyguard promised Azzam that Russians and Syrians would find and kill whoever shot him.

· · ·

The Terp took his eyes out of his optics slowly. "I think Azzam is in the rear MRAP."

Court said, "You've got the twenty-power optics. Mine is thirty-five, but I didn't see him get in. There are too many people down there running around. Are you sure?"

He looked at the two vehicles again. "The rear one." After a hesitation he said, "I think."

Court said, "You need to be sure. The Carl Gustaf takes a half minute to reload, re-aim, and refire. Those guys aren't going to be able to take out both vehicles before the enemy is on top of them."

The young man said, "I saw men in suits get in the rear one. They are the bodyguards. Why would they get in if Azzam was not—"

"That's good enough for me. Tell the other team Azzam is inbound to the airport."

Court took his eye out of the scope now and looked into the open sky. "Russian helos. Coming right at us."

A pair of Mi-24s approached from above the airfield, coming in hard and fast to the eastern portion of the city.

The Syrian held the radio to his mouth, but he didn't transmit. Instead he said, "I can't be sure it's the right vehicle. Why don't we get them to shoot down the plane when he leaves?"

"Negative," Court said. "That aircraft will be moving instantly, taking off to the west and farther away. At the range those guys will be firing from, they'll miss if the plane rolls at all. And there is no chance in hell of them hitting the plane in the air. The Carl Gustaf is not a SAM; it's a dumb rocket." Court raised an eyebrow. "A really big dumb rocket."

The Terp said, "So . . . do I tell Yusuf they need to fire at the rear Typhoon?"

Court said, "No, you watch both vehicles until they get on the tarmac. *Then* you tell him which one to hit. You have to make sure the vehicles don't switch positions on the drive." He then said, "Kid, those men should know: if they fire from where they are, out in the open like that . . . the Russians *will* see them. They will lose their lives, and they *won't* get another shot."

The radio crackled between the two men lying in the dark snipers' hide. A man spoke Arabic; Court recognized the voice as belonging to Yusuf.

The Terp said, "There are two towers at the northern edge of the airfield. Yusuf says they can't move any closer to get into range because the men in those towers will spot them."

Court looked back to the incoming attack helos. They would be here at the building within seconds.

"Northern edge?" Court clarified, and then he scooted forward in his hide, in front of his weapon, until he could see the entire northern side of the base. He spotted the two towers only when he brought his rifle to his new position and looked through the scope.

"It's one point four miles. I can probably get a hit on those guys from here, which will help out the other team."

The Terp said, "We are out of water. This area is very dusty."

Court replied, "Nothing I can do about that."

"The helicopters are near us. If you fire, the helicopters will see our position."

Court began steadying the massive rifle on his right forearm. "Yep."

The young Syrian crawled forward with the binos to position himself on Court's right. He looked through them.

Court said, "Tell the boys to be ready to move. When I take these guards, that's going to draw attention to their side of the base soon enough. Azzam will be at the airport in three minutes. Don't figure they have much more time than that to act before they're spotted."

The Syrian nodded and made the transmission. After he finished he said, "They will die proud Shahid."

Court dialed in the range for the farther of the two towers on his scope. Then he settled in behind the weapon. "Firing."

After the crack of the rifle, dust kicked up in the ruined apartment and obscured both men's views, but when they cleared, the FSA soldier said, "Hit! The guard is down."

Court had already shifted his aim to the nearest guard. Ten seconds later the man's head snapped back and a spray of blood misted the air above him.

"Hit," the FSA soldier repeated.

Court said, "Tell your guys to haul ass."

The two Russian helicopters streaked by the apartment building, just three hundred yards from where Court and the Terp lay.

CHAPTER 76

A minute after the two helicopters passed by Court and the Syrian's building, all was silent in their sniper's hide. The two Typhoons neared the airport to the southeast, and both men tracked the vehicles with their optics.

Then, from nowhere, Court saw a Russian Mi-24 streak by again at his eye level, within fifty yards of the opening in the apartment's wall. It passed by from left to right at speed, and Court could see the white helmets and black visors of the two men on the other side of the windshield.

Court tried to get his scope on one of the men, but the helo shot past the hole in the apartment wall too quickly.

The Terp said, "The transports will be on the tarmac in one minute."

"Right. Tell Yusuf that they need to—"

Without warning an explosion on the floor below him lifted Court into the air. The Syrian flew with him; they crashed into the bathroom on their right and slammed down on the floor there.

Rusty water drained out of a pipe and onto Court's pants. He looked around and saw the kid lying half in and half out of the bathroom on a floor that was buckled and broken.

"You okay?"

"Yes," he said. "I think we've been spotted."

"No shit."

Before Court could move, another explosion hit, this time just above them. Part of the ceiling collapsed, and dust filled the air. Court assumed these were rockets from one of the Mi-24s, and he knew each helo would have dozens more where these came from.

"You have your radio?" he asked the Terp.

"It's . . . I can't find it."

Court pulled his out of his chest rig and handed it over. "Tell Yusuf it's up to them now. We can't see the target any longer. Tell him the second vehicle has Azzam in it, but he needs to wait till the vehicle opens its hatch. If men in dark suits climb out, he needs to hit it with his rockets right then!"

The young man made the transmission, told the Carl Gustaf crew that he thought Azzam was in the rear vehicle, then grabbed his rifle.

Court climbed over the smaller man and back into the hall and put the sling of his AK over his head, and he had just started to reach for the Mc-Millan when the dust cleared enough for him to look out into the sky near his sixth-floor room.

A single Mi-24 loomed there, and the rocket pods on its pylons emitted a blast of smoke and fire.

"Incoming!" Court screamed.

The explosion hit below them again, but the floor gave way fully now. They fell an entire story down and crashed into another apartment.

Court landed with the Syrian on top of him; his arm and face hurt, and his ears rang. He fought his way to his feet again and pulled the kid up. "You okay?"

The man was stunned, covered completely in dust, but he gave a weak thumbs-up. Court pushed him towards the exit of the apartment, mostly obscured with dust now. "Just go!" he said.

They made it to the stairwell just as another rocket salvo destroyed the apartment.

A minute later they were down at ground level. Civilians ran through the streets, a few cars raced out of the area, and a Syrian Arab Army patrol vehicle streaked down the street right next to them. Court hid his AK from the passing vehicle, then looked at the interpreter. The kid was covered head to toe in gray dust, and his weapon and backpack were missing.

He had his radio in his pocket, and both men still wore their ammunition on their chest. Court imagined the equipment had been covered by the dust, or else the passing patrol just hadn't looked their way at all.

Court pulled the Terp back into the building and ripped off the man's military equipment. He pulled his own chest rig and pistol holster off, but he drew his pistol and crammed it into the small of his back under his T-shirt.

The Terp began trying to raise Yusuf on the radio. After thirty seconds he said, "I think the radio is down."

Court said, "We'll have to read in the newspapers about what the hell happened at the Palmyra airfield."

The Syrian stared at Court. "You . . . you are bleeding."

Court knew blood was pouring from the cut over his ear and a new gash near his right eye. His legs were bruised from the fall. "I'm fine," he said.

"What do we do?"

"We go."

"Go *where*?"

"We're going to the north."

"The north?"

"There are FSA units to the north in the hills, right?"

"I . . . I don't know."

"Well, we can't make it back to the southeast where your base is. North is the fastest way out of here."

• • •

Two blocks from the building, Court and the Terp walked as fast as they could, continuing north. The streets were surprisingly alive, even though every building Court saw was either partially or totally destroyed. It was clear civilians had been living among the rubble for some time.

Court began scanning for some sort of a vehicle, and within minutes he saw two Syrian National Defence Forces militiamen sitting on a pair of motorcycles just off the sidewalk. Court continued towards them, though the Terp grabbed him by the arm. Whispering, the Syrian said, "They are government militia."

Court did not reply; he just pulled his arm away and continued towards them.

At fifteen feet one of the two men stepped off his bike and reached for his AK hanging from his shoulder.

485

Court pulled the M9 pistol from the small of his back and shot both men twice in the head. Civilians nearby raced away, disappearing back into ruined buildings.

The young man started to pick up one of the dead men's rifles.

Court said, "Leave the AKs. We take one bike. Ride in tandem."

The Syrian climbed on behind Court, and the American fired up the engine, racing off to the north.

• • •

The two men made it just two miles before Court decided the checkpoints and SAA patrols were too thick on the roads to chance, so they walked their motorcycle up a gravel driveway in a residential area on the northern side of the city. Court picked the lock of a gate to a small courtyard of a shuttered home, and they hid the bike in a shed. Here the two men waited, deciding against breaking into the house.

A bank of fog rolled into the city in the midafternoon, and Court and the Terp decided they'd attempt to take advantage of the weather. They walked the bike off the property and then rolled out of the residential neighborhood, skirting a single roadblock before leaving the city proper.

Court took the bike off-road to try to avoid further checkpoints, and north of the city he began to hit the hills of the Mazar mountain range. These were rocky, dusty land formations with no trees, a desert formation just as the hills to the south of Palmyra had been. But the tight twists and bends of the road and the high hills and low passes made for good cover from the air.

They drove for over an hour, but the fog grew so thick Court began to worry about stumbling into a roadblock or enemy patrol, so he decided they'd start looking for a place to hide for the rest of the night. In the morning they would hunt for any FSA units in the area, but both Court and the Terp assumed they'd have to travel a lot farther north before leaving the security cordon. From what Court had learned from his time with the Desert Hawks, this entire area was under the security control of the Iranians, but so far he hadn't seen any military up in these rugged hills.

Court's motorcycle rounded a tight turn, cresting a rise in the fog that made it impossible to see what was just thirty yards ahead, and when they straightened out and began going down again, Court reached for the brakes.

A technical was in the middle of the road, blocking it off. In back of the vehicle was a .50 caliber machine gun, with a bearded man standing behind it.

And around the vehicle and the big gun, easily another dozen fighters stood with rifles on their shoulders. It was clear they'd heard the bike approaching for some time.

Court stopped the machine totally, just twenty meters from the truck.

Court said, "Tell me these guys are FSA."

The Terp did not reply.

"Kid? Are they Iranian?"

After several seconds the Terp said, "They're Daesh."

Court felt his passenger reaching for the pistol in the small of Court's back, but Court saw all the guns on him, and he knew the outcome of any resistance.

"No. Don't do it."

Both men raised their hands.

. . .

The young Syrian FSA soldier and Court were stripped of their gear, all the way down to their T-shirts and pants; even their shoes were taken off and carted away. The men who did the frisking said little. They moved with efficiency, and as soon as he and the Terp were led off the road, Court saw why.

A long Ural truck stood behind a stone outcropping on the hill, and inside it were over a dozen men. They all looked like FSA to Court, but he wasn't about to speak to his partner to find out for sure.

The prisoners were surrounded by five more armed ISIS fighters, putting the total number of hostiles here to nearly a dozen.

Court and the Terp were loaded into the truck. A guard standing in the bed lashed their hands behind their backs and shoved them into positions on the floor of the bed, next to other men.

Court looked around. Heads hung low. Some men had been physically beaten, and one older man, he might have been forty but his head was almost bald and what hair he did have was gray, had obviously been shot in

487

the upper shoulder. The wound glistened and bled unattended as the man lolled his head in immense pain with his arms fastened behind his back.

Court and the Terp sat there with the prisoners for several minutes, until another vehicle drove by the hilltop road; it, too, was stopped at the roadblock, and then three more terrified young men were led around the rock and onto the truck.

The truck rolled off in the late afternoon, heading north, deeper into the hills.

Court and the Terp did not say a single word to each other. Court just looked out at the deep fog. The fog that had saved him, and the fog that had condemned him.

CHAPTER 77

Twenty-four-year-old Yasmin Samara held Jamal Medina tight, looking down at the sleeping boy. She was worried about tonight, but Dr. Saddiqi had promised her everything had been arranged by a man in France who was in contact with Bianca.

Yasmin did not know, and she did not trust. But she did not know what else she could do but go along with the arrangement.

Now she stood in the lobby of the doctor's apartment building, watching the headlights of the approaching vehicle. The doctor had gone outside to make sure everything was safe first, and he said he would wave her forward if the coast was clear.

She watched him lean into the car. After a few seconds the engine was turned off and two occupants climbed out.

She started to panic, thought about running out the back, as had been the plan, but Dr. Saddiqi waved to her.

The car was driven by an Arab-looking couple in their twenties who wore civilian clothing and smiled at her, and the woman even stroked the baby's head in Yasmin's arms as the man loaded her bags into the car. Saddiqi wished Yasmin luck and told her *inshallah* she would be very safe, very soon. The young doctor went back into his building, and Yasmin climbed into the backseat.

The woman sat in back with her and the baby while the man began driving to the south. The woman explained that although there was no reason to worry, the entire city was looking for the boy in Yasmin's arms. To get through the checkpoints they would have to play different roles. They were sisters, Yasmin was the boy's aunt, and the driver was the woman's husband.

Yasmin was handed forged identity papers; her "sister" took Jamal and put him in her own lap.

Between Damascus and the Jordanian border they were stopped four times. On each occasion the husband calmly told the officers that they were heading home to Daraa. It was clear to Yasmin that the forged papers were good quality, because other than shining flashlights into the backseat, even on the baby, they had no problems. Each time their documents, and their stories, saw them through.

Yasmin had never been to the Jordanian border, so she didn't know what to expect, but after they passed through the Syrian town of Daraa, there were no lights, no buildings. It was just flat farmland, though if anything was being cultivated here now, the young girl could not see it out the window.

To her surprise the driver pulled the vehicle over to the side of the quiet road, parked, and flashed his headlights. The woman playing the part of Jamal's mother climbed out with the baby in her arms, and she beckoned Yasmin on. They stood there by the side of the road for a moment, and then a sound broke the quiet, coming in from the opposite direction of the glow from the city of Daraa.

Yasmin knew it was a helicopter, but when she looked into the sky she couldn't see any lights.

The helicopter was on top of them before she saw it; it appeared out of the darkness above the road right next to the car. A satchel was tossed down and the man caught it, then threw it into the vehicle's open window.

The tires of the helicopter touched the ground and Yasmin was rushed to it by the woman holding Jamal. She climbed aboard and was heaved in by a pair of strong arms and strapped to a seat. Around her were several men in military uniforms, rifles on their chests.

When the young couple and Jamal were aboard and strapped in, the helicopter took off again; it had not been on the ground for ten seconds. They turned around and flew back in the direction the sound had come from, and Yasmin watched while a soldier put a pair of headphones over the baby's ears. Just then Yasmin saw a flash of light behind her out the door of the helicopter. She looked back to see the car exploding in a fireball on an otherwise quiet farm road.

. . .

They landed after only fifteen minutes in the air. She was handed back Jamal and told she was safe in Idlib, Jordan, and the man and the woman who'd rescued her disappeared through a doorway.

She and Jamal were ushered to a private room and given food and blankets, she fed Jamal, and every few minutes someone would pop their head in and ask if she had everything she needed.

An hour after she arrived, Jamal was wide awake and in a playful mood. A woman brought a foam cup with some little rocks in it and a lid that had been taped closed. The woman apologized that this Royal Jordanian Air Force base didn't have any baby toys lying about, but she hoped Jamal would enjoy his new rattle nevertheless.

Yasmin was shaking the toy to Jamal's delight when Bianca Medina raced into the room, collapsed on her son, and held him tight. Yasmin began to cry and Bianca pulled her into the hug, while Jordanian intelligence agents looked on and wondered just what the hell they were supposed to do with a Spaniard and two Syrians without documents.

CHAPTER 78

Court spent the entire night in a cramped cell with what seemed like fifty or sixty men. He wore an orange jumpsuit, exactly like in his dream the day before, and he'd been given no food or water.

He had managed some sleep, but he woke thirsty and stressed. The cuts to his face and head stung and had been joined by dozens more scrapes and bruises where he'd been roughed up by the guards.

This was not because he'd been singled out for special treatment. He had not. In fact, all the prisoners had been forced to march down a long hallway with their hands tied behind their backs while, standing along the walls, a dozen ISIS men used their feet, fists, and rifle stocks to beat the prisoners as they passed.

Court looked to find the Terp in the crowd. The young Syrian was there, just feet away, his own face black and blue, but his eyes open and alert.

The young man leaned closer to Court and spoke softly in English. "I wish I knew what happened to Azzam yesterday."

Court said, "If he were dead, these guards would probably be talking about it."

"True, but if it happened at a Russian base, they could keep it quiet for a day." He thought it over. "I think."

Court shrugged. "I guess you and I will never know."

A guard walked up to the bars and began shouting to all the prisoners in the cell. He went on for a couple of minutes without stopping; Court couldn't make much of it out at all, and what he did understand didn't tell him anything about his predicament.

But he could see the fear and dread in the eyes of the others.

When the man left, Court looked at the Terp. "That didn't sound good."

The young man had a similar look on his face, although he tried to hide it. "We will be taken to a lake in an hour. Then we will be shot and we will be thrown in the lake so that it will be fouled with our corpses. Daesh is pulling out of the area, but they want to poison the water. A camera crew will film it all to show the world that ISIS is still fighting in Syria."

"That's nice," Court said, leaning his head back against the wall.

The Terp said, "Somehow I made it through seven years of war without getting killed." He smiled at the American. "Today I will finally find peace."

Court said, "Glad you're cool with it. I, on the other hand, am pretty annoyed about the whole thing."

The Terp was interested in this. "Why? Is your mind troubled?"

"When they kill me, that means they win and I lose. That means one more of those sons of bitches doesn't die at my hand." Court shrugged. "That pisses me off."

The young man said, "You were a lion yesterday. You are a true warrior. Even if we didn't get Azzam, we showed him this land will never be safe for him."

"Thanks, kid. You were pretty badass yourself. What's your name?"

The Terp smiled. "Abdul Basset Rahal. You can call me Basset."

. . .

Three hours later Court knelt by the lake, his head down in accordance with the orders of the men with the guns all around him. Once every forty to fifty seconds he heard the crack of a rifle, and the splash of a man falling into the lake.

A cameraman stood on the edge of the pier, and a second was positioned in a rowboat in the water. The gunmen were mostly behind the prisoners, except for the two walking the condemned up the pier and the lead executioner himself.

493

Eventually Court felt the guards cut him off the long rope lashing the prisoners together, then they yanked him to his feet by his shoulders. He was pulled through the brush at the water's edge, his feet just skimming the ground for the first few feet before he found his footing. Cord was wrapped tight around his wrists in front of him.

Behind him Basset shouted to him, but in Arabic, and Court missed most of it.

He'd picked up the words "friend," "fight," and "die."

Yeah, Court thought. That encapsulated the situation well enough.

He heard the crack of an AK's stock as it pounded into a head, and he figured the poor interpreter had taken another beating for saying good-bye.

Court ignored what was going on behind him and listened to his footfalls on the pier, counting them off. He passed the photographer on his right; the man was bored now, beyond the thrill of killing, just focusing on his job.

Then he looked up to see the executioner beckon him on.

At the end of the pier Court was pushed down to his knees; they slipped in the slime a little, but he caught himself.

The executioner was off Court's right shoulder; the two guards were each a step behind him, one on the right and one on the left, and from the sound of the movement of the sling swivels on their rifles, he could tell the muzzles of the weapons were within a foot of the back of his head, at 45-degree angles, equidistant.

The executioner himself raised his weapon and the sling swivels told Court where it was in relationship to his right ear.

Court relaxed the muscles in his back and legs, brought his shoulders back and his head up, and fixed his eyes in resolution.

"Here we go."

Court launched up from the kneeling position, pushing off with his left knee, spinning him in the air to his right. His arms fired out, the cord he'd managed to untie an hour earlier fell to his side. His hands swept around while he spun, and when he faced up towards the sky he arched his back, pulling his head back and down towards the dock, and his fingers clutched the barrels of the guards' AKs, holding them tight near the front sights. He shoved the weapons up and formed an X with them, and as part of the same movement he jerked both rifles hard.

The executioner had been startled by the blur of movement in front of him but he pulled the trigger now, just as both guards fired their weapons at the exact same moment. The executioner's bullet passed within four inches of Court's face, scorching his beard and cutting his lip with tiny bits of unburned gunpowder racing out the weapon's muzzle at two thousand feet per second.

Because of the X orientation of the two guards' weapons at the moment their rounds discharged, the men shot each other. Bullets ripped point-blank into one guard's lower torso and the other guard's genitals. They both teetered backwards off the side of the dock, and as soon as Court landed on his back on the wooden slats, he grabbed the executioner's rifle with both hands and yanked hard across his body, tipping the executioner over his body because he was caught by the sling around his neck.

The two guards splashed into the water as one, and just as the executioner shouted out, he, too, fell face-first into the lake.

Court rolled off the dock to his right, following the executioner off the boards. He crashed into and then disappeared under the bloodred surface of the water.

. . .

Basset had heard the gunshot, then the splash, and he knew it was his time to die.

Then he heard the shouting . . . and the second splash.

He looked up, his eyes focused on the end of the dock just when the American rolled from his back off the pier, fell one meter down, and belly-flopped into the water.

Around him the ISIS fighters began spinning towards the dock, their guns rising in front of them.

Basset had two guards just behind him; they were taking him to die next, after all, and now they opened fire on the lake at the edge of the pier. Both weapons were extended over Basset's kneeling form, so he stood up between the guns, leapt back, and yanked other men tied to him as he went. The two ISIS gunmen fell to the ground under the scrum of prisoners, and the prisoners kicked and bit and elbowed and shouted as they fought with them. Other men on the rope line fell back or jumped back, knocking into gunmen standing close to them.

495

Underwater, Court grabbed at the eyes of the executioner with one hand while he pulled on the AK with the other hand. The water was fifteen feet deep here, dark and brown, so Court felt his way forward, vying for the rifle before the man recovered and thought to reach for one of the ornamental knives in his belt.

It was clear the executioner did not swim; the panic in his actions had nothing to do with the fact that he was in a life-and-death struggle with another human, and everything to do with the fact he was underwater and unable to breathe.

Court pulled the weapon away as the executioner reached out for it, and then the American spun the barrel towards the thick man, pounded the muzzle into the man's solar plexus because he couldn't see him and needed to be sure of his target, and pulled the trigger at contact distance.

The weapon fired; the bullet slammed into the man's chest and blew out his back.

Court's feet hit the lakebed now, and he shoved off with them, launching back up towards the surface. His head broke the water and he sucked in a huge breath of air, but instantly he saw he was ten feet from the edge of the pier, and at least four men were running up it now, heading in his direction. The fighter in front opened fire, raking the water around Court with brass-jacketed lead.

Court dove again, kicked his legs, and shot under the pier. Here he spun onto his back while still below the surface, and he reached up with his AK. He kicked along, a backstroke without the arm movements, and he opened fire on the wooden dock right above him, sending dozens of rounds up, splintering slats, tearing through the legs and torsos of the men running down to the edge of the pier.

A man fell off into the water on the left, and Court tossed the empty AK in his hands and swam after the rifle that had been held by his newest victim.

. . .

Basset slammed his head back twice into the nose of an ISIS fighter lying under him on the lakeshore, and when he was certain the man was dazed from the pounding, he drew a knife from the man's belt. He cut his bindings free in seconds, although he also sliced into his own hand doing so, and then he grabbed the man's rifle and eviscerated him with a long burst of fire to his abdomen.

Up the row of prisoners an ISIS gunman shot two Kurds at close range and was aiming at a third, but Basset shot him twice in the pelvis, dropping him where he stood. The prisoners alive near the wounded man fell onto him, tearing at clothing and flesh with their hands. One man got the AK off the doomed terrorist while others in the line began untying one another's bindings by picking at the knots with their fingertips.

Basset and a prisoner nearby both had weapons now, and they poured fire into the ISIS gunmen near the Ural truck as well as those fighting amid the line of prisoners. The ISIS fighters fired back, of course, and soon the man next to Basset went down with a cry of pain.

Basset emptied his weapon and lunged for the gun dropped by the fallen prisoner. He got his hands on it and spun around but saw two gunmen aiming at him from higher on the hill. He knew he didn't have time to get off any shots before they gunned him down.

Gunfire cracked from behind, and both men launched backwards onto the rocky hillside. Basset looked over his shoulder and saw the American, fifty feet from the shoreline in the bloody water, firing his Kalashnikov, using a floating body to rest the weapon on.

Basset spun back to the ISIS men scrambling around the hillside and he fired, and by now two more prisoners had taken weapons and were in the fight.

. . .

Court staggered out of the water when the crazed shoot-out was over, then fell into the salty mud.

Basset limped over, holding on to his own right forearm with his bloody hand. The young Syrian had been shot in the arm and the foot, and he also bled from where he'd cut himself. But he ignored his injuries, dropped to his knees next to the American, and put his hand on the man's back. "My friend! We did it! You did it! But more Daesh will surely come. We have to go!"

Court looked up at him, coughed lake water, and vomited into the dirt. "How . . . how many did we lose?"

Basset helped Court to his feet. "I don't know. Many. But many more of us are left. We will take the truck and go."

"Go where?" Court asked. He barely had the energy to stand.

"Anywhere!" Basset said with a wide smile.

"I like this plan," Court said, and then he dropped face-first into the mud.

Basset called some men over to help move the American to the truck.

CHAPTER 79

Captain Robert Anderson sat in the main cabin of the UH-60 Blackhawk helicopter as it streaked impossibly low over the dark desert landscape, and he steeled his stomach to what was about to come.

Over the cabin intercom he'd been notified by the pilot that they were moments from hitting the hills, and when that happened, this low and fast flying was going to make life difficult for him and the eight other men here in the back of the helo.

Of course he knew the computers on board kept the machine from slamming into terrain, but he also knew that every time he flew nap-of-the-earth he got nauseous.

He almost never puked, but he *always* felt like he was going to puke.

Just as he told himself to put the motion of the helo out of his mind, his headset came alive again.

"Captain, we got a FRAGO comin' in from the JOC." A FRAGO was a fragmented order, meaning an addendum to an operations order in place. Their current order was to leave Syria, to head north straight up towards the Turkish border as fast as possible, and Anderson hadn't expected any FRAGOs to interfere or delay this order, because his Joint Operations Center had seemed very insistent he carry it out as soon as possible.

Anderson said, "Roger. Send FRAGO."

The captain listened to the transmission for over a minute, then made some notes on a pad he kept in his load-bearing vest. A smile grew on his face. "Copy all. Zulu out."

Seconds later, the UH-60 banked to the northwest, picked up even more speed, and entered the hills. It lurched upwards to miss a steep rise, and Robby Anderson immediately regretted eating the two candy bars he'd downed not twenty minutes earlier.

· · ·

A half hour after receiving his FRAGO, Anderson and the rest of his twelve-man A-team leapt out of their two helos in a rugged mountainous area to the northeast of Palmyra. He knew they couldn't remain on the ground for any time at all without endangering his men and his helicopters. Fortunately, he had no plans to hang out here for the rest of the evening.

With his weapon on his shoulder, he and his team pushed forward into a walled structure, where they found a large Russian Ural truck parked alone. The men cleared the area, making sure there were no hostiles, and then Anderson himself climbed into the bed of the vehicle. He found a man sitting Indian style, his hands in the air, and another lying on his back with his face partially bandaged. Anderson illuminated him with the flashlight on his rifle and confirmed he had the two he was looking for. "ID confirmed. I need two up here to help me move them."

The two men were carried off the truck and into the back of the helo; less than three minutes after landing, the helicopter rose into the air, then returned to its stomach-wrenching nap-of-the-earth flying to the north.

· · ·

Inside the Blackhawk, the new passenger prone on the deck lay still, until a Green Beret medic held smelling salts under his nose.

Then the man lurched a little, and opened his eyes.

Captain Anderson knelt down over him. "Sir? Sir? Can you hear me?"

The American Anderson only knew as Slick seemed to come to his senses quickly. "Oh, hey, Robby. What's goin' on?"

"You know. Not much. The usual."

The man smiled a little, and looked around. "Yeah."

"You've lost some blood, and you're probably dehydrated. We'll fix you up."

500

"Thanks."

Robby nodded. "Had a rough couple of days, I see."

"The usual. Where's Basset?"

Basset waved from the other side of the helo when the American looked his way. A medic was tending to his bloody forearm, hand, and foot.

Robby said, "He called my command about forty-five minutes ago and gave us your coordinates. We just happened to be passing through, so we swung by to pick you up."

"Passing through?"

"Yep. We're exfilling Syria. Getting the hell out before anyone knows we were here."

"I thought you said you'd be here a couple more months."

"Yeah . . . well, that was before."

"Before *what*?"

"Sir, if you don't know, then you're pretty much the only man on Earth that doesn't."

Court thought he understood. "He's dead? Azzam's dead?"

A slow smile grew on Anderson's face. "Ahmed Azzam is dead as dirt. State TV confirmed it this afternoon. Killed by terrorists while personally leading the fight on the front lines of Palmyra."

The American nodded. "Yeah, that's *exactly* what went down."

Robby turned somber now. "Yusuf and Khalid didn't make it."

Court nodded. "They are heroes of their nation."

"No doubt about it." Robby looked into the night for a moment.

The man said, "Someone gave you the okay to come get me?"

"Affirm. I've got orders to get you to Incirlik, Turkey. After that, you can do whatever you want." He smiled. "I suggest a vacation."

"You won't believe this, but this *was* my vacation, Captain."

Robby looked at him like he was insane, then handed him a bottle of water.

Court said, "You got a sat phone?"

Robby moved to the bulkhead and took a phone out of his backpack. He handed it to the man on the gurney. Court dialed a number, then looked at Robby, who took the hint and moved away.

After several seconds the line went live. "*'Allo?*"

Court put a finger in his left ear and held the phone hard to his right. "It's me."

Vincent Voland did not hide his shock at hearing the American's voice. "*Mon dieu*, you are alive!"

"Tell me about Jamal and Yasmin."

"They are in Jordan, with me, and they are safe."

Court blew out a long sigh of relief.

Voland said, "You did it, didn't you?"

"You mean Azzam? No, I didn't, but apparently it got done."

"Right," Voland said incredulously. Clearly he believed the Gray Man had assassinated the Syrian president, but he didn't press. Instead he said, "I have someone else here who wants to say hello, but first, I need you to believe me."

"About what?"

"I gave you some bad information when we last spoke, but I was acting on the best intelligence I had at the time."

"What are you talking about?"

The phone was silent for several seconds, and then Court heard a woman's voice. "Monsieur? This is Bianca. I want to thank you for everything you have done for my son."

Court couldn't believe it. "You're alive?"

"Yes. I am, Jamal is, and Yasmin is, as well. All thanks to you and Monsieur Voland."

Court just laid his head back onto the gurney and stared at the ceiling of the Blackhawk's cabin. "Well, I'll be damned."

EPILOGUE

It was a nice summer evening for Sebastian Drexler at the chateau in Lauterbrunnen, Switzerland. He sat on the deck and looked out at the stars, watched deer and rabbit run across the hectares of private land, and enjoyed a Cheval Blanc Bordeaux from 1970.

Things were nice, but they weren't perfect. This wasn't his chateau; it belonged to Meier Privatbank, but he was living here now. For the past month he had been in charge of the protection detail watching a client of the bank, a woman with a Swiss passport that claimed her name was Ara Karimi, and she was a refugee from the Syrian war.

No, things weren't perfect at all. Ara Karimi was, in truth, Shakira Azzam. The woman had arrived in country on a private jet with her children right after the death of the president of Syria, and through special circumstances arranged by the bank, she'd not had to appear in person at any consulate or embassy to obtain her documentation. She'd just flown into the country, gotten a few stamps on her visa and passport from an immigration official who was "a friend" of Meier, and then she'd come here.

Drexler had been on the same flight from Syria, and although she had been the last person in the world he'd wanted to see before he was put on board the ship in Greece, once he got to Syria and found out Azzam was dead, she became his ticket home to Switzerland. Her life was in danger during the tumultuous days after Ahmed's death, and she was one of Meier Privatbank's most important clients. They wanted her safe from harm, and Drexler was uniquely positioned to make that happen.

Accidentally so, but he was there, nevertheless.

He'd gotten the family out in an SAA plane to Lebanon, and from there they used the Swiss documents to make it into Europe. The kids had immediately been relocated away from the mother, for everyone's benefit. The two daughters were given new identities and sent to boarding school in Lausanne.

And now Drexler was back home in Lauterbrunnen, which was good for him.

But far from perfect.

Shakira sat in front of him now on the deck, the bottle of wine between them. She was carrying on about her plan to retake the reins of leadership in Damascus. As he looked at her, regarded her new short black hairdo, the Botox she'd gotten in Bern that puffed out her lips and fattened her eyelids, and the tanning she'd done to turn her skin several shades darker, he had to admit she looked different, but to him she was still the same Shakira. Drexler nodded along, engaging in her power fantasy just to keep her happy, because keeping her alive and happy was his job.

He felt confident in his skills to accomplish the former. Less so, the latter.

. . .

Drexler had been ordered by the bank to protect Shakira for the first few months of her exile. To this end he had a dozen men on the property at any one time, and he had every manner of alarm and sensor known to man.

He did not, however, have fighter planes in the sky, so there was no one to prevent a skydiver from stepping off a limestone cliff thousands of feet above the Ú-shaped valley where Lauterbrunnen sat, dressed head to toe in black, and then HAHO jumping, steering his parachute precisely so that he came down silently on the back deck of the chateau, not ten meters from where Sebastian and Shakira sat with their wine, plotting her return to power.

A pair of security men stood in the attached living room, and they saw the billowing black chute as it appeared over the man as he landed behind Drexler, and they pulled firearms and moved towards the windows.

But the man under the collapsing canopy saw the men and he was faster and more sure of his mission than they. He shot them both with a silenced Ruger Mark II integrally suppressed pistol, three times each in the chest and throat.

Both men died before they fired a round, and the gun that killed them was no louder than an electric typewriter clicking out a few letters.

Shakira and Drexler both stood and faced the man who expertly dropped his chute with one hand on his quick-release, while holding his pistol on them with the other.

"Don't make a sound," the man said, and Drexler remembered the voice.

"You." There was marvel in his tone.

"Me," the man said, executing a magazine change of the Ruger so fast Drexler had not even been able to take advantage of it.

"What do you want?" Shakira asked. She didn't know who this was.

The man said, "The kids. Are they here?"

Neither she nor the Swiss man standing next to her answered the question. Drexler said, "You are the Gray Man. You're quite famous."

"And you are Sebastian Drexler. You're quite an asshole."

. . .

Court held his pistol on the woman, and although she didn't look much like the photos he'd seen of Shakira al-Azzam, he knew it had to be her.

Drexler said, "You decapitated the Syrian government. But there's a new ruler, he's an Alawi, he's Ba'ath Party, and he says he will continue the war. What the fuck do you think you've accomplished?"

Court said, "Ask Ahmed. Ask Shakira." A pause. "Go ahead, ask her. I'll wait."

Drexler looked to Shakira, and then back to Court.

Court said, "Yeah. I know it's her. You can't go posing for *Vanity Fair* and then try to hide your identity." Court scanned the living room, made sure no one was there. He said, "Yeah, I didn't bring peace, love, and understanding to Syria overnight, and that sucks. But the new guy in charge knows the old guy in charge got fragged for being an asshole. It might not make much difference, but the status quo in Syria wasn't exactly working for anyone.

"Maybe I didn't end the war, but I helped kill Ahmed, I pissed off the Russians and Iranians, and I killed a bunch of jihadis.

"I chalk this up in the win column, even before today."

"What's today?" Shakira asked.

"Today is when I kill Sebastian Drexler and Shakira Azzam."

Drexler cleared his throat. Flashed his eyes into the living room. It was empty still. "Was this all for money? Or have you bought into the lies of the West?"

Court said, "Half million dead. Millions injured. Millions displaced. *Those* lies?"

"*All* lies," Shakira said, and Court could hear the cracking of terror in her voice now.

Drexler said, "You've won, Gray Man. You've *already* won. Why not take your victory, along with the spoils?"

"Meaning?"

Drexler said, "Listen, man. My bank can provide you with—"

Court fired once; the .22 caliber round slammed into Drexler's right knee, dropping him to the deck floor. He grabbed at the wound in pain.

Court said, "I promised Voland that I'd make it hurt. I'll give you a few seconds' agony, then end it for you."

"*Fuck you!*" Drexler cried out as blood appeared between the fingers clutching his knee.

Court pointed the gun at Shakira now, and although she did not move a muscle, he could see her face redden several shades as the panic began to well in her.

She said, "Sir . . . I could make you a *very* rich man."

"Did money buy *you* happiness?"

"It . . . well . . . it helped a great deal."

"At the end of the day, you'd have been better off poor back in the UK. The world would have been better off, as well."

She saw the bribery wasn't working, so she said, "As you know, I have children. Two daughters. I am all they have left."

The man with the pistol held it steady. "There was a version of me who would have cared. I don't really know where that guy went . . . but he's gone now."

"Let me show you photos of them. They are wonderful—"

"They'll have money, and whatever security that it will buy. And they'll probably have some sense that a great wrong was done to them. I hope they channel that rage into something productive, but I can't help them. I can only exact revenge for all those who are dead because of you."

Her voice grew with each word as she tried to alert security men to the danger. "Revenge? *Revenge?* Is revenge really worth any—"

Court shot Shakira Azzam through the heart. She fell back and landed next to, but facing away from, Sebastian Drexler, and their blood pooled together. He shot her still body twice more.

Court said, "It's not worth much, no. But it's worth more than you."

He started to shift back to Drexler, who had not moved and seemed resigned to his fate, but the door into the living room opened fifty feet away. A man saw Court standing on the deck and pulled his weapon. Court shifted to him to fire, and as he did so Drexler leapt up on his good leg and dove over the top of the deck railing.

It was two stories straight down to a steep hillside below.

Court shot the guard, but another came behind him a moment later. Court himself rolled onto and over the railing, scaled quickly off the other side, but stopped on a lower balcony. Here he ran to the northern side of the balcony, out of sight from where he'd climbed from above, and climbed down from there.

Court had to drop the last several feet and he landed in a roll, blunting the impact of the drop. He began sprinting away, pulling a pair of night vision goggles from a dump pouch on his hip as he ran.

He knew Drexler could not have gone far, even if he survived the fall, but where Drexler went over would be full of security men in moments, so Court ran off in the other direction.

• • •

Twenty minutes later he stood in the dark on Schlitwald Strasse, and a black BMW coupe pulled up next to him. Court climbed in, and the vehicle began moving again.

The man behind the wheel said nothing at first, and Court appreciated that, but he knew it wouldn't last.

Finally Vincent Voland turned to him. "So? It's done?"

"I don't know."

507

"You don't know?"

"Shakira's done. Drexler got the pain you wanted him to feel. Maybe more."

"But?"

"But I don't know." Court turned to the Frenchman. "I'd be locking my doors, if I were you."

"Merde." Shit. "Did he . . . did he say anything? What about her? Did she speak? Tell me, what did they say?"

Court said, "I don't remember, really. 'Don't shoot,' probably. That's usually what you hear. Trust me, you rarely get anything too profound."

Voland was clearly frustrated. "I see." It was silent between the two men as they drove along the narrow valley road. "Listen. I have been asked to reach out to you by members of the French government, who would like to pay you for everything you have—"

"Don't insult me, Vincent."

"No insult intended. They want to hire you again, they have more work, and you are the only man they will trust with it. It's a show of good faith, nothing more."

Court shook his head. "When I get out of this car at the train station, you'll never see me again." He turned to the older Frenchman. "And if you do, it's only because I've been sent."

Voland turned to the American. "You'd kill me if you were paid to do so?"

"If you hadn't gotten the kid and Yasmin out of Syria, I would have killed you for free. But you came through, and you linked Drexler to the bank, and found him and Shakira here. You served your purpose." Court drew his pistol from the small of his back, and Voland turned to look at it. "Just like I've served mine."

Court tossed the weapon into a backpack in the back of the BMW, then pulled a small Smith and Wesson revolver in a holster from the bag and strapped it to his ankle.

The rest of the drive was quiet. Court climbed out of the BMW at the station, gave Voland a half nod, and began walking inside.

As he entered, he pulled out his phone and dialed a number. He made it all the way to the train timetable in the main hall before the call was answered.

"Suzanne Brewer."

Court paused a moment. He knew once he spoke, he was committed.

"Brewer?" There was obvious annoyance in her voice.

Court waited another second as he fantasized about hanging up, but then he spoke. "It's Violator. I'm reporting in. You need me?"

The woman at CIA did not hesitate. "I'm afraid we do."

HAVE YOU READ THEM ALL?

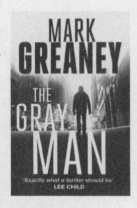

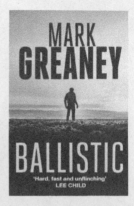

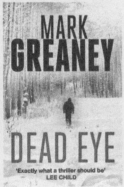

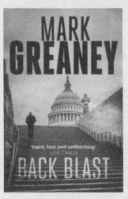

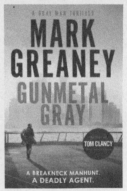

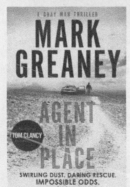

BP 2/19